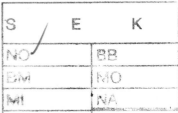
SONGLINES

THE SENTINELS OF EDEN

~ BOOK ONE ~

CAROLYN DENMAN

ODYSSEY
BOOKS

Published by Odyssey Books in 2016

www.odysseybooks.com.au

A Cataloguing-in-Publication entry is available from the
National Library of Australia

ISBN: 978-1-922200-60-0 (pbk)
ISBN: 978-1-922200-61-7 (ebook)

Cover design by Elijah Toten

For Dania

She is a tree of life to those who take hold of her,
and happy are all who retain her.

Proverbs 3:18 NKJ

Author's Note

My novel was set in a fictional town based on Jardwadjali Country and I would firstly like to acknowledge the traditional owners of this place. I would also like to express my deepest respect for all Aboriginal Elders, both past and present across this Great Southern Land. The Dreaming is the foundational belief system of Aboriginal political communities in Australia and I value and acknowledge Indigenous Ontologies and Epistemologies. I present my narrative ever conscious that Australian Indigenous Society is the oldest continuous culture in the world. *Songlines* is a speculative fiction story that draws upon the foundational beliefs of many religions, including Judeo-Christian and Indigenous traditions. However, I do not purport to represent or detract from either ontological perspective. My desire is that this tale reflects the co-existence and interconnectedness of belief systems and that you enjoy it, always conscious of my deep respect of Aboriginal country and Aboriginal society.

Chapter 1

The beast approached without stealth. Its diesel stench gusted in on the breeze that flipped around my leaves and I tasted death. My residents had no idea what was coming and I had no way of warning them, no way to escape. Vibrations travelled through rock and dirt and shook loose a thousand filaments from where they fed in the soil. When the machine hit, my foundation cracked, but I held on, so the metal blade bit into the ground around my roots and chewed and gnawed and loosened my grip. A section of bark was ripped away, revealing a clearer layer of a much older wound, its chevron pattern a reminder of my sacred duty. My branches shook and the family of ringtails in my hollow squirmed in fear. The beast backed away. But then it revved louder, and when it came at me again, it was as unstoppable as the tide.

I had failed. The bulldozer was not permitted here. With a silent outcry I was torn free from the earth and left to die as the metal monster continued to devour its way towards the heart of creation …

A blast from Mr Mason's whistle drilled a new hole in my skull, and I sat up so fast that my English essay tried to fly away. I snatched at the errant paper and then looked up to see if anyone had noticed me drifting off to sleep. Except I wasn't sure I'd actually been asleep. One minute I'd been silently laughing at the guys on the soccer team trying to hold their half-squats, and the next I'd been facing down a bulldozer. I'd had daydream visions before, but they weren't usually so … consuming. Nor had I ever been a tree. That was definitely new.

I leant back against the peppermint gum and extricated a few bits of bark from my messy plait. Perhaps the grassy edge of the school oval was not the best spot for doing homework after all.

On the field, the soccer team were thankfully ignoring me, distracted by a scuffle between two of the players. Noah was trying to break it up, but my friend wasn't having a lot of success because one of the fighters was flailing his limbs around like he had a spider in his ear. Bane's dark fringe flicked around as he swung his elbow at his opponent, and Noah almost copped the rebound when he tried to intercept it.

Bane, of course, was not his real name. Ben Millard. Bane of my life. Noah and I had nicknamed him years ago after he'd 'accidentally' set my locker on fire. Ever since kindergarten the tight-lipped guy with the freaky stare had picked on me in the most irritating ways possible. I tried not to take it too personally though because Bane seemed to annoy almost everyone with his random fits of temper. Most people had long since learnt to steer clear of him. He was like a socially inept child who became aggressive every time anyone inadvertently tripped over his schoolbag while carrying four red freezies. It wasn't like I'd asked him to try to catch me. It wasn't *my* fault one of the freezies had ended up down his shirt. He reminded me of a toddler who couldn't seem to grow out of the biting-people phase. In fact, were those *teeth marks* on Noah's wrist?

Mr Mason's whistle blew again, long and loud. He didn't stop blowing it until three of the other players came to Noah's aid and forcibly pulled Bane and Jake apart.

Scowling, Bane wiped the sweat from his face with his T-shirt while Mr Mason put on his serious schoolteacher voice. From where I was he sounded calm, but he was clearly angry because he kept clutching at his stopwatch and couldn't keep his feet still. After his rant he sent Bane jogging around the oval while Noah was sent with a key to unlock the school canteen for some ice. The rest of the team were given basic ball skills to focus on for a while.

Nalong College was the smaller and less funded of the two secondary schools in our Victorian country town. It tended to attract the rural families of the region, so over the last couple of years we'd seen many of our friends drop out of school to work full-time on their farms. They all seemed happy to still play on our soccer and footy teams though. It wasn't like every other country school didn't do the same thing. Otherwise there'd never be enough players.

The students who stuck it out, like Noah and I, were determined to make a life for ourselves outside Nalong. We both wanted to do well enough to get into one of the big universities in Melbourne or Sydney the following year, and our final exams were getting so close that I could practically hear the clock ticking towards the 'pens down!' announcement. So after laying out all my stationery into dancing stick figures, highlighting the quotes I was planning to use in four different colours, and interpreting the title into runes to decorate the border with, I finally ran out of ways to procrastinate and knuckled down to finish the silly essay. It was on the origins of faerie tales and whether they related to early legends such as the Epic of Gilgamesh or the Garden of Eden, and Snow White wasn't really all that complex—a pretty girl, a bunch of ethnic minority friends, an evil witch and an apple. It was certainly easier than the Biology assignment on Australian megafauna that was also due the next day. That one was likely to take me almost as long as the Late Pleistocene Epoch had lasted.

I was just tidying up my last tenuous argument when I heard someone approach, panting heavily. I glanced up just as Bane ran past me, staring with such a vile expression that I flinched. Sweat dripped from his black hair as he sprinted, legs pounding with stubborn speed, as if he was relishing his penance. He made a crude gesture when he noticed me watching him, and so I quickly looked away, trying not to blush. What on Earth had I done now? It wasn't like his punishment was my fault. And why hadn't I thought to gesture him back instead of cringing like a complete wuss?

Noah came over with a freezer bag full of crushed ice.

'Hey, Lainie. Mr Mason said I can finish early, because apparently facing down a vicious predator is enough of a workout for one afternoon. Can we go or are you still working on your essay?'

I shook my head. 'We can go. I'm done with Snow White. I really don't care if she's supposed to be an allegory for Eve, neither of them should have been stupid enough to eat—'

'One of these?' Noah asked with a grin. He held out an apple he'd nicked from the canteen.

I jumped up and pounced on it like a poddy lamb after milk. 'You are an absolute God-send,' I exclaimed as I bit into it, ducking sideways to avoid the handful of ice he was offhandedly trying to slip down the back of my school dress.

'Yeah, but do you really have to eat the core as well? Something's just not quite right about that, you know.'

I swallowed without needing to reply because we'd had this conversation in all its forms already. There was simply nothing anyone could say about someone eating too much fruit. Even Aunt Lily didn't bother telling me off for it, and she had the predictable over-protectiveness of the guardian of an only child.

As we crossed the oval and headed towards the car park, I felt a brief flash of nostalgia. Just four weeks of classes to go. I would miss the cracked patch of asphalt where we'd played Four Square in Year 8. I'd miss the trees slashed with white paint that marked the out-of-bounds area past the maintenance shed. I'd miss the fragrance of squashed Vegemite sandwiches, old bananas and even that unmistakeable waft from the boys' toilets. Sort of.

'So how's your wrist? Do we need to take you to see Dr Knox for a rabies shot?' I asked.

'You can't catch rabies in Australia,' Noah pointed out. 'Except from bats.'

'Yes, but it was *Bane*. Who knows what unholy germs he carries? You might catch whatever he's got and become a psychopath too. Every full moon. Hey, did we ever check that? Does he get worse when the moon waxes and the fog rolls in across the moors?'

'Australia doesn't have moors, either. All we have are creeks named after dead animals. And if Bane's mood swings come in monthly cycles then you have no right to criticise.'

At that point our discussion descended into an ice fight complete with hair-pulling, wedgies, and uncalled for bra-strap-flicking, until eventually Noah sought refuge in the driver's seat of his beloved dusty red ute. He slammed the door with a healthy Holden clunk before I could give him the nipple-cripple he deserved. I relented and dumped my school bag in the tray before sliding into the passenger seat. It was satisfying to see him flinch.

Noah had just earned his driver's licence a few weeks earlier and was enjoying his newfound freedom by hanging around every day after school. We lived on neighbouring farms that were three quarters of an hour's drive out of town and I was really enjoying not having to take the school bus. Sadly I was still nearly a year away from getting my own licence, on account of being too stubborn to stay in my own class when I'd started Prep—I had snuck into Noah's class so often that in the end the teachers had just given up and moved me ahead a year. Maybe that explained some of my social ineptitude with my classmates.

As I did up my seatbelt I noticed a colourful flyer sticking out of the glove box.

'Why do you have a hang gliding brochure?' I asked. 'Are you in it?' His pretty face framed with white-blond curls tended to find its way into all sorts of publications no matter how much he complained. Like the new billboard at the town Visitors Centre, right above the slogan that said that Nalong was 'Home to the largest grain silo in the southern hemisphere'. His older brothers still hadn't let him forget it. 'Grain silo' had become a euphemism for all sorts of strange things since the billboard had gone up.

'Yes, but that's not why I have it. I was trying to convince Claudia to come with me sometime.'

The apple I'd eaten suddenly turned sour in my belly. He'd been going out with Claudia for less than a fortnight but I'd already had enough of her.

'Don't look like that,' he complained. 'You won't come. Last time I went I had to spend the whole pre-flight lecture with some dude with orange sideburns and feet that smelled like cat food.'

'Why would he need to take his shoes off for a hang gliding lesson?'

'He didn't. I could smell them through his shoes. Besides, Claudia won't come anyway. Too chicken, like you.'

'I am not! I just don't want to spend my hard-earned birthday money on something that lasts less than an hour. I'd rather put it towards my new jumping saddle.'

'Oh, the one you've been saving for since Year 7?'

'Just shut up and drive, Noah.'

He seemed more than happy to stay quiet and not talk about his new girlfriend. Which made two of us.

For the next twenty minutes we were so busy not talking about Claudia that I really did drift off to sleep. It wasn't unusual. The last few months of gruelling study were steadily taking their toll. And perhaps my previous daydream wasn't done with me, because in one of my dreams, my aunt was sitting awkwardly against that same yellow bulldozer with her hands chained above her head. The machine was huge and she looked fragile against it, even though she was yelling at someone in a voice that could have drowned out a hungry cockatoo. The man she was arguing with wore a high-vis shirt and a white hard hat and looked like he needed a beer, but he wasn't backing down. Instead, he was trying to get a word in to tell her something he clearly thought was important but that my aunt didn't seem to want to hear. I knew exactly how the poor man felt.

The screaming got louder and turned into a wailing siren and I jerked awake just in time to see a police cruiser fly past us, kicking up a spray of gravel from the road.

A sick feeling grew, right next to my spleen.

'Noah, I just had that déjà vu sensation again.'

He glanced my way. 'Like that time when I got lost on my dirt bike in the state park?'

I nodded. I'd been twelve, and Noah thirteen when I'd pestered our farmhand Harry to go and get him. Noah's mum had bought me a box of chocolates as a thank you for raising the alarm and hadn't even asked me about how I'd known where he was.

Without a word, Noah sped up a little and I knew he was going to follow the cruiser. I didn't complain. We were far enough out of town that there were only a handful of properties between us and our farms, and past our turnoff was all designated state park. That left a very small sample of people that could be in trouble. And we knew all of them.

Ten minutes later, we both breathed a sigh of relief when we saw the cruiser's lights in the distance. It had continued to follow the road we were on instead of taking our turnoff, but Noah still followed it. He was as nosy as I was.

Luckily, with the recent rain we'd had, the policeman's tyre tracks were easy to follow, otherwise we might not have noticed where he'd left the road just past Dead Dog Creek in the state park. There was an old fire access track leading up a gentle ridge that had recently been widened. Very recently. There were still fresh bulldozer tracks corrugating the mud.

The sick feeling came back.

Noah's old ute valiantly managed the greasy track even at the insane speeds he was asking for, and when we reached the small clearing on the other side of the ridge, there were no less than five other cars crammed into it: the police cruiser; the ute belonging to our farmhand, Harry; a couple of shiny white four-wheel drives with Kolsom Mining logos on the drivers' doors; and my aunt's blue station wagon.

'Kolsom?' Noah asked, pouncing from the car and striding down a track that hadn't existed a few hours ago. The scent of crushed ti-tree was losing the war against the stench of diesel. 'The coal seam gas company? What are they doing here?'

'Apparently their exploration licence extends down as far as Chentyn now,' I said, hurrying after him through the mud. It was the half-hearted sort of mud that only reached down a few centimetres. Just enough to peel nicely away from the dry ground underneath and stick to the soles of my school shoes. 'Aunt Lily's been going nuts over it. She reckons their gas fields up north are poisoning the river. If they decide to start operating anywhere near here she might just have a conniption, whatever that is.'

The track curved where it got a bit steep.

'Does it involve chaining yourself to a bulldozer?'

'Apparently so,' I rasped, stunned.

It was *exactly* the same as in my dream, only less vivid, somehow. Maybe because the reality of it didn't convey the ominous sense of danger I'd felt. Now I wasn't certain if I was scared because my aunt was chained to a giant metal monster or if it was because I had somehow seen what was happening without actually being present. Was there also a fallen tree nearby with a family of angry ringtail possums huddled inside?

My aunt looked very uncomfortable. 'You either get your equipment off my land right now, or I'll have you charged with trespassing,' she growled. There were six men in hard hats and fluorescent orange polo shirts and all of them turned to Senior Sergeant Loxwood and shrugged helplessly.

The sergeant had been in charge of the Nalong Police Station for as long as I could remember, and after that incident with the Ashbrees's ride-on mower, I was still just a little bit intimidated by him.

'Ms Gracewood,' the policeman said, 'this is state park. Kolsom are within their licence parameters to—'

'They need to check their maps again,' she cut in. 'The state park boundary is farther west. This is private property.'

Her statement was met by dubious looks from everyone else present, including me.

'Harry,' I said softly, coming to stand beside the dark-skinned farmhand, 'do you need a hand?'

'No, I think your aunt has it pretty well sorted,' he said. His arms were crossed patiently but there was a tightness around his eyes.

'I mean, do you need a hand with her?'

'Do you have any suggestions?'

'Do you happen to have any chocolate-coated liquorice with you?'

He shook his head.

'Then, no.'

My aunt noticed our exchange. 'Lainie, what are you doing here?' Her jeans were coated with drying mud and her hair windblown. How long had she been sitting there for?

'Are you really surprised?' Harry asked her. She didn't reply but her face got that set look like it did whenever she caught me watching *Game of Thrones*.

I smiled at her. 'I just came to ask if you want yellow flowers or purple? You know, for the side of your car? I prefer purple. That way it will match your tie-dyed kaftan.'

'This is not some Hippie thing, Lainie! This is important!'

The sergeant crouched down in front of her and put on a very patient expression. 'Lily, please don't make me arrest you. I have enough legal paperwork from my ex-wife to deal with; I'd rather not have any more.'

Aunt Lily leant back against the machine again. Her hands were chained above her head. 'I heard Sharlene's getting married again. I'm so sorry, Mick.'

One of the Kolsom workers cleared his throat. 'Excuse me, but can I just point out that it's getting late. I have a two-hour drive home and an unpleasant report to make to the office. Can the catch-up wait until she's in jail, please?'

'She won't be going to jail,' Noah said. 'Because it's too late in the day for any more work to be done anyway, so you might as well take the equipment back to town.' He gave them the sort of smile he used when he was confident he would get his own way. Which was all the time. Noah had an uncanny way of getting people to suck up to him. He was fit, tall, had the brightest green eyes, and when he smiled that particular smile at you it was hard to remember that you hadn't actually planned on making him a triple-layer Nutella sandwich. Guys at school tended to offer him their places in whatever queue he was lining up in, and girls just followed him around and giggled a lot. Clearly they'd never seen him as a three-year-old, dressed up in my aunt's best negligee and high heels, or covered in blood and sloppy cow poo at the age of twelve with a massive grin on his face after he'd just assisted with his first calf delivery. I turned to the Kolsom employees to see whether Noah's magic would work on them too.

'We're supposed to leave it here,' said a thin man with a fat moustache and a hole in his jeans.

'Yes. Leave the machine here,' my aunt agreed, pressing her face against the metal with false affection. 'I'll take good care of it.'

The sergeant rolled his eyes, rather unprofessionally.

Noah cranked it up a notch, giving the Kolsom man a smile that said, 'I'm on your side, mate. Trust me.'

The guy sighed. 'I suppose it might be better to at least get it back down to the road before the serious rain comes tomorrow.'

'And you can't work safely in that weather anyway, right? So you might as well check in with the office to make certain the locations are correct. Imagine finding out that she's right about the boundary? That would look pretty bad in next week's newspaper,' Noah said.

'I doubt our lawyer will have any problems proving that the work we're doing is within our company's rights. We have approval from the state government to drill core samples throughout the valley. Besides, the access routes we're making will assist with the local fire prevention strategy. Surely that can only be of benefit to you?'

Something in his words gave me a metallic taste on my tongue. I wanted to say something, but I didn't know what. All I knew was that I didn't like the idea of them disturbing the area at all.

'The valley is too steep and has far too much vegetation,' Harry said firmly. 'You won't be able to get in there.'

'All the more reason for us to create fire access trails.' He nodded towards my aunt. 'Now she needs to either move or spend the night behind bars.' The words were stern, but his voice held a note of uncertainty.

'I'm not going anywhere!' Aunt Lily declared, trying to flick her blonde fringe out of her eyes with no hands.

Why did she have to be so stubborn? Noah was right. No more clearing was getting done today anyhow. A rock wallaby thumped past nearby, off for its evening graze, as if to point out to us what time it was.

Before anyone realised what he was up to, Noah climbed up onto the driver's seat of the dozer and within seconds, the beast rumbled to life.

At least three of us yelled at him in unison, while my aunt scrambled to her feet and Sergeant Loxwood leapt up after him.

'Noah, you moron! What the hell are you doing?' I screamed, tugging at my aunt's chains. They were fastened with a combination lock that I recognised. It was the one from my old school locker that Bane had set on fire, so I started to swivel the dial around while my aunt tried to push me away.

'Leave it, Lainie, Noah won't do it,' she said.

'Oh yeah?' I looked her right in the eye. 'Remember that time he threatened to walk through the town stark naked if his mum didn't let him watch the new James Bond movie?' Not only had he made good on his threat, but he had proven to everyone that he knew exactly how to drive his mother crazy. Mrs Ashbree was such a terrible prude that I'd often wondered how Noah had even managed to be born.

Aunt Lily's face paled, and she stopped jiggling around. The problem was, the reason I'd bought a new lock after the fire was because this one had warped slightly, and wasn't always that reliable. Beside us, the front bucket shuddered and began to lift.

'Noah Ashbree, turn the engine off immediately, or I will arrest you!' The sergeant's face had turned a peculiar shade and his hand was actually hovering over his gun.

The stupid lock jammed for the second time.

'Noah, it's stuck! Please don't hurt her!' I begged.

Just then, the chains slid down and rattled to the ground. They had been hooked around a part of the lifting mechanism that had released when he'd raised the bucket. They were still done up, but were no longer attached to the bulldozer. The machine puttered down to thick silence and I looked up to see Noah with his hands up, holding the key and grinning at the policeman.

Not for the first time, I vowed that I was never going to speak to him, ever again.

Chapter 2

I meandered down the crowded school corridor, yawning. I'd spent the last few nights cramming my study and then staying up even later to research coal seam gas mining, and so quality sleep was now a forgotten luxury. Kolsom had taken away the bulldozers on advice from their office but I knew the standoff was far from over. My aunt had been to see a solicitor the day after her near-arrest but didn't seem to have come away with any clear plan as to how to keep the miners away. Late last night I'd heard her in the study, rummaging around the old filing cabinet but had been too tired to get up and ask her what she was looking for, and I'd left for school before she'd returned from the morning feed run. Perhaps when I got home I'd see if there was anything I could do to help.

Pale green walls framed dented lockers all the way along to the main doors. It was Friday afternoon and everyone was clawing their way towards the weekend. As I was pummelled by a multitude of clammy teenagers I tried to pick up my pace a little because as tall as I was, I still felt as though I could trip and be trampled at any moment like a baby lion under a herd of stampeding wildebeest. Something squishy slid under my shoe but I didn't dare to look down.

Almost within sight of freedom, I paused as I distinctly heard the word 'fruitcake' hidden behind a cough from one of the girls, Tessa, as she pushed past me. Her friend giggled at her weak insult, but instead of feeling embarrassed or annoyed, I stumbled to a wonky halt with a sudden vision, almost clear enough to taste, of Tessa standing in front of her bedroom mirror in tears of utter despair about the shape of her eyes. What was that about? There wasn't even anything wrong with her eyes. They had that stunning Asian tilt from her mother's side of the family that had the rest of us girls wishing we had even a sprinkling of genes from somewhere more exotic than the arse-end of nowhere. I shook my head as the vision cleared, leaving me with the residual after effects of her intense jealousy. Typical. Like all the other girls, she was jealous of something I didn't actually have. Noah was my best friend, and he was dating Claudia, but somehow I knew Tessa still assumed there was more going on. Far more disturbing than that, however, was the sudden fear that what I'd just imagined might not have been just some random day-dream. The dream I'd had about my aunt and the bulldozer had been playing in my mind over and over again until I'd chosen to pretend that I had simply made it up somehow. It wasn't like I really could have seen what was going on, after all. That would be impossible.

I stared at Tessa's back, trying to suppress my insanity and find my way back to the much safer world of blatant denial.

Visions. No way. Sleep deprivation and too much study. Much better explanation.

Way ahead of me, I glimpsed Noah's pale hair just as he disappeared through the main doors, so I broke into a jog to catch up. My shoulder was jerked back and I felt my school bag rapidly become a lot lighter. I spun around just in time to see two pears, three apples and all my books spill out across the hall. Bane was standing right behind me, flicking closed a pocketknife. A knife? At school? That was going way too far. In stunned disbelief, I watched a series of emotions spread across his face. Instead of looking smug, he seemed just as shocked as I was. That was soon replaced with revulsion, and then a look of fury so vicious that my shout of righteous protest was cut off mid-breath. We both froze for a second, staring at each other, invisible sparks of mutual hatred glinting in the dusty air, before he took off back down the corridor at a run.

Most of the other students in the hall had stopped and were staring at me with looks of amused confusion. I had no idea what to think. His pranks were getting increasingly ridiculous—and dangerous. We were in our final year of school for heaven's sake, why would he slice open my bag halfway down a busy corridor? Trying to steal something? Trying to expose my not-so-secret fruit fetish?

A shrill cry of alarm followed by a loud metallic bang startled us all out of our eerie silence and then the entire school seemed to rush out of the doors like water down a plughole. Bending to hurriedly retrieve my books, I gave up altogether on the fruit and fought my way out to the car park, clutching my bag together as best I could. Noah was sitting on the kerb with his head between his knees, next to an old white hatchback that had backed into the school fence. Dropping my bag altogether again, I rushed over to see if he was hurt.

'Missed me by a country mile,' he said weakly, his pale skin almost translucent from shock. 'What does that even mean? Is a country mile supposed to be longer than a city one? Whoever decided that clearly hasn't tried driving through Sydney lately.'

I peeled back his eyelids to check for concussion.

'Stop it, Lainie! I didn't hit my head, I'm perfectly fine,' he complained, batting my hands away. At the top of the school steps, Tessa had fainted in a tangle of drama and glossy dark hair, and was being flustered over by her friends like the princess she was. Seriously? Playing the fainting maiden when Noah was the one nearly killed? That was just plain pathetic.

I turned back to my friend. 'You have no blood left in your face. Are you woozy?'

'Don't be stupid. I was just stressing because I assumed you were right behind me. I couldn't help checking just in case your mangled body was under the car. Where did you go?'

'Bane again is the one to blame,' I sang with false cheerfulness, trying to pretend I wasn't shaken up at all, but the world had taken on a pale tinge. If anything had happened to Noah ... 'The car hit pretty hard,' I noticed, screwing up my nose at the twisted cyclone fence. 'How's the driver?'

'I'm fine—for now,' said Jake, a thin-faced fellow VCE student with far too much hair product in his long faux-hawk. He was inspecting the damage to the rear bumper. 'But Mum's going to kill me.' He finally turned his attention to Noah. 'I'm so, so sorry, mate. My dog jumped onto my lap just as I started backing out. I guess he distracted me.'

In the passenger window I could see a sturdy tan Staffy staring at us and fogging up the window with his slobbery dog-breath. There was a look in his black eyes that creeped me out a little, as if he was trying to ask me a silent question and would be cross if I gave the wrong answer.

'He must have dug under the backyard fence again,' Jake continued, fiddling with his car keys as Noah stood up. 'I found him raiding the bin near the oval. I am so *dead*. Look at Mum's car! Oh crap, look at that. Crap crap crap. Yep, and here's Mr Davis, right on time. Hide me, someone?'

He shoved his pack of cigarettes into the glove box before the principal could see, and then we helped him roll the car back into the parking bay.

❧

'He pulled a knife on you?' Noah asked, trying to catch my evasive eyes. The crowd had dispersed and we were heading to his ute, which was parked in the street. His footsteps had become noisier as I'd outlined the incident.

'Well, sort of. He attacked my school bag, not me. Speaking of which, could you please help me carry this lot? There's not a lot of actual bag left to do much carrying …'

Noah stopped dead still, staring ahead.

'What now?' I groaned, craning my neck to see what he was staring at. Footpath. Street light. Mother trying to reason with a fractious toddler who was flatly refusing to keep his shorts on. Absolutely nothing out of the ordinary. Maybe he was still in shock? I turned back to him and realised that his eyes had glazed over a little, the way they did when he was trying to do quadratic equations, and he was chewing on his tongue. 'Noah, what is it?'

'Nothing. It's nothing. Let's just go home. This place is crazy and I think it's about to rain again.'

He grabbed a couple of textbooks from my arms and strode away on his long legs. Trying to get him to explain was pointless; besides, the idea of just getting home to the sanity of pulling stuck lambs out of angry ewes was starting to sound strangely appealing.

When we reached his car, Noah got into the driver's seat but then just sat there silently, staring at the windscreen. Perhaps he was more shaken up than he wanted to admit. I waited for him to speak and eventually he turned the full force of his charming green eyes on me. It would have been enough to make half our class swoon, but I was immune. More or less. He did look a bit unsure of himself, which was unusual enough to make me pay attention.

'Lainie …' He swallowed nervously. 'There isn't much of school left, and next year who knows where we'll be?' My chest tightened in sudden fear of where this was going as he cleared his throat. 'What I mean is, graduation is coming up and there's the dance …'

Ah, now it made sense. Claudia went to the Catholic school, and the dance was only open to Nalong College students. Going with anyone else would have been a bit … inappropriate, so he needed me.

'And, I know, we've more or less just always gone together to things like that automatically,' he continued, 'but I just thought it might be nice this time if I formally invited you. You know, 'cos it's our last one.' He smiled his best charismatic smile at me, his raffish blond curls framing his face. 'Lainie Gracewood, would you do me the honour of attending the graduation dance with me?'

My mouth wanted to laugh in his face for being so corny but there was no way I would let him down, no matter how much I would have liked to see Claudia squirm. So instead I took a deep, serious breath. 'Of course, Noah, I would be honoured to be your date, so long as you understand that I *will* dump you like a sack of potatoes if anyone prettier comes along and asks me to dance.'

'But nobody's prettier than me,' he said. I punched him on the thigh. Hard. He just grinned and started the engine.

The deafening roar of the rain on the tin roof finally began to ease up enough for us to hear ourselves think. My aunt and I had become thoroughly drenched finishing the evening feeds out in the dark. Not the best part of farming, but the wood heater was starting to do its job so all was beginning to feel right with the world again. I laid my wet socks over the edge of the couch to dry.

'Can I have some extra money to buy a dress for the graduation dance?' I called out to the kitchen in half-hopeful expectation. Let the negotiations begin. 'Noah asked me officially. So I need to officially pretend to be a real girl. That means a dress. And shoes. And maybe a manicure.' No way would I get all that, but negotiating meant starting high.

Closing the thick green floral curtains against the weather, I made a note to myself to clean out the gutters on the next dry day, then crammed as much wood as I could on the fire and slammed the door shut quickly so it wouldn't all fall out again. Inara, Aunt Lily's skinny grey cat, stared ungratefully at me as I brushed a burning ember from her fur with the poker.

'Sure, no problem.' Aunt Lily's voice sounded distracted.

When I finished choking I swung around the corner to see her sitting at the dining table, cradling a mug of tea and peering at large sheet of paper. She tucked her damp hair behind her ears, then looked over at a map held down by the fruit bowl and the pepper grinder.

I came over to the table. 'What's up, Aunt Lil?'

'Oh, nothing, really. I'm just having a bit of trouble interpreting this schematic.'

'Is this about Kolsom again?'

She nodded. 'I found the copy of our land title, but I'm struggling to work out where exactly on the map our western boundary is.'

Sliding over the floorboards in my woolly bed socks, I peered over her shoulder. 'The title doesn't show where the river goes, is that why it's tricky?'

'Yeah, and also because there aren't any proper roads to use as landmarks.'

I pointed to a small rectangle on the northern part of the page. 'Is this the Ashbrees's place?'

She looked at it, and then at the map, and then back to the page. 'Can't be,' she said. 'It's too small.'

'Unless you have the scale wrong.'

We both squinted at the tiny writing that showed the measurements. Then I looked at the scale of the map. 'See this thin squiggly line running down here on the right?' I pointed to the faint trace and then showed her the corresponding place on the map. It was the river, but it was not where we expected it to be. Which meant the title covered a lot more land than we had assumed.

Aunt Lily turned to me. 'This farm is four times the size I thought it was!'

I did some quick sums, and pencilled in the borders on the map. What I had previously thought was our farm only took up one small corner, adjoining Noah's place. My aunt's broad grin became positively evil and I quietly hoped the lawyer at Kolsom Mining didn't suffer from a heart condition.

⌒

Staring up at the dark green leaves of a manna gum, I watched a kook-aburra bash a snail violently against the branch it was sitting on. I was supposed to be cleaning out the pit pump behind the tractor shed, but I didn't really want to.

The morning was cool but sunny, and beside me the river swirled noisily, fat with last night's downpour. This used to be the place Noah and I hung out the most, when I could convince my aunt that we would stay out of the water. Even then she only allowed it because it was within shouting distance from the house and the water was slow and shallow for quite a long way here.

Noah and I used to play a game where he would try to launch vari-ous things into the river upstream at his place while I would wait at this spot for hours—or so it felt—hoping to catch his boat with its message. Somehow his homemade contraptions never made it this far. Either he was not as good at boat building as his namesake or there was a phe-nomenon something like the Bermuda Triangle going on somewhere in between. No guesswork as to which option we'd decided to believe. In fact, when I was nine I'd mistakenly referred to it as the Barramundi Triangle and Noah had laughed so hard the name had stuck.

These days, however, instead of building boats we seemed to spend all our time on boring things like memorising the process of turning bauxite to aluminium, and figuring out how mitochondrial DNA could help trace the origins of the human race. Noah had called me at eleven o'clock the night before because he couldn't read his own handwriting and needed me to read out half the term's biology notes. I couldn't wait for exams to be over.

I stretched, yawned, prepared to get up and go back to my chores, and then promptly flopped back down on the rock. It was quite warm in the sun when I focused on nothing but the feel of it on my eyelids. All around me I could hear evidence of the life sustained by the swollen river and deep earth. Magpies warbled raucously in stark contrast to the delicate sounds of elusive bellbirds. An almost-warm breeze made a stray strand of my hair tickle my lips.

The music lingered just out of reach when I woke with a strangled cry. There were tears streaming down my face and I realised I was sobbing. A heartbreaking sense of loss consumed me as the memory of the dream melted away. Not again. Every night this week I had been having these musical dreams. Tantalising, fading before I had a chance to remember. No wonder I was so tired. Drying my eyes and trying to settle my emotions, I peeled myself off the rock. Not as comfortable as it had seemed a moment ago. A moment? I checked my watch. Crap, Aunt Lily would be back from town any minute and none of my chores had been done.

I was halfway up the hill when I heard the argument. The words were indistinguishable but it sounded like Noah's mum. She only ever complained to Harry when Aunt Lily had given us permission for something she didn't approve of, so feeling only pea-sized guilt, I crept up to Harry's cottage. The old fibro unit was nestled behind a small hill farther along the driveway than our house. Mrs Ashbree's white Pajero was parked in front of it.

'I don't care how close Kolsom are getting, you need to go, Harry,' came her voice from inside. She was crying. Maybe not loudly, maybe not out loud at all, or with physical tears, but I knew. Somehow, I always knew.

I crept past the window and then plastered myself against the wall to hear more.

'It can wait,' Harry replied.

'Do you think I can just ignore it? Let me try again.' She was speaking through her teeth, biting each word.

'Enough, Sarah. It isn't working. Just let it go.' Harry sounded even more tired than I was. 'Besides, Lainie's just outside and I need to talk to her.'

Damn. No matter how quietly I moved I never seemed to be able to sneak up on anyone. I walked up to the front door trying to think of a reason to be there. Noah's mum opened it just before I could knock. My brain scrambled for an excuse she might believe, but she beat me to it.

'Oh. Hi, Lainie. I just stopped by to ask Harry's advice.' She looked annoyed. 'I was hoping he could tell me the best brand of pocket-knife to buy for David for Christmas.'

What?

Behind her, Harry's face went blank, as if he'd been hurt by her comment. What was that all about?

Without waiting for me to respond, she pushed past me and strode back to her car. Not even a goodbye.

Harry and I looked at each other rather awkwardly, and then he beckoned me inside and put the kettle on.

'I, er, was wondering whether Aunt Lily told you what she found out about our land title.' It was the best excuse I could come up with. At least I hoped it sounded better than Mrs Ashbree's weak one.

'No, but I can guess. I know exactly how big this farm is, and where its borders lie.'

'It's over three hundred hectares, Harry.'

'Three hundred and twenty-eight. And the back of it runs north as far as the Chentyn road. It's a bit of an odd shape.'

I fished a couple of tea bags out of the ceramic jar by the stove. 'Do you think showing someone the title will be enough to stop the miners?'

Harry looked at me intently. 'I hope so. Can I ask you a question?'

I shrugged.

'How did you know to come out to the bush the other day?'

'We saw Sergeant Loxwood fly past,' I said, far too quickly.

He made a 'hmph' sort of a noise, and stirred sugar into his tea. Then he handed me my mug and led the way out to his back porch. We sat down on the step and watched the river sparkle through the trees at the bottom of the hill. I was itching to ask him what Mrs Ashbree had really been doing there, but it was none of my business. I also guessed that there was something he wanted to know from me, but there was no way I was going to tell him I'd been having visions and weird daydreams.

'I have to go away for a while,' Harry said eventually. 'Possibly for a few weeks, but I'll wait until after your exams so you won't have to cover for me while you're trying to study.'

He might as well have announced that he was moving to Antarctica. The longest I had ever known him to go away for were his four-day fishing trips with his friend Stumpy Johnson.

'I need to make sure you know some things before I go.'

'Like how to bail Aunt Lily out of jail?'

He smiled. 'Actually, I just need to know if you remember any of the stories she used to tell you when you were little. The ones about the Garden of Eden.'

My blank stare felt a bit rude, but I couldn't seem to find a better reaction. I remembered the stories, of course. We used to always make up tales of what it would be like to live in Paradise, and they were probably what had ignited my love of fantasy novels—I'd had to be careful not to make references to our made-up stories in my English essay by accident. But I had grown out of my aunt's bedtime stories at about the same time as I'd discovered that Santa was really Harry climbing across the roof on Christmas Eve. What did they have to do with Harry leaving?

'I'm serious, Lainie, do you remember?'

'I remember her telling me that my mother was living with the elves in Paradise. She made it sound so nice that I used to ask if I could go too. I argued that the elves would miss me if I didn't visit. I even had names for some of them. Then when I was six, we went to Dayna and Tom's wedding, and after the service Noah and I played in the cemetery behind the church. I found my parents' graves and cried for hours. What's your point, Harry?'

His deep brown eyes were full of the sort of sympathy that you couldn't brush aside. It opened up a hurt that I thought had been long since dealt with. But his next words hurt even more.

'Your mother's grave is a lie. I'm thinking of going to Eden to find her and see if she can help me with something I have to do.'

Chapter 3

'Take it back.'
'I can't.'
'Take it back, Harry!'
'No. Your mother is alive.'
'Then prove it.'
'Come with me.'
'Where?'
'The Garden of—'
'SHUT UP!'

Chapter 4

I didn't remember getting up or leaving, but I found myself stumbling along the riverbank, fuming. I was furious with Harry for coming out with such a ridiculous and hurtful joke. What he'd said had made no sense to me whatsoever. My aunt had used her stories of Paradise to comfort a grieving child. That I could understand. But to say that my mother's grave was a *lie*? Why would he do that? It wasn't funny, and I had never known him to be insensitive in any way.

By the time I'd calmed down enough to return to the house, Aunt Lily was waiting for me to jump in the ute so we could check the lambs together. She asked me what was wrong but I refused to tell her. Harry didn't appear, thankfully, and for the next few hours we kept busy with the sorts of jobs that were exhausting and yet we could seldom say what we had spent all that time doing. Just stuff. Unblocking drains, cleaning out pit pumps, checking limping sheep, retrieving panicking lambs from the wrong sides of fences, retrieving panicking ewes from the wrong side of a clump of gorse, stacking hay bales, unstacking a pile of bricks like a high stakes game of Jenga because Aunt Lily was certain she'd seen a snake but it turned out to be just a blue tongue lizard, restacking the same pile of bricks … the endless tasks required for living on a farm. It helped. A lot. Because even though Aunt Lily was the only one with me, I kept feeling as if there were too many people around and all I wanted was to *do* and not *think*. By evening I crawled into bed utterly spent, but when I fell asleep, my dreams were choked by sad music and hazy memories of my mother.

By Monday morning, I had almost managed to fool myself into believing that Harry really had been joking. A part of me knew that I couldn't ignore him forever, but I simply didn't know where to start. Better to just wait for him to apologise.

At recess I had just put my lunchbox away in my locker when Noah came hurrying down the concrete steps of the breezeway. He was so agitated it took him two tries to undo his combination lock.

'Worried about today's practice exam?' I guessed.

'What did you make me pick Chemistry for anyway?' he grouched, wrenching a textbook out of his bag.

'Oh, I just wanted your company. It's entertaining to watch Tessa Bright blush whenever you get partnered with her. We've finished all the pracs for the year now though, so you can ditch it if you like. Unless, of course, you actually do want to get into Melbourne Uni next year.'

He pressed his lips together, and then changed the topic. 'Lainie? What did you decide to do about the incident with Bane? Will you report him?' He shoved the book into his locker and slammed the door, leaving half a tree's worth of paper sticking out at odd angles.

'I guess so. I should, right? I mean, he had a *knife*. I think he's a bit unstable. I really should.' And yet I felt strangely reluctant. I couldn't stand the guy but that didn't mean I wanted to get him expelled right before exams. But what if he really hurt someone next time?

'I'm not sure he's that unstable. I know it must seem like that to you but he's not usually like that, not around most other people anyway. He's really quite a nice guy. Don't dob him in just because you hate him.'

'*Nice guy?* Are you mental?' He didn't look like he was kidding. He would always see the best in people, but there was no way I could live with myself if Bane did hurt someone. 'Noah, he had a weapon. At school. I need to let someone know.'

My friend didn't argue further as he tried to poke some of his papers back behind the door, but it was no use. The poor things were just too determined to escape the stench of old bananas.

Just then a flock of Year 8 girls came giggling around the corner. When they saw Noah, the giggles became rapidly hushed whispers and one of the girls turned pink. We ignored them like we always did. Girls had been acting mental around Noah since before he'd even sprouted underarm hair. But then one of the girls approached us. She had her red hair straightened to within an inch of its life and wore mascara so thick it looked like she'd taped spiders onto her eyelids.

'Hey, Noah. Nicole said to tell you she's catching the bus home tonight, so don't wait for her.'

Something didn't sit right. Something about the way her words … *looked wrong.* She wasn't lying, but she was hiding something. I could often tell when someone was being deceitful. Noah called it my gift. My distrust was conveyed to him with the barest gesture—a long-practised language that felt entirely natural.

For a moment he looked so weary that I thought he might just let it go, but then he took a step forward so that he towered over her and stared her down. The poor girl looked ready to faint. Then he smiled, and she blushed.

'When, exactly, did she tell you this?' he asked. One of the other girls giggled.

'U … um … before maths.'

'And did she stay for maths?'

No answer.

Noah kept staring. Waiting.

'She has permission to do some research in town,' the girl said, her voice rising at the end like it was a statement that needed his approval. Even Noah could tell she was lying.

Damn. Not again. Nicole was Noah's precocious thirteen-year-old sister. The youngest of four kids and the only girl, Nicole had a tendency towards dramatic escapades. Since Noah's two elder brothers had moved to the city to study, it was up to him to rein her in. It wasn't an unusual thing to have to raid the town library for research, because our school was too small to have a decent one of its own, but in Year 8 that involved permission slips and parental consent that she clearly didn't have. This would be the third time in two weeks that she'd wagged class. She was heading for a suspension.

As soon as Noah stepped back, the girl fled, not even waiting for her friends to catch up. I could hear his teeth grinding.

'She just doesn't care about anyone but herself, does she?' His foot twitched like it was about to kick something. 'Mum's going to totally spit it. The two of them fought non-stop all weekend, you know. Dad cut the grass twice, just to get out of the house. If she gets suspended, I'm coming to live with you.'

'I'll find her,' I offered. 'I've already done a practice exam and did okay. Mrs Armstrong won't care if I tell her I'm studying in town instead.'

For a second he looked like he wanted to be gentlemanly and refuse, but my suggestion made too much sense.

'Don't worry, it won't take me long. She's probably at the lake,' I said, already heading to the staff room to sign myself out. 'Old Mrs Jackson at the newsagent dobbed her in last time when she went to the shops, so she's unlikely to risk that again.'

The lake was the centrepiece of the town. During drought years it hosted weekly fruit and veg markets and footy matches, and when there was water in it, well, we kind of just hung around there letting the mozzies feed on us and pretended we were at the beach.

When I got to the park that overlooked the water I found Nicole perched sacrilegiously in Nalong's famous Carved Tree. An Indigenous resident had sliced chevron patterns into the bark hundreds of years earlier, most likely as a warning that there was sacred ground nearby. I shook my head to clear it of the memory of my daydream. That tree had been carved too.

'You know I can set a curse on you for touching that,' I told her.

'That's bullshit,' she muttered.

'Yeah, it is. We don't curse people, but Harry might be a bit annoyed at you.' Harry Doolan was an Elder of the local Aboriginal community—or what remained of it. Most of them lived closer to Horsham now, but Nalong was on a part of the river that they still belonged to.

'Do you really have Indigenous blood, Lainie?'

'So Harry tells me.' I was reluctant to say much more because the truth was that I didn't even know what my mother's favourite colour had been, let alone anything about her family history. I didn't know the people, the language, or the stories. In fact, I had always been so certain that I would offend someone if I went around bragging that I had Aboriginal heritage that I had never been brave enough to try to find out any more. And after Harry's insane announcement the other day, I didn't particularly want to think about either him or my mother.

'What are you doing here, Nic?' I asked as I waved to the old homeless guy who spent his days hanging around the park. He didn't wave back.

'Researching our Civics assignment,' she declared with a defiant smile. 'The one about the Dreaming.' She pointed to a plaque the council had erected next to the tree, which outlined the local story, assuming she was being clever, but I was already a step ahead.

'Good, because that's what I told the school.'

Her shoulders slumped.

According to the legend, Nalong had been built on the banks of a river that flowed from the time of Dreaming and spent many, many years swirling around the bones of our country, until it came out into our land in present day. It was said that the water carried the music of the Dreaming with it, and that the music helped to heal the people. I had dutifully written my own Year 8 essay on it, as had every other Nalong student since about 1980. It was a Nalong College rite of passage that even Nicole wasn't going to escape.

'Can't I just pay that guy to write it for me?' she attempted, nodding towards the vagrant who was picking a thread from the cuff of his pale grey business suit—probably his first pick from the Uniting Church op shop. It went really well with his bright green T-shirt and greasy dreadlocks. 'Hi there, Mr D,' she called to him. 'Find any treasure today?'

The bearded man scowled and didn't answer, but got up from his park bench and began to wander around with his hands in his pockets, scanning the ground like he really did expect to find something useful. It was how he spent his days. Always in this park. Harry had once assured me that he had somewhere reasonable to sleep at night though.

'He looks old enough to have been around when this tree was carved. I'm sure he knows more of its backstory than—hey! Ow!'

She only just managed to save herself from landing on her head when I grabbed her ankles and lifted them, sending her sliding backwards down the sacred tree trunk.

With a resentful stomp, she followed me to the library.

∼

'Hi, Mrs Hamilton, could I please see the local papers from November and December, 1998 and '99?' I was whispering as softly as I could but it still felt like everyone was listening far too curiously. The library was in the same building as the council office, so there were a few people busy at their desks, working.

The librarian had a face so wrinkled it made me wonder if she had been heritage listed along with the old building she worked in. Perhaps one of the heritage restrictions prevented the town from letting the poor woman retire. At least it meant she was proficient at her job. She took less than two minutes to emerge from the back room with an arm-load of newspapers.

I sat across the desk from where Nicole was sulkily scratching out her essay and flipped to the obituaries in the first paper. It didn't take long to find what I was looking for.

> Gracewood, Lucas. 3.6.1973-21.11.1998. Lost to the river and sadly missed. To Lily he was the best brother in the world. Adoring husband to Annie, and loving father to Lainie, to whom he will finish reading *Snugglepot* under a more graceful sky than this one.

A vivid memory sprang up like a pouncing tiger, of Aunt Lily shaking her head at something I'd asked her and pulling a book from my shelf, which she clutched to her chest before leaving the room. She'd been trying to hide her tears but I'd known she was crying. I always knew when people were crying. I must have been very young because the room still had the pink curtains I'd accidentally torn when Noah and I had played sword fighting when I was four. I'd never asked her to read *Snugglepot and Cuddlepie* to me again after she'd taken it away.

'What's the matter, Lainie?' Nicole leant away from me as if my tear-filled eyes heralded some sort of contagious disease.

Hydrogen, Helium, Lithium, Beryllium … By the time I got to Sodium I was able to shake my head dismissively at her, my emotions back under control. She turned back to her essay with the tip of her tongue sticking out of the corner of her mouth, but she didn't chew on it like Noah always did when he was concentrating.

It took me a bit longer to find my mother's death notice, because it wasn't really an obituary. It was a bite-sized article in one of the 1999 papers, stuck below an article about Y2K, simply saying that the coroner had finalised his report and declared the death of Annie Gracewood as suicide by drowning. She had died exactly one year after my dad. I'd been four years old.

My aunt had always been gentle with me whenever I'd asked about my parents. I knew my dad had drowned trying to save my mother and me. There had been some flash flooding and my mother had lost her footing; she couldn't even grab onto anything because she was carrying me. Dad had managed to get us both to safety, but got swept away in the process. I'd also known my mother's death had been suicide, but the drama of it … one year exactly …

'East of the state park. Along Old Redwood Road,' came a smooth male voice behind me.

'You mean the Gracewood's place?' Mrs Hamilton asked, distracting me from my soap opera imagination.

Nicole and I looked at each other. She peered around me to see who was talking. *Kolsom*, she mouthed silently.

'Yes, I need to see a copy of their land title,' the man replied.

I turned in my seat to see a man in a dark suit leaning towards the librarian. He looked to be in his mid-twenties and had a serious chin, soft hands, and a briefcase with a Kolsom logo on it, and he was frowning at his mobile phone as if bewildered by the lack of reception. Mrs Hamilton flicked her eyes to me, subtly asking my permission. Kind woman. Smiling, I gestured to her to go right ahead.

For five minutes or so I sat with my hands behind my head, chewing on my pen and amusing myself by listening to the man's frustrated sighs as he checked, rechecked, and cross-checked the title with no less than three different maps. Eventually I gave Nicole's essay a quick skim-read and then we prepared to leave. I glanced back at the man holding his phone up to the window looking for Nalong's ephemeral reception, and a shiver ran down from my hair to my toenails. Just like I could tell when someone was crying or being deliberately devious, I suddenly had no doubt that this man was someone who made Nicole look as honest as the bathroom scales.

Chapter 5

The last class of the day dragged on and I kept feeling like everyone was invading my space. All I wanted was to get home so I could finish my Biology revision and then pretend I was going to yell at Harry for an hour or two. Which, of course, I wouldn't do because he might say something else I didn't want to hear.

Nicole had been given a detention when the school found out she didn't have permission to be in town, but being able to produce her completed essay saved her from a worse fate. Not that she seemed in the least bit grateful to me. Had I ever been that annoying?

I crossed out the maths problem that I was stuffing up and started again.

'I heard he was so upset he left town altogether!'

My head snapped up to see who was whispering. It was Taylor, one of the blonde Barbie dolls in the front row. She was using the sort of whisper that wanted to be heard by the whole class.

Tessa leant forward, her manicured nails gripping the edge of the desk as she whispered just as loudly. 'Who left town?'

'Bane. I heard he came in this morning, emptied out his locker, and just drove off again. Exams are only a month away!' Scandal dripped from Taylor's voice.

Personally I thought there was a bit of a jump between emptying his locker and leaving town. But what if he really had been expelled? I hadn't yet had a chance to report him for the knife incident but it had hardly been a private scene. Anyone could have dobbed him in. I should have felt relieved that I didn't have to be the one to do it but I actually felt a little bit worried. Okay maybe not *worried*, but I did want to know if it was the incident with me that had made him leave. I decided to just be an adult about it so after class I went straight to the office.

'I have a book that Ben Millard lent me that I need to return to him but his locker is empty and I haven't seen him today. Has he changed lockers?' Well, maybe a little false backstory wasn't so adult, but it seemed simpler.

'I'm afraid he's no longer attending this school,' Mrs Carpenter replied as she pushed her glasses up the bridge of her long nose with one hand and smacked her mouse against the desk a few times with the other.

That didn't really tell me if he'd been expelled or left voluntarily. More sweet-talking required.

'Did he change schools? Should I drop the book in at St Catherine's or will he come back for graduation?'

She stopped trying to move her cursor and peered at me. 'I don't think he'll be coming back. He just dropped out without any good reason that I'm aware of. You might just have to keep the book.'

Bingo. I knew it wouldn't take much to get her to sing. Lovely heart has Mrs C, but she keeps her mouth shut about as well as anyone else in a small country town. So, not expelled then. For some reason that made me feel relieved, and a tiny part of me felt a bit sad that he'd come so close to the end of VCE and not finished. Still, he must have had his reasons. I thanked her, reached over to plug her mouse cord in properly, and then left.

☙

Utterly ridiculous. Some sort of cruel joke? Unlike Harry. My fingers were going numb so I rolled over onto my back again. That made three whole revolutions since I had woken at 2.17am. I was like a lamb roasting on a spit. A sleepless, very annoyed roast lamb. Basting in the memory of Harry's words. *Your mother's grave is a lie.* At the time, his warm brown eyes had seemed so placid, so peaceful, like he was telling me that all I had to do was click my heels together three times and I'd wake up in my mother's arms.

Stubbornly, I kept my eyes shut because opening them would be admitting that I was awake. If only I could sleep without hearing that mournful music! It was painfully beautiful. At least, I remembered that it was beautiful but I couldn't quite recall the music itself. The conflicts were frustrating. I dreaded the pain of it, but still longed to sleep so I could hear it again, and I was exhausted, but too tired to endure any more of the sadness that came from sleeping. So I flipped over yet again. The backs of my eyelids were really boring.

Your mother's grave is a lie.

What possible reason could Harry have for saying something like that? There had been a coroner's report. Nothing mysterious. Hideous, sad, tragic, but not at all mysterious. But I couldn't keep pretending Harry hadn't said it.

The floorboards were freezing as I crept down the hall to the study. It took a while to dig under the piles of poultry magazines leftover from that time when Aunt Lily decided to enter her Orpingtons in the Nalong show, but I finally pulled down the old photo album with the faded green vinyl cover. I didn't have a lot of family history from my mother's side, and it was pretty much all in that album.

The desk lamp threw the old sepia photos into stark brightness, so that I imagined the young couples in the pictures were about to cringe away, squinting. I apologised for disturbing them as I flipped through to the back of the book. Just a few coloured pictures graced the pages. There was one of a man holding a child above his head by her ankle with a woman standing nearby tilting her head upside-down to look the girl in the eye. They were all laughing. There was a 1970's lime green Ford station wagon in the background, so the child was most likely my mother. She had wavy light brown hair, same colour as mine but not nearly as thick and crazy. There was another photo of my grandmother, riding a bay stockhorse at a country show, and the next page had a picture of a young guy standing on a beach with his wetsuit peeled down to his waist. He was leaning on a surfboard wedged into the sand and his wet hair was an explosion of long curls. Man, my dad had kind of nice abs.

The wedding photo on the next page made my eyes flood. My mum's dress was exquisite, and my dad couldn't take his eyes off her despite the two groomsmen behind him who were about to pour their glasses of champagne over his head.

The last photo in the book was slightly blurry, as if the photographer had tried to take a sneaky shot. In it, I recognised myself as a toddler, and my mother was clutching me to her chest with one arm and pulling back the blue curtains to open my bedroom window with the other. It looked like she was singing …

Eight seconds later I burst through the door to my aunt's bedroom, switched on the light and slammed the album onto the bed violently enough to make Inara hiss. I was too upset to speak. All I could do was point to the photo, my trembling finger tapping against the curtains in the picture. The blue curtains. The ones that had replaced my pink Barbie ones after I'd torn them with the plastic sword Noah had been given for Christmas. The Christmas *after* my mother had died.

Chapter 6

'Calm down, Lainie. Just breathe.' My aunt squinted at the photo, her eyes still trying to adjust to the sudden brightness. 'Yes, that's your mother. I don't understand what the problem is.'

To my suddenly suspicious eye, she looked kind of nervous. Her eyes drank in every detail of the picture.

'The curtains. The curtains are the problem. What year was Noah given his sword for Christmas?' It wasn't that I was unsure, but I wanted to see if she would lie or hedge. She did neither. Instead, she burst into tears.

'I'm so sorry, Lainie! I didn't know what else to do. The last thing I wanted was to lie to you, and I tried not to for so long, but the truth was going to tear your life apart!'

I stood with freezing feet and waited for her to explain.

'Your mum left us,' she sobbed, one hand clutching her bed sheet. 'She tried to stay, for you, but every time she came back it just made things harder for both of you. I took that photo knowing it would be the last time we saw her. You lot never like getting photographed. My brother used to laugh at that.' She wiped a tear from the page, and then her finger traced the edge of the photo of my dad on the beach.

'Is she still alive?' I asked through clenched teeth. Feeling confused and angry, I just wanted her to come up with an explanation that would put my mother safely back in the grave, because if she were alive that would mean she had abandoned me.

Aunt Lily answered with the deepest of sighs, the gentlest of tears, and the barest of nods. 'Pass me my Bible,' she said. 'And hop in here where it's warm. I'll tell you what little I know.'

Chapter 7

There were two types of special trees in the Garden of Eden. One was the Tree of Life, whose leaves were for healing the nations. The other was the Tree of Knowledge of Good and Evil. God told Adam and Eve that they could eat from any tree in the garden, except from the Tree of Knowledge of Good and Evil. But the serpent tricked them into eating from it, and so God cast them out of the garden He had planted for them so that they couldn't eat from the Tree of Life and live forever. Then He stationed Cherubim, and a revolving sword of fire east of it, guarding the path to the Tree of Life.

At approximately 2.30am, Tuesday 2 October, Aunt Lily told me that my mother was a Cherub, and so was our farmhand, Harry Doolan. My mother had gone to live in Eden a year after my father had died, leaving Harry to guard the pathway to it, and leaving my aunt to try to explain to a four-year-old why her mother was never coming home.

After patiently listening to her garbled explanation and numerous apologies, I kissed my aunt and told her I loved her, then I walked the nine steps down the hallway and slammed my bedroom door shut behind me so hard that the plaster cast of my hand I had made in kindergarten fell off the wall and smashed into thirteen pieces. One piece for every year my mother had not been around. One for every year my aunt had been lying to me. And she still didn't have the decency to stop with the faerie stories and just tell me the truth.

❧

Noah and I ate our lunches in our usual spot under the tree near the oval, where the peppermint-scented leaves helped to disguise the pervasive smell of hundreds of schoolbags. Noah finished off my second sandwich while I wove daisy chains out of cape weed—anything to keep my hands busy and my mind away from thoughts that I didn't want. Between exam study, stressing over my aunt's and Harry's insanity, and obsessing over the possibility that my mother might still be alive somewhere, I hadn't had any decent sleep all week. And when I had, the grief-filled music in my dreams left me so wrung out I could barely function. It felt like my mother was singing to me from the grave. It had been four days since I had spoken more than single words to either Aunt Lily or Harry. So long as I got my chores done before I could be asked, it was easy to avoid people on a sheep farm as large as ours.

Noah shifted the bony shoulder I was leaning against.

'Hey, how's Nicole doing?' I mumbled, trying to sound more alert than I really was. I tore up the chain I had made and began to collect more flowers so I could start again.

'Okay, I guess. Mum apologised to her, believe it or not. She's been cranky as a constipated cow for the last few weeks, but the other day she actually admitted that her volatile temper might be causing a few of their issues.'

'Good to hear. I'm glad they sorted it out. We won't be around for much longer to keep her out of trouble.'

'Yeah. Not much longer at all.' Noah watched the kids on the oval playing footy. From the look on his face I could almost hear the music to the montage of memories playing in his head. For a bloke he could be ridiculously nostalgic. So could Aunt Lily, refusing to read *Snugglepot* to me after my dad had died. And my mother? Had she even thought about me since she'd left?

I was becoming obsessed.

I wanted to ask Noah if he would help me to find her, but maybe I was better off not asking anyone anything. If I didn't bring it up, I wouldn't have to try to articulate what I was feeling. But how could I understand what I *should* feel without talking to someone? I needed my best friend's advice.

'Catch 22,' Noah said.

'What?' Had I been thinking out loud?

'You're really not listening to me, are you? I said I was hoping to get my tandem hang gliding licence before uni starts next year, but I'm running out of time. It's going to be hard to fit in enough practice hours. It costs a lot in petrol to drive all the way to the training centre only to find that the weather's no good. I need money to get my licence, and I need the licence to earn more money.'

'Tandem licence? They trust you to take some poor sucker up there with you?' I wove two golden daisies together and tossed them into the air so we could watch them crash-land. Noah gave a half laugh but looked just a little bit offended, so I relented. 'Perhaps in the holidays I *will* come gliding with you,' I suggested. 'I'll pay for the petrol if you can get me a deal on a flight.'

He looked a bit uncomfortable. 'Um, Lainie, it might be better if you don't.'

'Good on ya,' I scoffed. 'I'm not that unco. If I can ride a horse I can fly a hang glider.'

His blond eyebrows rose. 'It's hardly the same thing as riding ...' But then he sighed. 'That's not what I meant, anyway. I just don't think Claudia would be too happy if I took you flying, that's all.'

My lapful of yellow daisies scattered in a flurry of agitation. 'Oh, come on! You can't be serious! Who does she think she is? How dare she try to tell you what you can and can't do?'

'Because only you're allowed to do that?' he snapped back.

'When have I ever—'

'Oh, let's see. How about yesterday when you told me I should get my Psych homework done instead of taking Claudia to the movies?'

'And did you listen to me?'

He made a rude, dismissive noise. 'Of course not! My point still stands, though. And how about all those times you keep telling me to—'

'Okay, this conversation is going nowhere good,' I interrupted.

'You're jealous.'

'Why would I be jealous of you? I can't stand Claudia. Her fingernails are too long and she ties her shoelaces funny.'

Noah's lips twitched in spite of himself, but then he caught my eye with a challenging stare. 'What if I'd asked you to come to the movies instead? Would you have still stayed home to study?'

My mouth kept working but all of my words were hiding somewhere behind my uvula. The cowards. I knew the correct response was

'Yes, unless it was a movie by Peter Jackson or Tim Burton,' but there was a serious glint in his eyes that made me pause. What exactly was he *really* asking?

When I didn't answer, he pressed further. 'You've never had a problem with me going out with other people before. Weren't you the one who "accidentally" let slip to Marko's mum that he'd failed his maths test, and then faked being sick so Taylor and I ended up at the movies by ourselves?'

I clamped my lips shut so I wouldn't be tempted to tell him how much Taylor had paid me for that little scheme. Thankfully, just then, a country and western ballad blared across the oval, signalling the end of lunch, so I reached for my bag instead of answering. But he didn't let it go.

'Claudia's my first proper girlfriend,' he explained, as if I didn't know. His arms were crossed and his eyebrows had a little furrow between them. 'I'm not certain about what the rules are.'

Those cowardly words must have been tickling the back of my throat because my laugh came out as more of a splutter. 'Rules? Hasn't your mum given you that talk?'

'I mean with you! I don't know if it's okay for you to come gliding with me. I don't *know* if I'm allowed to invite you both to watch the Nalong-Chentyn game, or come night fishing at the lake. Or if it's weird for us all to go to a concert together.'

That hurt. We'd always done everything together.

'Let me make it easy for you, then, Noah. I'm not going *anywhere* with you. Not until you work out what you *want* the rules to be. I won't tell you what to do, and neither should she!'

As I stomped back to class I knew the stress I was under was probably making me overreact, but that didn't mean I could stop it. Even if I'd wanted to.

Harry hobbled into the kitchen on Saturday morning looking weary but satisfied. He brought with him two large water drums that weighed him down so much he limped.

'It's as much as I could carry, Lily. It should help for a while.'

Aunt Lily looked relieved and helped him lift the containers up onto a spare stretch of bench. Harry changed the caps for ones with taps, turned the drums onto their sides, and then poured out some water into a glass. He took a big gulp then burped noisily. Yeah, supernatural custodian of the Garden of Eden. Sure he was.

'Thirsty, Lainie?' he asked.

'There are bugs floating in your drink, Harry.'

'You look like you could use the protein, you're a bit peaky,' he threw back.

'I am reluctant to ask, but why are you drinking river water? I thought you believed that all our local water was contaminated by the mining.'

'That's why we need it. Let's just say that this water isn't exactly local. It comes from a bit farther … upstream,' he said, rubbing his shoulder to ease the strain.

As in all decent faerie tales, the elves in my aunt's stories lived at the bottom of the garden. Or, to be more precise, the gateway to Paradise where they lived had always been located somewhere between our farm and the Ashbrees's. The river had been the source of much magic, because it flowed out from the garden and carried wishes in the spring-time. Somehow my six-year-old brain had failed to understand that the river flowed all the way through the Ashbrees's farm as well, so it couldn't possibly have its source between the two properties. Nor had I known enough to question how the Garden of Eden could be here when the biblical account placed it somewhere in the region that had flooded around 8,000 years ago to form the Persian Gulf.

Enough was enough. Something had to be said. 'Are you implying that this water comes from the Garden of Eden?'

'Yes. Yes I am. Well, as close as I could get without crossing over the boundary.'

'So those are Eden bugs you're drinking?'

Harry gagged mid-gulp, spraying water across the kitchen. He threw me a dirty look, but then cocked his head to one side, peering at the water critically. Aunt Lily looked startled.

'Unlikely,' he decided. 'The water passes through a cave system and has plenty of time to pick up our local wildlife before it gets to where I collected it.'

Fine. I was up for a gag. I wanted to see just how far they were going to take it. 'Are you sure you should be telling me all this? Isn't this all a big secret? How do you know I won't start blabbing it all over school?' I asked with mock sincerity.

The two old friends looked at each other seriously. 'What exactly would you say, and to whom?' asked Aunt Lily, sliding onto one of the kitchen chairs.

'What if I confided in the school counsellor that I thought you were both turning into crazy bush hermits?' Yet even as I said it, I felt a twisting heaviness in the pit of my stomach. An overwhelming feeling of shame. I felt sick with it, and I hadn't even done anything. I honestly didn't think I could ever get the words out of my mouth to talk about Eden. It was a relief just to stop *thinking* about telling someone. The feeling was completely disproportionate to the circumstances.

'I don't think Scott Henry would see anything unusual there.' Harry grinned. 'Scotty used to call me the Nargun of Nalong back when we played footy together. He once came out of a bad tackle and said I was half human and half rock.'

The Nargun was a rock monster that kidnapped children who came too close to its cave. At least that was what Aboriginal parents used to tell their kids in order to keep them away from the forbidden site where it lived.

'Nargun? Really? How many more folktales can you throw at me?'

Harry's grin was gone in an instant. 'And who are you to decide if something's a folktale?' he bit back. 'Every yarn contains someone's truth. Don't ever disregard someone else's perspective. You're better than that, Lainie.'

It felt as though he'd slapped me. Harry never got angry. Ever. Except for that one time Noah and I had nicked his old model boat and lost it in the river. Even then, he'd seemed more sad than angry. I turned to Aunt Lily who looked, if anything, even more furious. That, at least, I was used to.

I lowered my eyes. 'I'm sorry, Harry. I didn't think. And you're right. I've been ignoring your perspective on this. If you believe it, then I need to stop being so …'

'Cynical?' Harry offered.

'Disrespectful,' I said.

He poured a glass of river water, and held it out to me, challenging me to make my apology a real one. It actually looked pretty clear – no visible swimmers. I'd been drinking from the river all my life and it didn't bother me. It was all the other implications that made me uncomfortable. Accepting the glass, I took a swig. It tasted amazing. Like home.

∽

Many restless hours later I swallowed my prickly pride and went to find the enigmatic farmer. The sun was just thinking about drifting towards the horizon and a mob of kangaroos were busy making the most of the crepuscular grazing time at the top of the hill. Harry had just put the tractor away and was bringing a mug of coffee out to his porch to enjoy the view. I quietly joined him. It was time I found out what he really believed.

We sat comfortably for a few minutes, as we had done hundreds of times over the years, but this time my mind was spinning with awkward questions. His kind eyes held a perception that felt so ancient I had to remind myself we had only celebrated his fortieth birthday a few months earlier, but on the other hand, his athletic frame and smooth dark complexion had often caused people to mistake him for someone much younger. According to some of the gossip in the pub, he was still one of Nalong's most eligible bachelors. Weird town.

I fiddled with a loose strand of my hair. I had a lot on my mind, but didn't have the foggiest idea where to start. Harry, as usual, knew exactly what I needed.

He cleared his throat. 'Your aunt told me about the photo,' he said. 'And that she told you about me.' His patient voice was irritating. 'You want to know three things. Firstly, am I immortal?'

My shoulders slumped. He did believe it.

'Secondly, do I have any superpowers? And thirdly, am I the only one?'

Actually, I had a lot more than three questions, but I wasn't remotely ready for even those three. Hearing him come right out and talk about it like he expected me to believe him was so disturbing that I just sat there in a sort of dazed silence, picking at the hole in my jeans.

'No, I'm not immortal. I'm not entirely human, but I am supposed to be able to pass as one, so physically at least I am more or less human, and have been since the day I was born. I doubt any medical tests would be able to tell the difference, although at the rate medicine is advancing, who knows what they might uncover? Doctors have always made me … uncomfortable.' The way he rubbed absently at his still aching shoulder made me wonder how often he had avoided getting medical attention over the years. Farm work wasn't always kind on your body, no matter how fit you were.

He peered at me as if assessing how I was doing so far, so I nodded. I was *not* going to lose my temper again. Or argue, if I could avoid it. I was going to sit quietly and listen to him try to explain how it was all supposed to work.

He took a long swig from his coffee mug before continuing. 'The only "superpower" I really know anything about is being able to feel when people are getting too close to the cave system. It makes me uncomfortable, and sometimes I kind of have … well, visions. I can sense where people are. It's a kind of warning system that even wakes me if I'm asleep. I also have some occasional insights into people's lives. Nothing very obvious or specific, just hunches. I think it helps me to persuade people to change their course of action if they get too close to finding out things they shouldn't. Usually just changing the topic of conversation at the right time is enough.' He leant forward in his chair. 'There are more … back up skills available to me if I need them, but luckily I haven't had a lot of experience with those.' A slight shudder went through him. Whatever experience he'd apparently had, it was obviously not something he wanted to talk about because he sat back again and looked away.

Frankly, that was a bit disappointing. He should have at least been able to fly.

'You look somewhat unimpressed,' he said observantly.

'Well, honestly, I'd hardly class those as superpowers. I mean, can't everyone kind of do most of those things from time to time?'

He shook his head, looking almost reluctant to continue. 'No, Lainie,' he admitted finally, swirling the dregs of his coffee. 'Most people can't do what you and I can. They are Cherubic traits, not human ones.'

Chapter 8

My mouth opened and shut itself a couple of times as the meaning of what Harry was telling me sank in. When my voice finally obeyed me it came out sounding a bit like one of the Chipmunks. 'You and I?'

'Don't tell me you haven't had your suspicions,' he said. 'Things have been changing since the miners started nosing around. Their activities have been triggering something in you. Visions, at least. Am I right?'

I thought back to the dream I'd had of my aunt chained to the bull-dozer. How it had been correct down to the way her bra strap had been slipping off her shoulder because her hands weren't free to fix it. There had also been the vision I'd had of Tessa in front of the mirror. But those were hardly the only visions I'd ever had. Ever since I could remember I'd been experiencing odd, random flashes of people's lives—especially if they were lying or being deceitful about something. Noah had told me it was just déjà vu but now Harry was implying it was something else. And I couldn't deny that the latest visions had been much more … specific.

If in doubt, fall back on sarcasm. 'And Aunt Lily too, I assume? Does she turn into a demon if we feed her after midnight?'

'You aunt is a completely normal human.'

'Now I know you're lying,' I said, but I knew he wasn't. 'Okay, so where is it?' I laughed softly.

'Near the river there's a—'

'No! Where's my letter from Hogwarts? I know Australia is a long way for an owl to fly, but they're very late. Still, I could probably agree to repeating at least some of high school if it means I get to—'

'Lainie, please don't. This is serious.'

'Not a witch then? Fine. How about a half-blood daughter of a god?

Can I control any of the elements? When do we leave for training camp so I can learn how to fight? Do I get to use a sword?'

The usually unflappable farmhand was so exasperated that he groaned and buried his head in his hands.

I stretched my legs out in front of me and tried again. 'Please tell me that I can at least hunt demons!' I peered around the small garden to find where Aunt Lily was hiding. Surely she was ready somewhere with a camera.

'Lainie, please, this is no game.' He looked me right in the eye. 'We can't do magic spells, we can't control the elements, and we're not demon hunters. We're just farmers with a sacred duty to keep humans away from the land we belong to, and we only get given the power we need to be able to do our job. No more, no less, and only when we need it.'

The bleak honesty in his gaze was a powerful thing, and once again there was a genuine sympathy there that completely undid all my sarcastic defences—way too quickly for me to be able to adjust. He was telling the truth.

Reflexive anger took over. 'I'm sorry, but are you trying to tell me that I'm not *human?*' I stood up, clutching my empty mug like a stress ball. My temper was becoming a slippery thing to hold.

'There is no good way to break this news to you, Lainie. I'm so sorry, but you need to know. Your soul is linked to this place. It's an undeniable bond that will shape every choice you make from now on.' Then he winced. 'You won't be able to leave.'

I slammed my mug down on the porch railing. I didn't know the correct etiquette involved in responding to the news that I was a Cherub appointed by God as a sentinel of the Garden of Eden, but I felt fairly certain that a dramatic storming out could probably be justified, just this once. I got about four angry strides away before Harry changed the course of my life with just six easy words.

'Can you hear the river crying?'

I stopped like I had seen a snake and turned, desperately searching his eyes for the truth. 'You hear that? In your sleep?' I whispered.

'I always hear it,' he replied, staring to the northwest. His ageless brown eyes revealed a deep longing that reflected the grief of the music far too well.

'Is it always so sad?'

He stood up and walked over to me, then took my hands in his. As soon as his calloused fingers touched mine, my head was filled with wordless song, beautiful and devastating, yearning for something lost, calling …

'No, Lainie, it used to energise and sustain me, like a drug. I could never stay away from the river for long, but now …'

'I just want to turn it all off!'

Harry pulled me into his chest and hugged me, letting me pour out all my tiredness and confusion. It was the most physical contact we'd ever had. It was what I imagined a father would do.

'Are you … ? Are we … ?' I struggled to stop blubbering and get the words out, but I just couldn't do it. I couldn't bear to hear any more. I hated that I was crying again. And I hated Harry for the simple fact that I knew he wasn't deliberately lying. I always knew. Harry believed that he was a Cherub, and so was my mother. And so was I.

The more questions I thought to ask, the more I realised I was afraid of his honest answers, so I shook myself free from his arms and backed away like he was some sort of dangerous animal. As I tripped over the edge of his rose garden, he made one last attempt to suck me in.

'I'm going to Eden, Lainie. I'm sorry, but I can't wait any longer. I'm going to talk to your mother and try to find out why the river is so sad. Then I'm going to ask her to help me to get rid of those miners once and for all.'

I refused to listen.

Chapter 9

High above the ground, the Sentinel stood right on the point of the tree branch between where her weight was supported easily and the bendy region where a sudden movement would surely send her to her death again.

The view was spectacular enough to distract her for quite some time, and she soaked it in as greedily as her lungs soaked in air—scented with pine and honey and blossoms—as she recovered from the climb. Under her feet, helpful rustling reminded her how deeply she was loved and cherished here, as the tree began to redirect its energy into growing faster beneath her toes, the branch thickening and strengthening with miraculous speed. The timeless pine hungered to keep her safe at least as much as it hungered for the sweet nectar of warm sunlight. Deep textured wisdom flowed up through the core of its massive trunk, tasting the atmosphere to assess her needs as well as its own.

She brushed her fingertips across the tips of the pine needles. Their scent tripped threads of elusive memories—decorated trees on Christmas mornings with ACDC echoing across the backyard and Dad yelling at Mum to turn it down and Mum yelling back that he must be getting old and would he like a glass of sherry and Dad teasing her back by saying he'd prefer a shandy … but those memories were best left behind. Still, something tugged at her, from the east, demanding her attention in a place where demands were meaningless. Something forgotten, and uncomfortable to dwell on. Something that made her want to stay distracted enough not to have to think about it, and death was very distracting.

Above her head, sparrows flicked around tiny gusts of air with each wing beat, throwing in random bursts of speed every time there was a hint of a pause in their song like they were playing musical chairs. Smiling, she pulled a slightly squished piece of Fruit from where it had been tucked under her belt, and then she launched herself from the branch, up towards the graceful sky.

Adrenaline washed away her lingering discomfort as she plummeted past the base of the tree and down into the rocky gorge that it leant out over. Remnant reflexes from another world caused her to gasp, and for a second her limbs became rigid in response to her body's perceived danger, but that only lasted for a few moments. She inhaled sweet life to drown the memories, and then let her breath out again with a laugh as she noticed the sparrows trying to follow her, unable to fall nearly as well with their hollow bones. Poor little things. Spreading her arms and legs in glorious celebration, she flew downwards faster than she could move in any other game, wishing she could somehow break the laws of gravity and move even more quickly. But then it wouldn't last as long. As it was, the ground was rising up far too rapidly. She would have to ask around to see if any of her friends knew of anywhere higher to jump from. They would laugh at her childishness, but to them she *was* still a child, and they loved to indulge her.

Below, the River sparkled, its curved body growing fatter as she approached it. The darker blue of its deepest pool called to her like a lover ready to fold her into his arms, and tears fell through her laughter. In her blurred vision, the River became a spiral of blue, curling around a plain brown shell. Lost. She had lost it, so long ago, and with it she'd lost her lover's embrace. As she hit the water with explosive force, bones broke, bruises blossomed like tulips at dawn, and the piece of Fruit she had been clutching floated away from her limp fingers.

By the riverbank, a tall Tree swayed in the gusty breeze, scattering out a flurry of dry leaves. A little while later, after the Sentinel had been found by her friends and had tasted life again, a silver branch cracked and fell.

The Tree was dying.

Chapter 10

The following morning, Harry's ute was still parked by his cottage, but he was gone. Unless someone had driven in to collect him during the night without me noticing, it meant that he must have gone somewhere on foot. But there was nowhere logical for him to go. Was he camping out in the bush somewhere just to prove a point?

No matter how many times I pestered my aunt, she never changed her story. 'No, Lainie, your mother hasn't been living as a bush hermit for the last thirteen years', went right alongside 'Yes, Lainie, the Garden of Eden was moved to Australia in order to keep it hidden', and 'No, Lainie, I can't tell you who moved it or how, because Harry can't talk about it openly to just any old human like myself. You should have asked him when you had the chance.'

I lost count of how many times she said, 'No, Lainie, you can't go and look for them because Harry once told me that when you cross into Eden you completely lose track of time, and I don't want you to miss your exams.'

After a while she started to sound kind of snippy. Which *might* have had something to do with the fact that all my questions were either sarcastic or just plain snide. It didn't work anyway; she still stuck to her story, so eventually I gave up asking. Harry was more than capable of taking care of himself and would return eventually. And if my mother happened to reappear at the same time, then I would play along with any fantasy they wanted. If not, then I would find a way to scrounge enough money to hire a private detective to pick up where my internet searches for her had fallen to dead ends. It was constantly in the back of my mind, to the point that I kept looking over my shoulder, expecting to see people there, invading my space, and half hoping one of them might look like the young woman in the photo who had been singing to me. It was driving me crazy.

So then I threw myself into a fury of exam study and avoided talking to my aunt about anything other than day-to-day, mundane things, and I avoided Noah too, because he'd spat the dummy with me after our little fight and had become unbelievably sulky. It was a lonely and fretful couple of weeks.

Muck Up day arrived with dramatic thunderstorms at the end of October—our last bit of fun before exams. It was ridiculous how we could go from years of drought to a season of flash flooding seemingly overnight. My last-minute costume of ripped jeans, fake wounds and mummy bandages looked fine until I had to complete the outfit with a Driza-bone coat.

We were supposed to arrive early but I still had to rely on the bus, so by the time I got to school the pranks were already in full swing. I was just volunteering to climb onto the roof of the staff room with some paint when Noah and Claudia arrived, dressed up as an angel and she-devil respectively. A flash of irritation shot through me and I shoved the tin of paint into the hands of another nearby student. Claudia wasn't even a Nalong College student—what was she doing here? To make matters worse, Noah was bare-chested but wearing the huge pair of wings that I had made him the previous month. It had taken hours to stick on all the chicken feathers. Wistfully I had to admit that they looked better than I had expected—wings kind of suited him—and I probably would have been even more annoyed if they had gone to waste. And yet I still fought the urge to go over and rip them from his shoulders and shove them somewhere that Claudia wouldn't enjoy. I was not usually so petty but something about that girl just made my fake blood boil.

Claudia was small, willowy, and about as clever as a toothpick. Pale and dainty as a dandelion, we were all just waiting for her to fall in love with a vampire, werewolf or angel. Instead she'd snared Noah, and now they were kissing over by the water bubblers and Taylor was giving me a revoltingly sympathetic look and Noah was pretending he hadn't seen me. What had happened to my friend? He'd always been so fervent in his ideologies, saying he wouldn't just behave the way everyone expected of a teenage boy, and I'd believed him. I just hoped he believed in himself enough to remember.

Suddenly I felt overwhelmingly tired, grouchy and could no longer deny how stupid I'd been to alienate my best friend just when I really needed someone to talk to. I kept my head down for the rest of the morning so I wouldn't be noticed, which worked fine until I needed the loo. Unfortunately the toilets had all been filled with gelatine or covered with sugar, and because of the intermittent hail storms, all the sugar and flour inevitably used in every prank was starting to form a sweet, cakey layer over everything.

As I was sneaking out of the staff toilets, Mrs Ashbree appeared in the foyer, talking to the principal. A sullen-looking Nicole stood nearby, trying to look invisible. It seemed that Noah's sister had been skipping school again. Naturally, it was just at that moment that the loud speakers started blaring out 'Eagle Rock' at a deafening volume. Mr Davis groaned, knowing perfectly well what was coming next, and sure enough, as I shadowed them out of the staff building we were confronted with students of every year level converging in the quadrangle and dropping their pants.

The 'Eagle Rock' de-pantsing tradition was compulsory for Muck Up day. Usually Mr Davis just hid in his office trying to ignore what he had no means to control, but this time he had Mrs Ashbree there. Nicole took full advantage of the distraction and was off like a bride's nightie, racing for the nearest building to hide. Mrs Ashbree appeared to be trying hard not to laugh—up until the moment the crowd of students parted and she saw Noah and Claudia. Noah had already been topless so everyone was now openly admiring the sight of him dancing in the rain in just his worn-out boxers and a giant pair of wings. Hardly anyone even noticed Claudia, who was wearing not much other than a red crop-top, knickers, and a predatory expression. Hardly anyone except Noah's prudish mum.

Furious didn't begin to cover it. In years to come Sarah Ashbree's tirade would become legend at the school. She went totally troppo and her shrill yelling lasted almost to the end of the song. Mr Davis dragged Claudia off towards his office—possibly for her own protection—while Mrs Ashbree continued to rant at her son, seemingly without drawing a single breath. The words 'disrespect' and 'flaunting' and 'that Jezebel' echoed around the brick buildings, and I was certain the phrase 'should have sent you to a monastery' came up more than once. Finally she whispered something in Noah's ear that made him shudder, and he meekly followed her to her car.

The rest of the students stood stunned with their pants around their ankles, all trying hard not to be the first to start laughing. As soon as the car pulled away though, all hell broke loose in the courtyard.

I just shrugged, did up my jeans and went to talk to Tessa, who looked like all her Christmases had come at once.

Exams came around with an anti-climax worthy of a long-awaited series final. Most of them were easier than I had expected, which I hoped meant that at least my lonely study time had paid off. Even English was all right; we had to write a poem about 'hidden beauty' and I started with some clichéd piece about the rugged countryside, which inevitably led to a description of a river. It flowed wherever it was welcomed. The sentient water revelled in the joyful play of the people, and was sensitive to all their hopes and longings, pain and fears. Then of course all the musical sadness I had bottled inside me leaked out into my poem until I had written something passionate and real. Perhaps more hidden misery than hidden beauty, but artistic enough to satisfy an examiner, I hoped.

And then that was it. School had finished and there were just a couple of weeks to go until graduation and then summer holidays, followed by the bright new existence known as university, which meant moving to the city. No rural student ever felt entirely ready for that. I didn't even like going to the city on holidays. I literally got homesick if I was away for more than a week or so. Actually sick, not just whiney. Embarrassing but true.

With just scant weeks to go, I still hadn't decided what I wanted to study or where. A firm decision would have to be made soon or I wouldn't have anywhere to live. I enjoyed science but couldn't see myself working in a research lab all my life. I had submitted applications for some environmental studies courses but I just didn't have a clear sense that it was what I wanted to do. The idea of travelling overseas for a while sounded glorious, but that took money, and I had struggled enough this year finding time to help on the farm—no way could I have managed a job in town as well. Maybe I could work in town next year, then travel, then study? I knew too many people who talked about that but ended up working for two years, then three, then meeting someone. That was a trap for sure.

And somewhere, in the very back corner of my brain lurked the memory of Harry's regretful words: *Your soul is linked to this place. It's an undeniable bond that will shape every choice you make from now on. You won't be able to leave.*

As the days grew hotter I threw myself into trying to catch up with the farm work. With Harry away there was always more to do but I couldn't believe how tired I was getting. Each morning I popped vitamins like lollies but it didn't help much. Every time I mentioned it to Aunt Lily she would hand me a piece of bland fruit and a glass of water. That had always been her thing, whatever was wrong with me, my whole life. From a headache to just a bad hair day, her remedy was always predictably the same: 'Have a glass of water, Lainie.' Sometimes I wondered if she would recommend the same thing if my head fell off. 'Have some water, Lainie, you'll feel better.' Now, of course, I realised why the ceramic water cooler had always been filled with river water. I'd always assumed it was just because she thought it was cleaner than what came out of our elderly rain-water tank. Problem was, the supply Harry had brought us from 'upstream' was now getting low and my aunt was rationing it—only adding a dash of it to each glass of water she poured me. It was hard not to wonder if that really was why I was getting more tired. Despite my determination to keep my conscious thoughts firmly refuting the existence of Eden, I often found myself subconsciously asking, 'But what if?'

And then came the day that I had another vision. In it, Harry was standing in the mouth of a cave, staring off into the bush. He was facing the sun, which was low in the sky, just about to fall below the line of the ridge to the west. His attention was on something he couldn't see, as if he was having a vision of his own. And I felt as if I knew what it was. There were people—just a couple of them—walking through a patch of red and yellow flowered egg-and-bacon shrubs. Their steel-capped boots left a graveyard of broken twigs behind them, disturbing ground that cried a warning to any who would listen. And someone was. Harry breathed in deeply, his face a study of such intense concentration that one of his nostrils twitched. He walked backwards a few steps, and then spun and stumbled back into the cave.

My eyes snapped open so fast I could almost hear them. Something was happening. Something ... *needed*. Because those people were just too close. They shouldn't be there. They had no right. I wouldn't let them come a single step closer ...

The ground shuddered, deep but faint, and my foot rolled under me as I realised I had been moving, heading to where I was needed. I looked up. The sun was sinking languidly below the ridge line far to the west, just as it had been in my vision, but from a slightly different angle. What I'd seen was not a premonition, or a memory. It was happening *now*. Feeling somewhat shaken, I dropped to a crouch and placed my hands flat on the ground. The rumble was settling, and with it went the sense of urgency that had made my feet move without my permission. I could no longer see what was happening out there, but I *felt* the two people stop, and then turn around. Perhaps they had noticed the ground shaking too. But what had caused it? Feeling a bit stupid, I closed my eyes and tried to get the vision back, but it was gone. A moment ago, Harry's presence had felt as solid as if he was standing beside me, but now the whole thing just felt like it had all been my imagination. When I opened my eyes again, one of the lambs was looking at me as if I had gone nuts.

Shooing it along with the last of the skittish sheep into a fresh paddock, I swung the gate shut and went to find Aunt Lily. She was just hanging up the phone as I entered the kitchen.

'Did you feel that, Aunt Lil?'

'I did. It was probably the mining company. They've been mapping and ground testing the area west of the fire track. They aren't supposed to come on this side of it but I don't trust them.'

'What do you think it was?'

'My guess is some sort of a landslide or cave-in. They aren't supposed to be using explosives—at least not until their environmental assessments have been finalised—but there are extensive cave systems around there, and maybe they drilled an unstable area.'

Cave-in? Like the cave from my vision? The one that Harry had gone into?

'Should we look for Harry?' I asked. 'I wish he'd taken the sat-phone! It's not fair on us to have to worry like this.'

'You know how much he hates phones,' she pointed out, staring out of the window as if she was trying to spot him out there somewhere.

It was true. Unless it was an emergency, Harry avoided the things like a disease. He didn't even have a landline extension to his cottage, but used ours instead. It wasn't really ever a problem because the only person who ever called him was Stumpy Johnson on the odd occasion that he needed to cancel their fortnightly fishing afternoon.

'Anyway, Harry is fine.' She smiled slightly. 'I could tell you how I know if you like.' She was doing some sample drilling of her own, trying to test my reactions.

My hands stopped rummaging through the pantry for snacks. Was it really possible that the legendary Garden of Eden was out there some-where? On our land? Even if our property was four times the size I'd always thought it was, I still couldn't quite see an entire Paradise fitting into it. Not to mention the fact that it was all thick bush, steep hills and utterly inaccessible valleys.

Perhaps it was because I'd had a few weeks to let the idea sink in, or maybe I was simply tempted by the idea that my mother was out there somewhere just waiting for me to believe in Eden so I could find her, but as I stood there, holding a handful of Nutri-Grain, I realised I was actually starting to accept the whole crazy story. The realisation frightened me so much that I started to cry. My aunt came and hugged me and didn't speak. She didn't push me, and didn't try to tell me I would feel better if I talked about it, and at that moment I totally loved her.

I didn't need a mother. Aunt Lily knew me much better than the woman who had abandoned me all those years ago.

Chapter 11

That week things got progressively worse. The sad melody of the river had become so addictive that it was starting to drift its way into my mind even when I was awake. It was an all-out struggle to focus on any sort of task properly and eventually I noticed my hands trembling as I was trying to cook dinner.

When we finished up our meal I carried my dishes to the dishwasher, watching my knife and fork jiggle about as I tried to keep them balanced on my plate.

'It's okay, Lainie, honey, I'll do it,' said Aunt Lily, catching my fork with her shoe as it fell.

I slumped back down at the table. 'What's wrong with me? Why am I always so exhausted?' Our supply of 'upstream' river water had run out and I couldn't help noticing that my tiredness had worsened significantly since then. There had to be a reason why, so I figured I might as well hear her explanation, if she had one.

She handed me a homegrown apple, and started filling the sink with hot water for the pots and pans. 'You're lacking an essential nutrient. Well, it's essential for you, not for me. It's a compound that's only found in this river, as far as I know. The contaminants in the water are probably reacting with it and changing it into something else. Up until recently the locally grown fruit has had enough of whatever it is to sustain you, but not anymore.'

I thought it must be something like that. At least now I knew where my fruit gluttony came from. 'Is that why all our fruit tastes weird these days?'

She nodded, looking defeated. 'I'll leave for Melbourne in the morning. The only thing I can think to do is to take the dregs of the water

Harry brought back from the Eden boundary and have it analysed. Maybe if they compare it to a contaminated sample, we can find out what the compound is that you need and then maybe we can figure out a way to get it from another source. I have a contact that might be able to help but I'll need to go in person to avoid a whole lot of unwelcome questions. I might as well check out the Gippsland sales while I'm down that way too. Can you manage here for a few days?' She placed her arm around my shoulders.

I thought about all the work there was to do outside and how bone weary I was. And what if Kolsom came snooping around where they shouldn't? What was I meant to do then? But she was doing this for me. How could I complain?

'Of course, Aunt Lil, it's me. I can do anything. I'm a Cherub, aren't I?'

≈

I lasted almost two whole days on my own before giving up and calling Noah. There wasn't really any choice. A vicious windstorm had ripped through like a freight train during the night and a massive tree had come down on one of the fences. I managed ten minutes of chain-sawing before deciding it was just too dangerous in my pathetic state. Despite our recent awkwardness Noah came straight away, and after we repaired the fence I invited him to come in for a coffee.

'Are you sure, Lainie? I mean, I'm happy to help but don't feel you need to cross any boundaries you've made.'

I chuckled tiredly at his choice of phrase.

'Just come in, Noah. I'm too tired to avoid you today.' Stripping my leather gloves off, I slapped him playfully with them before chucking them in the shed with the rest of the tools.

We headed inside and I put the kettle on while he raided the pantry as he had always done. The fruit bowl was nearly empty but I found some bottled pears in the bottom of the cupboard. We polished them off along with a whole lot of Vegemite toast, which we shared with the cat.

'Oh, mate, I've been so hungry lately! I ate an entire box of nectarines yesterday. It must be a post-exam thing,' Noah said, catching the toast I dropped as I juggled the last two pieces from the toaster.

'Nice to have them over with, though. And from what you said about the chemistry exam, I reckon you blitzed it.'

'So long as I did enough to get into Ag Science, I'm happy.'

The thought returned that if what Harry had said was true then there was a very real possibility that I might not be going anywhere next year, and I wasn't certain how I felt about that. I'd spent a long time preparing for the idea of leaving home and now I couldn't work out if I felt relieved or disappointed. A bit of both really. Noah looked a little lost too as he spooned some Vegemite straight out of the jar. He didn't seem comfortable with the idea of moving to the city either.

'It'll be great, Noah, you'll love uni. You're such a people person. City life will suit you. Then you can come back and make your millions revolutionising our farms.' He smiled in rueful confirmation that I had guessed his anxious thoughts correctly.

Tossing my crusts to Inara, I headed for the door. As much as I wished he could stay longer, I didn't want him to start asking me about my plans for next year. Had I just wasted all that effort on school? I had a thing or two to say to Aunt Lily if that was the case.

He picked up his car keys and started to leave, but stopped with his hand on the door handle and looked down self-consciously. 'Mum said that you aren't expecting Harry to come home for a while. I guess it's about time he had a holiday.' He cleared his throat uncomfortably. 'When does your aunt get back? Do you ... need a hand with anything else?'

Man, I had certainly made things awkward between us if he didn't even know if he was welcome to offer to help.

'She's not due back until Wednesday. I could use some help, I guess. That would be really awesome, Noah, thanks. But only if you aren't needed elsewhere,' I added quickly.

'They don't need me,' he smiled, fiddling with his watch. 'They have Nicole! She's trying hard to prove she can manage the farm entirely on her own. I think she plans on ditching school altogether as soon as she's allowed. Besides, Mum's been acting a bit weird lately. I'd rather stay out of the way of both of them.'

'What about Claudia? Shouldn't you be spending time with her?' I tried hard to keep the edge out of my voice.

'Claudia's out of the picture, Lainie. Mum kind of scared her off.'

I absolutely loved Mrs Ashbree sometimes. 'Oh. Your mum can be a bit scary. I'm sorry things didn't work out for you.'

He looked at me intently, his bright green eyes piercing. 'Are you, Lainie? You didn't seem all that enthusiastic about her.'

'Well, maybe not *her*. Maybe pick someone with more common sense than a peanut next time. Did she really ask your mum's opinion about the lingerie she bought?'

He looked pained. 'Mum told her she loved it and already owned a set exactly the same. It put us both right off.'

I laughed so hard that Noah had to give in and see the funny side.

'Anyway,' he argued, 'why would she need common sense when she's such an adorable tiny pixie?' he asked, batting his long blond eyelashes at me and flashing his dimples.

'Urgh. Get out of here, before I chuck,' I said, poking him in the ribs. He'd always teased me about my farm-muscled shoulders and height, so I knew we were reverting back to our normal friendly banter. But then he grabbed my hand mid-poke and held onto it. 'I've missed you, Lain. It just hasn't been the same without you around.'

For some reason, I couldn't meet his eyes. 'I know, Noah, and I'm sorry I yelled at you. I'll try harder to be reasonable next time, I promise.'

He held my hand a moment longer, and took a short breath as if he wanted to say more, but then turned and walked out the door. 'I'll see you in the morning.'

The moment Aunt Lily returned on Wednesday afternoon, I plonked myself onto the couch and lay there like a lizard in the sun. I never wanted to move again. My bones felt like they had been replaced with jelly crystals and my head hurt. Aunt Lily poured herself a glass of wine and joined me.

'How did you go? Any miracle cures for me?' Idly I plucked bits of fluff off the tired cushion I was cuddling and stared up at the ceiling. It had different cornices than the ceiling above my bed. I'd never noticed before. It was a reflection of the number of sleepless nights I'd spent staring up at it lately.

'Not yet, still working on it. It'll take a bit of chemical wizardry to find something unusual and then try to duplicate it without telling anyone why. My contact thinks I'm looking for mining contaminants. Luckily he's very much against the coal seam extraction process so he's genuinely enthusiastic about the opportunity to test the water. How did you manage here?'

'I had to ask Noah to help.'

She put her glass down gently. 'Oh. I understand. Is it still awkward between you?'

'Yes,' I said sulkily, 'but it's better now. I apologised.'

'About time. It's been weird not having him around.'

Something in my chest felt hot and swirly and unpleasant. 'Well, you'll have to get used to that. He'll be off to the city in a couple of months, after all.'

'And you too?' she asked tentatively.

'Me? How can I go anywhere? I'm stuck here, remember? Especially if I'm the only Cherub around to do whatever it is I'm supposed to be doing.'

'You'll still study, though. Most of the courses you applied for can be done by correspondence, with only a few trips into Melbourne each semester.'

'So you knew this was coming?'

'Lainie, even if Harry was still around I knew you would have some problems. Do you remember the last trip overseas we took?'

'Not really, I spent most of it feeling dizzy and nauseated.' Rotten homesickness. That had been a few years ago though, and I'd assumed it would pass as I got older. 'Was that because of the nutrient I can only get from here?'

'Possibly. I really will do everything I can to try to solve that issue, but I'm not confident that's all it is. I think you're *meant* to stay in Nalong.'

That was what Harry had implied, too. 'So that's it?' I snapped. 'I'm just supposed to settle down here and farm for the rest of my life?'

'Would that be so bad?'

In an unusual moment of clarity I realised that she had done exactly that, for me. Somehow I'd never considered that she might have had another life planned. Did she ever have a different career? A relationship with someone special? Just what had she given up to look after me, knowing we had to stay in this town permanently? I cuddled the cushion again. 'Sorry. I guess I just need some time to adjust to the idea. I don't like having my choices taken away from me. I didn't mean to sound so petulant.'

Her face softened. 'It's fine. Totally understandable. We'll find a way, Lainie. I want you to study. I want you to have every opportunity that your parents didn't. We'll work something out.'

She left to unpack her bag as I stared dejectedly at the non-matching cornices.

Chapter 12

Friday afternoon was stinking hot to the point where we could have easily cooked eggs on the pavement. We were all dressed formally for our school graduation ceremony and our assembly hall wasn't air conditioned. Some of the parents in the seating at the back were nodding off by the end of Mr Davis's address. I couldn't believe this was the last time we would have to sit through one of his speeches. Most of the girls looked teary as the ceremony ended and I became heartily sick of girls coming up to me for soggy hugs, congratulating me on making school dux and trying to make me promise I would Facebook them every day.

Eventually all the students headed down to the river for a quick swim before the after-party at the pub.

Noah made it into the water first, courtesy of the fact that he didn't bother to take off anything but his shoes. He and the other boys just dive-bombed in off the bridge. Loudly. We had all swum there for years and knew where it was safe to jump. I stripped down to my bathers, while on the riverbank the other girls squealed about how cold it was and that they couldn't possibly get their hair wet before the party. Which was probably just as well because there were a lot of bikinis that looked unsafe for any sort of decent current strength. Ridiculous.

The short moment of free-fall from the bridge was delicious, but as soon as I hit the water I realised I had a serious problem. The water was energising, but the music rippling through it was so overpowering that I burst into tears. The agony of its cry ripped through me like a shockwave. Lost! Something so lost, yearning to find … someone? So alone. So sad … With shallow gasps I floundered back to the riverbank, slipping painfully on the rocks. Trying to avoid eye contact with anyone,

I scrambled up on to the rough grass, trembling and hoping no one would notice my tears given that I was wet through anyway.

Noah did. He followed me out. He always seemed to know when I was trying to hide something.

'What's wrong, Lainie?' he asked as he sat next to me on the grass, his jade eyes brimming with concern.

'Nothing, I'm fine. You go enjoy playtime. I'm just going to lie in the shade for a while,' I said as I rummaged through my bag for my towel and sundress.

'Can I get you some water?'

'No thanks, I drank enough of the river.'

'Ah, Lainie, that's not really the best idea when there are eleven sweaty guys swimming in there.'

Groaning, I lay back and tried not to think about it.

'I think I might stay out of the water for a while anyway so let me know if I can get you anything,' he offered, taking off his drenched shirt. He looked a bit uncomfortable.

'Really, I'm fine, Noah, stop worrying. Go and show your abs off somewhere else.' I was confused and grumpy and struggling to keep my attention away from the dirge echoing around my skull.

Shrugging, he got to his feet and went off to join the game of footy that had inevitably started up. He looked about as tired as I felt, although he was hiding it well. The searing heat was obviously getting to him too.

∽

The late afternoon sun reflected in the beast's eyes. We crouched, facing each other, muscles tense and both staring hungrily at the prize. Under no circumstances was I going to allow the beast to have it. It was mine to protect, and my will was stronger because I had a far greater appreciation of what it was worth. It was awe-inspiring, legendary. Battles had been fought over it, the battle songs known by all.

The prize rolled, arcing slightly, but neither of us allowed the movement to distract our concentration. I was good at this game but my opponent wasn't the same species I was used to. My usual opponents didn't generally growl quite so convincingly, or raise their hackles to such a bristly ridge of tan fur. The slobber wasn't new though, sadly.

Jake's dog growled again, so I did too. His language was clear. *My ball. Back off.*

I crouched even lower until the end of my thick plait was trailing in the dust. The late afternoon sun still had a bite and I could feel the back of my neck burning. My fingers pressed against the hard soil, painfully trying to support my weight but I couldn't move because my face was already way too close to the animal's yellow teeth as it was. The dog looked like a Besser brick on legs. The sort of creature that could be three days dead and still keep its jaws locked around a rabbit.

My ball. Mine, I told it silently. *Your voracious instincts will only ruin it.*

Noah's voice entreated warily from behind me. 'Lainie, let it go. We should probably start getting ready for the pub anyhow.'

He almost sounded worried.

'My ball,' I growled, and Noah made a frustrated sort of gargle in the back of his throat.

At the sound of my voice the animal took its gaze from the prize to stare at me instead, growled again, and I made the mistake of looking straight back into its cold black eyes. Direct eye contact with a predator was not ideal and the creature had just shifted the game to much higher stakes. In retrospect, growling back at it had possibly not been the smartest idea. I was a threat now, and it was too dangerous for me to look away. The beast's lip curled upwards and a nice gooey trail of saliva dripped from its mouth. I almost expected the grass it fell onto to hiss and dissolve and for a second I was sure I could see a dull red glow behind the animal's irises.

Then one front paw twitched and I very nearly flinched away. My heart rate doubled.

Behind me, Noah was calling to one of the other guys who had started the impromptu game. 'Chuck us that tennis ball! Lainie's about to become puppy food!'

A few more tense moments passed, during which I wondered whether I should have made out a will, or if Aunt Lily would just toss all my stuff onto the next bonfire the way she often threatened to. But then out of the corner of my eye I saw a tennis ball begin to bounce, enticingly close.

'Here, boy. Check this one out,' Noah tempted. 'It's smaller but very tasty. Like a teeny, tiny little kitten.'

A tail swished, and it definitely wasn't mine.

When the tennis ball bounced right under its nose, the animal's canine consciousness just couldn't resist. It flicked its eyes away from me for just a second, and I shuffled back. Noah caught the tennis ball again and threw it as hard as he could along the riverbank. The Staffy took off after it, its muscles bunching with far too much power for its short strides. When it captured its prey the dog kept running, off into the bushland.

Dusting off my sundress, I watched it disappear, shaking my head in disdain at its cowardice.

My friend acknowledged my fierce bravery with a slap across the back of my head. 'What was that all about?'

It was a very good question. While I'd been messing around with the guys, pretending to have far more energy than I really did, I'd been thinking about Kolsom, and our farm, my *home*, and how easy it could be for them to just decide to start mining wherever they wanted, and how I wouldn't know the first thing about how to kick them out. Then the dog had bounded in and stolen the footy and my surge of possessiveness may have gotten a little out of hand.

Instead of answering Noah, I picked up the liberated ball and cradled it to my chest, growling at him with one lip raised when he reached for it, which made him laugh.

'Are you sure you want to do this?' he asked, crouching slightly as he prepared to tackle the ball from my grip.

I tossed it to him. 'Not really. I'm kind of stuffed,' I admitted. 'I might just go and get changed.'

He kicked the ball back to its real owner, who had been waiting patiently. 'Good plan. I'll just go and apologise to Matt for losing his tennis ball and then I'll join you.'

It was now late enough in the afternoon that the thirsty wind gusts had begun to settle and most of the local students had long since gone home to get ready for the evening's festivities. My legs trembled as I trudged up the hill to the bridge, where I saw Jake whistling for his dog. I pointed vaguely in the direction I had last seen it, and then crossed the street towards Noah's ute where I had packed my clothes for the evening along with a bag of frozen oranges—not that they would still be frozen after an afternoon in a hot car. I needed a dose of … whatever it was that I needed. Of course, I made it most of the way there before realising I would need the car keys. No one usually locked their cars in our town but Noah had started to do it after Nicole had taken to driving off in it while no one was looking. I turned back and whistled to him, the sound cutting across the noise of the river. One of the other guys heard me and tapped him on the shoulder, so I tried to signal that I needed his keys. All I got in response was a frantic waving of his arms. Did he really expect me to walk all the way back down again to get them?

The heartbreaking sound of a poor abused engine being over-revved intruded on our game of charades, and I twisted around to see where it was coming from. A faded blue sedan spun out of a side street and swerved into the main road, the angry squeal of its tyres sounding alien in the quiet afternoon. Stupid bogan drivers. With mindless unbelief, I watched it straighten and aim straight for me. I dodged to the right. It swerved the same way. So I stumbled left, and it followed me. It was like one of those awkward moments with an oncoming person in a busy shopping centre, only the sedan was travelling a heck of a lot faster than I was.

Snarling violence filled my ears.

Blue metal filled my vision.

The snarling sound grew into vicious growl inside my head as the mechanical blue beast charged for my throat and I felt something tug at my arm, but all my attention was focused on the death machine coming for me as I scrambled backwards, tripping over my own feet.

The car skimmed past me, its metal skin hot where it brushed against my shoulder as I fell.

An interrupted yelp and sickening crunch sounded simultaneously in my stunned ears, and I rolled back up to my knees just in time to see Jake's poor dog slide across the bitumen. Screaming brakes didn't quite save the sedan from mounting the kerb and hitting a street bin with a horrible metallic crunch.

Everything froze, and for a crystalline moment all I could see was the motionless form of the poor dog lying on the road, its limbs sticking out like spider's legs and its neck bent sickeningly. When I found the courage to look away, the sedan driver was stumbling out.

Bane.

Somehow he managed to look furious and terrified at the same time. Wearing old shabby jeans and a ripped T-shirt, he was sweat-soaked and shaking. He didn't even glance at the dog as he slammed his door shut and strode towards me.

'What the HELL is the matter with you!' I yelled. Any residual sympathy I'd had for him leaving school flew out the window with his apparent total lack of concern for what he'd just done. Finally forcing my limbs to move, I stood unsteadily and turned my back on him. I needed to see if the dog was alive.

Jake got there first and keened his grief-stricken conclusion. I stammered out something that sounded consoling, but I was too shaken to make much sense.

'Are you all right, Lainie?' Distress filled Jake's eyes as he looked up at me. His skinny arms lifted the heavy animal and I could see fresh blood smear across the half unbuttoned white shirt he'd worn for graduation. 'I don't know what got into him, he used to be so gentle. A bit of a boofhead and all, but always gentle! Lately he's been acting so weird, and it's not like him, I promise!' He held the beast's head on his lap, rocking back and forth. 'Bane, mate!' his voice cracked as he looked up. 'I tried to catch him but he was too quick, I'm so sorry!' As he spoke, Jake cringed away from the crazed dropout as he approached.

'Don't you dare apologise to him, Jake! He came out of nowhere! Seriously, Bane, what were you thinking?'

The shaken driver staggered towards us, sweat dripping from his hair and every muscle tense. 'I don't know. I had to … I don't know!'

He sounded confused and very angry. Maybe he'd hit his head?

Like some kind of raving animal he pinned me with his gaze and I froze. His voice became manic, hysterical, soaked in violence, with a depth to it that cut into my chest.

'I don't understand what's happening to me! I don't understand why I can't leave. I don't understand why I just can't leave you alone! I can't *stand* you! I can't stand to be around you!'. As he ranted he kept stumbling towards me, his expression terrifying.

Held motionless by his outspoken hatred, I couldn't even make myself step away. 'Why? Why me? What have I EVER done to you? Why do you hate me *so much?*' I yelled back, my own voice quivering with righteous pent-up anger for all his years of unsolicited abuse.

'*Because I hate who I am when I'm around you!*' he screamed, his voice splintering.

Silent seconds passed.

Mere inches from my face, he froze, looking even more baffled than I was. His pale grey eyes were locked on mine, tortured and intense. He smelled like strong alcohol.

'Stay away from me then,' I whispered. He was seriously frightening me now. It looked like every muscle in his body was seizing up as he took a deep breath in and reached for my left wrist. Blood dripped from a gory looking wound on my forearm that I hadn't even noticed. Had Jake's Staffy *bitten* me? Wincing from the suddenly noticed pain, I flinched away, but he grabbed me firmly.

'I *can't*, Lainie,' he snapped. He placed both his hands right on to the gash and I felt a flash of intense heat, as if my arm had just caught fire. Still he held on too tightly for me to pull away. It went beyond pain, like an electric shock that rearranged each one of my molecules. A split second before I could scream, the burning eased to a tingling warmth. He exhaled and all the tension drained out his body with his breath.

'Holey. Frickin. Swiss cheese!' exclaimed Jake, who had carried the dead dog to the footpath and was coming back to see if we were okay.

Looking down, I saw the smooth skin of my arm beneath a leftover smear of blood. The wound itself had vanished. Not a trace of a cut or even a graze. As my legs gave way, both boys grabbed me and lowered me to the ground just as Noah blew in like a cyclone.

'Lainie, are you all right?' he cried, shoving the others out of the way and kneeling down in front of me. His face was ashen and he was breathing hard.

'Apparently so. Why is everyone asking about me? Jake's the one who just lost his dog because of this maniac!'

'Thank God Bane arrived when he did! A split second later and you would have been dog meat!'

'What? What do you mean?'

'Did you seriously not notice the savage beast about to take you down like a bloody orphaned lamb? You were looking at me and I was trying to warn you but you just waved back at me like an idiot!' The obvious worry in his eyes softened the harshness of his words. 'Jake, do you *never* lock your gate?' he panted, still breathless from his sprint up the hill.

Jake had been staring at my arm but looked at Noah with a guilty expression. 'Of course I do, but somehow he always still gets out. I mean, got out. I am so sorry, Lainie.'

'Wait,' said Bane. 'Are you absolutely sure the dog was attacking her? I didn't just hit it for no reason?' His face was white and clammy and he looked like he was about to faint. It made no sense. Did *he* think he'd hit the dog for no reason?

'Yeah, mate, I know you saw it attack. What I don't understand is how you predicted it from so far away,' Noah said.

'We haven't told you the freaky bit yet,' Jake muttered, pointing at my arm.

'Okay. No. Time out,' I said, shaking them all away from me. 'I can't … I'm sorry. I just need to go home now. Bane, sit down before you fall down. I can't talk to you just yet. I don't know what you just did or whether I should be thanking you, apologising to you or suing you.'

He slumped down to the kerb, holding his head in his hands. 'Just stay the hell away from me,' he snarled.

Jake looked like he wanted to argue but Noah silenced him with a look and then held his hand out to me.

'Come on, I'll take you home.' He hauled me to my feet. 'You can tell me what's so freaky about your arm later. We'll leave these two to deal with the dog.' He winced at the blue sedan that was cuddling a rubbish bin. 'And the car. At least no one else is involved.'

The familiar feel of his arms steadied my trembling limbs as he guided me back to his ute.

As soon as we were on the road out of town I started gasping and swallowing down tears. At the end of such an exhausting and confusing week, including all the drama of graduation, my emotions were about as manageable as a broken shopping trolley.

'He healed me, Noah,' I sobbed, scratching frantically at my wrist, trying to feel for some evidence of the injury. 'I mean, *healed*. Like in the movies. He laid his hands on my arm and the wound just disappeared.'

Noah grabbed my hand to stop me scratching, but didn't say anything. I kept staring at where the wound had been, almost wishing it would reappear.

'I don't understand what's going on. How did he do that? And why? He'd just finished telling me how much he hates me and then he pulls some freakin' superpower on me in the middle of the street!'

Noah still didn't reply, and continued to drive one-handed, his other still gripping mine as if he was worried about what I might do if he let it go. Perhaps he thought I was having some sort of an episode. Which I guess I was.

'You don't believe me, do you?'

It took a few moments for him to answer. 'I believe you,' he said finally, although his jaw was tight. 'I saw you with a massive bundle of aggressive dog hanging off your arm. I just don't know what to say. I would like to give you answers but all I have is a crazy theory that I would never believe if I hadn't seen it for myself.'

'Theory?' I asked hopefully.

He thought for a few seconds. 'Do you remember that day at soccer training when he bit me?'

'Yeah, he's totally barmy, and—'

'No, Lainie.' He cut me off before I could launch into my usual guess-what-else-Bane-did rant. 'I don't think he's insane. I think he's … compelled.'

I raised one eyebrow at him.

'After a whole season of being one of our best team players, the one time you were there he went berko. The thing is, the player he tackled was in the process of kicking that ball directly towards you. I only noticed because I flinched, thinking you were about to get taken out by a ball in the face.'

Entirely possible. I had been entangled in a daydream about a tree and would have made a prime candidate for *Funniest Home Videos*.

'Somehow, I think he can tell when you're in danger and he's compelled to do something about it. I don't think he even realises what he's doing.'

I chewed over that for a few seconds and then shook my head. 'That's ridiculous, Noah. He's a psycho and he hates me. Did you forget that he pulled a *knife* on me?'

'Well, what would have happened if he hadn't?'

I shrugged.

'You would have caught up with me outside,' he said. 'Maybe just in time for Jake to reverse into you in the car park.'

'Oh!' My heart was pounding and it took a while for me to untangle my thoughts. My mind kept circling around the dead dog, the soccer incident, the knife attack, and the intense look in Bane's eyes when he'd grabbed my arm. I eased out of Noah's grip and grabbed an orange instead, rolling it around like a stress ball. The idea of Bane as some sort of guardian angel was ludicrous but I couldn't shake the feeling that Noah might just be on to something. There had to be some sort of explanation for his insane behaviour. Did all this have something to do with being a Cherub? Somehow I would have to find out what else Aunt Lily knew.

As Noah pulled up to the front gate I turned to him. 'I don't know if you're right about Bane,' I said, still fiddling with the orange, 'but I do know who I rely on to look out for me. If it wasn't for you I would never have made it through this week. And I really am sorry that I was such a pest about Claudia.'

He smiled, but the worry didn't leave his eyes. 'I get it, Lainie, I do. Things were a lot less complicated when we were younger, weren't they?' He looked almost nostalgic. 'Get an early night maybe. Or did you still want to come to the after-party?'

I shook my head. 'No, I don't think I could handle that. You go ahead.'

'What about tomorrow night? You'll still come to that, right?' Great big green puppy-dog eyes filled his face, melting my sombre mood. The next night was our formal graduation dance. Aunt Lily had followed through on her promise to buy me a new dress and I'd been looking forward to wearing it.

'Of course. I wouldn't miss it. And if you're very nice to me, I might even help you find a new Claudia. Pick me up at seven?' I asked, getting out of the car. He nodded, but didn't laugh like I expected. 'And, Noah?'

'Hmm?'

It was there. Right on the tip of my tongue. Those words. *I don't want you to go away next year.* But I was not that selfish, so instead I found safer ones. 'Thanks for believing me.'

He gave me his most melting smile and I knew we were okay again as I shut the door and watched him drive away. Just before he turned onto the road, he glanced back at me, and for just a moment his eyes were full of worry.

⌒

'We need to talk,' I declared to Aunt Lily as I entered the kitchen. As reluctant as I was to tell her about what had happened with Bane, there were things I needed to understand.

She started peeling an apple for me. 'What's happened, Lainie?'

'First tell me about my parents. Was your brother really human?' I sat down and placed my palms flat against the table to steady myself. Bane had healed me. Something supernatural was undeniably going on. Most likely because I was a Cherub. There was simply no longer any point in denying that I was not, actually, a human being. As if the hideous 'birds-and-bees' talk hadn't been bad enough, now I had to somehow ask her if I was even human enough to have a normal relationship. Was Lucas Gracewood really my father? Harry was just a few years older than my mother and I wasn't stupid. They were both Cherubim and so was I. Or was my mother supposed to be with Harry but fell in love with a human instead? Was that why Harry had remained alone all these years?

Aunt Lily looked at me for a stretched out moment. Assessing how much to tell me. Eventually she nodded and handed me the apple. 'My brother was human, just like I am. But when he met Annie, he became … something more, and everything changed for him. You're destined for a particular partner, Lainie, and when you find him, neither of you will care about being compelled to stay in Nalong.'

I raised my eyebrows. I had expected her to say I was destined to be alone, that I was the last of my kind and had a divinely appointed job to do and wasn't allowed to become involved with anyone who might jeopardise my task. Forbidden love was a tragedy that would have slotted seamlessly into my tragic life story.

Then the last part of what she'd said clicked into place and I felt the blood drain from my face.

'Compelled?' I spluttered. 'Bane? … DESTINED?'

Because who else would it be? I had no idea how his 'compulsion' fit into the scheme of things—only that I was supposed to guard the way to Eden but was apparently not able to protect myself from even the most mundane of dangers.

'Do you mean I'm destined to *fall in love* with him? That's more insane than anything else you've come up with so far. You have *no idea* how much he hates me. What happened to the whole idea of free will? You just can't play with people's emotions like this!' I was shouting and furious and ranting like an overexcited televangelist. My anger needed to go somewhere, and the apple was handy, so I threw it as hard as I could at the wall where it exploded into smooshy pulp.

Aunt Lily blinked. 'Who's Bane?'

Chapter 13

Bane had told his mother he would be home before dark, but he couldn't go back yet, so he sent her a quick text to apologise—which, given the reception problems in Nalong, she probably wouldn't receive until sometime the following day. He kept walking until he left the sealed roads and rows of tidy weatherboard houses behind. A couple of cars sped past him, coating everything in sight with choking dust and creating an eerie golden haze.

As usual, he ended up at the river. The events of the day had shaken him to his core, and the river was the only place he ever felt calm. He needed to think. What options were left to him now? He had promised himself it would end, even though it had meant giving up on trying to stick things out until the end of school. He'd convinced himself that if he just left town altogether, he could start fresh—maybe head for Sydney and try to make some sense of his life—but he'd only made it as far as Horsham before the nausea had made it impossible to keep driving.

It had happened before, but he'd assumed it was just bad timing, picking up some sort of a stomach bug just in time for his weekend away. Then it had happened again when he'd gone to his father's funeral last year. He'd put it down to nerves and grief that time, although he'd never really known his father all that well. He remembered going to visit him as a child and he'd had no difficulty leaving town then. So what had changed in the last few years? His father had stopped asking him to visit once he'd hit the teenage years, and his mother couldn't afford holidays to the city, so the furthest he'd tried to go since then was camping in the bush—no problems there. Horsham had been fine for him too until recently but whatever was going on, it was getting worse.

As the sun began to drag the day down with it, he took off his shoes and tiptoed along a sturdy log that jutted well out into the river, where the sound of the water drowned out all other distractions. Stretching a bit precariously, he doused his feet in the freezing current, feeling some of the tension flow out of him with the heat. Only then did he allow himself to turn his mind to Lainie. He had spent so much effort training his thoughts to stay away from her. She infuriated him. Why? Why was he always so obsessed with needing to know what she was up to? Why were there times when he just couldn't control his actions around her? His behaviour was ludicrous, and he hated her for it.

He remembered a time when all he needed to do was watch her for a while, hiding with the smokers and their stink amongst the clumps of bracken and cape wattles on the far side of the school oval. No one had cared about that. He wasn't the only guy who watched her when he could get away with it. But things had been getting worse. For over a year now, every time she'd played footy at lunchtime he'd been yanked away from whatever he'd been doing and forced to watch her, filled with inexplicable and impotent rage. That time when she'd gone up for a specky, launching herself so gracefully from Noah's shoulder to make the catch before she was set upon by no less than four opposing play-ers … his sudden shocking urge to wreak violence on anyone near her just then had sent him running for the bushes, gasping and vomiting. What the hell was the matter with him?

Reluctantly he reasoned that his two problems had to be linked, but it still made no sense whatsoever. All he knew was that when she was hurt today his whole body had felt like it was on fire until he touched her. Had he really healed her? He had no idea how he had done it, only that it had been such a relief to finally give in to the pull. It was the same pull that had been tugging at him for a good hour before the accident. He had *needed* to get to her, long before he ever saw the stupid dog. Trying everything he could think of to distract himself, he'd even resorted to drinking a shot of his mum's vodka, but eventually he just had to get to where she was—fast. It was probably the vodka that had caused the acci-dent. He almost wished that were true. It didn't explain why he'd felt the pull in the first place, or how he'd known where to find her.

Even now, he knew he could have spun around with his eyes closed and still been able to point to exactly where she was. And as often as he told himself he was just imagining it, he knew perfectly well that he'd been able to do that for years. She *pulled* at him, constantly, and he was beginning to realise that the farther away he got from her, the stronger the pull affected him, even to the point of physical illness.

Lifting his numb feet back up onto the log, he drew his knees up to his chin and hugged his ankles, perching as still as he could. He closed his eyes and once again wished that someone would just tell him what a sick bastard he was and lock him up before he hurt someone. He'd tried to get help, to talk to someone, but he could never get the words out without choking on his own guilt. And why should he be the one to feel guilty? He hadn't asked for this. It *had* to be her fault in some way. Everyone knew there was something strange about her; he could feel the way the air in the room always became slightly hushed whenever she and Noah walked in. She … distracted people, somehow.

Had she been the cause of today's little miracle? Used him somehow? No. The look of fear in her eyes had been genuine … oh God, how that look haunted him! He'd *healed* her arm, but that wasn't the image replaying in his mind over and over. Instead all he kept seeing was the way she'd flinched away from him. For as long as they'd known each other, and all the bitter clashes they'd had, she'd never once looked afraid of him until today.

Mosquitoes drifted around his ears, signalling the frenzied onset of evening. Conflicting thoughts tangled themselves, refusing to find resolution until he succumbed to the only course left open to him, short of breaking the law just to get himself arrested. For a moment he genuinely toyed with both options, until he had to admit that only one of them had any hope of providing the answers he needed.

Somehow he was going to have to convince her to talk to him. Maybe then he could figure out how and why his illogical instincts had saved her life.

Chapter 14

'Come on, Lainie, it's the last thing we have left, we should at least try to get there more or less on time,' Noah begged, throwing me his best dimpled smile as he peered around the corner into the bathroom. 'Wow!' he exclaimed, walking around me like he was inspecting a new car. 'You should wear your hair down more often, you look incredible!'

'Are you kidding me? Do you have any idea how annoying it is when I leave it down?' I grumbled, trying to flatten down some of the curls that were threatening to strangle me.

'There really is a lot of it, isn't there?' he conceded as he pushed me aside to use the mirror to straighten his tie.

I shoved him back, brandishing the hair straightener like a cattle prod. 'Just give me a few more minutes to try to tame it, I won't be much longer.' Another curl attacked the straightening iron like a python trying to swallow its prey and I scorched my fingers trying to untangle it. Noah just laughed at me. He knew I was dawdling because I was lacking enthusiasm. I usually enjoyed dances but only because he and I would always muck around so much. This time I had promised myself I would hold back, and prove I really could be mature by giving him enough space to find a new Claudia. But infinitely more distressing was the possibility of running into Bane. His mum was the local piano and singing teacher and she had taught her son to play keyboard and guitar. As a result he was usually called upon to play in the student band and I wasn't confident that dropping out of school would have changed that.

A minute later, Noah kidnapped my hair straightener, forcing me to give up on my unruly mane and kiss Aunt Lily goodbye. She took a couple of hurried photos of us, complaining that she'd paid for my new gold dress and deserved a picture of me in it.

'You make quite a striking couple,' she said, and then stared at me meaningfully. The previous evening, after I'd explained to her who Bane was, she'd given me an uncomfortable lecture about behaving myself around Noah. She seemed to be under the impression that Bane's animosity might somehow be caused by jealousy. As if maybe he saw us as something more than good friends. I thought about that one afternoon we had nicked Aunt Lily's bottle of port, well over a year ago now. The make-out session that had resulted in the back of the shearing shed was never to be spoken of again. Nothing had happened since that day. No one had any reason to be jealous.

I ducked out the door before she could unleash any embarrassing innuendoes.

The hotel reception centre that the school had booked for our graduation dance was the classiest venue in town. That was a sad thought. It had been renovated the previous year so at least the silver textured wallpaper was no longer there. The dance floor was small but there weren't many of us anyway so that was probably a good thing.

We were served a posh meal that had all the good bits sliced too thinly and propped up into little tepees, but it was tasty. Noah polished off his food in record time and looked wistfully at Tessa's plate. She had manoeuvred her way on to our table by simply moving Taylor's handbag to her own spot and ignoring the resultant complaints. Smiling sweetly, she offered Noah half her steak and I shook my head in disappointment. She was going to have to develop a better immunity to his natural charisma if she hoped to spend any time with him. Either that or starve. Personally, I would never have relinquished an eye fillet no matter how much he begged.

Towards the end of dinner the music morphed from a CD to the live band and sure enough, Bane stepped up to the keyboard. He was wearing a plain black shirt and black pants as if he was trying not to be noticed but I felt his eyes on me immediately. Forcing myself to eat rather than just fiddle with my fork, I finished my meal and sat humming along with the music. I didn't know where to look. Luckily Taylor grabbed my hand and dragged me to the dance floor with the rest of her friends—probably so she could sneak back and steal my spot at the table—and I fumbled after her, gratefully attempting to get lost in a sea of gyrating high school graduates. Dancing cautiously, I concentrated as hard as I could on not tripping in my heels because all I could think about was what Bane would do if he thought I was about to go arse-over-breakfast-time on the dance floor. I could feel his broody eyes on me the whole time.

Half an hour later the band took a break and a CD came back on for the first of the slow dances. Noah sought me out and offered me his hand with a dramatic flourish, but I frowned in stern disapproval. He was supposed to be flirting with all the pretty girls.

'Please, Lainie? You're my best friend. I can't *not* dance with you tonight. You're being irrational.'

He caught my eye and refused to let me look away until I relented. He was right. We were adults now. Surely this didn't need to be so complicated. In resignation I put my hand in his and curtsied, so he batted his eyelashes and curtsied back, and I laughed. Out of the corner of my eye I could see Tessa staring at us with her lips pressed together. Her eyebrows were too delicate for me to tell if she was annoyed or disappointed. Probably both.

'You'd better make it up to her, Noah, she looks upset,' I remarked as we swayed our way to the middle of the mob.

'I will, I promise. She can have me all to herself for the rest of the night after this,' he smiled, twirling me around effortlessly.

'Really? All night?' I teased.

'You know what I mean. Tessa's nice. Did you know she volunteers with the Country Fire Authority? She's smart, too,' he said slyly.

'Well of course she is. She's not Claudia! And she's clearly smart enough to have out-manoeuvred the three other girls that tried to sit at our table tonight,' I pointed out. 'Not to mention how incredible she looks in those heels. They must be five inches at least. Don't let her stand on your feet when you're dancing, whatever you do. And take care of her. She's going to be in agony by midnight.'

'So why wear them?' he asked in exasperation.

'So she can look you in the eye, pea-brain! How else is she supposed to get you to notice her instead of looking straight over the top of her head?' Honestly, boys could be so dense.

'Oh, I notice her all right,' he replied with a grin, then saw my raised eyebrows and cleared his throat self-consciously. 'Well, all the boys do,' he clarified. 'She's almost as pretty as you are.'

I rolled my eyes at him. 'You need to stop teasing me like that. People get the wrong idea. They think you mean it!' Now that I was paying attention, I was beginning to see where Aunt Lily was coming from. Our easy-going banter could easily be misconstrued.

'But I do mean it, Lainie! You look incredible in that dress, and the last thing you need are high heels to get anyone to notice you.'

I laughed in relief. Hearing him tease me about my height was much more acceptable.

We danced for a while in silence and when the music slowed to something very couple-friendly I refused to feel weird about it. He pulled me in against his chest and I let myself absorb the familiar feel of his presence as if I could store up his texture like a memory. I would miss the dancing. I didn't think there would be many more opportunities for it in the future. He was one of the few people I could dance with who was taller than I was. It was hard to feel graceful if your partner was a head shorter than you. Regretfully the song ended and as we both looked around for Tessa I felt a tap on my shoulder.

I froze.

Deep breath. Even Bane wouldn't pull any freaky crap in the middle of all these people, would he? I could do this. I would just speak to him like a mature adult. Easy.

But when I turned around, it was Jake Evans waiting nervously, not Bane.

'Hi, Lainie. I just wanted to see if you were okay. You know, after yesterday.' He scrubbed his fingers through his ridiculously high hairdo, presumably to mess it up more perfectly. 'I'm really sorry about Frawley. I don't know why he went after you.'

'I'm sorry he died.' It was hard to know what else to say.

'He was just a stupid animal,' Jake mumbled, sounding resentful. 'And Bane was the one who hit him.' There was just a hint of venom in his voice to reveal how upset he really was. Enough that it carried through to his next words too. 'How did you do it, Lainie? Was it him or you?'

A noise came out of my mouth that could have sounded something like an answer if we'd known how to speak Chicken.

'Was what her, Jake?' came a dark voice from behind Noah. We all turned to see Bane standing nearby, glowering as only he could.

'Her arm,' Jake challenged.

'The one that got covered in left over bits of your feral dog? She should charge you for having to dry-clean its blood off her dress.'

Jake's ears turned the same shade of crimson as his shirt. 'Are you trying to imply that all you did was wipe Frawley's blood off her? And since when have you ever come that close to her without trying to spit at her, anyway? That's bullsh—'

'Okay! That's enough, mate,' Noah interrupted quickly. 'This is the last time you two ever need to see each other, so how about we just leave things nice and friendly?'

Both Bane and Jake took a small step back, probably obeying Noah out of habit more than anything else. Then Jake took one last annoyed glance at me and walked off, pretending to have spotted a friend to talk to, while Bane continued to stand there with his hands in his pockets and look even more sullen than usual, impossible as that seemed. He eyed Noah warily, like he would watch a tiger that was about to attack at any second. It was not the sort of look Noah ever got from people.

I laid a hand on Noah's arm. 'It's okay, I'll need to face him eventually,' I said.

He nodded, still looking troubled, but turned away to find Tessa.

I didn't really know what to say to Bane so instead I tugged his hand out of his pocket and led him to the centre of the dance floor. It was the simplest way I could think of to stop him from talking. He looked stunned. We had never been even remotely friendly to one another, so inviting him to dance was clearly the last thing he expected from me. Everyone else who noticed us looked equally confused. Bane was one of those guys who was extremely good looking—especially with those gorgeous illegally long eyelashes—but far too intimidating for anyone to actually consider flirting with. Everyone knew he was slightly dangerous and unstable, and not in that sexy arrogant bad boy way either. He was the sort of guy that looked so surly and unsure of himself that parents automatically steered young children away from him on the street. As far as I knew no one had *ever* seen him dance. It was risky but I didn't know what else to do. I simply wasn't ready to talk yet.

An upbeat Preatures song began to play, and I breathed a massive sigh of relief that it wasn't another romantic slow one, but as I let go of his hand and began to dance awkwardly, he frowned. Perhaps he thought I was somehow trying to embarrass him in front of everybody. So he just stood there. Perfectly still.

Just staring at me.

Bastard.

Was he really just going to stand there for the whole song while I danced around on my own with everyone watching us? It was mortifying. But just as I was about to stalk away in a huff, he reached for me, grabbed me firmly around the waist and pulled me in close.

For a couple of seconds, we both froze and I found myself blinking at his collarbone.

When had he grown so tall? Last year he had been in the front row of the class photo and didn't seem to have any shoulders, but now apparently God had finally gotten around to finishing blowing him up. And how had he spent all that time up on stage and still managed to smell like fresh linen? The ridiculous observation didn't do much to help me think straight as I felt a deeply disturbing sensation, like my heart had just reversed all its rhythms and was now beating backwards.

'If we have to dance, let's at least do it properly,' he almost spat, and I didn't get an opportunity to reply because he swung me around and led me in a complex pattern of movement that made no apology for the fact that everyone else had to move aside or be bulldozed by us. Furious, I didn't even bother trying to think about how I was going to keep up. If he wanted to see me fall on my face then I was just going to have to make damn certain that I took him down with me. Relaxing into his firm grip, I let him swing me recklessly around and after a few moments I had to laugh when I saw that he was just as surprised as I was that we were still both upright. My backwards heart was thumping wildly, but it was actually not all that difficult to move in time with his audacious steps. So this was what it was like to have someone lead! Seriously *lead*. I was only an average dancer, and he swung me around as if he was challenging me to keep up, yet at the same time he always seemed to know when I was about to trip and supported me easily. His mother must have made certain his musical education had included some form of dancing to go with it. Did all professional dancers hold their partners this securely? I could feel the resonant heat of his skin like an intricate lace of energies, seeking, flowing ... searching for something to heal? Cobwebs made of light and life coursed through me wherever our bodies connected—from his hands, his hip, his thigh—pure enough to taste.

Every pair of eyes in the room was fixed on us; I could feel them boring into my back. I couldn't remember why that was a problem. At least it meant that the people around us instinctively began to give us space, because Bane certainly wasn't trying to remain inconspicuous anymore. As he spun me to a breathless halt I was amazed to find that the song had ended. His hand trembled on my shoulder blade but he still held me firmly while we both stood there gasping, and I wondered whether his heart was doing the same weird thing mine was. The expression on his face was unreadable, sort of confused and cross and startled all at the same time, which made me want to laugh. For once I didn't. Eyes of chipped ice held mine, as he in turn tried to gauge my mood. Pity I didn't know it myself.

I bit my lower lip and extricated my fingers from his. 'Can we go outside?' I mumbled. 'I think we'd better talk.'

Nodding grimly, he took my hand again and led me out the front door, attracting even more surprised glances from the other students. Practically yanking me along, he strode all the way down the street to a small playground, away from all the smokers and couples. I quietly hoped Noah was right about him trying to protect me, otherwise I was headed for a secluded area with someone who had recently pulled a knife on me ... sort of. I started to have second thoughts.

Sensing my reluctance he let go of my hand and backed away from me, a puzzled expression on his face. 'You aren't in any danger. What's wrong?' He looked confused, then frustrated as he realised that he was the one I was worrying about.

Leaning forward, I peered at him in the dusky yellow light of the street lamp. 'How do you know? How do you know whether or not I'm in danger?' My inquisitiveness was quickly winning over my reticence.

He hesitated before answering, his hands finding his pockets again. A lock of velvet-black hair fell into his eyes as he lowered his gaze again. 'Because I don't currently feel like a junkie desperate for a hit,' he said, clenching his jaw and looking down at his shoes.

I pondered that for a moment. He stayed silent. Annoyed, I realised he wasn't going to volunteer any information and that I was going to have to steer the awkward conversation. Great. I sat down on the edge of a seesaw shaped like a bee.

'Are you trying to protect me? From what? And why?'

He looked up sharply. 'I have no idea. I just … need you to be safe. I didn't even realise that's what it was until yesterday. I've tried to stay away from you, I really have. I just can't. It makes me sick.'

'*Physically* sick?' I asked incredulously, eyebrows reaching for the sky. He nodded. Oh great, how lovely. What was I supposed to say to that, exactly?

'Um. Okay. So how close do you need to be?'

He looked down again. 'It seems to be more dependent on time than on distance,' he said thoughtfully. 'I mean, if I'm in or near my car I feel more comfortable than if I'm on foot. Maybe because I can get to you faster that way. I've driven almost as far as Horsham before throwing up, but I can only walk as far as the grain silos on Tarin Street if you're at home. It's hard for me when you leave town.'

My eyes bulged. Man, he must have been struggling with this for a while. I had no idea it was so powerful, or so controlling.

'When did all this start?'

He looked away, staring at the ancient swings, unable to meet my eyes. 'It's been getting stronger over the last couple of years. I've always felt … sort of … drawn to you, but you make me uncomfortable. I keep doing strange things when I'm around you so I try to keep my distance. It's been getting harder.' He looked accusingly at me. 'I always know where you are. *Exactly* where you are. Why? Why you?'

I glared right back. 'Why me? I've been asking myself that since primary school! Why do you always pick on me? What have I ever done to upset you? Why was it *my* locker you had to set on fire? Honestly? Until recently I thought it was about Noah … you know, because you act a bit like the girls in class would if they didn't have any self-restraint …' It was my turn to study my shoes.

He was quiet for a moment, then started to chuckle. I couldn't remember ever hearing him laugh before, and I started chuckling too. I think we were both a bit desperate to see a funny side to the situation. He took a deep breath and the corners of his mouth twitched into an almost- smile.

'No,' he assured me, 'this *definitely* has nothing whatsoever to do with your pretty boyfriend. You can keep him. I'll keep as far away from you both as I can.'

Damn, I hated it when my aunt was right, although the idea that Bane was *jealous* was still taking it way too far.

'He's not my boyfriend. He never has been. Didn't anyone notice him going all cow-eyed over Claudia? How can you have been at school with us all these years and not know we're *just friends*?'

'Whatever. Friends then,' he said cynically. 'I'll still try to leave you alone. But please, could you, maybe, call me or something if you're going to do anything … risky? It's easier if I'm close. Or at least I'll know not to do anything I need to concentrate on that day.'

If I didn't already believe that there was something supernatural going on I would have told him where he could stick it. Instead I just felt kind of bad for him. He didn't deserve this. We were both caught up in something completely outside our control. I thought about what Aunt Lily had said about being destined for him, which was laughable—I would have been less surprised to catch Noah knitting—but I thought I'd better at least try to get used to having him around.

I shook some tan bark out of my shoe. 'Ben, what are your plans? Do you have a job?' I asked.

His shoulders relaxed slightly, as if he'd actually been worried about my reaction to his request. 'No, I'm still looking,' he admitted. 'I've been doing some odd jobs around town since I can't go to the city to find work. I'll find something though.'

I took a resigned breath. 'Are you any good on a farm? We happen to be without our farmhand at the moment and some of the less urgent jobs are starting to pile up. My aunt and I could use some help if you're interested. We'd pay you, of course, and feed you. I'll ask if you can use Harry's cottage until he gets back.'

He looked at me as if I'd grown an extra nose. 'Seriously? Just like that?' He blinked. 'After everything we've … You would just invite me to come and live on your farm and work?'

How could I explain to him there was no real choice? I just smiled and nodded. I had found that usually worked well enough when I didn't know what else to say. Just smile and nod. I wondered if there was a way I could just do that instead of having to tell Aunt Lily.

Chapter 15

The next morning my vivacious aunt fluttered around the house like a butterfly on red cordial. She tidied, she cleaned, she polished. In short, she fretted. It was obviously difficult for her to prepare to meet the boy she believed I would marry, and I was more than a little worried that she would blurt out something inexcusably embarrassing in front of him.

She'd set up our guest bedroom for him to stay in because she didn't feel comfortable letting him use Harry's place without being able to check with him first, but she didn't seem too happy about us living under the same roof either. In the end she probably figured that it would be inevitable anyway so she cleared out the back room and then proceeded to clear out every other loose item in the house as well. When I caught her trying to vacuum the veranda I had to say something.

'What are you doing? Why does everything need to be so clean? Honestly, it's only *Bane*. You have no idea how … how … irritating he can be.'

'I'm just trying to make a good first impression! We only get one chance at that.'

'Or else what? He won't think I'm a suitable match? Isn't that a good thing? Maybe his disgust at our housekeeping abilities will override his compulsion to fall hopelessly in love with me.'

'I just want things to go as smoothly as possible. This doesn't need to play out like some TV daytime soap opera. I just want things to stay simple.'

Stay simple? Which part of any of this was simple?

A cloud of dust billowed up from the road behind a blue sedan.

'Please just don't say anything to him, Aunt Lily. He might not care about my housekeeping skills but scaring him off by acting crazy certainly won't help to keep things *simple*.'

Humming nervously, I tried to look busy when our new employee knocked on the front door. Aunt Lily introduced herself and welcomed him inside, leading him down the short hallway into the kitchen where I was rearranging the knives in the knife block. Bane took one look at me and scowled, so I meekly sat down. The three of us were so much on edge that we all jumped a mile when the phone rang. Aunt Lily excused herself and took the phone into the other room.

'Tea or coffee?' I asked, trying to sound casual.

'Coffee would be great, thanks.' It was the first time he had ever said thank you to me for anything. In fact, in the last two days he'd spoken more to me than in our entire high school lives. If you didn't count all the yelling. It was going to take getting used to.

For the next few minutes I pottered around the kitchen trying to find something other than fruit to offer him to eat. We had been so busy with lambing and graduation that we hadn't had a chance to go to town for groceries for a while. All we really had were things we grew at home, currently consisting of eggs, lettuce, cauliflower and a glut of snow peas.

'Nutri-Grain? Or some pears?' I offered awkwardly.

'Er, no, thanks. Just the coffee would be great.'

I put the milk and sugar out for him but he drank it plain and black. Sitting down with my cup of tea, I pried open a jar of bottled pears and poured some into a bowl. We were starting to run low on those too.

He watched me try to stab a slippery piece of the fruit with my spoon. 'Listen,' he said, clutching his coffee mug like he wanted to strangle it. 'You and I both know that we don't get along, and this is probably the last place on Earth I want to be.'

A pear slid off my bowl onto the table.

'But I want you to know that I'm grateful. And I'll try to ... I mean I'll try not to—'

'Be such an asshole?' I volunteered, wondering what he'd say if I still ate the pear. Popping it quickly into my mouth, I decided that since he hated me anyway I didn't care.

He recoiled slightly, but nodded. 'So, what sort of things will you need me to do?' he asked after a moment.

Well, let's see, take care of a few thousand sheep, protect me from all harm, keep the secret of Eden from the world, marry me and help me raise children who will probably not be human.

'Oh, you know, just the usual things that keep a sheep farm going,' I told him instead. 'Have you driven a tractor before?'

'No. But I can learn. What else?'

If I didn't know better I might have thought he almost sounded enthusiastic. He was in for disappointment if he thought it was going to be exciting work.

'Well, the new sheep need drenching. We'll give that a go this afternoon and after that we'll just see what jobs turn up. There's always something.'

We sat in awkward silence for a minute. Aunt Lily was still on the phone. Why couldn't she just take a message?

I fished around blindly for something to talk about. 'So, um, do you have any hobbies? Interests? Extra skills we should know about?'

'I play keyboard and guitar. And I used to play soccer,' he reminded me.

Ow. He'd played soccer until I'd ruined it for him.

'But what sorts of things do you do with your friends?' I tried again.

He just stared out of the window, his face managing to look both sulky and irritated at the same time. Right. No friends. I knew that. He had always more or less kept to himself at school and was a bit of a loner. Oh dear God, please tell me I hadn't just invited a budding psychopath to come and live with us …

That was when I decided that I had a new mission. Like it or not, I was going to have to get him to lighten up a heck of a lot if we were going to have to spend much time together. In fact, any time together. My eyes narrowed evilly as I studied him studying his coffee. Clearly I wasn't going to be able to irritate him until he laughed like I did with Noah. I was going to have to be sneakier than that. I was up for the challenge.

⌐

Later, when Bane was unpacking his things, I noticed Aunt Lily slumped at the desk, doodling absently on a notepad. She'd drawn the Kolsom logo and was adding devil's horns to it.

'So the phone call was bad news then?'

'My friend from Melbourne,' she explained. 'The contaminated water sample only shows very small amounts of mining by-products. All within safe levels. Nothing we can use to argue against Kolsom.'

'And the other sample?' I asked. 'What's in it that I need?'

She leant back in her chair to look at me. 'The only differences he could see between the two samples were slight variations in some organic compounds that were impossible to identify. He just said that it would be difficult to prove if the contaminants had caused them to break down faster than normal. I'm sorry, Lainie, but whatever it is, it's not anything we can find anywhere else.'

So not only was I stuck in Nalong indefinitely, but if Harry didn't return soon to replenish my magic water potion, I was basically stuffed. And we were also no closer to getting rid of Kolsom. Our local council representative had been politely frustrating when we'd met with him, assuring us with all the right words that he would uphold our right to deny the miners access to our property, but he hadn't offered any practical suggestions whatsoever.

Aunt Lily handed me another notepad and a pencil, and together we came up with some pretty creative logo variations until Bane returned and cut short our art therapy session.

⌒

That evening when we all returned exhausted from the paddocks, he began to appreciate what it was like for us when he realised we still had to cook dinner and do all the usual evening chores.

'So where's your usual farmhand? Harry, is it? Will he be away for long?' he asked, holding a bunch of snow peas as if he'd never seen such things before.

My aunt and I looked at each other uneasily. We hadn't even thought about what we were going to tell him. That was when I found out how good Aunt Lily was at coming up with cover stories without lying.

'He had some personal business to attend to. He couldn't give us a timeframe but I think it'll be at least a month until he returns. Will you be able to stay that long?' she asked, taking the snow peas from him to give them a rinse.

This time Bane looked at me nervously. This was going to be annoying, keeping secrets that didn't really need to be kept. 'Sure, I can stay as long as you need me,' he replied.

I didn't even want to think about how long that might be.

After our uncomfortably quiet dinner I went outside with Aunt Lily to put the chooks away in their fox-proof shed.

'How much do you know about this compulsion he has to protect me?' I queried, nudging the obstinate rooster with my foot to hurry him up.

'Only what little I know from your parents. Lucas protected your mother. With his life, eventually,' she said, leaning on the gate. Her flash of grief for her lost brother tightened the air around her.

'Just my mother? Did Harry have someone to protect him too? Someone he was "destined to be with"?' If only girls needed protectors then I had a whole flood of arguments ready, and Bane could just go and do his scowling somewhere else. I had never seen Harry in a relationship with anyone, and I wondered if Aunt Lily might have had the role.

She glared at me, her blue eyes flashing like ice crystals at dawn. 'Harry's business is his own. You'll have to ask him yourself.'

Although I had clearly touched a nerve there, I couldn't let it rest. 'I can't ask him though, can I? Are you certain he's not hurt somewhere? There was a *landslide* after all. What if he didn't make it to Eden?' I didn't want to push but it had been playing on my mind for such a long time.

'He's fine, Lainie, I promise. I'm just concerned that he might not come back,' she said, staring off to the northwest.

'*At all?*' I panicked. 'Doesn't he have some sort of compulsion to get back here? He has a job to do, right?' My voice climbed about an octave.

'You're here now. He might not … remember to come back. Harry said that once you cross into Eden this world can sort of fade from your list of priorities. If you weren't here it might be different but since you're around to guard this side … well, I'm worried he might forget how unprepared you are.'

That was unthinkable. I needed to talk to him. I had way more questions to ask him and we hadn't even finished with the three he was prepared to answer yet. I clenched my jaw. 'I'll just have to go and remind him then.'

All the colour drained from my aunt's face, and she stared at me, like she was about to cry.

'What is it now?' I asked, shoulders slumping. 'Do I have to slay a dragon to get into Eden or something?'

'What? No! Not as far as I'm aware. I just don't want you to go, that's all.' She fiddled with the gate latch. 'I wasn't kidding about this world fading from your priorities. I mean, look around you, Lainie. Do you really think this place can compare with Paradise? Why would you bother coming back?'

A bit self-consciously, I wiped some chook poo and feathers off the edge of my shoe onto the dead grass.

She didn't notice because she was busy staring at nothing with tears welling in her blue eyes. 'What if you decide to stay there too? I'm not ready to lose you yet, honey. I know I have no right to keep you here, but I can't just wave goodbye to you and not know if I'll ever even see you again …'

Her tears felt hot against my neck as I hugged her. 'Okay,' I soothed. 'I won't go. I think you're wrong anyway. Harry will be back soon, I'm sure of it.' She sobbed and crushed my ribs and I realised how she must have felt when my mother had left us. 'Besides, I would never do that,' I mumbled into her ear. 'This is my home. I don't care how pretty the Garden of Eden is—I would never just abandon you.'

She sniffed and wiped her eyes as she let me go. 'Don't make promises you can't keep.'

&

The following week was spent trying to teach the bane of my life all there was to know about farming. Astonishingly I found it was kind of fun when he wasn't shouting at me. It wasn't until I tried to teach someone else that I realised just how many skills I had that I'd taken for granted, from fixing water pumps to simple things like opening hay bales and feed bags without a knife. I laughed openly as he practised driving the tractor around one of the smaller paddocks, having to pop it into reverse each time a corner came up. He only hit the fence once. Then I had to teach him how to re-strain a fence.

The day he couldn't find one of his shirts I told him it was in the hay press. He gave me the usual scowl but didn't ask, so I sighed in mock exasperation, led him out to the hay shed and lifted off the top couple of bales. Somehow I kept a totally straight face as I revealed a stash of freshly cleaned laundry that had been neatly folded and pressed under the heavy blocks of meadow hay. I really hated ironing.

The next day when he took his work gloves off he found that his hands had turned bright red because someone had filled them with the powder we used to mark the lambs with. He tried to get me back by putting snails in my work boots but picked the wrong ones. It still worked though because Aunt Lily refused to believe he'd done it and blamed me anyway.

As we argued our way through the endless jobs, I noticed he was becoming much more at ease. He barely looked down at his shoes any-more and was starting to make regular eye contact when we spoke. Surly, angry eye contact, but at least it was honest. The looks he threw me when he thought I wasn't watching were distinctly less vicious, which made a nice change, and by the end of that first week we were almost civil to one another. His eyes were still serious, the grey taking on a bluish tinge when he was outdoors, and he still never spoke to me unless he had to. Finally, however, I had a major breakthrough on the day he agreed to help me tie-dye Aunt Lily's pyjamas, although he had no idea why it was so funny. I was smugly encouraged by his progress, until he ruined it.

As I hung them up on the clothesline, I noticed him staring at his bright purple fingers in confusion, probably wondering how he had ended up in such a strange situation.

'Do you always do this?' he asked.

'Dye my aunt's sleepwear? Nope. First time. Looks good though, don't you think? Maybe we should dye something else. Do you own anything that isn't black?'

For a brief second his face almost softened into a smile. Almost. But then his thunder-face reappeared.

'I mean, do you always play these tricks? I thought you were only doing it to embarrass me, but now you're targeting your aunt as well. If I'd realised you didn't have her permission to do this, I never would have agreed to help.'

Embarrass him? That stung. Just because *he* hated the universe and everything in it didn't mean that *I* was that cruel. In my mind's eye, the rinse bucket of bright purple water tipping triumphantly over his head made a glorious sight, but instead of indulging my fantasy I tried to see things from his point of view. I had to try. I couldn't start a fight that would end with him leaving and suffering the ridiculously unfair paranormal consequences. So I took some deep breaths. Hydrogen, Helium, Lithium … Once I had a semblance of control back again, I opened my eyes and smiled as politely as I could.

'I play tricks to make people laugh, Ben, not to embarrass or irritate. Despite what you think I would never be that nasty. Not even to you.'

The look on his face was one of astonished disbelief, but I just had to walk away before he could see my hurt and angry tears betray me. There were not enough elements in the Periodic Table to calm me down.

If anything, he became even crankier after that. The snarky comments and fits of temper he tried so badly to control made my worst days of the month seem as charming as Snow White at a tea party.

'We'll be here all day if you don't hit the stupid thing properly!' I snapped at one point, frustrated with all his muttered cursing when yet another staple pinged away from the semi-petrified ancient fence post and disappeared into the netherworld.

'I can't hit it when you're holding it like that!' he shouted straight back, throwing the hammer down and only just missing his own foot.

I swore loudly with my mouth clamped shut. It had been a long morning and Aunt Lily had gone into town, leaving us to fix the latest hole in the gully fence on our own. The stupid sheep always managed to find the weakest spot in any stretch of fence, and this time one of them had managed to tangle herself in it, dragging a good forty-metre length of rusty ring-lock with her across the paddock before giving up and waiting to be rescued. She was fine now, although prettily graffitied with purple antiseptic spray. The ring-lock, however, was proving to be unbelievably fractious, bending in ways it was never designed to. That meant hammering in a lot of staples. Staples were just plain evil.

'How else am I supposed to keep it tight?' I asked with patience that was fizzing away like a bath bomb. I peeled my leather gloves off and rubbed my fingers where the wire had bitten into them. 'Please can you just let me do it?' I begged yet again.

He literally growled. I'd only hit my thumb once, but that had been enough to trigger one heck of a tantrum until I'd finally relinquished the hammer. Swapping jobs had been fine until we'd reached the end post. I was struggling to get the mesh to cover enough of the post for him to be able to hammer it on, and so I was pulling it as tightly as I could, gripping it very close to where he had to whack the staple in.

I tried to be reasonable. 'Either let me do the hammering or trust yourself not to hit me,' I said.

'I can't!'

'Oh for the love of—'

'You don't get it, Lainie! I literally *can't!*' He threw his own gloves away in utter frustration. 'I don't have the control to guarantee that I won't hit you, so I can't make my hands do it!'

As his words sank in, I sat down with a graceless plop, and the ring-lock escaped and ran away in curly glee. 'Really?' I asked, surprised.

He refused to even look at me. 'It feels as impossible as if I was trying to hammer my own thumb. Hard. On purpose. I honestly believe I would feel twice as much pain as you if I hurt you. I can't make myself do it.'

My eyes narrowed thoughtfully. 'Reeeally?' I asked again. 'You *can't* hurt me?' I stood up and looked him squarely in the eye, assessing. And then I punched him on the shoulder.

'Agghh! You *cow*! What the *hell* was that for?' he yelled, hardly breathing in his fury.

'For calling me a cow!' I shouted illogically, dancing on the balls of my feet with my clenched fists in front of my face, the way I'd been taught by watching all those stupid *Rocky* movies that Noah had forced me to sit through. Then I hit him again, but he was ready this time and didn't flinch. He didn't speak either, he just screamed at me with his eyes. I grinned evilly. 'That one was for dobbing on me last year when I climbed up to get the ball off the roof of the toilet block for the grade six kids!' He flipped me the bird, so I stomped hard on his foot. 'And that was for all the crude gestures you've made to me over the years!'

'What's wrong with you? You stupid—' He grunted when I elbowed him in the stomach, and wisely didn't try to finish his sentence.

'That one was for biting Noah!' I yelled, surprised to find that I was actually still a bit genuine in my anger at that one. He was doubled over now, but didn't retreat or try to fight back.

'What the hell is your problem?' he gasped, grey eyes flashing. The tendons in his neck were so tight I was worried they might snap.

'*My* problem? I have no problem! I just figure that if you're going to hate me anyway, I'd like to deserve it! Don't you think beating someone up who can't fight back deserves a bit of hate?'

He stood straight. Painfully. Gritting his teeth he said, 'Don't worry, you've done plenty to deserve it.'

'Such as?' I challenged, readying my fists again.

'How about dragging me away from detention just because you wanted to play footy at lunchtime? That earned me a week-long suspension!'

I slapped him, trying not to let him see my relief.

'And what about all the times you went to Melbourne for the weekend and left me puking my guts out, trying to prove to my mother that I hadn't been drinking?'

My carefully controlled punch hit him squarely on the jaw. Rocky would have been proud.

'Aagh! And what about the time I had to tip over your beaker in Chemistry to stop you from adding water to your sulphuric acid instead of the other way around?'

Now he was getting it. I kicked him in the shins and smiled.

'Damn, girl! That one hurt,' he said, stumbling back a step. 'Why couldn't you just have waited for Noah to help you that day when you needed to get the stupid poster paper down from the top shelf in the art room? Why'd you have to make me throw that paint?'

He caught my fist a split second before it connected with his cheekbone. Wow. He had incredible reflexes. I hadn't even seen him move.

'*That* one would have sprained your finger. You have terrible technique.' Warmth flooded my fist where he gripped it, making me gasp. Quick as a flash, he picked up my other hand and slid his fingers across the back of my thumb where I'd whacked it with the hammer. Fire spread through the bruised joint, fading to a light tingle within moments, and even my ever-present weariness eased a little.

Swaying slightly, he closed his eyes and took a few deep breaths, fighting off dizziness. When he opened them again, his eyes looked subtly different. I turned my hand so that I was gripping his instead, and concentrated hard. The excruciatingly sharp self-loathing I'd 'seen' every time I'd hit him had diminished to a bearable ache. Each punishment I'd inflicted for every relived memory had resolved something intrinsic in his ragged ego. He wasn't healed yet, but at least some of the bitterest strain seemed to have finally been mitigated.

Maybe now we'd be able to get some work done.

'Lainie?' Aunt Lily found me a few days later leaning on the side of the door to the hay shed, playing with the cat's ears and chewing on the end of my ponytail. Inara, who was perched on the shelf by the door, mewed happily and left me to suck up to my aunt instead. She was a pretty and affectionate cat but a faithless companion.

'Hmmm?' I was watching Bane stack bales. He had his shirt off. I really should have stopped him to let him know that was a bad idea because he was going to end up with a terrible rash from the hay, but I couldn't seem to make myself interrupt him. His lean torso showed new tan lines from all the time he had been spending outdoors lately. Steadily he made his way through the pile, checking underneath each one in case there were more unexpected items of clothing. Pfft, as if I would ever use the same prank twice. Besides, I had backed right off the practical jokes since he'd told me they embarrassed him. The strange thing was, when I'd refrained from taking advantage of him the previous day when he'd thought the garden hose was blocked, he'd almost seemed disappointed. Perhaps he'd just been hot. I chewed on my hair some more.

It was tricky to get the bales to the top of the stack, but he and his muscles were doing just great. Despite the fact that working with him was like being followed around by the world's most miserable thundercloud, I had to admit that at least he never backed away from putting in the hard yards. He was no bludger. Startled, I suddenly realised he'd finished the last bale when he turned and caught us both watching him. I tripped over my aunt as I fled out the door.

'What was it you wanted, Aunt Lily?' I asked as we hurried away, trying hard not to sound flustered.

'I honestly don't remember!' she admitted, laughing. I laughed too as I head-butted her playfully on the shoulder. So what if I looked a little? It wasn't until much later that I remembered that he would have known I was there the whole time.

∽

As the week progressed we learnt more about each other's skill set, and we both made an effort to be more polite, at least to each other's faces. He taught me to play 'Lainie had a Little Lamb' on our old piano and I taught him how to wrestle a sheep.

His protectiveness was kind of handy sometimes too—at least when he wasn't trying to convince me he should be the one to use the chainsaw. Honestly, did he think he would be any safer? He'd never even touched one before. Besides, I really didn't mind watching him stack the wood.

While I rested, waiting for the machine to cool down, I gently placed a large Huntsman spider on his shoulder so it could get a better view of the world. He still didn't laugh as he stumbled over the woodpile trying to get it off, but instead of the angry tantrum I was expecting, he just looked resigned. So later, when I'd finished cutting up the pile I was working on, I carved him a present to celebrate.

'Because the last spider wasn't big enough?' he asked while I emptied some of my drink bottle over my head to cool down. 'You had to make me a bigger one?'

'Spider?' I despaired. 'It's supposed to be a Batman logo!'

'I know.' His mouth twitched in something that would have resembled amusement if I didn't know better. 'I was watching when you entered the chainsaw carving at the Nalong Show last year. The judge said you would have scored better if you'd given it the right number of legs.'

He somehow managed to evade the water I threw at him.

After a bit of training, I did let him start cutting up some of the bigger logs. They looked harder but were actually much safer to cut, and I just no longer had the energy to do it. It was just as well I wasn't trying to run the place on my own anymore. We'd finally run out of bottled fruit and if Harry didn't return soon, I was going to have to be taken out to the back of the shed and dealt with humanely. It was Bane who finally made me take action a couple of days later.

I was filling the ride-on mower with petrol—badly—when he took the canister away from me and put it down. He took my hands in his. My skin buzzed warmly the way it always did when we touched and I felt better immediately, but I knew it wouldn't last for long.

'Your hands are trembling again, Lainie. What's going on?'

I'd been wondering how long it would take him to pluck up the courage to ask about it.

'It's getting worse,' I mumbled, trying to pull away. He wouldn't let me. There was no point trying to avoid it any longer, I would have to tell him something, but I felt sick at the thought of telling such a ridiculous story to the one person who I knew hated me.

'I'm not entirely … normal, Ben.' He raised one eyebrow as if that should have been common knowledge. I suppose I deserved that. 'There's a reason you and I are linked that I don't exactly understand, and I'm going to sound mental if I try to explain it.'

'Well you may as well try me. I'm kind of used to you being mental.'

Not this mental. How do you tell someone you're not human? I still wasn't entirely convinced myself. I was done with waiting for Harry to come home. The last thing I wanted to do was upset Aunt Lily, but I needed to find some answers of my own.

I peered up at him. If I couldn't explain it, then maybe I could show him instead. 'Have you ever paddled down a river on a blow-up mattress?' I asked with a sly smile.

It was time to enter Nalong's Barramundi Triangle.

Chapter 16

The familiarity of the rendered brick farmhouse with its clipped roses and homemade garden sculptures calmed my jumpy nerves as we climbed the three steps up onto the Ashbrees' porch the next day. It was a relief when Nicole answered the door. With a bright expression that showed she was hoping to get a reaction out of me, she told us that Noah was in town with his new girlfriend, and I could see her smugness grow as she scrutinised Bane hovering behind me. She clearly assumed there was gossip to be spread. Luckily I'd already told Noah about him coming to work on the farm.

'It's "Ben" now, is it?' was all he'd said. I'd been trying hard to get used to calling him by his real name, out loud at least. Still, Noah hadn't sounded pleased at the news and it would have been more than awkward if he'd answered the door and I'd had to ask his permission for us to go for a swim without him. Especially after the last argument we'd had. It was bad enough having to ask Nicole as it was. Luckily Mrs Ashbree found a job for Nicole to do before she could ask to come along. Naturally she assumed we wanted time alone. She wasn't wrong, just not for the right reasons.

The Ashbree kids and I had paddled down the river on mattresses plenty of times before, but we always stopped and got out before the river got down to our fence line. This time we would need to explore a lot farther. We had brought with us a small plastic drum with a screw-on lid for our supplies, so we took off our shoes and socks and stuffed them, with our phones, into a plastic bag inside it, and then tied it to my mattress with a bit of rope. I left my T-shirt and shorts on over my bathers, having long since learnt that bikinis were not reliable when you hit the rapids. Then Bane put his shirt into the drum as well and I tried not to look but it was hard not to appreciate the view. He had really bulked up in the last couple of weeks of farm work. Possibly because he wasn't throwing up anymore.

As I did a last minute check for air leaks, Bane eyed the mattresses dubiously. 'Are you sure this is safe?'

Launching myself with a delighted yodel onto my mattress, I started to paddle downstream. 'You tell me, Ben. Am I safe?'

I laughed as he scrambled to get on board his own restless mount to follow, because he made a sound like a squeaky toy when his chest hit the freezing water.

'Please just don't get too far ahead. I haven't done this before, you know.'

'Seriously?' I spluttered. 'How have you survived the summers here?'

'In the river, like everyone else, just not on unsafe floatation devices. How the hell do I steer this thing?'

'With your hands. But only if you have to. Let the river take you, it's more fun that way ... Oh, but watch out for sharp rocks.' The current picked me up and sped me around the next river bend and I had to lean heavily to one side to avoid a huge slimy log that could have impaled my steed. I had forgotten how much fun this could be. I hadn't done it in years. I missed having Noah there to race me. Somewhere behind me, I heard a squawk and a splash as Bane tried to figure out how to steer past the log.

Twenty minutes later we drifted slowly down a wide section of the river. We were surrounded by open paddocks and the sun was scorching, so naturally I dived off the mattress to cool down. Bane soon joined me. Bracing myself, I got ready to dunk my head underwater. Perhaps if I was prepared for the music I could prevent myself from crying like a weaned calf. Cool water drew the heat from my scalp deliciously.

Nothing else happened.

Holding my breath and pausing just beneath the surface, I could still hear the music, but it was far off, nothing like it was after graduation. It made a certain sense. The music must join the river near the cave somewhere. I could always try dunking my head in the river every few metres until I found where it started. Sadly that was the best lead I had.

We swam alongside the mattresses for a while, enjoying the feel of the insistent current. I watched Bane floating on his back, looking more relaxed than I had ever seen him before, and all of a sudden I realised I was genuinely anxious about what his reaction would be if it turned out that Eden was real. He just looked so serene and gentle, and I didn't want him to go back to being so … hateful. It was obvious that things were easier for him now, given that he didn't have to deal with nausea just to walk down to the shops anymore, but what was he going to say when he found out about me? About Eden? And what if I didn't find the path at all? I was going to look like a right dork then.

Not long after our swim we reached the boundary between the Ashbree and Gracewood farms. We ducked under the token bit of wire fence and kept floating. None of the land had been cleared from here on in, until the river got much closer to our house, so I really didn't know what to expect up ahead. We both started to look out for rocks that might puncture our little rafts. The bush gave us some shade, which was lovely, but it came with a plague of mosquitoes as payment.

A few minutes later Bane called out to me, sounding very agitated. I had been concentrating so hard on peering into the water that I hadn't noticed the sound of rapids getting louder. These ones sounded messy, too. Within seconds he was calling me frantically so I began to back-paddle to let him catch up, and then the drum decided to take a different path around a rock than the one my mattress had taken and I was swung around with a jerk. Pulling hard on the rope, I tried to drag myself back to the rock to untangle things but the current was too strong. Still, I figured that at least it would give him a chance to get over to where I was. The rock had other ideas. The rotten thing turned out to be just slippery enough to let the rope slide over the top of it once it was pushed by enough water, and suddenly my mattress was free again. Of course, in its excitement, my wild beast of a mattress slipped out from under me and I spent the next few moments trying desperately to climb back on and failing miserably.

That was when I realised we were in real trouble.

As we came around a bend in the river the rapids got rougher and I could hear a roaring sound that was definitely unwelcome. The last thought I had as I plummeted over the edge of the waterfall was that I should have thought to bring the old bike helmets.

Chapter 17

I tried to hold my breath as best I could but as I slammed into the water at the base of the falls, all my precious air was forced out of my lungs like a violent sneeze, and the tenuous grip I still had on the air mattress wasn't enough to stop it from escaping. Fighting hard not to breathe in again, I felt rocks pummel me from every side and then a stabbing pain tore into my back.

It was hard not to panic.

Who was I kidding? I was panicking like a fifteen-year-old at her first B&S ball. I had no idea which way was up so I just curled up and hoped like crazy that I wouldn't hit my head. My lungs began to scream and I sternly reminded them that I was good at holding my breath. Better than anyone I knew. Even Noah had given up trying to challenge me during our primary school swimming lessons. Another rock hit my face, I took a reflexive gasp, choked, and all residual self-control was lost. Flailing madly, I felt the rope brush my shoulder and made a grab for it with one hand, hoping that the drum still tied to its end would still be able to float. But which end? The pressure of the water was unbelievable. Like a schnitzel steak I was being pummelled ruthlessly from every direction.

My progress was agonisingly slow as I pulled my way along the rope, and my limbs felt feeble as I continued to struggle ... until the deliciously desolate music began to filter through the swirl of violent water around me, its familiar sorrow distracting me from my battle. It overwhelmed my thoughts with tender grief as if I had already died, so that it became almost impossible not to just give in and let it happen. The beautiful symphony of sadness saturated every cell in my body with its melancholy echo.

The world stopped. Peace beckoned me with sad longing, calling me to just let go of the burning in my chest. If I would just let the water in, the fire would be quenched, and the loneliness would be gone forever … but I couldn't give in to it because something powerful was blocking my way. A pressure around my waist, tugging and burning and hauling me away from the siren's call. Certain that I was being dragged sideways, I tried to compensate but then my left ear broke the surface of the water.

Air was the best invention ever.

Gasping and spluttering, I thrashed about with reflexive greed for more oxygen, and had to forced myself to relax. Apparently it was difficult to help a drowning person when they were panicking and wriggling around, so I just concentrated on breathing in the deliciously abundant elixir. Strangely, I felt quite calm with the feel of Bane's arm around my waist.

He dragged me up onto the riverbank and pried the rope from my clenched fist, and both of us coughed for quite a while. Somehow he managed to haul the drum in as well. There was no sign of either mattress. In utter relief I lay back, gasping, but as soon as I touched the ground, I cried out in agony. Turning painfully, I raised my shirt and tried to see what had happened. Just under my shoulder blade was a jagged wound where I had been gouged by a rock and it was bleeding everywhere. That was going to need stitches. How queasy would Bane get if I made him stitch me up? Looking at his face I remembered that might not be necessary. He looked like he was about to have an aneurism.

'Wait!' I gasped, putting my hand on his chest as he reached out to me. His skin felt like it was on fire. 'It makes you dizzy, remember? Maybe you should just wait and recover a bit first.' Another coughing fit suffocated me as punishment for trying to speak too soon.

'Lainie, you're bleeding like crazy! I can't just sit here and watch you!' he rasped through gritted teeth, panting. He sounded furious and I didn't blame him one bit. We both could have easily been killed because of my stupidity. Muscles bulged in his shoulders as he held his fists clenched, trembling. He clearly wasn't going to recover until he'd worked his freaky mojo on me, so reluctantly I turned my back towards him, wincing as I felt the wound open further. He lifted my T-shirt over my head and I bit my lower lip to keep from squealing again. It *really* stung.

As before, he placed both his hands over the wound and I felt an intense heat, almost as painful as the wound itself. It was so hard not to jump away that I found myself swearing like a trooper. Then it was done. I gasped at the absence of pain as much as from the shock and looked over my shoulder to try to see what had happened. It was perfect. Not even a red patch remained to show where it had been. Astounded, I turned back to thank him, but he'd passed out.

A couple of minutes later I watched him shudder as he came to. Having found the contents of the drum still dry, I had propped his head onto his rolled up shirt as a pillow but I didn't think it had helped much. He had a large purple bruise forming on his elbow and probably more elsewhere, but I was too shy to look.

'How do you feel?' I asked.

'Like I jumped off a cliff, landed on some sharp rocks, and then burst into flames,' he groaned, sitting up and holding his head in his hands. 'How about you?'

'Unbelievably good,' I said, prodding at my cheekbone where I was sure I'd been bruised, but there was nothing there. 'I mean, I actually feel better than I did before we got into the river. If we could just bottle that healing power of yours we'd make squillions.' I didn't even feel tired anymore. 'Thank you, Ben,' I said seriously. 'You saved my life, again. I'm sorry you had to heal me; it's obviously hard on you. But in my defence I did try to get you to recover a bit first. You really should have listened.'

'No, Lainie, I'm afraid that just wasn't an option. You have no idea what it feels like for me when you're hurt.'

'Well, then, I'm sorry I let myself get hurt.'

'Was it worth it?' he asked unsteadily, assessing some of his ribs with his fingertips and then inspecting his elbow with a sour look on his face. 'Are we any closer to what you wanted to show me? I wish you would just tell me what's going on.' He was still fuming, but seemed to be making an effort not to let it show.

I looked up at the waterfall again. It was at least a five-metre drop. No wonder our little childhood boats had never made it through. What an idiot I'd been, bringing us here without knowing what the conditions would be like. My father had died in this river, after all. The thought made my chest hurt.

'I'm trying to find a cave. And hopefully some evidence that someone else has been around. The problem is, I'm not sure if this is anywhere near where I'm meant to be looking,' I admitted.

'Well I'd say we must be close, given that there's a canoe on the other side of the river.'

I looked to where he was pointing and sure enough, there was an old brown canoe tied up to a cape wattle on the western side of the riverbank. It was tucked well under the low branches so it wasn't easy to spot. My appreciation of his eyesight was quickly followed by a surge of relief as I realised I hadn't risked our lives entirely for nothing. We had to be close.

Bane finally agreed that we would have to cross the river again and this time we didn't take any chances, wrapping the rope around our hands and using the barrel for support. With both of us kicking it wasn't hard to get across, and we only had to walk back upstream a short way to get back to the little boat. Discouragingly, it had no stories to tell. It was empty, so we kept going until I noticed a small creek draining into the river that just begged to be followed.

We slipped and staggered our way upstream for quite some time, fighting off swarms of gnats and prickly branches. Just as I was considering giving up, the creek rounded a bend and disappeared under an outcrop of rock. I turned to Bane and smiled wickedly. A rocky path betrayed where the creek probably used to run in ages past and we followed it into a cave, which felt very familiar.

The cold air that hit us as we entered was like a breeze from Antarctica. Except that it smelled amazing. Sort of like chalk dust. In the dim light I could just make out where the creek flowed through the cave to head outside.

It suddenly hit me that this was most likely where Harry had sourced our 'upstream' water supply, and sure enough when I tasted the water it had the satisfying tang of home. It tasted *right*. I emptied our water bottles of the nasty stuff we had brought with us and refilled them from the stream, wishing I had thought to bring something bigger.

Bane, in the meantime, had been exploring the back of the cave. In case there were drop bears. He returned and looked at me quizzically.

'What did you just do?' he asked.

'I just drank a magic potion.'

'You feel better.' It wasn't a question.

'There's something in this water that I need. And the mining has been contaminating the river, so I can only get it here, close to its source, before it joins with the river water.'

'Should I drink some too? Will it cure me?'

Cure him? I hadn't thought of his compulsion in that way before, but I shouldn't have been surprised that it felt to him like something that needed to be cured. For some reason I felt a bit hurt by that, although it was fair enough. Who would want to live chained to another person by gut-wrenching nausea? I offered him the bottle.

'Tastes just like normal water to me. Nice and cold though. Is it supposed to taste different?'

'It tastes delicious to me. Like a cold beer on a hot day. Almost addictive. My hands have stopped trembling.'

'I think I've found something at the back of the cave,' he said, handing me back the bottle. I followed him further inside to where the pale rock face fell into shadow, revealing the start of a narrow tunnel.

'I feel like some sort of treasure hunter looking for pirate's gold,' I sniggered.

'Right. Pirates of the Wimmera. Careful, the floor isn't very even.'

Sure enough, in the dim light I could see that a lot of loose rock had been shaken down from the walls.

'There was a landslide somewhere near here a couple of weeks ago,' I warned him.

'You tell me this *after* I've entered the dark gloomy cave?'

'Or possibly a cave-in.'

'Awesome. Thanks.'

We travelled down the tunnel for what felt like a long time but probably wasn't. At times we had to duck quite low to avoid stalactites that looked like booby traps from a computer game, and at one point Bane grabbed me just in time to stop me from falling into a freezing pool of water. He could definitely be handy to have around. It was a pity he had to be so smug about how useful his phone was as a torch after I'd teased him so thoroughly about how pointless it was to have it when there was no reception whatsoever.

We stopped at the threshold of an uneven cavern, where the sound of the tiny stream echoed in hushed tones like a patient sigh. Bane's harsh light slipped across the flowstone floor to reveal a much drier area beyond. The glow stretched up for a long way above us with only vague shadowy protrusions of rock to indicate that it even had a ceiling somewhere. Creeping forwards in muted respect for the secretive atmosphere, we finally found what must have caused the ground to shudder that day. There had been a serious rockslide. The way forward was blocked. The huge pile of debris looked so overwhelmingly immoveable that I sat down on the rubble and started to cry. Now that I was faced with its solid reality, I couldn't help imagining that Harry was crushed under it somewhere. Aunt Lily had been so confident that he was okay but I just didn't know how much to believe. I needed to see for myself, or find something—anything—to reassure me that he was alive somewhere.

Bane came and sat next to me. 'Sorry, Lainie, I don't know what you were hoping to find but we can't go any further. Please don't cry.' His unexpected kindness stung.

'I'm crying because Harry was around here when the rock fall happened. I'm terrified that he might be dead!' I sobbed into his shoulder, too distressed to care what he thought about my girly blubbering.

'I thought your aunt said he was away on personal business? Why hasn't someone called the police?'

'Aunt Lily said she had some way of knowing for certain that he was all right. I'd hoped that maybe if I got close enough I might have a vision of him to prove it, but I can't sense him at all!'

'Vision? What are you talking about? Since when do you have visions?'

'Well,' I sniffed, 'all my life, I guess. I just never thought they were important.' I tried to dry my eyes on my shirt. 'They always felt perfectly natural to me. I just assumed they were just sort of … spontaneous figments of my imagination, and that everyone had them.'

He didn't reply. I let him think on it while I tried to compose myself. I had made his shoulder all wet again. Poor Bane. I felt him shift around a little.

'Do you feel that?' he asked. 'These rocks are warm.'

Suppressing my undignified snivelling, I reached across him and felt a couple of them. He was right. The cave was freezing but the rocks felt like they had been out in the sun all afternoon.

'Do you think there might be daylight on the other side of this?' I asked.

'Move away a bit, I'll see if I can shift a few. Let me know if you see any of the rocks at the top start to move.'

Great. Very reassuring. He started pulling some of the smaller rocks out of the way, until he had made a small tunnel in the wall. Then he hissed and started blowing on his fingertips. The rocks were getting really hot.

'What's going on here?' he asked.

He rummaged around some more, wiggling each little stone to find ones he could safely remove. Suddenly a few of the rocks cascaded down, opening up a small hole.

A piercing, pulsating light and a blast of hot air came through from the other side, blinding us for a moment, but that didn't stop us both from cramming our heads into the gap to see what was going on. We looked into a bright cavern and gaped, because floating just a few metres away was the thing I had been both searching for, and hoping I would never, ever see. The mere fact of its existence grounded every wild thread of my imagination, weaving a reality that I had to swallow down in one gulp.

It was a huge sword, nearly two metres long, made entirely of a shiny, white metal I had never seen before, with an intricately carved handle. The crosspiece was encircled by a piece of metal so bright it reminded me of an angel's halo. It was revolving slowly, and it was wreathed in bright, flickering flames.

Chapter 18

As I stared mesmerised by the sight of the spinning weapon, I wondered whether there were any forgotten stories or traditions of my mother's people that could have helped to prepare me for what was happening now. Suddenly my lost heritage weighed heavily, and yet I knew that nothing could ever have really prepared me for what I was seeing. The sword had a huge presence, filling both the chamber and my heart with its glow. So real, so exquisitely beautiful and pure. Profoundly *alive*. My lamed spirit bathed in its dazzling majesty, entranced far beyond simple tears while the world lost its lustre to the sword's deep mystery.

When my legs began to cramp I wondered how long we had been watching it for and I tore my eyes away to glance at Bane's face. He remained utterly still, his large grey eyes unblinking, reflecting the dancing flames. In the eerie glow, his fine-boned features looked unearthly, and kind of … beautiful. After a while he pulled away and sat down.

'What the *hell* is that, Lainie?'

Hmm, poor choice of words maybe, but an understandable reaction all the same. I was suddenly grateful that Harry had been patient enough to tell me what he could despite my rude behaviour. It made it all a bit easier to come to terms with now. Bane had no such advantage.

'Um, I don't suppose you've ever been to church, Ben?' I asked slowly.

'Church? Yeah, Mum and I have been going to the Anglican Church on Main Street ever since Dad left.'

It took a moment for that unexpected fact to sink in, but I tried not to let it show. 'Have you heard the story of the Garden of Eden?'

'Yes, of course. The Fall of Man. God cast out Adam and Eve when they disobeyed Him and He's spent the rest of history on His plan to redeem the human race.'

He had been to church a lot then. That made things a *whole* lot easier, but I still struggled to reconcile the image of him faithfully attending church with his mother. He used to get in trouble at least twice a week for swearing.

'The pathway to Eden was supposedly guarded by creatures called Cherubim and a revolving sword of flame,' I explained with slow, clear words.

He squinted back through the hole in shocked amazement, but instead of the automatic denial and disbelief that I had been struggling with for weeks, all he said was, 'Isn't Eden supposed to be somewhere in the Middle East? The Bible specifically mentions four rivers that flow out of it. The Tigris and Euphrates, and I can't remember the other two but I'm sure I would have noticed if the Nalong and Glenelg had been mentioned.'

I couldn't help chuckling at that, despite the sombre atmosphere. 'Some scholars believe the four rivers used to originate from a place that's now in the Persian Gulf,' I said.

'Lost in a massive flood?'

'That might explain why it got moved,' I mused, staring bug-eyed at the spinning sword with its tantalisingly familiar golden fire.

'To *Australia*? Are you mental?'

'Yes, I am. I did warn you.' Then I tilted my head towards the improbable sword to remind him that I wasn't the one instigating the craziness. 'Seriously though,' I said, my lips pursed slightly, 'you would think if Paradise was to be moved anywhere it would at least go somewhere in New Zealand. I mean, have you *seen* the south island?'

Reverting back to his typical grouchiness, he glared at me with a look of outraged consternation. 'If this is another one of your practical jokes, Lainie, I don't find it in the least bit funny. Some topics are sacrosanct ...'

So maybe he wasn't quite ready to see the lighter side of this yet. I, however, was feeling strangely uplifted. The sword was not natural. Every fibre of my being *knew* it. It was not just some cool trick, or a fake. It was real and it was alive. Something supernatural was right in front of my nose and I could no longer make myself deny that the Garden of Eden actually did exist on our farm. Which also meant that Harry had been telling the truth, so I really was not a human being. And yet instead of cowering into a trembling ball of frightened Cherub, all I felt was relief. All my confusion about why Aunt Lily and Harry had been telling me ridiculous stories had now gone. And maybe the stories I'd been told as a child weren't so crazy after all either.

'What if Adam and Eve weren't the only people living in the Garden?' I proposed, fiddling with my bottom lip.

'Just stop, Lainie.'

I grabbed his wrist. He had to listen. 'I guarantee you that this is no hoax. *Look* at it, Ben. No way could I ever manage something this awesome. Please, just help me think this through.' He looked down at my hand clutching his, and I let go awkwardly. 'What if there are still people in there?' But even I wasn't game enough to mention the word 'elves'.

Bane shook his head. 'The Bible doesn't mention anyone else.'

'Yes, but there might be a good reason for that.'

He glanced back at the hovering sword, biting his lower lip. 'If there were, then they would still have access to the Tree of Life. And they would be pure and innocent people. Sinless.'

'And when the Garden was about to be flooded?'

He stared at the weapon, lost in thought, then admitted, 'They would have needed protecting. And not just from the water. People have been searching for the Tree of Life for thousands of years. So you think it was moved here to keep it secret?'

'Keeping it secret would have been the best way to keep the people in there safe from the rest of us,' I agreed.

'Which would also explain why there's no mention of them in any Jewish records,' he said. He sat back and shut his eyes, as if he wanted to think without being influenced by the incredible spectacle on the other side of the wall.

But I couldn't tear my eyes away from it. I leant further into the tiny opening again to try to see if there was some evidence that Harry had been there. There was nothing. I figured though, that if the existence of Eden was true then I might as well believe that my aunt would be right about Harry as well. She had seemed so convinced that he was safe.

I looked up at the immense wall of boulders blocking the way through to the sword, and it dawned on me that the rocks had fallen in a very convenient location. Had Harry somehow caused the landslide? That would be some superpower. My imagination was spiralling way out of control. Perhaps he'd simply used some explosives or something.

'So what does Eden have to do with you and me?' Bane eventually plucked up the courage to ask.

Perching on a large boulder, I hugged my knees to my chest and peered over at him cautiously. I couldn't put it off any longer.

'I am not, entirely … human,' I said, trying hard not to cringe. To avoid looking at his reaction, I squeezed my eyes shut as I spoke. 'I am, apparently, one of the Cherubim appointed to guard the pathway. I'm supposed to make certain no humans ever find it.'

With a sinking feeling I realised I had just done exactly that. Bane was human. He had a bit of a weird supernatural compulsion thing going on but I was pretty certain he was fully human. And he was currently staring through a hole at the flaming sword. I *really* hoped we weren't about to be struck down by lightning. It was turning out to be one of those days after all.

'Is Harry a Cherub too?'

'Yes, he—wait.' My eyes flew back open. 'You sound like you actually believe me.' My distrust must have sounded pretty clear because he looked away from the sword and leant towards me, his silver eyes searching mine.

'I believe you,' he stated definitively.

'Why?'

He shrugged. 'Already a Christian. Not a big jump. Plus, I already know there's something strange about you because I've healed you, more than once, but what I do doesn't seem to work on anyone else. Your aunt didn't even laugh at me when I asked her if I could try the other day when she whacked her elbow.'

My aunt hadn't looked at all surprised when it didn't work, either.

'Plus, you're clearly … different.' He said the word 'different' like it was coated in chocolate. It made me feel as if 'different' was a good thing. The moment stretched so thin that our eye contact finally shattered, and I cleared my throat awkwardly.

'I think Harry might have gone in there and then caused the rock fall to block the passageway behind him,' I said. 'There have been far too many people near here lately, and it was making him nervous.' And me edgy, I realised, thinking back to all the times I'd felt like someone was invading my space.

'But a few minutes ago you were worried he might be dead. Now you say he caused this?'

I began to fiddle with one of the smaller heated pebbles. 'I honestly didn't know it was all true. About Eden I mean. Harry only told me what I was a few weeks ago, but I didn't fully believe him until now.' It was all a bit overwhelming. I could only imagine what he was feeling.

'So I'm supposed to protect you because you're some sort of an angel creature?'

'No, not an angel. I Googled it. Cherubim are different.'

'Yeah, aren't you supposed to have four faces and two pairs of wings?'

I had been a bit concerned when I'd read that particular description in Ezekiel. 'Harry told me we were made to look like humans so we could do our job better.' I grinned naughtily. 'And yes, I really am seventeen.'

'I don't understand.'

I fiddled with the hem of my T-shirt. 'It runs in the family. My mother was a Cherub too, apparently. I found out recently that she didn't commit suicide like I had always thought. She crossed over into Eden a year after Dad died. My aunt implied that she forgot all about me. About this whole world, really.' Shaking my head, I tried to clear away such morbid thoughts. I had Aunt Lily; I didn't need my mother. All the same, I did wish I knew the truth about my parentage. Was there a way to get in? There were some significant, if uncomfortable questions I wanted to ask both Harry and my mother, if I could find them. With cold determination I tried to wiggle a rock to widen the hole, but it wouldn't budge.

'You could help,' I suggested, trying not to sound too bossy. But Bane shook his head.

'No. I can't. The same way I couldn't risk hitting you with a hammer. It's too dangerous. Please stop before the whole thing collapses on us.'

He had that look on his face that made me think he was going to chuck. I'd seen it a couple of times now. It meant that I was probably about to get hurt, so I held my hands up in surrender and backed away.

Through the small gap in the rocks the sword seemed so close, and beyond that, the cavern seemed to narrow down to another tunnel. But the rock fall between us and the sword sat there, resolutely crossing its arms and denying us passage. If it had been Harry's doing he had certainly done a pretty thorough job of it. We weren't getting through this way. Maybe that was it. Maybe this was the only way in and Harry had made sure it was blocked so I wouldn't have to do very much to guard it. That seemed just a little too convenient though, somehow.

'I'm sorry, Lainie, about your parents. I lost my dad last year but we weren't exactly close. He lived in Sydney. I still miss him though, I guess.'

'Oh, I'm sorry,' I said, squeezing his hand in sympathy. I felt bad for him. We barely knew each other really, and now he was being forced to hear all my family's personal dramas. He quickly looked away so I figured he didn't want to talk about it.

'We should head back,' I said. 'Aunt Lily just thinks we're swimming at the Ashbrees's. She'll freak if we're not home before dark. I'll find another way into Eden somehow and try to find some answers for us both, but I don't think it'll be this way.' I'd also told my aunt that I wouldn't try to cross into Eden, but I was going to have to talk to her about that. The Garden was real, and just a rock fall away …

After one last regretful look at the gracefully spinning sword, we both started to pile the rocks back into place. It got very dark and cold again.

'Here, Lainie, take my hand, I'll make sure you don't trip. I do need to guard the guardian, after all.'

In the dark it was impossible to tell whether or not his face had its usual sarcastic smirk, but I was more shaken up than I wanted to admit, from both fear and excitement, and so it felt reassuring to let him lead me with his warm, steady grip.

After eating the soggy ham sangers we'd stashed in the drum, we refilled the water bottles and then argued about using the canoe to head back downstream. Bane was uncomfortable with the idea of riding any more unknown rapids, so instead we fought our way through the thick scrub until we reached the fence line where the river left our farmland. It looped back into our paddocks much farther downstream. The quickest way home would have been to cross back over the river again and then follow the fence south until we hit our western track, but I was starting to get that edgy feeling again so I bullied him into detouring farther west. We left the drum behind and just took Bane's nearly dead phone, which he refused to leave behind.

It wasn't long before we found what had been bothering me. A familiar patch of egg-and-bacon bushes stretched out across a gentle hillside, their bright flowers almost spent. This was where the intruders had been in my vision, prompting Harry to block up the passageway and hide the sword. I hurried up to the tree line, and sure enough every hundred metres or so the trees had been marked with pink plastic tape. Kolsom had been trespassing. Furious, I proceeded to rip all the tape off and stuff it into the pocket of my shorts. The Garden of Eden was real. I could feel the truth of it every time my mind drifted back to the memory of the glorious burning sword. The Garden was real, it was close by, and it was my responsibility to keep it hidden. I wanted no evidence of human interference anywhere near the place. Bane eventually had to stop me.

'Lainie, it's getting late. Are you planning to unmark every tree in the state park today?'

'This is *not* state park here. I own this!' I had never felt so possessive of the farm before. It had always felt like it belonged to Aunt Lily, but now I felt like a possum defending its territory. A fleeting imaginary vision of myself trying to wee on every tree the miners had marked made me realise it was probably time to go home and rest, so I let him drag me back to the fence line where we retrieved the drum and began the trek south.

Once she had finished squeezing all the air out of me, Aunt Lily finally let go long enough for me to explain what Kolsom had been doing. She was as angry as I was. I told her about finding the blocked cavern, and how I thought Harry had caused the landslide, and that Bane now knew everything. I kind of left out the part about the near drowning, though, and avoided too much detail regarding the location of the cave and the sword. I didn't want to get her into trouble with some higher power as well, so I was reluctant to say too much. She told me she didn't want to know the details anyway, and was just glad we were home.

'Is it all right that I took Ben there?' I asked worriedly.

'Yeah, I guess so. Lucas knew where the cave was too,' she explained. 'Can you see the irony here, Lainie? You are a Cherub and you're asking permission from a human to show someone else the cave.'

I pressed my lips together. I didn't want to be reminded that I wasn't human. 'What do we do about the miners?' I asked to change the subject.

'I'll head into town first thing tomorrow and speak to a lawyer about it. They have no right to be there. I wish there was some way to fence it but even then it wouldn't stop them.'

Suddenly the idea of chaining ourselves to a bulldozer didn't seem so outrageous, but there had to be a better way.

Chapter 19

We spent the next few days trying to finish our farm work as soon as possible so we could head out into the bush to remove pink tape and look for another way into Eden. We made a couple of trips back up the river to fill the water drums—and sneak some more peeks at the incredible sword—so at least I had a bit of energy back in my step. No matter how Bane really felt about the whole Eden story, he couldn't deny that drinking the water made me feel better, and he was at least willing to follow me on my tape-removing missions without grumbling too much.

In fear of attracting any more attention to the area, I refused to take out the noisy dirt bikes, so instead Bane got a crash course on how to ride a horse. Literally. It only took a couple of falls from my thoroughbred, Alonso, before he gave in and let me put him on my old galloway instead. He wasn't impressed. It hurt his ego to be on the smaller, safe-looking mount while I was on my shiny fat gelding. Too bad. I wasn't going to risk his neck for the sake of his pride.

By the third day he started to ride more like the dancer I knew he was, instead of looking as stiff and awkward as someone trying to ski for the first time. He even mastered a relaxed canter and almost looked like he was enjoying himself, so I boldly tried racing him up a nice steep hill. The surge of all that equine muscle straining to reach the top made me feel vicariously fit. For just a moment, I closed my eyes and focused on the sound of hooves chipping granite and pounding the dirt. My fingers scrunched a bunch of reins and mane, and my calves strained to take all my weight in my heels. It felt like I was the one running on four legs, leaping and pushing, working sleek muscles to move faster as the hill reached its peak. All I wanted was to keep going and leap into the air as if I could simply unfurl a set of wings and fly away.

Alonso and I won, of course, but Bane managed to keep up just fine, looking carefree and joyful for the first time in, well, ever. He laughed in relief as Charlie slowed of his own accord at the top of the hill and I caught my breath in astonishment. His playfulness was more subtle than Noah's, but definitely there, in his smile, just waiting to be released. If the girls at school had even once seen that expression and all that it promised, Noah might have had a bit more breathing room from his ever-present fan club.

Pulling up his puffing mount to a relaxed walk in front of mine, he deliberately held back a leafy branch he was riding past so that it flicked me in the face, flinching with me, but then grinned at my pretend out-raged reaction. Inside my chest, my heart did a little victory lap with its T-shirt over its head. It was a massive step forwards.

We rested for lunch at the top of a small ridge before it blended into an even bigger climb. The weather was mild so we'd decided to use the whole day and search farther than we had before. I felt pretty relaxed so I hoped that meant that no one else had been nearby for a while.

After tethering the horses, we sat and ate near a temporary billabong in the shade of a peppermint gum, its hot leaves giving off a strong heady scent. It reminded me of lunchtimes spent with Noah at school. I'd only seen him twice since the graduation dance and hoped that meant things were going well with Tessa. That would be good. Despite her tendency to make the odd snide comment behind my back, she actually seemed quite nice to everyone else. And I did like the way she always volunteered to take care of any exchange students or new class-mates. She could get fiercely protective if she thought they were getting picked on. Like a lioness guarding her cubs.

Bane noticed my wistfulness. 'What are you thinking about?' he inquired as he picked the cucumbers out of his sandwich and flicked them into the water.

'Just how much I miss school. Well, maybe not school, but certainly my friends. Graduation feels like a lifetime ago.'

'You miss Noah,' he stated flatly, watching his cucumbers float away like tiny lily pads.

'Yeah, I've hardly seen him since he hooked up with Tess.'

'Are you jealous?' He peered at me sideways, his face blank, but slight tension knotted his jaw despite his casual tone.

'Of Tess? No, of course not. I told you we were just friends.' My water bottle suddenly became very interesting.

'Sure,' he said sarcastically. 'The two most attractive people in the school spend every waking moment together—are practically joined at the hip, in fact—but are just friends. Right.'

Righteous indignation caused me to splutter and dribble water down my chin. Aunt Lily had been right after all. Did everyone at the school really believe Noah and I were together or was it just Bane? Swallowing quickly, I framed a beautifully snarky comeback but he interrupted before I had a chance to utter it.

'Wait, you *were* just friends?'

'He'll be off to uni soon. I can't go anywhere. We're unlikely to see each other much from now on.' I remembered that he was in the same boat, trapped in Nalong because of me. It felt like it was my fault.

He reached his hand out to mine as if he wanted to console me but then stopped and rubbed at his shoulder, looking a bit uncomfortable. He was still sore from riding.

'Third day is always the worst,' I sympathised. 'You'll start to feel better tomorrow.'

'I'll start to feel better when I can stop riding. How much longer do you think we'll need to do this?'

'As long as it takes. I never said you had to come.'

'Right. Like I have a choice.'

My sandwich suddenly smelled horribly sour. I chucked the rest of it into the water after his cucumbers and got up to put my rubbish in the saddlebag. Why did he always have to ruin everything?

'Oh, come on. Don't do that,' he complained.

'Do what?'

'That sulky face. Ever since you found out you're a Cherub you've been looking for a pity-fest.'

'*What?*'

'You said Harry told you what was going on weeks ago but you refused to believe him. Did you give him that sulky face too?'

'No!' I lied, remembering that I'd stormed off. Twice. And I was getting tempted to try the tactic one more time. 'Maybe,' I amended.

'How long had he been waiting to tell you, do you think?'

All my life. I said nothing. I glared really well though. We were both standing with our arms crossed, facing each other like we had done at least once a week for the last six years.

'He probably hoped you'd be excited to find out, but I bet you didn't even give him a chance to tell you what you could do. Knowing you, you probably stormed off.'

Damn. I untied Charlie's lead rope and handed it to him so it didn't look like I was trying to leave without him. Even though I wanted to. 'We can't do anything,' I argued. 'Visions. That's all.'

'Bullshit.'

'Fine. Visions and PMS when people trespass on my property!' I untied Alonso's lead rope from the tree and knotted it under his neck.

'I bet there's more.'

'Harry said we only get what we need to do our job. No more and no less.'

'Well what if you need more than visions? What if you need to move some more rocks?'

'You're really starting to piss me off,' I muttered, swinging back into the saddle. What he was suggesting was extremely disturbing, and I didn't want to talk about it anymore.

It wasn't until we were halfway through a thick stand of snow gums and I was irritably replaying our arguments in my head that I realised he'd implied I was attractive.

An hour or so later we made it to the very top of the razorback, far to the northwest of the farm, and I guessed that somewhere beneath us was the same cave system that held the incredible sword.

The view was beautiful, in a rather ordinary way. There was nothing particularly spectacular about it. The hills were clothed in green and grey, and clumps of Mallee wattles still clung to the last of their golden fluff balls, dotting the drying hills with splashes of yellow in every direction. The sky cradled the hills like a sapphire crown, and off to the south pastureland stretched out in dusty greens that faded to yellow all the way to the horizon. There were better views to be had down in the southeast where the real mountains were, but this was *my* view. My home.

We climbed up onto some large boulders that allowed us an uninterrupted view across the next valley. It was a breathtaking drop down. A sheer cliff ran pretty much the whole way along the ridge. The other side of the valley looked just as inaccessible, if not worse. It was impossible to even tell how deep the ravine went because all we could see were the tops of eucalyptus trees before the terrain dropped away even more steeply behind a rocky overhang. Two magnificent pairs of wedge-tailed eagles soared in lazy circles, riding the air currents.

We stared out for a long time, even using an old pair of binoculars I had brought along, but there was no evidence of any human presence. Just how much of this area did I own? At least the valley region. It was a humbling thought. I wondered if anyone had ever been down there, and if so, how the hokey they would have made it back out again. At least the thick vegetation and steep gullies meant that the miners wouldn't have a hope of trespassing there.

'Looks like a perfect place for base jumping,' Bane pointed out, hopping down from the slab of granite and leaning over the edge to look straight down the cliff face.

Joining him, I followed his gaze, drinking in the feel of open air all around me. 'Or hang gliding,' I agreed. 'Except for all the trees at the bottom. I expect if it wasn't for that, Noah would have flown here by now.' I hadn't picked Bane for an adrenaline junkie. Idly I wondered if he would ever let me do either of those things.

'Noah knows how to hang glide?' he asked, sounding slightly resentful.

'Yeah, he's always been a bit obsessed with flying. He did a course last year and has been working with an adventure tours mob in the high country on holidays. Pity we can't tell him about all this. Do you think Eden is down there somewhere?'

He stared down into the gorge as if he could pierce the dense foliage with x-ray vision. 'Maybe it's in another dimension, and can only be entered by passing the sword, like a portal of some sort.' He actually sounded serious and I looked at him with genuine admiration. Could he possibly have read and watched as much science fiction as my aunt and I? I could beat that though.

'Or maybe it's like a dimensional bubble, and all we have to do is to step off the cliff and we'll step safely onto the ground in Eden,' I suggested.

A frantic look lit his smoky eyes and he took an extra step towards me, making me laugh.

'Relax. I'm not planning to jump just yet.'

'Just yet? Just what are you thinking?' he asked suspiciously, fingers twitching as if he wanted to drag me away from the precipice.

'Well, I need to get in somehow. Maybe hang gliding *could* work. If it is a dimensional thing then the worst that would happen is that I'd look pretty stupid appearing out of nowhere, running like a maniac with a hang glider strapped to me.'

His eyes widened even further. 'You're serious, aren't you, Lainie? No way! I couldn't let you do that!'

'Ben. Listen to me,' I said, stepping back from the edge to help ease his tension. 'We can either find a way for me to get into Eden and try to bring Harry back, or spend the rest of our lives stuck on my farm with no one to ask about how to escape. Is that what you want?'

He looked stricken. Obviously he hadn't realised he might be stuck with me long term. He turned away, gazing out over the quiet valley with his hands tucked into the back pockets of his jeans. It was a while before he spoke.

'I couldn't let you go alone, if it is even possible. We would have to jump tandem.' His voice was rough, almost conflicted, and he wouldn't meet my eyes.

'You can't,' I reminded him. 'Humans aren't allowed in there.'

'Well that's just too bad!' he snapped. 'I'm not left with a lot of choices here. Either we do nothing and continue as we are, or I let you jump alone and die leaving me in goodness knows what kind of agony, or I go with you and hope that we both make it. Which would you suggest?'

It was harsh, but he had a point.

Wearily I slumped down to sit on one of the rocks. I hadn't a clue what to say. We were both trapped and I just couldn't see any way out.

Chapter 20

On advice from the police, we decided to put some 'Private Property' signs up along the boundary to the state park. It was a huge undertaking, but if Kolsom came nosing around again it would be difficult to prosecute them for trespassing without them. So we enlisted the help of Noah and his family. Thankfully, his two older brothers Liam and Caleb were home from uni for the Christmas holidays. The twins had always been like big brothers to me. They had taught me to fish, to shoot and to drive. I had missed them terribly.

'Hey, Lainie. You get prettier each time we see you. Has that little brother of ours netted you yet?' Caleb teased automatically. Noah pretended to ignore him as he threw a box of tools into the back of his ute with a loud clatter. Caleb winced as a couple of ratchet heads bounced out and rolled across the tray. Above us a Currawong warbled out its early morning greeting and our rooster answered. We had decided to try to beat the heat by starting as early as possible.

I yawned again. 'Nah, his ute's the wrong colour. I only go for the black ones.'

Caleb clutched at his heart dramatically, looking mightily offended, and I could see Noah's lips twitch in amusement. The twins had made no secret of their distaste for shiny black cars. They were for townies. Real utes had rust.

'What colour car does the new farmhand have, then?' Liam asked slyly, putting his arm around my shoulder as if inviting me to confide in him. Luckily Bane was out of earshot. I thought about his faded blue sedan that still carried the scars from the altercation with Jake's dog and the bin.

'I'm not sure, it's too beaten up.'

'And where is he anyway? He is coming to help, isn't he?' Caleb asked, looking around the yard eagerly. He had taken the cue from his brother and wanted to see the newcomer for himself, with the expectation that Bane would provide him with endless opportunities to tease me with.

'Splitting wood. And yes of course he's coming to help,' I defended, trying subtly to remind them that just because he wasn't farm bred didn't mean he was useless.

The twins glanced at each other disdainfully. 'Splitting wood in the middle of summer?' Caleb asked.

Liam's eyes lit up with an evil gleam. 'Maybe he's trying to impress someone.'

I made a rude noise. 'Resounding no. He kind of went off in a huff, actually. We collected the tools from the shed but as soon as I got off the ladder he just sort of stormed off and—'

'He held the bottom of the ladder for you?'

I nodded warily.

'And then had a sudden urge to go and split firewood in forty degree heat in the middle of summer?'

'Well, yeah, but—'

'Perhaps he needed to let off some excess energy,' Liam suggested, giving his brother a wink.

I rolled my eyes. Trust the twins to see it that way. Bane was always grouchy when I climbed things but I could hardly explain the reason for that.

'It's not forty yet,' I grumbled, 'but it soon will be and I'd rather not waste the coolest part of the day standing around here yapping. Are we ready to go or what? It's going to take us ages to get this done.' I felt myself blush and hoped like crazy they would leave Bane alone.

'Yep, we'll be doing this today, tomorrow, and a few after that I expect, especially if the new guy gets distracted so easily!' Caleb spluttered, not even bothering to pretend to suppress his laugh.

In fact, the job took the rest of the week. There was an old fire access track that marked the boundary line but it hadn't been graded for years so the rain had gouged out deep crevasses along it, and much of the encroaching ti-tree was so big that we needed the chainsaw to get the cars past. It was heavy work. We worked in two teams, one car leading and clearing the track, while the people in the other car nailed signs to trees. It was hard to keep up with hour after hour of hammering without my fingers taking a pounding every now and then. Bane was suffering for each missed stroke more than I was, so I tried to do the driving as often as I could instead. I only needed to be winched out once. Caleb, whose ute it was, just laughed and shook his head.

By the end of the second day my bodyguard and I had worked out a nice little system where he would cough loudly if I was about to injure myself, so I would freeze when I heard him and concentrate extra hard on what I was doing. It mostly worked. Except once I froze so long I got bitten by a bull-ant. Typical case of a causality loop. Hopping around like a frog on a rock, I yelped as I tore off my boot and sock and Bane, Liam and Noah all came bounding across to me. Bane got there first and laid one hand on my ankle while he squished the monster with his heel, before I even had a chance to show everyone how freaking huge it was. Of course, then I had to pretend that it still stung while Liam tried to find the bite. Noah peered curiously at Bane. Bane smiled right back at him kind of smugly, but at least he didn't faint.

Finally we made it to the north end of the track where it turned on to the main road leading to the next town. The Ashbrees's farm ran east of there so we put some signs along that road as well, just to make sure.

That evening Aunt Lily invited the Ashbrees over for dinner to thank them for all their help. I felt bad for Liam and Caleb having to spend an entire week of their summer break on such heavy work.

'Don't worry about it, Lois Lainie, farm work is farm work and that track needed clearing. They're predicting a bad bushfire season this year. If anything, apologise to Dad because now we won't have time to clear the back paddock for him.'

'I can do it!' Nicole piped in.

Caleb gave her a serious look. 'You might break a nail though, Nic. Better leave it to the big boys,' he provoked. She stomped on his foot. Hard. As they chased each other around the back yard I noticed Noah watching Bane irritably. Bane was looking at me. Our eyes met for a split second before I looked away self-consciously. Noah probably assumed there was something going on between us, and I was so annoyed by the idea that I went to help Aunt Lily with the roast.

After dinner Noah excused himself and went for a walk on his own outside and Liam and Caleb exchanged knowing glances. They were waiting to see if I would follow. Then when I didn't, Caleb glared at me and drummed his fingers on the table. This was getting ridiculous. Nothing was going on, with either of them! Irritated at all of the boys of the world in general, I poked my tongue out at Caleb, dumped my plate in the sink and went out to find my friend.

He was waiting for me at our usual spot by the river, tearing leaves from a dead gum tree branch and tossing them one by one into the water. All the lovely spring rain we'd had was now just a memory and the river was a pathetic shadow of its former glory. Slimy broken logs and clumps of muddy leaves clogged up the edges where the water had receded. It could change so quickly. Tonight the music sounded calmer, as if the river was too tired and hot to cry anymore and just wanted to sulk for a while. Noah looked a bit sulky too. He had dark circles under his eyes; the week had been a tough one working out in the bush every day in such scorching weather, and the nights were so hot it was diffi-cult for anyone to sleep. Sadly I was growing accustomed to that.

'How are you doing, Noah?' I asked, sitting down and leaning com-fortably against him. 'You got better results than you were expecting. Have you made up your mind about what you want to study next year?'

'Not really. I think I might study by correspondence.'

That was a shock. I knew how much he'd been looking forward to going to the city. He'd spent years talking about his plans to share a house with a bunch of mates and get a part-time job in a local pub.

Picking up the end of my messy braid, he twirled a loose curl around his finger. It was a familiar gesture. 'I'm a bit reluctant to leave Nicole here with just Mum and Dad. She needs someone around who she can talk to, and the three of them can't run the farm without help.'

Lame excuse. Harry, Aunt Lily and I had always done okay and our place was bigger. Much bigger, in fact. I knew that overdeveloped sense of responsibility would get him into trouble one day. Still, he was a big boy now and didn't need me to talk him into leaving. Especially given that the thought of him going off without me was so depressing. In fact I felt so selfishly relieved that he might stay another year that I couldn't think of what to say. As a supportive friend, was I supposed to sound pleased or disappointed for him? So we sat quietly for a while. Until Noah found the courage to ask what had clearly been bugging him all week.

'So, um … was I right? About Bane?'

I nodded as vaguely as I could. How much was I allowed to tell him? Luckily he seemed to be more annoyed than curious.

'It's brave of you to take him in after everything he's put you through over the years. He healed your bite the other day, didn't he?'

I slipped off my shoes and perched cross-legged on the rock. 'Yeah. I don't pretend to understand how it all works but apparently he gets sick if we're too far apart, and he *has* to heal me when I get injured.' I showed him my hands. My nails were still as raggedly broken any rural kid's, but my skin was totally unblemished. Even my old burn scar from the wood heater was gone. 'Sadly for him I never was very good with a hammer; he gets really dizzy each time he has to repair my thumb.' That made Noah grin a little.

'I suppose that explains why he watches you all the time. He can't seem to take his eyes off you.' He was glaring at the end of my braid as if he was furious with it. 'Has he tried to kiss you yet?'

'What? No! Of course not. He hates me, remember? I literally make him sick after all.'

Noah looked up at me hopefully. 'Then you and he are not …'

I glared at him in exasperation. 'Noah. Nothing's happened. As if *he* would be interested in a lanky farm girl like me. Be serious.'

He pinned me with his bright green gaze. 'You're not just some farm girl, Lainie. You should have heard what some of the guys at school used to say about you when they thought I couldn't hear them.' Flinching his eyes away, he cut me off just as I opened my mouth to ask. 'Actually, no, you should never *ever* hear that. Forget I said anything.' Wavy blond hair masked his face as he turned away to stare at the river. With incredible self-control, I chose not to pursue the topic.

'How are things going with Tessa by the way? Made any, um, progress?'

'Nothing I want to tell you about,' he snapped primly, as if he hadn't just been prying into my own personal life.

'Fine. Just let me know if you need me to cover for you with your mum.'

'Actually, Mum's been great. She adores Tess.'

That was a surprise, remembering the wobbly she'd chucked at school over Claudia. We watched the river slip past for a long time while I wondered what Tessa had done to win her over.

❧

Lainie, there is always a choice.

Standing stupidly in my rubber gloves, I fretted at the note scrawled on Harry's fridge. He'd been gone for a few weeks and the cottage was starting to get a bit funky. Aunt Lily was giving the bathroom a bit of a scrub while I took kitchen duty, but all I'd done so far was stare at the fridge. What was that supposed to mean? Did I have a choice whether or not to take up the role of a Cherub? Surely not. The sorts of compulsive behaviours that Bane and I had experienced were not the sort of things you could just choose not to participate in.

If he knew he was just going to leave me here and go off to Eden, then why couldn't he leave me a more useful message? His one line phrase was about as helpful as a Chihuahua rounding up cattle. Irritably I disinfected the sink and threw out the few items of food that he'd left behind. There had to be a way to get into the Garden, somehow.

❧

A couple of hours later Bane found me in the shopping centre trying to push my sweaty hair from my eyes while carrying an arm load of bags and a red icy-pole. He'd spent the day visiting his mum and Aunt Lily had dropped me in town for some last minute Christmas shopping. We hadn't even needed to arrange where to meet, which was handy. He reached out as if to tuck my hair behind my ears but then thought better of it and relieved me of some of the bags instead. I bought him his own icy-pole as a reward for his gallantry. We dumped the shopping in his car and then headed towards the park. It was always a bit cooler by the river.

'How's your mum?' I asked, kicking off my thongs and walking with tiny careful steps along a massive tree that had fallen across the river. Icy bliss numbed my feet and ankles as I dangled them into the lazy current. Unsure as to how much information he might have shared with his mother about his link to me, I was fishing for information.

'Great. She's very happy with me, actually. I just bought her a new portable air-conditioner. I've never earned much money before so it felt nice to buy something for her.'

I wouldn't have considered that what we paid him was 'much money' either, but I suppose it helped that we were feeding and housing him as well.

'How does she feel about you working on the farm?'

He peered at me sideways through his long lashes. 'You mean, did I tell her that I live with a heavenly creature who is a sentinel of the Garden of Eden?'

I blushed a little. He was learning to read me way too easily. And 'heavenly creature'? Good grief.

'I haven't said anything,' he assured me, as he took his own shoes off and joined me on the tree. 'And given that I dropped out of school and had to sit my exams in the back corner of the library at Horsham Secondary College with all the other students wondering who I was and why I always looked so green, I think she's just happy that I'm working at all.'

I felt miserable as I looked out across the shallow river. I really had messed up his life and no free icy-poles were going to make up for that.

'Perhaps when Harry gets back we can try spending some time together in the city,' I suggested. 'I could just take a few water drums with me. If it works out we could try renting flats that are close together and still ... study.' Awkwardly I realised I had never asked him what his plans for next year would have been.

He stared pensively across the glimmering water, taking his time to decide what to say. 'Actually, I was planning on joining the army. That's not possible now.'

'Oh! Did you really do that badly? I thought you could still be a regular army guy without VCE at all. Just not an officer. Or you could sit your exams again next year,' I encouraged. 'I mean, it isn't that you aren't smart enough or anything.'

He looked me in the eye. 'My results were fine. That isn't the problem.'

Oh yeah. I think the army officials would notice if I had to stay within an hour of his location at all times. What a mess.

'I'm so sorry, Ben. About everything. I treated you so badly when we were at school and now I've ruined all your career plans as well.'

'*You* treated *me* badly? You weren't the one setting lockers on fire and stealing homework,' he pointed out, his graceful fingers plucking at a piece of bark.

'That's what happened to my geography assignment? I knew I hadn't just lost it somewhere!' I started poking him accusingly with my icy-pole stick.

'It was my divinely appointed task to be the Bane of your life, don't blame me!' He laughed as he pinned my elbows to my sides with one arm and relieved me of my weapon with the other. I slumped in his arms.

'You caught that, did you? I'm so sorry,' I said again, losing the precious moment of frivolity.

'Everyone caught that, Lainie. Even the teachers picked up on it. They didn't even notice they were calling me that too. I don't mind, you know.' He glanced away. 'It does fit.' His arm was still holding me loosely and when he looked back at me, his astonishing blue-grey eyes trapped me like a leaf in a cobweb. 'At least I know the reason why I did those things now,' he continued. 'You have no idea how much of a relief that is.' Beneath his confident demeanour, I could still sense his nervousness, but he didn't back away. 'You and Lily have been unbelievably generous, letting me stay with you.' This time he did move the hair back from my face. 'I have a better understanding of who I am because of you. I'm happier now than I can ever remember ... aside from maybe the Huntsman spider incident,' he qualified. 'You ... you aren't the person I thought you were.'

Sparkly little shivers ran down my spine at his touch. 'Well that's hardly surprising,' I said. 'I'm not the person I thought I was either. In fact, I'm not even the *species* I thought I was.'

His chuckle held the same subtle playfulness I'd glimpsed on those rare occasions when he forgot to be him. I liked it, and realised that he wasn't the person I thought I knew either. He was so different when he was happy. I was getting lost in his closeness, and I found myself wanting to get closer so I pulled away determinedly. I wouldn't do this to him too. Happy or not, he should still be left with some free will, not just hook up with me because it was supposedly 'pre-destined'. As Harry had said, there was always a choice.

He let me go, and the usual broodiness clouded his eyes once again.

Chapter 21

Gasping panicked breaths, I jumped right out of bed before I even realised I was awake, tripping over the denim shorts I had left on the floor. I looked at the clock. It was 4.25am and something was very, very wrong. I dressed so fast I whacked my elbow on the corner of my desk twice, and then headed down the hall to wake the others, but Bane was already up.

'What's the problem?' he asked in a husky voice. 'I just woke up needing to find you. Why are you up?'

Rubbing crusty sleep tears out of my eyes and trying to focus, I stumbled into the kitchen. 'There are people where they shouldn't be. Just a couple of them, but they're up to something. I ... saw them. I need to check it out.'

Just then the phone rang. Aunt Lily emerged from her bedroom looking rumpled and confused as I lunged for the phone. It was Noah.

'Bushfire, Lainie! Northwest of here. Liam and Caleb are here so Dad's sending me over to you. We've already called the CFA.' I could hear the sound of a dirt bike starting up. Was he riding and phoning me at the same time? I glanced out of the kitchen window. I couldn't see anything but blackness, broken by a few washed out stars, but that didn't mean much.

'Can you help Aunt Lily with the generator?' I asked him. 'Ben and I need to take a look.' I couldn't think of any good reason to give him as to why I was abandoning my aunt and heading straight into the bush during a fire so I just hung up. All I knew was that I had to go. After I explained what was happening to Aunt Lily, she handed me the bushfire pack that was always ready by the back door. It was a backpack that contained water bottles, a battery operated two-way radio, a fireproof blanket, a first-aid kit and torches.

'I know you have to go, Lainie, but please try to keep some common sense while you're out there,' she pleaded, looking vulnerable in her cotton summer nightie. Nodding as confidently as I could, I kissed her on the cheek and ran out of the house. Bane was still trying to pull on his second boot as he stumbled out to the shed to catch up to me.

The shed was full of birds. Every rafter fluttered with wings fighting for a place. They knew what was coming and were seeking out whatever shelter they could find. They were much more sensible than me. After a quick check that the petrol tank was full, I wheeled my dirt bike out from behind the ute and started it up just as Bane handed me my helmet. I hoped the spare one would fit him.

As soon as he was settled behind me I took off across the paddock towards the track to the state park. At least he hadn't argued about who was driving. I knew where I needed to be and I didn't have time to give directions.

The ride was torture. It was just as well we'd spent so much time exploring the area recently because tearing through the bush in the dark at full pelt was not very OH&S friendly. And yet somehow I could sense exactly where to go. Sweaty palms made it difficult to keep control at times but Bane's arms were locked around my waist reassuringly. When he tugged on my sleeve to make me veer slightly, I realised he was using his sense of threat to me to guide us past hidden obstacles, and at one point he frantically pushed my head down from behind just in time to avoid a sharp low hanging branch. He never put me off balance, or asked me to slow down. My heart raced as if trying to set the pace, calling me to move *faster*. Loose rocks and dust scattered behind us in a cloud of petrol fumes while the wind gusted through the branches above us.

Three quarters of a stretched out hour later we finally reached the top of the ridge that overlooked my valley. The sun should have risen by then, but everything was still dark due to the fat cloud of smoke blanketing the world. The only thing visible was an eerie glow from behind the next hill, a little to the north. The air was so sharp that it hurt to breath. The fire was definitely headed our way, and despite the length of time it had taken us to reach the ridge, I knew that the fire would race its way back to our farm much faster. Worse than even that horrific thought, however, was the realisation that the valley below me was about to be decimated.

The wind whipped the trees into a wild frenzy as if they knew what was coming and were trying to uproot and run away. They had more chance of leaving than I did, and I was terrified. Or was I? My brain was filled with nightmarish scenarios and logical arguments for turning tail and running, but my body felt strangely calm.

'Ben. Please. You can't stay. At least head back down to the caves. Please?'

He just stood next to me and took my hand in his. It was way too late to get away anyhow. Fire travelled quickly when it got to steep inclines, and the bush was incredibly dry. It would reach the far side of the valley in a matter of minutes. The top of a hill was one of the worst places to be. And yet I felt his strong hand gripping mine, soothing, reassuring. Which was strange considering he couldn't even watch me clean the gutters out without getting snippy.

Looking down at my valley I thought about the devastation that was about to occur and began to feel deeply angry. The one pocket of truly undisturbed land that I was custodian of was about to be torn apart by violent winds and flames. Already I could see the fire front writhing its way towards us like a red glowing snake, searching for prey to devour in the dim light. I imagined it burning its way down, seeking a way into Eden so it could swallow it up, and the thought was so distressing that an uncanny sense of purpose wrung the fear right out of me. I knew what I wanted to do and I suddenly felt like it was the most obvious thing in the world, so I closed my eyes and started to whisper. I had no idea what I was saying, I just pleaded with the world to listen to my request. Words were pouring out from my lips that I had never heard before. I didn't know what they meant and yet at the same time I did. Before long I was shocked to feel tears streaming down my face as I begged, commanded and authorised. I thought about Eden, and all that it promised, and I *cared*.

Gradually I felt a sort of ... cool heaviness press in from the sky to the south. I pulled on it with my words and with my spirit, but it was so heavy that I felt as if my heart was made from brittle clay and would just shatter under the weight of it at any moment.

I risked it anyway.

Standing entranced on the edge of the cliff, I lost all track of time. I could have been there for minutes or years. Desperately I raised my voice from a whisper to a cry, and then to a shout until my throat was raw and slowly, slowly, I felt the heavy cloud mass fight its way across the sky towards us. Electricity stabbed me viciously as the cooler moist air clashed with the warm wind. It felt like the lightning was passing right through my body as I struggled to keep hold of the storm, pulling it with agonising violence through the high pressure system. Thunder rattled my bones at exactly the same time as the lightning bolts struck me, but my ears didn't catch the sounds until seconds later. I was inside the heart of the storm itself, but at the same time the storm was too far away. Terrified, I knew I would never be able to bring it fast enough before the cold air was overwhelmed by the desolate heat from the north. My fear fed on itself until doubt crept its way back into my mind. *What did I think I was doing?*

Another cloud dissolved away and I felt so tired. It seemed as if I had been struggling for an eternity. As soon as I gathered one storm cloud in, another would be wrenched from my grasp by the selfish northerlies. My skin quivered with tension and when I stole a glimpse of the fire I saw no less than four places where burning embers had started new spot fires along the far ridge. At any moment now, the multiple fire fronts would join up and tear the valley apart. Despairing, I fell to my knees, lost in my madness but screaming at the sky to do my bidding anyway.

Strong arms lifted me to my feet. I opened my eyes to tell Bane to leave me alone but it wasn't just him.

'Noah?'

He smiled grimly, his pale hair slick with sweat from his helmet and his green eyes wild with fear—or was it anger? He had ridden his dirt bike right up to where we were. Perhaps he had come to force me to take shelter, but how could I explain to him the overwhelming need I felt to stay and fight? All three of us were in terrible danger now because of me, but how could I have stopped either of them from coming? For that matter, how had Noah even known where to look for us? I hadn't felt him approach despite being so close to Eden—the storm had taken every shred of my concentration. Even now I could sense it slipping back to the south, unable to make war on the northerly gusts without a commander. Slamming down my doubt and guilt, I closed my eyes and started to pull patiently again at the tangled threads of air currents. Giving up was simply not an option.

To my intense relief they began to move much more easily. I felt Bane's hands gripping my shoulders, holding me up, as well as Noah holding my hand. A distant part of my overwhelmed brain noted that Noah was speaking confidently in the language I had never known existed until now. His words joined with mine, wrapping my appeal in powerful expressions of uncompromising support as together we commanded and cajoled the clouds into submission. His self-assurance was exactly what I needed. He was Noah. The same Noah that always, always made me see things the way he did. I trusted him much more than I trusted myself. I always had. And now his words were throwing out the same call to arms as mine were, and everything became absurdly easy. Quickly now, the cold air pummelled its way to the north, building up moisture as the storm system grew. A sharp crack of thunder split the air and madly I fought to bring the clouds closer. Lightning without rain would be disastrous. But finally a welcome splatter hit my face as we both shouted at the sky.

With a cry of relief I threw my heart out to the storm, and the rain obeyed and began to pelt down like a volley of arrows on a war host. Very soon we were soaked to the skin, laughing hysterically at the sky in the innocent way children do when they're chasing bubbles. I couldn't believe we had done it! Bane picked me up in his arms and spun me around, utter relief shining through his laughter while Noah fell to his knees with a gigantic grin on his face, looking out over the drenched valley where the impossible tempest was soaking the dry foliage.

Putting me down, Bane whispered in my ear. 'I told you so.'

I tried to stomp on his foot, but he was ready for it and danced aside. But he didn't let me go. Instead, he began to waltz me around the rocks, his wet cotton shirt clinging to him in a very intriguing way. He sang as he spun and twirled me around, making me laugh.

'Is that Boom Crash Opera?'

'Well we are dancing in a storm,' he defended. 'If you can hum the *Man From Snowy River* theme whenever you're nervous, I can have this.'

'Is that what I hum?'

He just laughed, deep and throaty, and I finally got a real taste of what he was like without all the angst, and he was glorious. We danced with rain pouring down our faces and I wanted it to last forever, but as we passed behind a massive granite boulder, he stopped singing and froze. Lightning reflected from his silver irises, as if they were backlit by something deep in his soul. Utterly lost in his intense gaze, I couldn't even blink away the rain. Could he see what I was feeling? It wasn't fair! My defences were non-existent in the aftermath of what had just happened! After a long moment he drew a deep breath and shut his eyes, breaking the dazzling hold he had over me and turning away. His fingers slid from my elbow to wrist as he started to let me go, and an instinctive stab of despair shot through my chest in blatant defiance of what my brain was trying to lecture me about.

At the last second he paused, and his warm fingertips lingered on my palm.

He murmured something huskily under his breath, and then with a sudden firm grip he tugged me in against his chest. Rain dripped from his hair as his lips boldly found mine, and I immediately forgot all about the storm and the fire, and found out just how quickly an entire world could fade from memory.

Chapter 22

A sharp crack of thunder brought us back to our senses way too soon, and Bane pulled away from me, looking as regretful as I felt. The ecstatic light that danced in his eyes was still there but his posture had become tense and protective. Standing on the top of a hill in an electrical storm probably wasn't the safest place to be, and it would be typically ironic of me to be struck and fried by my own summoned lightning. A lingering yearning for his touch pulsed through my racing heart but I forced myself to untangle my fingers from his. For a few seconds neither of us could move but then another brilliant flash streaked across the sky like a giant electric cattle prod. Guiltily I kept my eyes away from his face as we made our way back around the giant boulders that we had climbed upon the first time we had come. I couldn't believe I had let that happen. He deserved so much better. He should be with someone he *chose*, not someone who was chosen for him.

Noah was still kneeling at the edge of the cliff, staring out over the valley, unblinking, so I carefully knelt down beside him. For all I knew he might have been in such a daze he was in danger of falling off the edge. He turned to face me with a frenzied look in his eyes.

'Lainie? Did we just call a *storm*?' he asked in a shaken voice.

'Yeah. Apparently so. The fire's going out. We're safe now.' I tried to sound calm, the way you were supposed to with accident victims, but my head was spinning with unanswered questions. I'd felt the power Noah had summoned with his words as clearly as I'd felt my own. He must be a Cherub too. Had he known? What did that mean? Were we somehow related? The sudden thought that we could be siblings just numbed my mind. Not possible. No way.

'How exactly did we do that?' he asked.

'No idea. I just knew I had to do it. How did you find me?'

'I can always find you, Lainie. Maybe I'm compelled to protect you too? Like Bane?' He looked dubious, and sort of childlike in his confusion.

I shook my head. 'I don't think that's it. I think you had to be here too. Do you think you would have still come here if I wasn't around?'

He looked back over the valley. 'Yeah. I had to come. I just woke up and I knew I had to come out here. The quickest way was through your farm so I convinced Dad to let me go to help you. I knew there was a fire without even seeing anything.' Worry and guilt clouded his face. 'I can't believe I abandoned both our families in a bushfire!' He buried his head in his hands and his shoulders were trembling.

'Noah, no! It's okay! You *saved* your family from a bushfire, and everyone else,' I assured him, standing up so I could pull him back from the edge. 'I need to call Aunt Lily, tell her everything's all right.' I went to find the backpack with the radio. The rain was still pelting down and thunder still shook us every few seconds, and I shivered from the sudden drop in temperature. Bane started to put his arm around me but then changed his mind. Suddenly I was relieved that Noah hadn't seen us kissing. I didn't think he could have coped with any more surprises. I wasn't sure I could either.

After reassuring my aunt, we started the bikes up again and headed back down the hill. This time I let Bane drive. As we began the long trek back I huddled behind him, my arms clutching him too tightly around his waist. I just wanted to hold him and not have to think about what I had just done because my brain kept trying to come up with alternate explanations for what had happened, and I just couldn't trick myself into believing any of them.

When we finally pulled up by the house, Aunt Lily was waiting for us. There was a CFA pumper in the driveway and Bane quickly offered to put the bikes away, probably so he could hide in the shed until the fire crew had gone because they were all frowning at us. To them we just looked like three foolish teenagers who had headed out into the bush to sticky-beak at the fire. Beyond irresponsible in our community. Tessa Bright emerged from behind the truck dressed in her CFA jacket and thick yellow over-trousers that somehow made her look less likely to faint than usual. In fact, the way she was strangling her helmet and glaring at Noah made me think that perhaps he was in for a lecture that his mum would be impressed by. He glanced back at her, shamefaced, but as she started to stride towards him, he turned tail and practically ran into the house. Apparently cranky girlfriends were a lot scarier than bushfires or unexpected supernatural powers. I happily let Aunt Lily shepherd me inside as well, while she went back out to talk to the volunteers. I was indescribably grateful to her for dealing with them.

Noah called his mum to make sure everything was okay at his place while Bane snuck in through the back door and came to sit with me at the kitchen table. I smoothed my hand over the wood and listened to the fire crew outside arguing about the impossible weather. The old wooden table had heard its fair share of crazy discussions lately and it was about to witness another one. After a few minutes I found the energy to get up and change into a dry set of clothes and Bane generously found something for Noah to wear. After that I put on a pot of coffee.

Eventually we heard the pumper leave to join the crews at the fire scene; they would still have a long day ahead of them assessing damage and ensuring the fire was completely quenched. It certainly could have been a lot worse. Without the miraculous rain, that fire could easily have taken out any number of farms as it headed south towards the township. I wasn't sure if Eden would have been directly impacted by the fire itself; however, the thick bush was our best defence against intruders. A fire would have opened up access in all sorts of ways. For starters, the CFA crews would have been automatically required to inspect the area to ensure there were no spot fires, and I didn't doubt that others would have had no problems sneaking in at the same time. I sincerely hoped that the fire had stayed far enough away from the ravine to keep the fire crews from nosing around too closely. I would have to keep a mental eye out.

'The pumper made it here in record time,' Aunt Lily said as she came in and poured herself a coffee. 'They arrived about half an hour after you left, Noah.'

Realising how completely we'd all abandoned her made me feel a little ill.

'Why didn't you tell me Noah was a Cherub?' I asked bluntly, watching her. She froze mid-sip, staring first at me, then at Noah. The utter shock on her face told me what I'd been hoping for. She'd had no idea.

'Noah's a *Cherub?* What happened out there? Where did this amazing storm come from?'

The ground was still shaking every few minutes from the thunder, and the rain kept shifting between pelting downpours and a steady soaking. Noah squirmed a bit, but stayed silent. Once again, it was up to me to steer the conversation.

'Noah and I … pulled it up from the south,' I said hesitantly. I still couldn't quite believe it was our doing, but I couldn't deny the immense power I had felt. It wasn't a random lucky coincidence. I knew we had made it happen. 'What's the deal here, Aunt Lily? The Bible only talks about two Cherubim.' Although, it dawned on me that if my mother really was still alive then that already made four of us, including Noah. How many more?

'What's a Cherub?' Noah asked, confused.

'Cherubim are the sentinels that guard access to the Garden of Eden,' I explained. Noah looked at me blankly. Great. I *knew* he hadn't done the research for that English essay. We were going to have to start from scratch. Aunt Lily had left the computer tablet switched on to check for the latest updates on the fire so Bane searched up a copy of the Bible and slid it over to Noah.

'Time to brush up on some Judeo-Christian history, my friend,' he advised with his wry sideways smile, showing him where to read from. Other than being on the school soccer team together, they were not what I would have considered 'friends'. He seemed to be trying to make an effort to connect, given that Noah was apparently going to be part of our secret little world.

We left Noah to familiarise himself with the Creation story while I poured a couple of glasses of river water. Noah gulped his down without noticing how brown it was because he was too engrossed in what he was reading, but he held it out to me for a refill. He read the story three times before leaning back in his chair and rubbing his forehead.

'Are you implying that I'm one of the Cherubim that were appointed to stop people from getting back into Eden? 'Cos I'm pretty sure I would have remembered if I was thousands of years old. And I didn't realise the Bible was set in Australia.' The confusion on his face was almost comical.

Aunt Lily turned to me. 'Are you sure about this, Lainie? Are you sure you didn't just tap into his energy or something?'

I was pretty confident it was more than that. 'Noah and I pulled that storm in together. And he told me that he woke up and knew there was a fire even before I did. I don't understand though—I thought it ran in the family? Didn't I inherit it from my mum?'

'Yes, you did.' She turned to Noah, twisting her fingers through the handle of her mug. 'I've known for years about your mum, Noah, but I had no idea that you were a Cherub. I think it would be best if you talked to her about all this. Trying to get a straight answer about Eden from anyone is difficult for a mere human like me. I only know bits and pieces. But it was your mum who told me that Harry had crossed over there.'

Mrs Ashbree was a Cherub now too? Just how many of us were there? And where had she been that morning if she had just as strong a compulsion to protect Eden as we did? Harry's words played hauntingly in the back of my mind. There was always a choice. Sarah Ashbree, who was so protective of her family, had managed to stay home to help them rather than go haring off into the bush like a lunatic. It was nice to think we might one day learn to have a bit of control over our compulsions. Particularly if it would otherwise put people's lives at risk. I glanced guiltily at Bane and my aunt while she explained to Noah about Harry being a Cherub and how he had caused a landslide to help safeguard the pathway.

'So now he's stuck there?' Noah surmised. 'Because he blocked himself in?'

Everyone else looked about as defeated as I felt. Harry had been gone for weeks. If there was another way into or out of Eden other than through that cave, he probably would have found it by now, which meant that either there wasn't one, or he didn't want to come home. And surely the threat of a bushfire in the valley would have lured him out if anything could.

'We'll get him back,' I said with far more confidence than I felt. 'If he can cause a landslide and we can call a storm, then unblocking a cave should be a piece of cake.'

But Noah just stared at me, his face rather pasty. He didn't have to say it. What we'd done had been spontaneous and instinctive, and I had no idea how to replicate it. And it had shaken me like a box of Hundreds and Thousands on to fairy bread. I wasn't ready to even contemplate doing anything like that again any time soon.

'Have you been tired and shaky too, Noah?' Bane asked, handing him his third glass of water and breaking the awkward moment. It was a good question. Noah was an eighteen-year-old guy. He ate like an elephant. Certainly for all the fruit I consumed he could polish off his fair share too, but he ate plenty of everything so it didn't seem out of place.

'Yeah, totally stuffed. Tessa keeps telling me to go to the doctor. Why?'

'Apparently there's something in the water you need that's been messed up by the local mining,' he explained.

'Is that why Harry brought around those drums of water before he left? I thought it was a bit strange at the time. Mum refused to answer when I asked about it.'

'And did you?' Bane asked. 'Go to the doctor, I mean.'

Noah smiled ruefully. 'And say what, that my girlfriend doesn't think I'm energetic enough?' Then he groaned. 'I shouldn't have dodged her just then, should I? She looked furious with me.'

Bane looked at me, his eyes going wide. My mouth dropped open as a suspicion began to form. He subtly put his finger to his lips and I nodded. We would want to be pretty certain before we told Noah that Tessa was supposed to be his bodyguard. He was a sweet guy but I was pretty sure his male ego would struggle with that one.

A heavy feeling settled in my chest as I thought about what that meant. Tessa Bright? Linked to Noah the way Bane was linked to me? But Noah was *mine*. I had always looked after him! Where had *she* been the day he'd burnt his leg on the exhaust of his first dirt bike? Or the day his Aunt Kelly had been killed in that car accident? When had she ever bullied him into studying for a maths test? The ferocity of my sudden jealousy shocked me into silent retreat. There was simply too much that I had to think through but I just couldn't get my head around it all.

As Noah went back to reading the tablet to research his new role, Bane and Aunt Lily went out to put all the fire-fighting equipment away. I moved over to the couch in a daze, staring out the window at the rain. My mind was flipping like a fish out of water between the calling of the storm and Bane's kiss. There just didn't seem to be any room left in my brain to think about anything else, and anyway I refused to let myself think about skinny little Tessa Bright for even a second.

A little while later Noah found a blanket and wrapped it around my shoulders. I must have been cold but I hadn't noticed. Outside, the rain was starting to ease off, which came as a massive relief. I had been quietly concerned that it would keep going until I sent it away and I honestly didn't know how to do it. I'd even had a panicked thought that maybe one of my predecessors had done something similar and accidentally been responsible for the Great Flood because they couldn't switch it off. Maybe Noah really was named after one of his ancestors ...

Aunt Lily shook me awake. 'Are you all right?'

I nodded, wiped away the usual tears and mumbled something about a bad dream. Someone had wrapped me up like a burrito in the blanket and as I untangled my legs I noticed that the rain had stopped. Just as well.

Noah had already left to check on his family and I wondered what he would say to his mum. I felt like I should have at least given him some sort of booklet titled *Cherubship For Dummies*, but no one had given me one either so there wouldn't have been very much in it. His mum would most likely be able to do a much better job anyhow. Hopefully she could clear up some questions for me too.

I yawned and stood up, deciding that I could really use a shower. My clothes and hair stank of smoke. As I passed the kitchen I could feel Bane's eyes on me but I chickened out of looking back. What was I supposed to tell him? Loved the kiss, let's do it again but just please ignore the fact that you don't actually love me, you're just compelled to make out with me so we can have little Cherub babies together and continue the line? I had visions of the traditional fat baby winged putti flying around the farm. People might notice. Maybe we could dress them in woollen jumpers and tell people they were sheep. Flying sheep. It was a bit startling to realise how relaxed a mood I was in. The nap must have done me a lot of good. Or maybe it was the euphoria from creating my own personal weather system to quench a bushfire. Or maybe it was the other thing.

We got a call from the Country Fire Authority late in the afternoon to give us the all clear and ask if we could take in any injured wildlife. They warned us to remain on alert and not hesitate to call them if there was anything we were unsure about. Even if they saw no further evidence of flames they wouldn't declare the region as officially safe for at least another 24 hours, just in case. Luckily Noah and I had managed to drown the blaze fairly quickly before it had been given a chance to really take hold. The CFA only considered it a minor incident, as bush-fires went. Everyone knew it could have been a lot worse and so they were checking things out pretty thoroughly.

I'd spent the day trying to concentrate on my 'spidey-sense' to feel if anyone was getting too close to Eden, and all I'd felt were vague impressions of people driving around, far to the west. My mood continued to lift so I took that as a good sign. It probably helped that Bane and Aunt Lily seemed to be doing their best to do all my chores before I could. They were babying me terribly and I didn't know why.

As the evening progressed I began to wonder if I really had 'seen' two people out there when the fire started. Considering I had been asleep at the time, perhaps it had just been a regular dream, rather than a vision, yet somehow that just didn't feel right. Fire bugs were not unheard of but everyone knew how deadly bushfires were, and the punishment for arsonists both from the law and from the community was severe. It just seemed so unlikely that two people would be involved if that were the case. Maybe kids? I didn't think so. The people I saw didn't seem to be all that young. Still, I could hardly call the police and tell them I'd had a vision of two suspicious people out in the bush in the middle of the night just as the fire started. I hoped the CFA investigators would find something. So long as they looked well away from Eden, of course.

As I slipped into bed that night I cranked up the music in my head-phones to try to distract myself from thinking about it anymore. It didn't really help.

✐

Relishing the brief coolness of the new day, I sat huddled on the old tractor tyre that used to be my sandpit as I bottle fed an orphaned joey and squinted hard at the clouds above me. A soft chuckle came from behind me.

'Are you trying to make it rain or send the clouds away?' Bane asked, bringing me a steaming mug of tea. I passed the pillowcase full of wrig-gling joey over to him so I could warm my frozen hands around the mug. It was still early and I had hardly slept. The young wallaby had been found in its dead mother's pouch not far from the edge of the burn zone and still needed feeding every four hours. Luckily she hadn't been injured herself, and was fully covered in hair so she had a good chance of survival, but she would need some serious TLC for the next few weeks.

'You have to admit, we could run a great sheep station here if I could control how much rain we get.' I puffed out a wistful sigh.

'And? Any luck?'

'I honestly have no idea how I did it. I know I was saying something but not in any language that I know. I just knew that I had the authority to do it.'

'But not anymore?' he asked.

'Only the power we need, when we need it, remember? Just as well, I suppose. Who knows what havoc I would wreak otherwise. Let alone Noah—he would probably start parading around with his undies on the outside just to let people know what he could do.'

He waited.

'Okay. Fine. You were right when you said there might be more to being a Cherub than just visions, but seriously, who would have expected that?'

I watched him cradle the tiny joey as it guzzled down the milk. It was hard to believe he was the same person that everyone had been so intimidated by at school. I really didn't know who he was at all. Staring into my mug, I procrastinated for a full minute before choosing to do the right thing.

'I'm sorry about yesterday. I should never have put you in danger like that. And also ...' I struggled to say the words.

'I kissed you, Lainie,' he said softly, still looking down so that his dark hair hid his eyes. 'I'm the one who should apologise. I had no right, not after everything I've done to you.'

How could I explain this to him? As frightened as I was about his reaction, it would be unfair not to tell him. Inside my brain, my conscience wrestled bravely with my unruly teenage hormones. Then Bane smiled at the baby marsupial, his lips making a quirky little shape in the corners, and my hormones nearly won but my conscience managed a sneaky body slam and pinned them down mercilessly. I ran the tip of my finger nervously around the rim of my tea.

'Ben,' I choked. No sound came out. I cleared my throat and tried again. 'Ben, Aunt Lily seems to think we're supposed to be together. And I mean, *be* together. Like your compulsion to heal and protect me. It's not your fault—it's part of this whole weird package. I will find a way to break it though, somehow. You should be free to be with whoever you want, not forced into something like some old-fashioned arranged marriage.'

He looked up at me in shock, confusion in his large pale eyes, along with ... hope? He glanced away before responding.

'But Noah's a Cherub ... I mean, I was sure that meant that it would be him you would end up with. You've always had a strong connection.' He thought for a moment, and then looked up at me. 'You want to break it? This compulsion I have?'

'Of course I do! I could never keep you here. You should be out in the world, making your own choices, not stuck here at the back end of nowhere your whole life.'

For a second he stared at me in utter confusion.

'Wait,' I said. 'If you thought Noah and I ... then why did you—'

'Because I thought it would be the only chance I'd get,' he interrupted, hiding behind his fringe again. My heart stuttered for a few beats before I reminded myself that none of it was real. You can't be 'compelled' to love someone.

He frowned at the baby marsupial, which was sucking so hard on the bottle it threatened to pull the rubber teat right off. He seemed thoroughly miserable.

'Your feelings are not your own right now, Ben. Please, if we can just figure out a way to break this you will be grateful, I promise.'

'Money back guarantee?'.

'Of course. I'm a Cherub of integrity after all,' I said with a relieved smile.

Chapter 23

Christmas morning dawned clear and hot. The storm system was long gone and the northerly wind whipped everything into choking dust again. We were feeding out massive amounts of hay because all the grass had turned to short dry stubble. Despite the sweltering heat we kept up the ridiculous traditions of a snowy Christmas by preparing a huge roast complete with baked potatoes and mulled wine. The woolly stockings hanging from the wood heater and the fake snow sprayed on all the windows were totally out of sync with the scorched landscape, but for us the decorations just meant Christmas, not winter.

We had always celebrated Christmas by having lunch with Noah's family, so after we finished all our morning chores we packed up all the presents, the food and one rambunctious joey, and headed over to the Ashbrees's farm.

Nicole greeted us at the gate wearing shorts, thongs and a Santa hat and beard. She trotted and bounced her way around the garden trying to catch hold of their dog, Blue. The kelpie was doing a good job of evading her so she could check out the interesting looking creature in the pillowcase I was holding. Kelpies just can't be caught unless they want to be. I couldn't wait until the pups we'd ordered were ready to be picked up. Our last two dogs had run away. Bungee had been about to turn four when he disappeared—he was a ripper little dog—and Gerdie was only eight months old when she went out for a walk with Harry one day and didn't come home. We'd never had much luck with them.

Liam's sharp whistle called Blue away, and she obediently skipped over to sit at his feet. I handed the joey over to Nicole, who went all gooey and suddenly looked like the thirteen-year-old girl she was instead of the stoic tomboy she always tried to be.

Noah came out of the house and caught me in a massive hug.

'Merry Christmas, Lainie.' He held on to me for a second longer than was normal. I hadn't had a chance to speak to him since the fire and I wondered what his mum had put him through. Surely she'd understood why he'd left home to protect Eden? Knowing her though, she'd still probably told him off for putting himself in danger.

'Merry Christmas, Noah. How's Tess?' I asked, extricating myself from his embrace and pulling out an armload of platters from Bane's shabby old sedan. All morning I had sternly disciplined myself to try to come to terms with having Tessa around. If Noah really liked her then I would support them both and try to behave like the grown up I wasn't.

'Ask her yourself—she came for lunch.' Had he figured out the connection between them? He had certainly figured out what Bane's problem was before I had. It wouldn't have been hard for him to put two and two together.

Caleb came out to help unload the car. 'This your car, Ben?'

'Yeah. It used to be Mum's.'

'It's not a ute.'

'Nope.'

'Where do you put your stuff?'

'Inside. Where it doesn't get covered in road dust,' he replied, lifting his chin slightly.

'How much can it tow?' Caleb teased.

'No towbar, but there's room inside for passengers. See? Actual seats. With seatbelts. So Lainie doesn't have to get bumped around in the tray.' He pulled out four bottles of soft drink from the backseat.

'Personally, I've never needed room for more than one girl before,' Caleb responded, his mouth twitching with suppressed amusement.

Aunt Lily stomped on his foot as she walked past him with a giant Pavlova dessert. 'Leave him alone, Caleb,' she scolded.

We all followed her meekly into the house.

'Hi, Lainie. Merry Christmas,' Tessa greeted as I entered the kitchen. Her pretty face looked thin and pale, but her smile was relaxed. At least she didn't have that pinched jealous look anymore. As soon as I found a bit of room on the table to put the platters down, I gave her a polite hug.

'Merry Christmas, Tessa. How did you go with your ATAR score?'

'Not great. I don't think I managed to get quite enough for what I wanted. I was hoping to do a nursing course next year, but it'll be touch and go as to whether I've done enough to get in.'

Nursing. Perfect. She would be a great healer. I wondered if she would be able to heal me, and Bane heal Noah. It would be an interesting experiment.

'How about you? How did you go?'

Noah handed us both a glass of sparkling pink wine. 'She could probably get into Cambridge on her score, the nerd.'

I peered at the drink, certain that something so pink and bubbly couldn't possibly be tasty. I took a sip and tried hard not to think about what Cambridge might have been like. All vaulted ceilings and stone buildings that smelled like wood polish and Skirlie mash for dinner. Tessa's face began to darken in a familiar way.

'He's exaggerating, Tess,' I said quickly. 'Noah did almost as well. Besides, I haven't even decided on a course yet. I'll probably ...' But there was no point in finishing my sentence because Tessa was no longer listening. Bane had just walked in and she actually stepped backwards in surprise—or possibly that was just the self-preservation reflex that came from being at school with him for so many years.

'Bane?' she croaked.

'Hi, Tessa. Merry Christmas,' he said, avoiding eye contact by busying himself with finding space in the fridge for the drinks.

'Uh, hi.' She turned back to me with eyebrows that were clearly asking, 'Why is *he* here?'

Another sip of the pink stuff didn't win me over to it. 'Bane's working for us on the farm,' I explained.

Tessa just looked from Bane back to me, then at Bane again, and I didn't need any insightful visions to know what she was thinking.

'And I haven't even set anything on fire,' Bane mumbled to the milk.

'Yet,' I mumbled back.

'What would be the point?' he muttered, making Noah crack up silently from behind where Tessa was standing.

When Bane shut the fridge and turned around, Tessa took a step closer to Noah. I tried not to smile as I realised she still saw him as a bit of a threat. Now that I knew what I was looking for, Tessa's possessive behaviour really was quite protective as well. Bane turned to leave but I grabbed his hand. She would have to get used to him at some point and it wouldn't hurt for her to think we were together. I hoped it might make her less defensive toward me, but all it did was make her blink at us in a sort of confused stupor so I let go again. I couldn't exactly blame her. I didn't believe it either.

As we continued to chat about our plans for next year I found myself getting distracted as I saw Noah's parents outside, his dad's arms around his wife, both laughing as they watched the twins wrestle on the lawn. They looked so happy and relaxed. How had they felt about being forced together by some supernatural compulsion? They didn't look like it bothered them one bit, but maybe it had been different in their generation. Regardless, they seemed to have embraced the situation in a way that made me feel a little wistful, and I wondered once again about my own parents. I shook my head to dispel my overactive imagination before anyone noticed the tears that welled in my eyes. It was Christmas Day, and not a time for dwelling on my dubious past and even more uncertain future.

Lunch was long and gluttonous and choc-a-block full of honeyed carrots, dumplings and inappropriate winter puddings. Afterwards we sat down to exchange presents on the front lawn in the shade of a huge hollowed out rivergum that had been there for centuries. Its bark was peeling like a Scottish tourist and a column of sugar ants were doing parade drills along its lowest branch. I wondered how many Cherubim it had known. Just how many of us were there? Aunt Lily had been confident that Noah's siblings were not Cherub-kind. They didn't know anything about it. Even just imagining talking to any of them about Eden produced a queasy sense of guilt at the base of my sternum that seemed to support that assumption. I was itching to talk to Noah's mum, though.

Stretching out on the tartan picnic rug, I started chucking gumnuts at the back of Noah's head, just to see if Tessa would notice. She did— when I missed and hit her by accident—so I sat up and concentrated on what I was supposed to be doing instead. I hadn't been very inventive when it came to presents. I'd bought Aunt Lily her favourite perfume and Bane and Noah the latest video games: a soccer one for Noah and an army-themed one for Bane. Like the slacker I was, I'd left Aunt Lily to buy all the rest, and in return, I got pampered very unfairly. Noah had bought me the latest book in a series I had been waiting on—for which I mouthed a silent thank you to my aunt who had clearly been the one to suggest it to him. She, in turn, had given me two tickets to see a band that I liked in Melbourne. My wrestling hug very nearly bowled her over as I showed her just how much I appreciated her subtle message. She was telling me how confident she was that I would still be able to travel, and have a more or less normal life. I was not trapped. Of course, the twins saw it as a slightly different subtle message, and Caleb asked me in an overly innocent voice who I was going to take with me. I told him it depended on who sucked up to me the best and then asked Liam if he wouldn't mind fetching me a glass of water.

While Nicole distracted everyone by starting up her 'new-hand-me-down' dirt bike, and getting told off by her mum for filling the air with exhaust fumes, Bane quietly handed me a small jewellery box tied with a ribbon. That was a bad sign. Liam frowned when he saw it but Caleb beamed at me with a smug 'I told you so' expression as I tentatively opened the box. There was a delicate golden bracelet inside, pretty but without too much bling. It had a plate with an inscription, '*Shalom*'. I had never heard the word before and I wondered if it was in the language I had used to call the storm, but Bane wouldn't have had a chance to have had the engraving done since then—it had to have been done earlier. He clasped it around my wrist.

Caleb gave his brother a nudge. 'Well that's going straight to the pool room.' Liam laughed.

'It means "peace" in Hebrew,' Bane explained, watching me carefully to gauge my reaction. It was a pretty gift, and I had long since become immune to Caleb's teasing so I hugged Bane in authentic appreciation. Out of the corner of my eye I could see Mrs Ashbree grinning at us.

We survived our traditional Christmas cricket game in the shallow part of the river without anyone biting the hostess' son, and rewarded the winner with the bone from the roast. While Blue skulked off to bury his prize, and the others were trying out the new games in the lounge room, I came out to the veranda to sip mulled wine with Noah's mum and Aunt Lily. The currawongs were shouting their lonely cries to each other as the wind began to settle for the evening and the bush started to wake from its somnolence. Usually around this time we would all be taking bets on who would nod off to sleep first, Harry or Noah's dad. I missed Harry.

'So how are you feeling about the other day, Lainie?' Mrs Ashbree asked, fiddling with her silver bangle. 'Noah tried to tell me what you both did, but it's hard for me to get my head around. You *called* the storm?'

Rats. I'd been hoping she would be able to shed some light on what had happened. Still, Harry had been rather vague about what powers we had, too. I wondered if they really had any idea just how much we were actually capable of.

'I don't know what to tell you, Mrs Ashbree. I just sort of knew what to do. I certainly couldn't do it again. Unless Eden was under threat, I suppose.'

'Please, Lainie, I think it's high time you started calling me Sarah. And yes, I agree. Cherubic powers only manifest when they're needed. Until now, none of us have come across anything so extreme. Only visions and feelings. We might have spent the rest of our lives not even experiencing anything unusual if there hadn't been a fire.' She sounded resentful, and Aunt Lily shifted uncomfortably, perhaps trying to come to terms with how potentially dangerous this was all becoming.

'I dunno about that,' I said. 'Harry told me Kolsom's activities triggered some things. At least in me.'

'True, but your gifts have always been there—latent or dormant maybe. When he was little, Noah occasionally mentioned that he had daydreams of people, out in the state park. And he could always find you without any problems.'

It was true. Hide and Seek was not a game we'd ever bothered playing because we always just found each other straight away. I'd never thought about it that much and had assumed that we simply knew each other too well, but now I realised that my instinctive hunches about where Noah was at any given time were probably not that normal after all. And I had known when he'd been lost in the bush on his dirt bike all those years ago.

A triumphant shout echoed out from the living room where Tessa had apparently slaughtered Bane's avatar in a PlayStation bloodbath. I could see her wiggling around doing a little victory dance. I felt a bit wistful that I was missing out, but the questions that had been rolling around my skull had already been waiting too long for answers.

'Have our families always been around to guard this area? Even before we became sheep farmers?' I knew my family had Indigenous blood in its history but Noah's family were all blond and fair with those startling green eyes. I was fishing for information shamelessly.

'What?' asked Aunt Lily, chuckling. 'You don't think being a shepherd is an appropriate job for a biblical character?' She winked at Noah's mum.

As I choked in response to being referred to as a biblical character, Sarah kindly answered my question with a little more reverence.

'Our families have lived here for a very, very long time,' she explained, understanding what it was I really wanted to know. 'Apparently we take on the physical characteristics required to blend in to whatever people expect to see.'

That fit with what Harry had said about us having human bodies in order to pass unnoticed, but it led me to another thought. 'Does it keep happening? Changing our appearance to blend in?'

'Quite possibly. I've always had my suspicions about your height. I think Noah just expected you to keep growing as much as he did, so you did. Why, has anything happened to you recently?' she inquired, peering at my face.

'No, not that I've noticed,' I said, leaning back self-consciously. 'I was just a bit worried that I might wake up one morning to find myself with sparkly skin or something. I don't suppose this job happens to come with some sort of an instruction manual? Are you sure there isn't some huge dusty tome hidden away in the attic somewhere? Or maybe my parents left me a mysterious package only to be opened on my seventeenth birthday that you forgot about?'

Sarah slid a napkin and a pen over to me. 'Here,' she said, 'Write down something about Eden. Perhaps something that you might like your own kids to know.'

I cringed at the thought that in her mind she already had me settled down with kids, but tried to do as she suggested. It would have been nice to find the cave without having to nearly drown. Maybe a map could have been handy. The pen froze at the end of my fingers. Something deep in my chest began to tremble as the guilty feeling rose up, swamping any desire I had to draw or write anything at all. I dropped the pen, feeling sick to the stomach. I couldn't even write the word 'Eden'. No wonder I'd had so much trouble with that English essay.

'I see.' So that was why there was so little information to go on; we couldn't speak openly to anyone that wasn't a Cherub or bodyguard, and evidently couldn't write anything down either. Personally, I was having enough trouble even talking around the edges of it while Aunt Lily was sitting with us. I wanted to ask more direct questions about Eden itself, but I couldn't even frame them in my mind without feeling like I was trying to murder someone. I could hardly blame Aunt Lily for wanting to hang around, though. I knew how concerned she was for me.

'Aunt Lily, how is it that you know anything at all about Eden if we can't even talk about it? Are you one of us too?' I had been wondering whether she really had been Harry's bodyguard, as ridiculous as that seemed, but she shook her head.

'As I mentioned the other day, getting information is almost impossible for me. I only know as much as I do because my brother became bonded to Annie and got caught up in something supernatural, and then I ended up raising you,' she explained. 'I actually know very little. Harry wasn't one to talk much at the best of times—he never said anything he didn't have to. Everything I know I've pieced together from things I've seen myself. I'm sorry I can't be more help.'

Sarah laid her hand on my arm. 'And I'm afraid I've never really been very involved. As you said before, things only happen as needed. With Harry around, I … wasn't needed.' She suddenly looked a little lost, almost regretful. Perhaps she was quietly jealous of what Noah and I had achieved.

My next question was a bit of an awkward one, but I bravely ploughed ahead. 'Speaking of not being needed, do you happen to know if there's a way to break this bond I have with Bane? I can take care of myself, and—'

Suddenly there was mulled wine everywhere, and Noah's mum was standing up. She'd dropped her mug from shaking hands.

'Don't *ever* say such a thing! *Don't you dare!*'

Perhaps storming away in anger was a natural female Cherub trait, because she did it even better than I ever had.

My aunt and I sat in silence for a long time after that, both of us wishing that Harry would just come home.

Chapter 24

A delicate giggle woke Harry from a sound sleep. He shouldn't have let his guard down for so long but his body could only cope with so much these days, and it was so hard to keep remembering why it even mattered. He crept back into the bushes, hoping the girl would lose interest once he was out of sight, but she followed him curiously, her large blue eyes showing no trace of fear. He should have known his furtive behaviour would only spark her inquisitiveness. He sat down and tried to look as bored as possible instead. It usually worked with young children at home, not that he'd had much experience with those, really. He only knew that when Lainie was a child she tended to lose interest most quickly when they were doing something that even he found tedious. Like trying to teach her to drench sheep. But this girl wasn't nine years old. She was probably more like fifty. Then again, she could have been four hundred. How could anyone tell in this place?

The girl smiled and came to sit down, practically in his lap. She hugged him tightly and her glossy dark hair tickled his nose, and then she looked him in the eye, curious to see what he would do next, so he kissed her on the cheek and smiled.

It had taken a while but he was slowly becoming re-accustomed to these people. The day he had arrived he'd been energetically embraced by a hulk of a man with legs like gate posts and a thick black beard who wouldn't have seemed out of place at the Nalong pub. Except for the hugging. There was nothing kinky in it—that almost made it harder. If there'd been some sort of seductive motive behind the intimacy he would have had no trouble knowing how to throw a good punch, but when he'd backed uncomfortably away from the man, the Edenite had just looked confused. The behaviour of the people here was completely innocent and natural. He might just as well get offended by an infant burping at him as with anything these people did. They just didn't get it.

Harry shifted away from the girl and tucked a couple of flowers into her hair. No matter how adult she appeared, he just couldn't think of her as anything but a girl. Everyone here looked like a young adult except for the very occasional true children, who were doted on by everyone. But they all behaved as children. Very, very intelligent children.

Pulling himself to his feet, he tried not to look as tired as he felt. The pain was getting worse. The girl watched him in delighted amusement. As he knew she would, she reached out and picked a yellow Fruit from a nearby tree and offered it to him. He shook his head, trying hard to keep his face passive. She looked surprised but tossed the ripe golden treat carelessly over her shoulder. *Great, here we go again.* Now she would follow him around to see when he would eat, until she eventually got bored and gave up. Perhaps he should talk to Annie again. She would know how to send the girl away without being rude.

He looked across to the lake where he knew she was busy collecting water chestnuts for the evening meal. Speaking to her had its consequences. He reminded her of a past life, and despite her enthusiasm for his company, his visits always ended the same way. He had come to Eden to try to address the problem of the sad music in the River, but his presence only seemed to be making it worse.

A gentle nudge reminded him of his friendly shadow. The girl had noticed his less than chirpy expression and was holding out another piece of Fruit, expecting him to eat it.

But no matter how bad things got, he refused to do anything that would make the River cry for him.

Chapter 25

On the Friday after Christmas I called the fire department to ask if they had completed their investigation into the cause of the blaze. They said they had found no trace of accelerants in the area where the fire started and suggested the most likely scenario was that hikers had left some cigarette butts around. I was pretty confident that innocent hikers wouldn't be wandering around in the bush smoking at 4am but I could hardly prove what I'd 'seen'. It would have been easy enough to start a fire without using anything more than a couple of matches with the bush so dry.

Even though I was not naturally suspicious, I was sure the fire had to have been arranged by someone at Kolsom. It would have been an easy way for them to gain access to the valley if they were trying to obtain more data for their report. Once they were in they could collect more samples and then just backdate the findings. I could only hope that meant that they didn't have enough data yet. Was this mining project really worth risking lives for?

In the afternoon we had a meeting with Senior Sergeant Mick Loxwood.

'I'm telling you that if any of those miners set so much as a big toe on our land I *will* prosecute.' Aunt Lily's jaw was clenched and I could hear the thinly suppressed fury in her voice. I hadn't heard that particular tone since I was eleven years old and Noah had thought it would be funny to open a couple of gates in the portable sheep yards so the sheep came around in a big circle and re-presented themselves for drenching. I had a healthy respect for that tone of voice now.

'With all due respect, Ms Gracewood, we only have limited resources here and I can't afford to send a patrol car out into the bush every day looking for stray mining surveyors.' The sergeant sounded patient, but he was spinning his pen around the base of his thumb much faster that he had been when we'd first arrived.

'I'm not asking you to patrol it, just give them fair warning and remind them that the law is on our side,' my aunt argued between clenched teeth.

'Them who, exactly? Do you believe the company executives are after revenge because you threatened to sabotage one of their bulldozers? Or is it a particular surveyor?' The sergeant's calm demeanour was starting to crack.

Aunt Lily narrowed her eyes dangerously. 'The "who" is Mr Alex Beckinsale. He's the young Property Liaison Lawyer at Kolsom who is trying to bully his way onto our land.' She leant toward him, her eyes pleading. 'I've been advised by my solicitor that if the company gains enough evidence of gas pockets they may have the right to a compulsory acquisition for that part of our land because it isn't being actively farmed.'

I looked at her, aghast. No way could they take our land by force, could they? How was I supposed to stop them? If there was one thing superpowers couldn't help with, it would have to be a scheming lawyer. I thought back to the man I'd seen in the library checking our land title and remembered the impression I'd had of him. If he really was Alex Beckinsale then his devious ambition could be a big problem for us.

The police sergeant sat back in his chair, running his fingers through sandy hair that betrayed just one or two greys. His frustrated frown stood out in contrast against his reassuring blue uniform. He had been living in Nalong for decades and understood just how attached farmers were to their properties.

'Okay, Ms Gracewood. All I can suggest at this point is that if you have any indication that someone might be trespassing, call the station immediately and we'll send someone to investigate. Your best bet is if we can catch people who are knowingly in the wrong place, then maybe you can press charges. You did put those Private Property signs up like we discussed?'

'As many as we could. No way could they use that as an excuse.'

'Assuming, of course, that the damage hasn't already been done. If they managed to get the information they needed before you put the signs up they'll only plead ignorance at the time it was collected,' he explained, shaking his head slightly.

'Sergeant Loxwood?'

He turned to me politely.

'Just hypothetically, if the bushfire had come through our place last week, would we still have had the right to stop people from coming on to our land?'

He glowered at me as he put down his pen. 'In the event of a natural disaster there are certain people who are legally authorised to have access to private property. Emergency services obviously, as well as certain other personnel who would be required to assess the safety of the area after the fire has passed. Please tell me you aren't suggesting what I think you are, Lainie. You would want to have some pretty hard evidence before accusing someone of lighting a bushfire.'

'Of course. I was just making sure I understood our rights if the fire had come through, that's all.' I tried to smile sweetly at him but I wasn't very good at it. He kept frowning.

'Thanks for all your advice, Sergeant,' Aunt Lily said, standing to leave. She probably wanted to get me out of there before I got myself into any real trouble. 'I wish I'd realised what was happening sooner. I just didn't think it could be possible in this day and age to use legal loopholes to take away someone's property rights. I feel so foolish.' She shook his hand and then hooked her handbag over her shoulder.

'I understand. I'm sorry I can't do more to help,' he sympathised as he showed us out of his office to where Bane and Noah were waiting. 'Just make sure you call us straight away if you think they might be snooping around again.'

I certainly would, and I'd know the minute they tried.

The next day I helped Bane to build a temporary enclosure for the joey who had just about had enough of her fake pillowcase pouch unless she was being carried around, and she was getting too heavy to do that too often. We were arguing over the best way to build it. Bane wanted to build solid fences so she couldn't see out and get tempted to escape, but I argued that she wasn't stupid and already knew perfectly well that there was more to the world than her little patch of grass. The fences were going to have to be as tall as we could make them, and even then we weren't going to be able to keep her in for long. Hopefully just long enough for her to mature to a point where she could survive on her own. I was happy enough to care for her as long as needed, but she belonged in the bush, not in a pen.

The sun was as bright as a tradie's wardrobe and was turning all the tools into branding irons, so I was grateful for the break when Noah arrived carrying a thick official-looking envelope.

'The postie asked me to bring this to you because it didn't fit in your letterbox,' he said as he walked up. I reached for the package but he held it above my head. He was one of two people I knew that could. It was rather annoying.

'Sorry, Lainie, this one's for Bane.' He laughed as he tossed it. I winced, thinking it looked too important to be thrown around like that but Bane caught it easily with one hand. Noah hovered inquisitively but I dragged him away to let Bane open his mail in peace.

'Noah, we need to talk,' I said, figuring now was as good a time as any. 'About Tess.' He stopped dead in his tracks and stared at me, horrified.

'Um, Lainie, Mum's had this talk with me already,' he said, his ears going a little red.

I laughed and kept pulling him along. 'Not that, bonehead. I wouldn't touch *that* topic with a cattle prod.'

We found an empty concrete drinking trough to sit on, far enough away to provide Bane with some privacy. 'So what exactly have you figured out about her?' I asked bluntly. I found blunt was usually best with Noah.

He fiddled with my bracelet, looking resigned. 'Apparently Tessa Bright is my Guardian,' he replied. He said it like it was an honoured title. I hadn't thought of it quite like that before.

'Is that what your mum calls her?'

'You mean Tessa or Guardian?' he asked with a laugh. Noah's sense of humour could never be suppressed for long. 'Mum thinks the world of her. She would be more devastated than Tess, I think, if we ever broke up.'

I highly doubted that. 'And what have you told Tessa?'

He fidgeted a little. 'Nothing, yet. I don't know where to start. What am I supposed to say?'

I remembered back to when Bane first arrived on the farm. It had certainly been an awkward situation.

'Can't you tell her?' he pleaded.

'Noah! You chicken! She's *your* girlfriend. We hardly even spoke to each other at school. How am I supposed to tell her?'

'Maybe Bane can, then. You know, Guardian to Guardian. Secret Guardian business. I should probably leave it to them, right?'

'Nice try, buddy, but no. If she's had to go through anything like what Bane has, then you owe it to her to do this right.' I placed my hands solidly on his shoulders and looked into his eyes. 'My friend, I'm afraid it's time for you to man-up and tell your tiny girlfriend that she's destined to be your bodyguard.'

'Why do I need a bodyguard anyway?'

My eyes narrowed.

'Well, come on, Lainie. You know what I'm talking about. What's Tessa going to be able to protect me from that I can't handle myse—'

His sentence was cut short when I demonstrated the answer to his question and about twenty seconds later, Bane hauled me off him.

'Let go of me!' I yelled. 'I don't need your help!'

Bane had my elbows pulled back tightly so I bit my lower lip hard enough to draw blood.

'Ah! For the love of—' He released me so fast I nearly fell over. For a few seconds none of us moved. In fact, I was too angry to even breathe properly. Then, of course, Noah's phone rang.

'What were you fighting about?' Bane asked while Noah listened to whatever lame excuse for calling that Tessa was trying to make up.

'I don't need a bodyguard,' I stated. 'Any more than Noah does.'

'Well of course you don't,' he agreed. 'You're the most capable person I know. You're never afraid of anything, even when you should be. The only thing you're ever likely to need protection from is the occasional random accident, and everyone has those. If Noah's male ego is a bit bruised then you have just as much right for your female ego to ... I mean, for your pride to be ... oh shi—'

'Just stop talking, Bane,' I interrupted, smiling in spite of myself. 'Noah?'

He glanced up from where he was still sitting in the dust with his phone to his ear.

'Tomorrow's Sunday. You'd better invite her over for lunch.'

Noah grinned. 'Fine. But first, let me see how Bane's going to fix your lip.'

It was a good thing for Noah that Bane had such good reflexes.

～

Later that afternoon as I was placing my orange peel in the kitchen bin I noticed the envelope Bane had received. He had thrown it out unopened.

'None of my business,' I said to the empty kitchen. 'Really, none of my business. Leave it alone, Lainie. He's entitled to his privacy.'

But then I noticed the Army logo.

Chapter 26

A gentle awareness alerted me to Noah's approach even before I heard his ute rumbling towards the house. My senses seemed to be getting more acute, maybe because I had been practising a lot, or perhaps I was just getting better at recognising what my feelings meant. I set the table and started to pull things out of the fridge. I had no idea whether Noah had told Tessa anything yet but if not, I would at least make sure she was well fed before we sent her screaming from the house.

'Calm down. It'll be fine,' Bane said as he opened the oven. The mouth-watering smell of rosemary and roast lamb filled the air as he poked at the potatoes with a fork.

'I am calm. I have nothing to worry about. It's Noah's turn to do this so it'll be fun to watch.' I tried to sound amused.

'Then why are you humming?'

Darn stupid Guardian empathy. Not that he needed it when I had such obvious giveaways. Inara looked up at me with typical feline optimism, volunteering to taste-test the roast, but I ignored her.

'What if she doesn't believe us? Or worse, what if she thinks we're all crazy and tells someone? Why can't we just make Noah's mum tell her?'

Bane grabbed my wrists and relieved me of the bread knife I was clutching. I really must have looked nervous.

'Do you really think it would be a good idea for Mrs Ashbree to be the one to announce to Tessa that she's destined to marry Noah?' The bread knife clattered to the floor as he realised what he'd just said. Out loud.

I sat down rather abruptly while he picked up the knife. He spoke quickly in an attempt to move the conversation along, which I was heartily in favour of. 'Tess won't be able to tell anybody. The words would just stick in her throat. I know. I've tried. Not once I knew about

Eden of course, but when I was younger. The school counsellor tried very hard to get me to talk about my issues, and I really wanted to, but I just couldn't. Tessa might not like it, but she will appreciate finally having an explanation for how she feels.'

Biting my lower lip, I smiled up at him. 'You'll help us explain things to her, won't you? You probably understand her best, after all.'

'That depends on her. I don't think she trusts me, and I don't blame her. I didn't really make the best reputation for myself at school.'

I hadn't exactly helped his case either, given how vocal I'd always been about his unfair treatment of me. He gave my hands one last reassuring squeeze as I heard the car pull up. *Poor kitchen table, here we go again.*

≈

Tessa knew something was going on. We were all a bit too quiet. Even Aunt Lily was having trouble acting naturally. Munching on my corn-cob, I found myself assessing Tessa as shrewdly as if she was a potential employee. She was tiny. Not really short, but to me most people seemed tiny. She had delicate features that highlighted her part-Asian heritage, and lustrous black hair that hung straight down almost to her waist with large soft curls at the very ends. And she had the sort of voice that banks could use to apologise for keeping people on hold for three hours straight and still retain loyal customers. I tried to picture her in a Lara Croft sort of way, and thought maybe it would help if she wore some camo gear instead of that skimpy tank top, but she just didn't look very capable of protecting herself, let alone Noah. Maybe we had it all wrong. Wasn't she prone to fainting? She'd fainted dead away that day when Jake nearly hit Noah in the school car park. Oh. In hindsight that made sense, actually. It must have been awful for her to feel the strong urge to do something but not know what, how or why.

Tessa shifted in her chair and Bane nudged my foot with his. I had been staring again.

She put down her knife and fork. 'Lainie, I'm sorry if this is difficult for you,' she said, her voice sounding as stern as I had ever heard her, 'but Noah and I are together now. If you have anything to say to me, just go ahead and say it.'

I could feel my eyebrows climbing into my scalp and across the room Aunt Lily had her lips clamped shut, but her laugh was escaping through her eyeballs instead. I still couldn't tell how much Tessa knew so I fell back on the old faithful. I smiled and nodded.

Bane kicked me again as I gripped the table for moral support. Why did it always come down to me to have to lead these discussions? It wasn't fair.

A big gulp of river water bought me the few precious moments I needed to find my voice. 'You're right, Tessa. This is a bit weird for me, but only because I've never seen Noah this taken with anyone before.'

She looked at me with a hopeful sort of astonishment.

'But I'm afraid it's only going to get weirder.' I looked at Noah. He was looking at me hopefully too, the coward. 'I think I know why you and Noah are so attached to one another. It's going to sound strange but I think I can guess some of the things that have been happening to you lately.'

She squirmed in her seat. I was relying on the fact that if we were all wrong about this, I wouldn't be *able* to say the next words out loud.

'I think you've been drawn to Noah in a really powerful way. Physically, even. You can always find him, and it makes you sick to be too far away from him.'

Her face paled and a sliver of hysteria coloured her words. 'You feel that too? Do you have to stay close as well?'

'No. No! That's not it. I mean, I know I can find him easily at any time too, but I'm not drawn to him like you are.'

'So what makes him so special? Why can't we stop thinking about him?'

Spluttering, I could see Noah's expression out of the corner of my eye and I made a heroic effort not to throw my bread roll at him. 'It's not just Noah, it's me too. We're not entirely human.' I couldn't believe I had to utter those words. Out loud. Again.

Tessa drew her perfectly shaped eyebrows down. I threw a pleading look at Aunt Lily, but she just shrugged her shoulders unhelpfully. Fine. 'Noah and I are Cherubim. We only found out we were different from everyone else a few weeks ago.'

'Actually, I only found out last week,' Noah piped in.

Very helpful. Thanks mate.

'You and Ben are our Guardians,' I continued. 'You're both fully human but have somehow developed a supernatural compulsion to protect us. You, obviously, are linked to Noah, and Ben is linked to me.' I gave her a few moments for that to sink in because it had all come out in a rush and sounded confusing even to me. It had sounded a lot smoother when I'd practised it in my head.

'How are you doing so far?' Noah asked her, picking up her hand like it was a fragile flower.

'Actually, that kind of explains a lot,' she nodded, looking at Bane as if seeing him for the first time, but then she frowned again. 'Sort of. What did you say you are?'

'Cherubim,' Noah stated, with a hint of pride that was immediately followed by a panicked expression as he turned to me. 'Wait. Not human? I mean, does that mean we can't ...' The look of disappointment as he glanced at Tessa told me a lot. 'We're not the same ... species,' he finished weakly.

'What? Horrified at the thought of me being the only female of your species you're not related to?' Generously then, I put everyone out of their obvious distress. 'Don't worry. We're Cherubim, but we're made of human,' I clarified. 'Both our dads are human, remember?'

'Made of human?' My aunt shook her head in dismay at my choice of words. Luckily Bane took over at that point, explaining the story in Genesis and even adding a few other Biblical references to the Tree of Life that I hadn't found yet. At some point I would have to find time to do some more homework.

Incredibly, Tessa accepted everything we said as if she was just pleased to be part of the story. Even when we told her about the fire and the storm.

'Is that why I was so sick last Saturday? I was supposed to be helping clear away scrub but I *needed* to come here so I just jumped onto the other pumper. I got suspended from the crew for six months for that. No volunteer has ever been suspended before.'

Bane looked at me pointedly. He had been absolutely right. It wasn't fair to keep the truth from her.

Noah put his arm around her and cradled her head against his shoulder. 'I'm so sorry, Tess. I honestly had no idea. I won't let that happen again, I promise.'

A sudden stab of jealousy felt like ice down my neck, but I brutally suppressed it. It would take time to get used to seeing them together, and that was okay. Just move on.

'How did you find out about all this?' Tessa asked. 'I mean, how come now? Although I've felt this way around Noah for a long time,' she admitted, nuzzling into his chest.

As clearly as I could, I explained about how Kolsom was trying to gain access to the valley, and that Harry had gone to Eden to try to get help but had trapped himself behind a rock fall. I left out the part about my mother, even though the image of her hugging and singing to me seemed to fill my thoughts whenever I inadvertently left room for it.

'But Noah didn't find out until the fire. Why didn't you tell him at the same time as Lainie?' she asked Aunt Lily.

'Actually, Tess, I didn't know that Noah was a Cherub. For years I assumed he was Lainie's Guardian.' That was news to me. She smiled crookedly at Noah. 'Until the day he came up with that brilliant plan to go ice-blocking down the hill paddock.'

Oh yeah. The first time we'd taken turns sliding down the hill on a giant ice block covered by a towel, we'd tried it standing up. I broke my arm. Since then we only rode them sitting down, with a nice thick rope frozen into the front for steering. Still probably not something a Guardian would have condoned. That must have been a bad time for Bane.

Aunt Lily stood up. 'If you'll excuse me, I think it might be better if I left now. You're going to want to speak about things that will be difficult to say with me here. And Tessa? I know this is all a bit hard on you, but let me just say that you can trust what Lainie says. You can trust all of us. I'll do anything I can to help you understand this.' And with that she abandoned us to explain the rest on our own.

We spent a long time talking through the details, comparing notes and stories. Tessa wanted to know every single thing Harry had told me and I felt terrible that I had spent so much effort avoiding him instead of taking the opportunity to find out more. Bane was particularly interested to find out if Tessa had the same range of distance before feeling ill, and why she'd had less trouble at school than he had. Apparently she'd experienced all sorts of problems, but instead of acting on her impulses she'd usually managed to suppress them, which had just left her feeling sick and dizzy instead. No wonder we'd never gotten along so well. I was usually the one putting Noah in danger and I just saw her as a pathetic doll who fainted at the drop of a hat, when the truth was she probably had more self-discipline than the rest of us put together. When she explained how she used to lock herself in the girls toilets to resist watching Noah play footy, Bane started to get that self-recriminating cast to his features again.

'So it must be so much easier for you now, Bane. Now that you can touch her any time you need to.' Tess smiled, sitting on Noah's lap and wrapping her arms around his neck.

I raised one eyebrow at my Guardian, who was taking a sudden interest in clearing the dishes from the drying rack.

'What do you mean?' I asked.

'It's not like that for me,' Bane intercepted, slamming the cutlery drawer shut. 'Anyway, shouldn't we get moving, Lainie? Are we going to go to show them the cave today or what?'

Clearly there was more to this than he wanted to say but I chose not to hassle him about it in front of the others. I could be patient.

Noah held Tessa back from following as Bane hung up the tea towel and quickly left the room. 'Bane and Lainie are not … *together*, Tess,' he confided, but she just laughed.

Too right, why did everyone automatically make these assumptions? Possibly because I'd held his hand on Christmas Day. Fair enough. My stupid mistake. Just as well Noah had sorted that out before Tessa said something that might have offended the poor guy, because I was certain that in all Bane's confusion about his unnatural feelings towards me, the bottom line was that he still didn't actually *like* me. He never had, and I'd be the worst kind of fool if I ever let myself believe that would really change.

Chapter 27

We packed Noah's ute with some supplies and the empty water drums to be refilled. It was difficult to guess how accustomed Tessa was to hiking in the bush so we made certain to pack a few essential items, like drink bottles, a bag of oranges, insect repellent, sunscreen and chocolate. We planned to drive as far upstream as we could and then hike our way to the waterfall. At least this time we would have more people to help carry the full drums of water back home. It was a gruelling trip, and there was no easy trail to follow.

Noah drove, with Tessa in the passenger seat, leaving Bane and me to ride in the tray. I glared at him for a full two minutes before he gave in and told me what Tessa had meant.

'There are times when the pull gets stronger,' he finally admitted, wedging the bag of oranges behind Noah's toolbox to prevent it from sliding away. 'I don't know why. Maybe you're in more danger somehow but I don't think that's it. It feels less about you and more about me. Don't worry. I can control it.'

'Just tell me what you need, Ben,' I said exasperatedly. 'I know this isn't your fault. If I make you uncomfortable just let me know what I can do and I'll do it.'

He looked away and laughed ruefully to himself. As we hit a particularly bumpy bit of ground he fidgeted, and then sat on his hands, looking frustrated. 'Lainie, what I need you to do is to stop calling me Ben. Everyone else calls me Bane now. I'm kind of used to it.'

'But I—'

'I know you think it offends me. It doesn't. It fits. It's who I am. I really am the bane of your life, and you still put up with me. I'm genuinely grateful for that, but I'm not sorry. I *like* being linked to you, it feels right.'

I thought about that for a while as we bounced across the paddock. Did he really not mind or was it just the relief of not being sick anymore? Could he even tell the difference? He had made plans for his life; surely he couldn't throw them away so easily? And yet I'd done the same. I wasn't going anywhere while I was needed here. Every cell in my pseudo-human body knew one thing instinctively: keeping Eden a secret was the most important thing I could ever do.

Bane waved his hand in front of my eyes, snapping my attention from trying to sense what was going on in the valley. 'I don't think you need to do that,' he said.

'Do what?'

'Listen so hard. I mean, it's just that if I understand it correctly, you'll know when there's a threat whether you're actively paying attention or not. The people starting the fire did wake you up, after all.'

'True, but not until it was too late. Perhaps if I'd been paying attention I could have stopped them sooner.'

'I doubt it. You can't predict what people are going to do in the future, only what happens in the present. Otherwise you really *wouldn't* need me at all,' he said with a wry smile.

I hadn't fully thought that through before. He really could predict the future to a small extent, at least in regards to me, and I wondered if there might not be a better way to make use of that ability.

'Besides,' he said, sounding concerned again, 'you can't stay up all night listening for what *might* happen. Tell me that isn't why you haven't been sleeping?' He sounded very disapproving.

'How do you know I haven't been sleeping well? Are you spying on me?'

'No, of course not. Nothing like that.' His ears turned red. 'It's just that I can feel when you're awake. It doesn't keep me up exactly, I just have a part of me that always pays attention to you and that part sort of … wakes up when you do.'

'You mean you don't sleep if I don't?' I shuddered at the thought. As if I hadn't messed him around enough, now this too?

'No, not exactly. I can still sleep, if I choose to. I'm not explaining this very well. It's more like a … gentle alarm … that I can hear in my sleep. It brings me out of a deep sleep into a lighter one, that's all. It's fine, really. I'm sorry I mentioned it.'

The rest of the ride was pretty quiet after that.

&

Tessa had no problems scrambling with us through the thick scrub. She even whistled a tacky pop song as she went. Noah refused to do anything about it and Bane told me bluntly that he was my Guardian, not my hitman, and that if I wanted her assassinated I would have to do it myself. But just as my patience ran out and I was about to grab her ponytail, Bane relented and began to explain to her how he was using his precognitive intuition to steer us around the worst of the evil blackberry snares. At least it kept her interested enough to stop the whistle torture.

By the time we reached the base of the waterfall, we all peeled off our boots and socks, ready for a much needed swim, but Noah hesitated at the edge.

'It's not too bad if you keep your head out of the water,' I murmured.

'You hear the music too? Do you know what it means?' he asked hopefully.

I shook my head and glanced at Bane, who was listening avidly. 'It's the reason I haven't been sleeping,' I explained to them both. 'When I do, the music takes over and it's so sad that I can't stand it, so I only sleep when I have to.'

'Same here,' Noah murmured. 'Ever since graduation when I couldn't stay in the water. But you couldn't either, right? Is this normal for us? Feeling so sad about the river?'

'Harry said the music used to be pleasant, so I think this is recent. And I think it's not right. That's one of the reasons why he went … away.'

'Then what are we waiting for?' Noah asked. 'Let's go and find him.'

With utmost care we waded into the swirling current as if we had frozen glass hearts that might shatter if we didn't gently acclimatise to the searing sound of the melodies. One tentative step at a time, we allowed the sweet sadness to reconcile with our souls—and then got shockingly doused by the icy cold fountain of water that Tessa produced when she came yodelling past us to dive bomb her way in. So much for my expectation that she would stand around in the shallows squealing with her shoulders up near her ears. Tessa Bright had always looked so thin and pale that I'd sort of assumed she wouldn't be very tough, but then I figured that if I threw up every time I moved more than an hour away from Noah I'd look pretty thin and pale too. Maybe she would start to put some weight on now. She caught me frowning at her thin frame.

'I'm not bulimic,' she defended, trying to untangle her hair tie.

'Of course not. Why would you assume I would think that?'

'Everyone thinks that. Especially my mother,' she replied.

Oh boy. Sliding further under the water, I eased my way over to her. 'I'm sorry, Tess. For what you've had to go through. If I'd known any earlier I would have tried to help.'

'Lainie. Stop apologising for all this. It's not like it's your fault, you know. And it's not all bad either.' She smiled, looking cow-eyed over at Noah whose headlights were on high beam from the cold water.

At least that part would be fairly straightforward for them. They seemed totally accepting of the fact that their relationship had just sky-rocketed to an intense level of commitment. Noah's eyes widened at the sight of her shaking out her wet hair. I just hoped my friend knew what he was getting himself into.

⁓

'I'm not ready for this,' Noah said huskily as he stared at the entrance to the cave.

'What's in there? Is this The Path?' Tessa asked eagerly, putting extra emphasis on the title.

I grinned at her obvious excitement. 'We thought you should both see the sword for yourselves. There's a tunnel at the back of the cave that leads to a sort of chamber, which is where the rock fall is. It's pretty cold in there though, so maybe we should wait until our clothes have dried out a bit more,' I suggested, patting my T-shirt to try to estimate how long that would take.

Bane shook his head. 'We don't have all that long, Lainie. We'll want to get home long before dark. That hike isn't easy at the best of times,' he pointed out.

Suddenly Noah started backing away from the entrance. 'I'm *not ready!*' He spun and stormed off into the bush. Tessa looked accusingly at us like we'd done something to upset him, and then ran off after him.

Bane and I just stared at each other helplessly.

⸺

The Sentinel greeted Harry with a hug. He'd known exactly where to find her. She'd been sitting by the River weaving a basket out of reeds. Holding her close, he felt as if their long years apart had just been a cruel joke. It made him feel old. He let her go a little wistfully.

'Hello, Annie,' he said softly.

'Hello!' she said with a laugh. 'What a funny word. Why did we always say it?'

'It's a greeting. It means I'm pleased to see you,' he replied. She kissed him on the cheek, making a point. So many of his words were unnecessary here, and yet back home people had considered him laconic.

'Can I ask you something?' Harry asked, picking up some reeds to help with her weaving. She looked confused. No point asking permission, she didn't understand the concept—or didn't remember it. He pressed ahead anyway.

'I haven't touched the Fruit but I still keep losing track of time. I need to go home but I can't.'

'Okay,' she agreed.

'No. Not okay. How do I go home?'

'You are home, Harry. Finally.'

She showed him how to weave as if they had all the time in the world—which was true—but he felt a little bit sad, as if each day that passed was making him lose something he wanted.

'The Fruit makes us forget what it's like to feel sad,' she stated after a minute. 'You can eat. Then you won't be sad, and you won't hurt!' She stood up, looking around for the Tree that was always close by.

He shook his head regretfully. 'I can't eat that, Annie. I can't afford to forget what's going on out there. It's important. I never should have come here.' As he listened to her humming, something tugged at him, rippling his remaining sense of peace. 'Lainie needs me to find a way home.'

⸺

Noah and Tessa had been gone for close to an hour and the sun was starting to ease down behind the hill, giving the air a deep golden hue. Bane and I sat back against the warm rocks near the cave entrance, feeling drowsy now that our clothes had dried.

'So, do you think Noah's having some sort of crisis of faith?' I asked Bane, stacking pebbles out of sheer boredom. 'How does that work? He helped me call a storm. He was there. It's not like he can deny that it happened.'

'Yes, but he was compelled to act last time. Now he has a choice. And he knows that what he sees will change everything for him. At least, it did for me.'

'He is what he is, Bane. Whether he looks at the sword or not,' I pointed out.

'Of course, but that doesn't make it any easier to accept. Just give him some space. We can't help him with this. He'll have to figure it out in his own time.'

'But time's running out; he's quite far away.' I knocked over my miniature castle in a burst of redirected aggression. Noah should have known better than to just run off like that.

Bane looked annoyingly relaxed. 'Tess will have no trouble finding him, and he would never leave her on her own out there. I'm sure they're fine. Are they still moving away?'

'No. I can't feel Tess very distinctly, but Noah's been in the same place for quite a while. They'd better come back soon.'

'I think we should consider staying here tonight anyway,' Bane said, standing up and brushing dust from his jeans. 'It took us nearly two hours to get here and there's only about half an hour of daylight left. I don't think it would be a good idea to hike along the river in the dark.'

He helped me up and then I fished the sat-phone out of its plastic bag. It was a good thing Harry had thought to bring the canoe up here otherwise the phone would never have survived all the river crossings. I gave Aunt Lily a quick call to explain what had happened. She agreed with Bane: Noah would have to come around in his own time. It would be unhelpful to try to rush him. She promised she would have a hot meal waiting for us when we returned in the morning.

There wasn't much we could do to prepare for the night. There was no food to cook and lighting a fire at this time of year was out of the question. The day had been bright and hot and the sky was clear, which meant that we were likely to have a chilly night ahead of us. I wondered if the cave would be better or worse than outdoors.

'Lainie, can I ask you something?' Bane was leaning against a tree, shredding a gum leaf into tiny fragments, obviously uncomfortable.

'Of course,' I replied. It would be hard to keep secrets now anyway, even if I had any, other than Eden.

'How do *you* feel about everything that's happened?' The leaf was in tatters. He picked another one.

I thought for a little while. It was a fair question that deserved a fair answer. It was also a complex one, but eventually I turned to face him.

'At first I was pretty angry, I guess, when Harry told me what I was. It seemed as if I hadn't been given a choice in anything that was happening. And I felt pretty stupid for not having known what was going on. I mean, how could someone not know that they aren't human? But I didn't have anything to compare it to, so how *could* I have known?' I picked my own leaf and started plucking at it ferociously. 'So now I'm starting to question everything about myself. Which traits are human? Which ones are Cherub? I *feel* human but that doesn't mean anything anymore. And then there's the bushfire. I still can't really process what happened. Just what am I capable of?' I could feel my emotions getting rapidly out of control but I couldn't seem to stop now that I was actually talking to someone. 'Did you know that the moon has a massive effect on storm systems?'

'The moon?'

'And it's really heavy!'

'You moved the moon?' His voice sounded a bit strangled.

I hurled the fragments of leaf away in a flurry of confetti. 'Of course not! That would have been catastrophic! I just told it to stop pulling so hard ...'

Bane's eyes looked a bit wild, and he opened his mouth as if he wanted to reassure me but couldn't find any words.

'I had the power to argue with the moon! No, that's not quite right. I had the authority to *command* the moon.' My voice was going all wiggly, and felt like it was coming straight from the pit of my stomach. 'What if I can't handle all this and I go crazy or something? I don't want to end up in an asylum! How will I get psychiatric help if I can't even talk about anything? Or what if I inadvertently destroy the planet? I'm scared, Bane. You want to know how I feel? I'm mostly just plain scared!' There were torn off clumps of gum leaves all around my feet that looked as if they had been angrily ripped from a nearby branch. I didn't remember doing that.

He drew me into a hug and held me while I let the tears flow. I had thought I was past all this, but no amount of logical reasoning could prevent me from reacting like a teenage girl faced with a ridiculously bewildering future.

'This is about as human as it gets, Lainie, trust me,' he said in a voice calmer than the summer sky, 'and you'll always have my help. It may not be professional, but at least you can talk to me. I won't let you go crazy, I promise.'

Full blown panic began to subside as his comforting words soaked in. He held me until my sobs eased off and I was breathing normally again, but I didn't want him to let go because if he did I was afraid I might just scatter into a flurry of confetti like the leaves.

He touched the bracelet on my wrist. The word *Shalom* sparkled in the low afternoon sun. 'It means more than just peace, you know,' he explained. 'In Hebrew the root word has several meanings. It can mean "worth it" or "fully paid for". It can also mean completeness. Wholeness. Harmony. Tranquillity. Health … safety.' He wrapped each word in unabashed compassion and my heart began to flutter as my fear melted away with each comforting trait he was offering.

'That's a lot of meaning in one word,' I muttered, unable to avoid his luminous grey eyes. I usually forced myself to steer clear of his direct gaze, but I had to see if what I felt was truly reflected there, or if he was just being kind. The honest devotion I saw pulled at me harder than the moon had.

'It's everything I want for you.' He wiped a tear from my cheek with his thumb, and then he brushed my lip very gently, healing the pain I'd inflicted on us both the day before. 'Shalom is the way things are *supposed* to be.'

It summed up everything I wanted. It also summed up everything he had come to mean to me over the past few weeks. I just hadn't wanted to admit to myself how much I'd been relying on him, and not just for physical safety. Bane had supported me through everything without hesitation, and without so much as a hint of resentment. I didn't know how I would ever cope without him. Maybe he was right, maybe this was the way it was meant to be.

'And what is it that *you* need? Will you tell me this time?' I pleaded, pressing my fingertips carefully against his.

He drew my hand to his cheek and sighed.

'This is what I need. Just to be touching you,' he whispered, closing his eyes. 'You have no idea how good this feels for me, not to have to hold back from reaching out for you. Just to be this close. It's like an unexpected release from a headache.' He stepped back with a twisted smile. 'I'm sorry. As I told you, I can control it. I certainly don't expect you to let me—'

I didn't let him finish. I threw myself at him and kissed him soundly. He stumbled but grabbed me as securely as if I had been about to jump off the cliff. His touch was everything I had tried to make myself forget from the morning of the fire, but I hadn't stood a chance. That kiss had become the backdrop to every thought I'd had since that day, waking or sleeping. It coloured everything gold.

This one could have burned the sun.

As if it were a dance, Bane quickly took the lead, his hands gripping the back of my neck gently as if he actually thought I might pull away. He spun me around so I was leaning against the tree. When he eventually drew back, his breath was hitched and he was watching me so warily that I was afraid to move a muscle in case I scared him off. My knees were weak. It was just as well the tree was holding me up. Actually, that was probably no accident.

Smiling at the ecstasy that was reflected in his pale eyes, I watched as his wary demeanour was replaced with sheer joy and he smiled back. At that moment I would have happily juggled the stars themselves to keep him looking like that.

'Shalom, Bane.' I laughed.

'Shalom, beautiful Lainie,' he whispered, and then he kissed me again.

Chapter 28

Half an hour later, as the kookaburras heralded the coming evening with their cackling challenges to each other, Noah returned with a weary looking Tessa in tow.

'Sorry, guys, for running off like that. I guess it all just got a bit too much, you know?'

I threw a chocolate bar at his head but Tessa intercepted it deftly and smiled at me.

'I hope you ate enough for lunch because we'll be staying here until morning,' I accused. 'Unless someone feels like hunting for some dinner? Didn't think so.'

Standing up, I gave Noah a relieved hug to take the sting out of my words. I was still in a state of euphoria, which didn't fit at all with our current predicament. Noah, of course, noticed straight away. He watched me as I tore into a packet of biscuits, and then looked questioningly at Bane. Bane ignored him. This was going to confuse the hell out of poor Tessa.

After we had all refreshed ourselves with a drink from the stream and what little food we had, Noah stood up and made his way determinedly towards the cave. As I knew he would, now that he had decided to step ahead into the unknown, he didn't hesitate to see it through. Bane took out his phone to light the way through the tunnel, showing the others where to avoid the worst of the pitfalls.

As we entered the echoing chamber, my anticipation of seeing the sword again grew. Its impact on me had been profoundly moving and I couldn't wait to share it. We carefully pulled away the rocks, hoping that the disturbance wouldn't cause a dangerous collapse. It couldn't possibly be safe to do it too often, but Bane kept going so I took that as a good sign. Finally the rocks became almost too hot to touch and when I knew the moment had come to shift the last one, I honestly tried to behave myself but it was just too hard. I pushed Bane aside and stood before the wall, facing the others.

'Behold!' I cried, thrusting my hands out dramatically. 'The Kingdom of Eden is at hand!'

Tessa rolled her eyes at me and Noah groaned, but Bane's lips twitched in subtle amusement. Ha. Knew it. He did appreciate my humour. He was just too stubborn to admit it. Noah pulled me aside and removed the last rock, and the sudden light had us all blinking furiously as the hole opened up into the cavern beyond.

'Holy shi—'

I clamped my hand over Noah's mouth before he could get the words out. I still felt like we might be punished if we said the wrong thing and I simply wasn't willing to risk it. If I could call a storm, I had no doubt at all that God could manage lightning inside a cave. Possibly should have been more respectful myself, in hindsight.

We all stared, mesmerised by the massive spinning sword, its white-silver edges laced with flames. All four of our faces were crammed into the narrow gap between the rocks until I reluctantly pulled out to give Noah and Tessa more room to look.

Tessa was crying openly. It was a deeply spiritual experience to come face to face with a story from Genesis, so I moved back a bit to give them time to let it sink in.

'I wonder what it does?' Bane mused after a minute or so.

I glared at him. 'What else does it need to do? It's a sword. It spins. It's *on fire*,' I pointed out.

'Yeah, but you could just walk past it, couldn't you?'

Something deep inside me shuddered. 'Would you try? It would be a bit of a risky thing to test out, don't you think?' I peered past Noah's head to study the narrow gaps either side of the sword.

'I suppose so, but I don't sense any danger,' he said.

'Just because it isn't dangerous to *me* doesn't mean that it's safe, Bane. Think about it.'

'Good point.' His smile was smug. 'Just don't try to go without me, and then I won't have to find out.'

As he kissed my fingers I looked away. At some point I would have to go to Eden. He knew that. And he knew he couldn't come. Realising what I felt for him didn't change that. If anything it made me more determined to find answers. I cared for him too much to keep him trapped here. It was not an argument I could start then, however, so I stayed silent.

Noah watched the sword for a long time, presumably coming to terms with what it meant for him. Tessa, if anything, looked relieved and I understood exactly how she felt—I'd had much the same reaction. It was good to finally find answers to questions you had been wrestling with for so long. Noah's biggest problem was that up until this week, he had never needed to wrestle with anything much. His worldview had been complete, or so he'd thought. Now he had to reassess everything.

The light from the sword gave a soft glow to everything it touched, sending reflective sparkles off all the walls, but most of the cave was still full of deep shadows. It gave the place an unearthly beauty but with a slightly creepy feel. Unlike the tunnel leading in, there weren't many stalactites or limestone deposits inside the chamber. The heat from the sword had kept the place too dry for the deposits to form, leaving the floor of the cavern relatively smooth. Only the tiny stream seeping up through the rocks along one side kept the place damp. I had been hoping that the chamber would be warm enough to sleep in, but the rock fall blocked out too much of the sword's heat. The tiny hole we had made was nowhere near enough for even that to warm such a large underground area. Perhaps if we left it open for a few hours we could always see if it was better during the night if we got too cold outside.

I started to shiver but none of us felt ready to leave just yet. Bane felt around for a few of the smaller rocks on the far side of the fall and handed them around for us to warm our hands on. They were too hot to hold for long but he pointed out that they should retain their heat for quite a while and might be useful to take with us.

Eventually it was Tessa who managed to articulate what we were all thinking. 'What happens now? Are we supposed to guard this place our whole lives or just while the miners are here?'

Once again I mentally berated myself as I realised I hadn't bothered to find out what her future plans had been either. Nursing, she'd mentioned, but what else? Great friend I was. Three questioning pairs of eyes all turned to me.

'How would I know? You all think I know how this works but I only found out about Eden about three months ago,' I said a bit petulantly.

'Surely Harry must have told you something,' Noah complained.

I thought back to all the times I had avoided him, expressly to prevent him from telling me anything. Bane was right. I had reacted pretty childishly. It made Noah's little hissy fit seem positively mature by comparison, and we were all paying the price for it.

'Harry wasn't one for saying much of anything but even if he had, I wasn't ready to listen, so I never gave him much of an opportunity,' I admitted. Tessa put her hands on her hips and frowned at me, so I tried to think of something more useful I could offer. 'As far as I know, Harry didn't seem to have a lot to do in the way of active duty until recently. I'm not certain he even really knew what we were capable of, or he would have warned me. Noah, your mum told me that she's never had a lot to do with Eden. She's never been inside, and doesn't know very much at all. I'm hoping that might mean that if Kolsom leave we can get on with our lives, more or less.'

Harry had also managed just fine without a Guardian, but I wasn't sure about the reason for that. Had they found a way to break the bond or had something happened to her? Certainly Aunt Lily had slammed the door shut the one time I'd tried to find out.

'The way I see it, we have two choices,' Bane said. 'Either we wait until Harry comes back or we can try to figure this out by ourselves. You don't actually need to get in there, do you?'

All three of us looked at him as if he was insane. The Garden of Eden. Paradise. Who could resist trying to get in?

Tessa inspected the wall of rocks very seriously but it seemed pretty obvious to me that even with four of us it would take years to clear away enough to get through. Even excavating the small hole we had made was dangerous. Moving any more would have to be done very methodically if we wanted to avoid ending up like the Wicked Witch of the East.

'Couldn't you two just sort of ... un-rock-slide it?' she asked, reaching for Noah's hand. Noah looked disconcerted, like he was trying to decide if he should be scared, excited, or eager to show off his abilities to his girlfriend. Bane seemed disappointed that she wasn't trying to talk us out of trying to get inside.

I stared at the rock wall. Somehow Harry had done this. Perhaps it was possible. Squeezing my eyes shut, I tried to remember what I'd felt during the bushfire. I had spoken out confidently, but for the life of me I couldn't remember what I'd said, or in what language. My mind stayed completely blank. Well, not completely. No one's mind can stay totally blank, and the harder I tried to clear mine, the more it kept defaulting back to thoughts of Bane, and kissing, and how it was nearly dinner time and I was kind of hungry. After a minute or so I let out my breath in a puff and opened my eyes. Everyone was staring at me expectantly.

'Sorry, guys. I've got nothin'. Any other ideas?'

'Could we get some sort of message through to Harry?' Noah peered through the opening as if expecting to see Harry there so we could have a chat. 'Somehow let him know that we need him back so he can move the rocks again?'

'Actually, Bane's right. We really only need to talk to him. I don't suppose he has a phone?' Tessa asked hopefully. Noah just laughed while I shook my head. Even assuming Eden could get satellite reception, Harry and phones were like opposite poles of a magnet. Besides, it was easy for her to say we didn't need him back; I would have given anything to have him home so things could go back to the way they were before. Well, maybe not quite everything.

Bane looked intrigued by the idea. Looking around for a small pebble, he tapped Noah on the shoulder so he could get close enough to toss it through the hole. It landed a couple of metres on the other side in a disappointing anticlimax.

'You need to get it past the sword,' Tessa said, stating the obvious in her enthusiasm. Bane tried again. This time the stone clattered past the sword and bounced a little farther, and then disappeared in a shimmering haze.

'What happened?' Noah asked, bobbing about trying to see past our heads.

'Event Horizon,' I said, trying to sound knowledgeable by giving it a technical sounding title. 'So it *is* like another dimension. There could be a whole universe in there.'

Noah groaned. As if stories from the Bible weren't enough, now he had to put up with my sci-fi jargon as well. Personally I felt less disturbed by the idea of a bigger-on-the-inside-other-dimension than I did with a Bible story coming to life. What did that say about me, exactly?

Backing away from the gap, Bane started fiddling with his phone. 'Lainie, I know you said Harry doesn't have a phone, but does he know how to use one?'

'Yeah, he's not *that* bad. He hates them but he isn't stupid. In fact he could probably figure out how to reprogram the thing if he wanted to. Why, what are you thinking?'

'What if I could get my phone in there? Do you think he would call you?'

'Only if he had reception.' It was funny how even after being faced with all these crazy supernatural circumstances, the idea of getting phone reception in another dimension was just too ridiculous to accept.

'Even if he doesn't, maybe we could still communicate.'

'How? No message bank either, remember?'

'True, but he could look at texts and notes. And we could set an alarm for a rendezvous time.'

Okay, so that was pretty brilliant. He offered me the phone and I tried to think of what note to write. What was I supposed to say? Hi, Harry, hope you're enjoying your holiday. Come back soon so I can still enrol for uni and by the way, are you my real dad? Instead I wrote, 'Harry, I'm ready to talk now. I have lots of questions. Meet me here. We've set the alarm for you.'

I had tried writing 'Meet me at the sword', but of course even trying to type the word 'sword' was impossible. Even what I did write made me feel as guilty as if I had run over a kitten. I badly needed this meeting though, so I mentally sacrificed the kitten and hit save.

Bane set the alarm for 6pm the following day, then wrapped his phone tightly in a sock. Tomorrow's hike home was undoubtedly going to be very uncomfortable for him.

With pedantic care, he widened the hole a little more and just managed to squeeze one arm and his head through. My heart skipped a few beats and something deep inside me stirred restlessly as he leant towards the threshold between worlds. I fought to suppress my compulsion to drag him away from there, while behind me Noah was pacing the floor like a weaned calf.

It was almost pitch dark with Bane blocking the sword's light, so we couldn't see him throw the phone to the other side, but he pulled himself out quickly, blowing on his scorched fingers. Hopefully he'd tossed it gently enough not to damage it but far enough away from the sword not to be affected by the heat.

'Should we try to call it?' Noah asked, squinting through the gap to try to see where it landed.

'Are you nuts? Bane can't even get reception here, let alone in another dimension.' I dialled the number into the sat-phone anyway, just in case Eden was actually a super-technologically-advanced civilisation, but it wasn't and I was strangely comforted by the idea that at least some of the laws of the universe still seemed to apply.

'Well, I guess that means we're coming back tomorrow,' I said as I slumped down onto a lumpy rock.

~

By the time we stumbled out of the cave the sun had almost completely set, leaving a dull golden haze against the top of the hills. Tessa was eager to explore and look for other ways through the ridge but we all talked her out of it. Not all caves began horizontally, and discovering the vertical ones in the dark didn't seem like a great idea.

We polished off the rest of the oranges and tried to make ourselves as comfortable as possible for the night. The warm rocks we had brought from the cave were great but not the cosiest things to cuddle. After some amusing experimentation, I ended up putting two small ones into my socks and cuddled a bigger one against my chest. It made me feel surprisingly safe. I thought about gathering some sort of bedding material but felt too lazy. Chances were I would probably regret that before morning.

We tried to settle ourselves near the mouth of the tunnel so the over-hang would keep the dew off us. Noah and Tessa curled up together on a flattish bit of almost grass. At least they would keep each other warm. I was relieved, however, when Bane chose a sleeping spot well away from mine—I still wasn't sure if I had done the right thing by him ear-lier so I was grateful not to have to decide between what I wanted and what I felt was sensible. My rebellious body ached to close the distance between us but I was determined to suppress such a selfish idea. If he could keep his distance then so could I.

Tessa lasted almost half an hour before the mosquitoes drove her into the cool tunnel. Noah followed to help her find somewhere dry to sleep. Mozzies had never bothered me much, which made me wonder if it was a Cherub thing, but Bane didn't seem to be too bothered either. Unless he was just hiding it well.

We lay there for a long time listening to each other breathing. It was obvious he wasn't asleep. Then I remembered that he could always feel when I was awake so I tried really hard to relax. It wasn't easy, and when I finally began to drift off all I could hear was the poignant echo of the river. The melodies wove themselves inexorably into my mind, far more powerful now that we were so close to the cave.

I dreamt of my mother. She was crying. Holding me but crying as if her heart was broken. Irritably I pushed away from her and climbed onto Aunt Lily's lap instead. She tickled me and sang me songs. Songs that made me laugh. But I could still hear my mother crying. Now she was crying because of me. Because she had lost me as well, so I tried to go back and comfort her but Aunt Lily held on to me too tightly. She pulled me away as I tried to reach for my mummy. I wanted to tell her I was still here, and that she hadn't lost me. I wanted to hug her and make her better, but Aunt Lily carried me out of the room. In my childlike distress I screamed at her to let me go, to take me back, and I struggled frantically to get her to release her hold but she held me like a vice. I wanted Mummy, *not* her. I needed to make her better; why wouldn't she listen? I screamed louder. Mummy needed me, she was so sad!

'Lainie! Listen to me!' Aunt Lily was shaking me. You should never shake a child, I thought angrily as I continued to struggle.

'Lainie, please listen, you're just dreaming!' Bane's voice sounded frantic and his hands burned where they gripped my shoulders.

I sat up with a jerk and blinked at him in utter confusion.

The grassy clearing glowed eerily in the moonlight while a trillion stars looked down disapprovingly at the tears that were streaming down my cheeks. Someone was sobbing loudly and I hoped futilely that it wasn't me. I needed time when I woke up to compose myself before anyone could see me, but Bane was *right there*. There was nowhere to hide.

A few hiccupy breaths helped as I tried to dry my face with my hand. My salty tears made my fingers sting, and looking down at them I realised it was because they were covered with grazes. Bane pried the fingers of my other hand away from the rock I was still clutching. I must have been wrestling with it in my sleep if I'd made myself bleed. No wonder I'd woken him up.

'Oh! Sorry, Bane, I'm so sorry, I didn't mean it. Here,' I said, offering him my hands as if I was under arrest.

He held my wrists and we both watched as the cuts closed over. I was dazed by the sight, and it distracted me nicely from the sorrow still lingering in my ears. Tingling warmth spread up my arms and my shoulders began to relax. I hadn't realised how cold I was.

'The music's worse here,' Bane guessed, his fingers lingering on my palms.

I nodded. I should have shrugged him off. I should have played it down and made some smart remark. Instead I just stared at his hands holding mine as if they were made of fragile crystal. Despite my emotional exhaustion, I knew it was unlikely that I would get back to sleep again. For his sake I should have at least been willing to try, but I just didn't want to move. At all. Ever. My watch had given up after one too many river crossings, and Bane's phone was lying in a stinky sock in another dimension, so I couldn't even check what time it was.

A violent shiver broke me out of my stupor and I considered picking up the rock again but I didn't dare, and it had probably long since gone cold anyway. Wordlessly Bane leant back against a granite boulder, drew me into his arms and pulled me against his chest. He was so warm. Breathing in the scent of him helped me to ignore the poignant echoes of the symphony that still bounced around my skull. He smelled like eucalyptus and sweat and ... well ... Aeroguard. It was ludicrously comforting. Pulling my head down onto his shoulder, he sighed as he felt me relax. He was far kinder to me than he needed to be. I was messing with his emotions big time and it was not going to end well. I felt as if I had slipped him some sort of love potion and I knew that at some point we would find a way to break this hold I had over him and then he would wake up with a massive case of 'the morning after'. He was really going to hate me then. I should be protecting him from himself. It would be the honourable thing to do ...

His heart beat a steady rhythm under my cheek.

Maybe if I just avoided the kissing. I had managed for seventeen years to live without this feeling he was giving me; surely I could survive without it, but until I had to, just being held by him would be okay, wouldn't it? I closed my eyes, selfishly relishing the feeling of being wanted, and cared for, and protected. And I tried like crazy to ignore the fact that it wasn't real.

∽

A flock of cockatoos screeched from the top of the cliff, waking us both with a jolt. Those birds were seriously loud, especially when there were about fifty of them together. Blinking stupidly, I was surprised to see the sun starting to rise. I had never expected to get back to sleep at all. My face was wet again, and sure enough, Bane's shirt looked as if someone had thrown a drink at him. How embarrassing.

My first attempt to peel myself off the ground resulted in a nasty reminder of the stones I'd put in my socks. When I tried again, so many leaves and sticks were imprinted onto my skin that I looked like a Year 8 art project. Stretching the kinks out of my back, it cracked so much it sounded like someone had stepped on a bag of chips and I hoped Bane wouldn't feel the need to have to heal me again. He looked up at me appraisingly, obviously trying to decide the same thing, and the mussed morning look of his dark hair almost had me leaning back down to smooth it out for him. Instead I backed away clumsily and went to wash up in the tiny creek.

When I felt capable of acting more or less sensible again I returned to the cave, but Bane was gone, so I sat down and daydreamed about bacon and eggs and wondered how long it would be before Tessa would wake up. She wasn't farm-bred, so she could sleep until midday for all I knew, but she emerged from the tunnel a few minutes later with more bounce in her step that any of us had a right to.

'Noah's dead to the world,' she said brightly. 'Where's Bane?'

'No idea. It doesn't work both ways,' I replied, trying not to sound grumbly.

'Do you think he'd mind if we did some exploring now? Just for a little while?'

As eager as I was to get home to my hot shower and breakfast, I couldn't help thinking that there could be some other tunnel, just around the corner somewhere, that might give us another way into

Eden. The memory of my dreams … my mother crying her river of sadness … She could be just around the corner. All we needed was another cave like this one.

'We don't need his permission, Tess. Come on. It isn't like he can't find me if he wants to, and I expect you'll feel it when Noah wakes up, so we'll know when to come back.'

Enjoying the freshness of the new morning, we made our way along the base of the cliff, trying to understand the lay of the land. The uneven wall formed part of the lower edge of the massive ridge that we had ridden up on the morning of the fire. It was possible that the cave kept tunnelling right under the ridge and exited into the ravine beyond, although how closely that matched what happened on the other side of the Event Horizon was anyone's guess. Was there another way into the valley? And was it a normal valley or was it filled with the Garden of Eden? I wanted to know if there were more caves. And more ways in.

We hiked for nearly half an hour before Tessa found another possible cave entrance, which turned out to be a shallow dead end. We kept going. The day was warming up quickly and I knew Bane would come looking for me soon, but each time I thought about turning around I would see another promising overhang that I just had to check out. None of them were any good. Then Tessa discovered a small gap between some rocks we were climbing over. It was barely large enough to squeeze into and yet she plunged down into the hole like she'd seen a magic ring, totally ignoring the nice long scrape she gained on her thigh when she slipped on the way down. Yet again, I realised that going to school with someone for years didn't necessarily mean you knew who they were. She was proving to be much tougher than she looked.

We wormed our way through the shaft using Tessa's phone as a torch, listening to the echoes of underground water nearby. Falling into a subterranean river didn't seem like a safe idea to me but Tessa led the way boldly, squeezing through tight gaps and twice needing me to pull her back out again to find an alternative route when she got stuck. The girl had no fear. When she started going backwards and headfirst down a skinny chute I had to say something. She told me not to be such a wuss and wriggled away before I could get to her.

'Ah, see, I told you not to worry,' she said, her voice bouncing around. 'Hurry up.'

I took a deep breath and shimmied down after her, silently cursing Noah for expecting me to grow so tall. The chute opened out into a nice wide passageway—big enough for us to stand up easily—and I could feel an icy breeze blowing up out of it. The air was just like in the cavern with the sword. It smelled like limestone and unsafe promises. It gave me a feeling of such deep reverence that when Tessa's voice blurted out from the darkness ahead, I jumped a mile.

'He's awake,' she announced. 'That's amazing! I really can tell when he's awake! I think he's heading towards us.'

'Congratulations, Tess. You are now officially as creepy as the rest of us.'

Her pretty face, reflecting blue light and shadows, looked delighted. And then, without even needing to discuss it, we both totally ignored our resolution to head back.

We clambered up and through another twisting tunnel that opened out into a chamber full of delicate straws hanging down from the low ceiling. Each one was gravid with a precious drop of moisture ready to fall. We were reluctant to move around too much in case we broke any, so we stayed close to the driest-looking side wall, and what we discovered there almost made Tessa drop her phone.

Chapter 29

The boys took forever to get to us. Bane stumbled in looking somewhat flustered, although to his credit he tried to hide it. I was grateful that he was trying to give me some independence. He reached for my hand but I shied away, pretending not to have noticed. Bouncing past him, I moved to the low wall where Tessa was holding up her phone to show off our discovery.

'No way!' Bane's deep voice sounded hushed and awestruck. His eyes drank in the series of cave paintings that coated the wall like ancient graffiti.

'Incredible. They could be thousands of years old,' Noah whispered.

Taking care not to touch them, I tried to decipher whether they had anything to do with Eden. At first I thought they were mostly hunting scenes, but then I noticed that the humans in the pictures were all injured. One had clearly stepped on a snake, one was drowning in a river, and one showed a man being chased by what looked like a giant emu.

'The world's first episode of *Funniest Home Videos*?' I asked.

Tessa shook her head. 'More like the first version of Dumb Ways to Die. These are warnings. Maybe for children?'

'Check this one out,' Noah breathed, pointing to a man and a woman standing on the top of a hill with their arms stretched up to the sky. A great flock of birds—thousands of them—were descending on a group of people who were cowering under their spears. There was a circle drawn around the hill, and the birds were attacking the people who had crossed into the circle, but there was another group of people just outside it who were left alone. The warning was clear.

Noah nodded thoughtfully. 'Birds, huh?'

'Could work, I guess. But it might attract a bit of attention,' I said. We moved along to see if there were any more tips for us, and Bane stared curiously at one picture of a stark naked, brave-looking warrior. I said it looked eerily like him, making him blush and press his lips together. Then I made him put his hand up just in front of a hand stencil and laughed when the outlines matched perfectly. After an intense search, however, we all had to admit that none of the pictures looked like they were of a hidden paradise. Our ancestors must have had as much trouble drawing as we had writing about Eden. I wondered if the paintings meant that we were standing on some sort of sacred site, but decided it was more likely that they were simply a warning that we were close to one. Still, I felt a bit sacrilegious as I took some photos with Tessa's phone so we could study the paintings better once we got home.

After that we were all too excited to just leave. After seeing both the sword and the ancient paintings, Eden felt real enough to taste. There had to be another way in. The chamber had two passageways leading from it, so we decided to split up. Noah and Tessa climbed down into another shaft, while I used the light from the sat-phone Bane had remembered to bring to lead him down a passageway just wide enough to wiggle through. It was difficult to concentrate on where we placed our feet and at the same time avoid low hanging rocky outcrops and stalactites.

Ancient water seeped patiently down from above, pooling in unexpected nooks and crannies, and sometimes we had to duck low and twist our bodies around awkwardly to get through. It was a winding route, which made it impossible to tell how far we were travelling, but eventually the tunnel widened again, revealing stalagmites laden with too much vanilla icing that kept trying to trip me over. Suddenly I was faced with a solid wall of glittering rock. How could such a wide tunnel end so abruptly? I searched above and below but I couldn't find any other way through, so I moved closer to examine the wall for any small openings. A couple of metres away from it I felt a shiver go down my spine. It was as though something was moving through my skin and wrapping around my bones. It wasn't cold or warm, it just felt like everything sort of *shifted* through me. For a long moment I just stood there feeling confused, trying to remember what I had been doing, like I had walked into the bedroom to get something but couldn't remember what it was. I shook my head to clear away the fuzziness. The wall. I was trying to find a way through. I examined it from top to bottom in the torchlight but it really was a dead end.

'I think that's as far as we can go, there's no way through here.'

Bane didn't answer so I moved back to see where he was, again feeling the strange sensation as I moved away from the wall.

'Bane?'

'Lainie! Are you all right? Where have you been?' He sounded frantic. To my immense surprise he was also behind me again. How had he managed that? He swept me into a crushing hug, startling me—he usually controlled himself much better than that.

'I haven't been anywhere! And of course I'm fine, you should know that too.' I tried to peel him off me but he refused to let me go and I realised he was trembling. 'Are you okay?'

'You were right in front of me,' he said. 'But then the light went out and you disappeared. And I mean totally. I couldn't even … feel you. I almost passed out from shock, Lainie. What did you do? How did you get behind me again?'

'I was just going to ask you the same thing. All I did was examine the wall. How weird is that? Let's see if it happens again!' Did it have something to do with the odd sensation I had felt? I tried to check it out but Bane clung to me like a baby possum.

'You're not going anywhere without me. Not again,' he stated flatly. His familiar scowl was back.

'Seriously? I was only gone for a few seconds! There's nothing to worry about.'

'Lainie, you're not listening. *I couldn't feel you at all!*'

Suddenly my heart was racing. Had I crossed the Event Horizon? The poor guy was really freaking out, which I couldn't blame him for if he really had been plunged into sudden darkness deep below the ground, but nothing was going to stop me from checking it out again.

'Hold my hand,' I coaxed. 'I'll go exactly where I went before so you can see.'

Once again, about two metres out, I felt my skin tingle. I didn't remember letting go of his hand but suddenly it just wasn't there. The whole of him wasn't there. I turned and felt the air. My fingertips tingled and I could feel a smooth wall of … something. Subtle. Like a fragile spider's web, but with a sort of shiny, soapy texture. I stepped back through it and sure enough he was behind me again, examining the rock. He spun around as the link between us was re-established.

'Cool magic trick, huh?' I teased him, wiggling my eyebrows.

'No. Not cool at all. Please don't do that again.' Extremely grumpy eyes met mine in a way that made him look a lot like his mum when she'd taken our class for recorder lessons in Year 3.

'So you just crossed through it and didn't feel anything?' I asked. 'Does it look the same on that side for you?' I was intrigued. Obviously I had crossed into Eden but Bane hadn't. Not that it did me much good since there was still no way through the rock.

'Crossed through what? You left me with nothing but a few glow worms. I couldn't see anything,' he grumbled. 'And even if I could, how would I know if it looks the same? I couldn't see whatever you did.'

'Everything looked the same as from here.' We both studied the impassable wall.

'But you were in Eden.'

'Yep. And you couldn't feel … me.' My excitement came crashing down like a manna gum in a drought as I realised that we had the answer we'd been looking for. There was a way to break the link. To set Bane free.

He stared at me with wide pale eyes, but in the dim light I couldn't work out what his expression meant. All of a sudden I felt like I was struggling to breathe. Conflicting emotions swirled around my chest and tied themselves into one giant knot that I couldn't seem to get any air past. I turned away from him, unwilling to let him see the confusion I felt. I would *not* let him feel guilty when the time came for him to leave, not on top of everything else I had already put him through.

I started to head back down the tunnel, hoping he hadn't noticed my hesitation. 'We'd better tell the others,' I said, trying to make my voice sound normal. He followed silently.

⌒

By the time we got back to the chamber with the paintings, Noah and Tessa were waiting for us and were eager to get going. Noah didn't even ask to go back to copy what I had done with the Event Horizon, and he led the way out at such a cracking pace that Tessa asked him if he was feeling claustrophobic. I knew that wasn't it. Something was making all my joints itch and I couldn't quite pin it down. I tried to sense if there were any miners in the area, but everything was a bit hazy. When I slipped and whacked my hip climbing back to the surface, Bane begged me to slow down. I couldn't.

When we got back to the first cave, we refilled the water drums and then rushed back to the river. Noah was so much on edge that he gave Tessa an irritated look when she started to lag behind. Someone was nearby. Two people, in fact, although only one was bugging me, and they weren't together. We moved through the scrub like mythical pumas, and practically slid down the embankment to get to the canoe. Someone was approaching and I didn't want the trespasser to see where we had come from. We threw the drums into the boat and Noah and Tessa paddled across while Bane and I melted back into the bush.

They had just managed to hide the canoe in a thick patch of ti-tree when Blue came bounding out from behind a cape wattle wagging her tail. She sat in front of Noah looking very pleased with herself and I smiled in relief. Noah visibly relaxed too and started to give her a tummy rub just as Nicole came stomping out of the bushes, looking smug.

'Good girl, Bluey, I knew you'd find them!' she exclaimed, throwing herself into Noah's arms. Noah kept his face neutral but I could tell from the way he had his lips pressed together that he was tempted to throttle her.

I could feel someone else approaching, still a few minutes away, but I didn't feel edgy so I figured it was probably Sarah. I would have to get used to what she 'felt' like.

'Nic, what are you doing out here on your own? Does Mum know where you are?' Noah asked. Nicely covered. As if he couldn't feel his mum heading our way.

'You've been out all night. I was worried!' She glared at Tessa.

'And so you decided to go out bush on your own to look for us?' Noah admonished her.

'Like you've never done that. Besides, I had Blue. And the phone. I would have called if I'd been in trouble, unlike some people.'

'I did call. Mum would have told you if you'd asked, but you chose not to run this by her, didn't you?'

She grinned at him, totally unashamed. 'What were you doing out here, anyway?'

'None of your business! Besides, we're on our way back. I'm starving.' He tried to distract her from asking too many questions, but it was never going to work.

'What are the water drums for?'

'Carrying water,' he replied unhelpfully.

He picked one up and Tessa took the other. I winced in sympathy at the sight of them struggling with the heavy water drums, but we couldn't help. I didn't want Nicole to know Bane and I were there. Better to let her think Noah and Tessa had come out for some time alone, but Blue was standing by the edge of the river staring into the bushes where we were hiding. I closed my eyes and whispered at her to go away. She did, and I wondered if I could have made us invisible if it had been necessary to keep Eden hidden. That might have been kind of fun.

Noah, Nicole and Tessa started to head back along the riverbank, and I knew they would run into Sarah as she tried to catch up to her daughter. Knowing Sarah, there would be some serious consequences, and I almost felt a bit sorry for Nicole. Almost.

Once they were well and truly out of range we began the long trek home. I carried our backpack while Bane limped along beside me in one sock and damp boots.

Chapter 30

After a morning to recuperate, Aunt Lily sent Bane into town to visit his mum and pick up some supplies. It was New Year's Eve and I had totally forgotten. We had originally planned to go into town for the fireworks but I'd had to explain to Aunt Lily about the potential meeting with Harry. It was a long shot, but on the off chance our plan worked, I wasn't going to stand him up for the sake of a fireworks display. So instead, Bane went to buy hot dogs, gelati, and fresh batteries for our torches in case we found any more caves to explore. This time we would pack properly, knowing we would be spending the night up there again. The minute Bane drove away, however, Aunt Lily pounced on me.

'So it's "Bane" again, is it?' she asked with a naughty glint in her eye as she ate a spoonful of Nutella straight from the jar. Her smooth golden hair was tucked behind her ears and she had tell-tale bits of wool clinging to her jeans from a morning spent vaccinating stock.

'He prefers it, apparently,' I said, blinking innocently. Had we been acting so differently that she had noticed something had happened? I had no reason to keep any secrets from her, but that didn't stop me from feeling awkward. She just smiled and drummed her fingers on the table, waiting for me to spill the beans.

'Okay, so we had a bit of a "moment". Happy? I succumbed to his dazzling charm, is that what you want to hear? I feel bad about it enough already, you don't need to rub it in,' I sulked, laying my forehead on the table.

'What's to feel bad about, Lainie? You two are clearly meant for each other! Why are you making this so complicated?'

'Because he would never have picked me if he'd had any say in the matter, that's why! I've done nothing but ruin his life since we were kids and now he's stuck here in the middle of nowhere instead of living the life he deserves!'

My aunt sat down opposite me with a look of wise sympathy in her steady blue eyes, so I got up and started tossing things around the kitchen to make up some milk for the joey.

'I don't think he sees it quite like that, honey. He adores you. Everyone can see it but you.'

'I see it. I just don't believe it's real. You never knew him at school. Since this has all started he's been compelled to feel … that way. It's wrong and unfair on him. I feel like an evil witch who's cast a love spell. Somewhere out there is the girl he really wants to be with while I'm holding him hostage here.'

'And what about you? Do you resent him hanging around you all the time? Do you want to ditch him so you can start seeing other people?'

I stopped shaking the bottle of milk formula and stared at her in astonishment. See other people? Was that what I wanted? Not even remotely. Did I want him to leave? My chest hurt just thinking about it, which was unexpected. I wasn't being compelled in any way, was I? Maybe it was just the idea of having someone so dedicated to protecting me—that was a powerful thing—but deep down I knew that wasn't all it was. I shook my head sadly.

'No. I don't want him to go. But I can't keep him either.'

With a heavy heart I pulled open the bottom drawer of the kitchen, the one with all the junk that didn't have a proper home, and handed her the envelope I had saved from the bin.

Annie Gracewood stood at the entrance to the tunnel, reluctant to go in. Despite the fact that she felt drawn to this place it always brought back memories for her, and that made her sad, so she avoided it. How could she be drawn here and not want to be here at the same time? It made no sense. She should go in. The thought surprised her. There was no 'should' or 'shouldn't' in Eden. That was a concept from Before. She rubbed her face. Harry wanted her to remember. He needed her help, and helping other people was more like what she knew. It was what people did here. Not because it was the right thing to do, but because it was what people were made for. The people here had Life breathed into them, and they acted according to the instincts that brought. It was natural, and easy.

It had been a long time since she had thought of the people here as different to herself, but they were. She was not really one of them. She wasn't one of the dead ones either. She had loved them too, and had left them behind a long time ago.

Harry had talked about one of them. Lainie. She had died like the rest and so she'd had to leave her precious baby behind, with all the other dead people. She'd *had* to leave before she died herself—she'd promised—but she missed Lainie terribly.

Looking wistfully at the bright yellow Living Fruit on a nearby tree, she considered taking a bite. The Fruit was a source of Life. She'd avoided eating it for so many years before finally giving in. Eating it made it difficult to remember things that hurt. If she ate it now, she would stop missing her baby, but then she wouldn't be able to help Harry. So she steeled herself and entered the tunnel instead.

When she saw the sword she nearly turned and ran back out again— too many memories writhed amongst its breathtaking flames—she forced herself to keep going. The light from the massive weapon flickered around the cavern, and what it showed made her eyebrows lift in utter bewilderment, and then she burst out laughing.

That afternoon I received a message from Noah to say that he and Tessa wouldn't be coming back to the cave with us that evening. It would look far too suspicious to have to explain to Nicole why they were going to miss out on the New Year's festivities to go out bush again and she was nosy enough as it was. So after an early and massively unhealthy dinner to make up for missing the party in town, Bane and I packed some basic overnight gear and torches and wearily trudged all the way back to the cave system. We arrived with almost half an hour to spare and I used it to stare at the legendary sword, daydream about pouncing on Bane again, and try to conjure up the language that I knew could be used to crush the rock wall to dust—if only I could remember it.

Hot rocks stung my fingertips as I peered through the gap, trying to see if anyone was in the cavern behind the sword. Was that a slight movement?

'Harry?' I whispered loudly. 'Harry, are you there?'

'Why are you whispering?' Bane asked. 'Sound doesn't even travel across the boundary, remember?'

Good point. Feeling sheepish, I pulled back and blew on my sore fingers. So what now? Bane's phone alarm had been due to go off a couple of minutes earlier, and I'd been excited when I hadn't heard it in the cavern beyond, thinking that meant someone must have picked it up. I'd forgotten that I wouldn't have heard it anyway. There wasn't any point trying to see anything either, as I had been invisible to Bane as soon as I had stepped across the threshold in the other tunnel. I let out a frustrated groan.

'What's the matter, Lainie-Bug?' Harry's voice came out of nowhere and I jumped a mile. Suddenly I could feel his presence, like a familiar scent of home.

'Harry! You came! You're really here!' I wanted to squeeze right through the hole and throw myself at him, but I only managed to get my head halfway through before a couple of rocks shifted ominously. Behind me, Bane growled under his breath.

'Yes, I came. Someone handed me a stinky sock containing something unpleasant,' he laughed. 'Here, you'd better have it back, it's nearly out of charge anyway, and it keeps bleeping at me.' He passed Bane's phone through the hole. 'And who does it belong to, anyway?' he asked, as if he couldn't sense that I was not alone.

'Ben Millard.' I paused, feeling my ears go pink. What to say? 'He's my Guardian.' I leant back and Harry tilted his head to see past me. Bane gave an awkward little wave.

Harry raised one eyebrow at me. He was not one to pry, but there was a definite smug twinkle in his brown eyes.

'Wait, someone handed you the phone? So there really are other people in there?'

He nodded. 'Of course. You don't think this has all been set up just to protect some exotic plants and animals, do you?'

If those exotic plants included a Tree that gave immortality, then I didn't see why not, but I was happy to trust him on this one.

'Lainie, how is everything? What's been happening with Kolsom?'

There was so much to tell him, but I tried to sum up as best I could because he was beginning to look pained as the heat from the sword behind him radiated through his clothing.

'The miners are still here. They lit a bushfire to try to burn the valley to gain access to it but Noah and I put it out.' I almost laughed at the incredulous expression on his face. There was a lot to take in from that one sentence. 'You knew about Noah though, didn't you, Harry?' I guessed. How could he not have?

Shielding his face from the heat, he looked as uncomfortable as he had that time I'd caught him planting roses in his little garden. 'It wasn't my place to talk about it. I was waiting for Sarah to tell him first.'

'She didn't. He found out when he started yelling at rain clouds. It was a bit of a shock. For both of us.'

Harry muttered angrily to himself, probably regretting the fact he hadn't told us himself.

'Harry, is there some way I can get in, or can you get out? Can you move these rocks again?'

'I've tried, but as I told you, that sort of power only manifests when there's a need for it.'

'But I need you to come home! Please?'

'It's not our needs that matter. It's whether Eden needs it. And if there is even just one Cherub available to protect it from your side, then I'm not needed there.'

Let alone if there were three of us around.

'Well, if not through here, is there some other way in?' I asked. 'We found another Event Horizon in a different cave, but it's a dead end on the other side. I could cross it, but for Bane it didn't even exist.'

Shifting around like a frog on a hot rock, Harry looked intrigued. We were running out of time; he would have to go back before his clothes caught fire.

'Really? I always assumed there was only the one way in. How are we supposed to protect this place if there are more?'

'I think only Cherubim can cross elsewhere. Everyone else would just walk straight past without realising, but we cross over. I expect this is the only place ... humans ... can even potentially get through, so this is the only place we have to really guard.' What I was saying was pure conjecture, but it was the best I had. It still felt disconcerting to talk about humans as if I wasn't one, but I pretended not to care.

He nodded thoughtfully. 'Let me think about it. This cave leads to another tunnel behind the sword, which opens out into ...' His face twisted into a grimace, and his eyes flicked up to where Bane was standing patiently behind me. So even the Guardians weren't allowed to know everything, then. 'I'll do some exploring and see what I can find,' he said instead. 'Will I meet you here again the day after tomorrow?' He was looking very uncomfortable and sweat was pouring from his chin.

'We'll be here. Make it earlier, around lunchtime. You'd better go before you lose your eyebrows. But Harry ... ?'

He started to back away.

'Harry, what about the music? And my mother, did you find her?'

'Say hi to your aunt for me,' he called back, pretending he hadn't heard me, 'and to Sarah, too.'

And between one step and another, he disappeared.

It took me a good half hour to forgive Harry for evading my questions, even though Bane sensibly pointed out that it was probably because he couldn't say anything while a human was around. He promised to give us a bit more space the next time, and then proceeded to demonstrate how that was done by doing his best to ignore my existence as we set up camp for the night. I knew he was grouchy because he was fretting about me going to Eden without him, but I was determined to see it through. He would thank me for it one day. I tried not to think about how I felt about that. Remembered images of his past venomous looks sickened me now. I had once been fairly de-sensitised to them—and I had honestly forgiven him for each and every one once I had understood what I had put him through—but if he ever went back to hating me that much, something in me would shatter beyond repair.

As the river music filled my head with its poignant sorrow, I longed for him to hold me again, and promise me that he would try to be as nice as he could, but he stayed on his side of the dusty grotto, as far away from me as he could get. I had been sending him so many mixed signals lately, I was sure he was about to derail. Resolutely I disciplined my thoughts—I couldn't have things both ways. I had already let things go way too far between us. It was time for me to wise up.

Scrunching down into my sleeping bag, I prodded at the bag of clothes I was using for a pillow until it wasn't quite so lumpy. Above me I could just see the Southern Cross from beyond the overhang. Bits of gravel dust blew in with the breeze, peppering me as I tried to get comfortable, but I refused to turn my face away from the view of the sky. Was Harry watching the same stars I was? And my mother? Was the river music as sad there as it was here? Rather than try to block it out, I decided for once to just let the music fill me, riding its currents to see where they would lead me. Burning tears erupted as I knew they would and I was too tired to bother fighting them. The new approach didn't help me sleep, but it did replace my confusion and anxiety with numb emotional exhaustion. Hours passed. Slower than a school speech night.

'Lainie?' The softest of whispers overlaid the backdrop of cicada and frog songs. Had he been awake the whole time too? Twitchy heartbeats had to be firmly disciplined. The two of us spending the night alone in the bush was dangerous enough without me giving him any more of the wrong reactions.

I kept my voice to a low whisper so it wouldn't betray the longing I felt. Or the sadness. If he tried to console me again I was going to cave for sure. 'Yeah?' was all I managed to breathe.

'Happy New Year.'

That was when I realised that it was the first New Year's Eve I hadn't spent with Noah.

⸺

The following morning over breakfast, we showed Aunt Lily the photos of the cave paintings Tessa had emailed me. She was appropriately awe-struck, and kept glancing sideways at me as if trying to come to terms with the idea that I really was descended from an ancient Indigenous clan. And I wasn't the pale-skinned green-eyed Cherub.

'Harry said hi,' I remembered. I had briefly outlined our meeting with him but found it difficult to give her any details. She was content to know that he was all right and understood why I couldn't say more.

'Do you think he'll come home?' she asked carefully.

'He wants to but he really is stuck. We're working on it, though. We just need to find …' I struggled to spit out the words. All the specific details were getting tangled in my throat with my two-minute noodles.

Aunt Lily just shook her head. 'It doesn't matter. Just make sure you stay safe.'

It was so frustrating. She might have had a brilliant suggestion for getting into Eden but I couldn't even talk about it. Bane was no use; he wasn't likely to offer any ideas. Just as I decided I would have to go and see Noah, the phone rang. It was Sarah again. Apparently she'd called the night before and a couple of times that morning already. It made sense. She would have felt Harry suddenly turn up near Eden and then disappear again, so I told her I would come over and explain.

When I arrived, she led me to the far end of the backyard to talk, away from any prying ears.

'Your aunt told me you and Bane set up a meeting with Harry. I felt him return briefly last night. How did you manage it? How did he get past the rock fall?' she asked.

'The rock fall is still there, right in front of the Event Horizon. Harry just managed to fit between them but it was very hot, so he couldn't stay long,' I explained. When I told her how we had managed to get a message to him, she snorted at the irony of Harry having to use a phone.

'So is he going to come home? He never liked the idea of crossing over after what happened to your mother. I'm surprised he's stayed there this long.'

That caught my attention. 'What happened to my mother?' I asked, trying to sound casual. Just how much did she know?

'Oh, honey, sorry,' she said, laying her hand on my arm. 'I suppose no one has ever really told you the truth about that. It's not right. You should know.'

'It's not Aunt Lily's fault. She only knows bits and pieces about Eden. She's told me everything she can.' I felt a bit defensive. After all, Sarah could have filled me in at any time if she really believed it was important enough.

'I know. I'm not blaming her. Harry should have told you more. Although I know Lily wanted us to wait until you were a bit more mature to find out about all this, so I guess it was right that he deferred to her judgment.'

We sat down on a rickety garden bench that had seen better days. At least it was in the shade.

'Your mother fell into a severe depression when your dad died,' she explained, moving along to give me a bit more space on the bench. 'She started to cross over into Eden regularly. She said it made her feel better, and it worked ... for a while, but there was something about the place that messed with her mind. She began to stay there for longer and longer periods of time. Each time she returned she would be a little bit more disconnected. She began to forget things and became ... irresponsible. She just couldn't seem to get her priorities straight. One minute she would be all over you, saying how much she'd missed you, and the next we would find her wandering by the river, having forgotten that she'd left you in the house alone. Lily did an amazing job of trying to keep her grounded, but eventually she ... slipped away. The last time I saw her she was in tears, saying that you had died. She was holding you in her arms at the time and you were sleeping peacefully. We tried to explain to her that you were fine but she'd finally tipped over the edge. She left for Eden that day and I never saw her again. Harry went after her ...' Her olive eyes glazed over as she got lost in her memories. Then she gave herself a little shake. 'When he returned he told us your mum had all but forgotten this world and didn't ... want to remember.' She squeezed my hand. 'Even though your aunt would never admit it, I think she was relieved. Watching what you went through each time your mother left you again ... and having to pick up the pieces each time ... I'm so sorry, Lainie. This can't be easy for you to hear.'

It matched what Aunt Lily had said, but that didn't make it any better. My mother had still left me alone. Suddenly the rickety bench I was sitting on felt a lot more stable than the rest of the planet. So many reactions fought for priority that I just squashed them all down to deal with later, and tried to focus on the questions I had instead. 'So that's why you and Harry avoid going into Eden? It sends you crazy?'

She shook her head. 'Not so much crazy, it just makes you forget. You're in another world, so this one just sort of fades away. I've never been there. I don't want to risk losing my family.'

We sat silently for a while and I reflected on the way I had struggled to pay attention to what I was doing as soon as I had crossed over the boundary. It was easy to see how quickly memories could slip away.

Perhaps it was a good thing though—I wouldn't miss Bane and Aunt Lily so much if I couldn't remember them. That was the moment I realised that I was actually contemplating what it would be like to live there. Another world. A whole other life. In Paradise. And it was calling to me louder and louder every day. There had to be a way in.

'Sarah, is it really possible to resist these compulsions? If it protects the ones we love?' If she was able to avoid going into Eden then perhaps I could go in and avoid the temptation to return, despite my ties to this world. My attachment to Bane wasn't necessarily compulsive, but it felt awfully close.

'I would do *anything* to protect the people I love. I believe we always have a choice, even when it comes to Eden.' She was on the verge of tears and I could see how conflicted she was between following her role as a Cherub and doing what was best for her family. Her words echoed Harry's so closely that I wondered how many more 'choices' they had both been forced to make. I tried to shift the subject to a less painful topic.

'I think Harry would like to come home if we can find a way, and I think there might be one. Bane and I found another cave. There was an Event Horizon there, but it was a dead end on the other side—in both worlds.'

She looked up at me, a fascinated expression brightening her serene face.

'Bane couldn't cross it,' I continued. 'He walked through it but nothing changed for him. He just couldn't sense me at all when I crossed.'

'So presumably there is still only the one place humans can get in to Eden?'

A shiver of revulsion went down my spine at the thought; it was the same feeling I got when people tried to lie to me. Humans. Crossing over the Event Horizon. The mere idea of it made my teeth ache. 'But they're not allowed.' The bleak flatness of my rebuke seemed to startle her almost as much as it did me.

She was quiet for a moment, and then asked in a subdued voice, 'So if we can find another place for Cherubim to cross, would you go?' Her gaze was as piercing as my answer was quick.

'Of course. I want to find her, and I want to know why the river music is so sad. And I want to help Harry to get home, somehow.'

'No,' she said, fiddling with her silver bangle. 'I mean, if you want to go, that's up to you, but Harry ...' She breathed in very deeply, and there were emotions swirling around her that I couldn't decipher. When she relaxed again, her voice was steady. 'If Harry wants to stay there, then please don't try to talk him out of it.'

Chapter 31

I carefully fed the rolled up fire blanket through the hole to Harry. He draped it over his head and crouched down so it gave some protection from the sword's heat.

'I've felt the boundary in a few places,' he said. 'It's always right up against the cliff face, though, so there's nowhere to go. I've spent all day exploring caves and tunnels with no luck. They all either stop or twist around and head back out again. I get the impression the boundary runs along the full length of the cliff. At the southern edge I felt nothing. Like a wall that just finishes where the cliff starts to descend to the river. I haven't been to the northern end but I would guess that the same thing happens. The Event Horizon has been neatly set up to coincide with the one place that's physically inaccessible.'

'Except for this tunnel,' Noah pointed out, moving my hair aside so he could see what was going on.

'Correct, except for this tunnel, which is guarded by the sword,' Harry confirmed.

'Clever design, really,' I noted, elbowing my best friend away. I had to appreciate the tidiness of the system. Although why would there be an entire stretch of boundary wall that Cherubim could pass through if there was no way for us to do it? I had a theory but Bane wasn't going to like it. And if I was right, it would only work from this side, so there was still no way to get home again. 'So what's the landscape like where you are?' I asked him, checking over my shoulder to make certain that Bane and Tessa had remained outside as promised.

'Magnificent. Everything a garden should be. It's quite open, but the fields are lush and green, not like home. There's a bright river running through this valley, lined with trees so tall that you feel like an ant under them. And flowers everywhere. The air smells …' He shook his head, at a loss for words. 'I haven't been out of the valley area, but I believe there's a whole world here. I wish you could see it.' His eyes had a new shine behind them. I had never heard him speak so effusively before, and I could hear the passion in his voice. I wanted in. And if the landscape was as open as he said, my idea should work.

'Is there any way for you to get to the top of the cliff, Harry?' Noah asked, making me wonder whether he had arrived at the same conclusion.

'Not easily,' he replied. 'I would take me weeks. As I mentioned, the river cuts through it to the south of here. The northern end just gets higher till it joins a mountain range—a pretty spectacular one, actually.'

Noah's gaze flickered to me. He had the same look on his face as when he had come up with the ice-blocking plan, and I knew exactly what he was thinking. Even if Harry had been able to get to the top of the cliff, he couldn't jump off it through the boundary because it was the wrong direction, but we could. The next step would be for us to try to find out if the boundary ran vertically as well. Could we cross into Eden somewhere along the top of the ridge?

While Noah stepped back to draw himself a little map on the floor with his finger, I took the opportunity to ask Harry as many questions as I could before he disappeared again.

'Please,' I begged. 'I need to know if you found her.'

His smile was sad. 'Yeah, she's here.'

'But?' I prompted. There was definitely one coming.

'But she doesn't believe me when I tell her you want to see her.'

'*What?*' I spluttered. 'Why wouldn't I want to see her? Does she think I'm angry with her?'

'Aren't you?'

I hesitated. 'Well, yes. Of course I am, but that doesn't mean I don't want to see her.'

Harry shook his head. 'That isn't the problem anyway. The reason she doesn't believe me is because she thinks you're dead.'

I found I had somehow sat down, and Noah's face was close to mine, full of concern. His luminous green eyes were brimming with tears.

'Lainie, are you all right?'

'My mother. She really is alive,' I told him in an unsteady voice.

'I know. Mum told me. I've been waiting for you to bring it up.' He seemed a bit hurt. 'Why didn't you talk to me?'

My hands were trembling, but I wasn't crying, thankfully. 'Because I wanted to know for sure. If I'd said it out loud and then found that she was dead after all, it would have been worse.'

'Lainie logic,' Harry said to Noah, as if he was trying to be helpful. And Noah nodded back as if he actually had been.

'Why does she think I'm dead?' I asked Harry.

'That's a bit hard to explain. I honestly don't have the words.'

'Then what about if I come to her?'

He smiled. 'That might convince her.' He adjusted the blanket, shifting his feet about. They were bare and most likely burning. I was running out of time again.

'And the music? Did you find out why it's so sad?'

All three of us automatically looked over to the tiny streamlet, trickling its way between the rocks over by the wall. Poignant echoes of loss and tragedy bounced silently around the cavern, heard only in our minds.

'I did,' Harry said. 'But that one is even harder to explain. And even harder to fix. Maybe if you come, it will help.'

As if I needed any more excuses.

Then I broached the last of my most urgent questions, the one that had been filling my brain with all sorts of panic-inducing scenarios.

'Harry,' I muttered, leaning into the hole again, 'just what are we capable of, exactly?'

His eyes flicked up at me, but he didn't answer.

'I mean, what happened that morning, with the fire ... I don't really know how I did it. What if I do something wrong next time? We were messing with things we weren't prepared for. Shouldn't we have some sort of training or something? I mean, I can't even have a pet snake without a licence, so how is it that I'm allowed to mess with the weather?' Beside me, Noah nodded, fiddling with my braid the way he often did when he was worried.

'Your authority frightens you.'

'Damn straight!' I agreed in a strangled voice. 'How did you learn to control it all?'

'Control it? Lainie, I hate to tell you, but I didn't even know what we could do until I ... built ... this!' he said, waving his hand at the huge pile of rocks separating us. 'And I was terrified. I've never even heard of any of us doing anything so …' He hunched deeper into the protection of his blanket.

'Never? So there's no precedent for any of this? But how do we know what we're supposed to do? What if I go crazy and destroy the universe or something? Surely there are some rules, or limits, or something!' My voice was getting unattractively squeaky, even in the hushed tone I was trying to stick to.

Harry pushed me back gently, reached through the hole and picked something shimmery and small from one of the rocks. It was a Christmas beetle—they were everywhere at this time of the year. Biting thoughtfully on his tongue, he examined it with eyes that held the very essence of peace. 'My uncle used to love these. He used to spend ages just watching them. He was fascinated by their shine, and incredible colours. I asked him once why he wasted so much time watching bugs walk around, and he said, "*When it all becomes too much to handle, I ground myself with the things of the Earth. The small things. The scent of the dirt, the feel of the rocks, the dance of the insects.*"' Harry smiled and placed the beetle on my shoulder. 'We belong to the Earth, Lainie-Bug. We were sent here in human form for a reason. If you don't know what to do, then just be human.'

Right. Like that was ever a simple thing to do.

'Eden bugs, Harry?' I rescued the poor creature before it crawled under my collar, and he laughed at the reminder.

'Actually, yes. After all, Eden is just a compilation of the best the Earth has ever had to offer, didn't you know?'

I told him that if that was true, then I was going to be very disappointed if there weren't any dinosaur-related fire-lizards.

We arranged to meet again in three days' time. We needed a chance to explore. I also had a meeting in town to attend the following day. Councillor Lleyland had requested a meeting with the Kolsom representative. It was time for me to meet Mr Alex Beckinsale properly.

⌒

The dusty old receptionist showed us into the councillor's air-conditioned meeting room and I poured myself and Aunt Lily a glass of water from the jug on the table. My hands trembled with uncharacteristic nervousness. There had to be a reason we were called to attend a meeting in person and it wasn't likely to be a positive one. Humming under my breath, I fidgeted like an ant on a hot plate as we waited for Councillor Lleyland and Mr Beckinsale. The water tasted weird.

The moment they walked in together I knew we were in trouble. Not just because I recognised the lawyer as the same man I had seen in the library, but also because they had obviously just held a separate private meeting without us present.

The mining executive was again dressed in an expensive suit and tie that looked mighty uncomfortable in the heat. He looked like the sort of man that clipped his nose hair every Friday, and his chiselled features were backed up with a charming smile that would have fooled most people. I was not most people.

The councillor introduced us all politely, but as I shook hands with the young lawyer a multitude of images smashed into me that were so vivid I struggled not to react violently. As it was I held onto his hand a bit too long as I tried to absorb everything I was seeing. His smile widened, probably assuming I was being swayed by his charm, and I snatched my hand back awkwardly.

The first few minutes of polite chitchat were a complete blur to me as my mind frantically tried to sort and filter the information I had been hit with. Never before had I seen such vivid images of someone. Usually I only got fleeting impressions, but like a super-fast preview to a movie, I had just seen jumbled images of this man being picked on as a boy by his classmates for being too clever at school. I had seen him get drunk and cheat on his girlfriend. I had also seen an image of his father hitting his mother as he screamed in frightened outrage, cowering under the kitchen table with his toy dinosaur. Later that night his mother had bundled him up, and they had snuck out of the house as she'd rescued them both from an abusive situation. I watched him as a teenager again as he arrogantly asked the school counsellor which career would be the most likely to make him rich, then in the same moment saw a vision of him years earlier, crying because his mother had sold his computer so they would have enough money for rent. There were plenty more. Including a frighteningly familiar scene out in the bush during the night.

The vivid splattering of images was random and confusing, but they all had one thing in common. In each vision I could *feel* exactly what he had felt. Sitting as still as I could, I struggled not to either burst into tears of sympathy or stand up and slap him across the face. This man was incredibly ambitious—and not in a healthy way. Too many of the images contained intense feelings of either fear or fury. I had no doubt that Mr Beckinsale was capable of violence. It bubbled just under the surface, controlled more by his intelligence than any real self-discipline. I wished I could just dismiss the images as some sort of wild daydream, but they felt far too *real*, and I knew I was getting the information because he was a threat to the one thing I was born to protect. I remained frozen, wondering just what this man was scheming to do next. I didn't have long to wait.

Councillor Lleyland cleared his throat. 'Now that the shire has decided to back Kolsom's application for a full mining licence, I believe it is my duty as a council officer to ensure the relevant landowners are fully informed,' he announced to us with an ingratiating smile. 'I'll provide any assistance you require to negotiate a mutually beneficial arrangement with Mr Beckinsale here.' He was trying hard to ignore the icy glare that Aunt Lily was directing at him and I wondered what he had been offered to make him change his attitude so completely from the last public meeting he'd attended—or had he just been telling the community what we wanted to hear? Generally I tried to assume the best of people but after what I had just 'seen' of Mr Beckinsale I couldn't stomach the idea of seeing any of the councillor's dirty laundry.

'And just what area of land are you applying to mine?' Aunt Lily asked in a dangerously saccharin voice.

'The area south of Mokin Road down to the southern end of the state park, and extending east to the river,' Mr Beckinsale stated smoothly. My heart thumped wildly. That included my valley, and the caves. Even though I had known it was coming I could still feel the anger churning inside me like a waking beast. Drilling holes and extracting gas wasn't even the real problem. The problem was simply that no one was allowed to be anywhere near that area. Ever. Narrowing my eyes, I wondered how well hard hats would protect the miners from an attack by a thousand angry cockies.

'Here are the documents outlining the reasons we think the

government should agree to the compulsory acquisition of a small part of your land, including a *very* generous offer of compensation.' He slid a thick pile of papers over to her with a smile, as if he genuinely expected us to be convinced by the offer of money.

My glorious aunt looked him directly in the eye. 'Not a snowball's chance in Hell!'

'Ms Gracewood, this isn't an access agreement. There's nothing for you to sign. This is an application to the state government for the *compulsory* acquisition of the land. I'm simply informing you of the process as per company policy. Our full licence will be approved in the next week or two and then mining will commence straight away.' The electricity in his voice could have made a dead frog jump. He was not going to be at all intimidated by anything we said. Or so he thought.

'Excuse me, Mr Beckinsale,' I said, trying to sound demure. 'Would you please outline the major arguments in the document for your application? I will read it all as soon as I have the chance, of course, but if you could just save us some time?'

He threw me the barest glance and then addressed his answer to my aunt. 'We've discovered a subterranean gas pocket in the area that's of a size and grade that will be a viable source of fuel for many years to come. We believe that it's in the best economic interest of the community to mine this resource.'

'And just how did you obtain the data on this area?' I asked. 'Your exploration licence didn't permit you access, and no permission was granted to you by the landowners.' My voice didn't usually sound this composed when I was angry, but all I could think of was the way Bane had accused me of always storming off instead of listening.

'Kolsom surveyors tried their best to remain in the area specified in the licence, but without appropriate signage it appears that they followed the seam too far to the east. They stopped their activities as soon as they realised, and the error was duly reported to the relevant authorities.'

Aunt Lily glared at the 'relevant authority', who was fiddling with his pen and pretending not to notice.

'Nevertheless, the data collected provides sufficient evidence that there is a very large pocket in the heart of the ravine and so we felt it appropriate to submit the application to mine it.'

'How will you get to it? That valley is inaccessible. And it's all old growth forest so you won't be allowed to just bulldoze your way in.'

I gasped as I suddenly realised why he'd tried to burn it. To get past the environmental restrictions. Land that had already been cleared by 'natural' disaster would be pointless for the environmental agency to try to protect. I knew what he'd done. And by the razor sharp look he gave me, he now knew that I knew.

'Nothing is ever really inaccessible,' he said. 'We'll find a way.'

Words buzzed just under my tongue at the threat in his voice, but they were unformed and directionless. I just couldn't think of what to do. If we had been outdoors, he might have copped a good swoop from a magpie though.

'I see. Well, I expect there are all sorts of hoops you still have to jump through to get this application approved. Just the Native Land Act alone would be quite a hurdle, I imagine.'

'This area is not listed on the Aboriginal Heritage Register, so it shouldn't take too long,' he smirked.

My tongue flipped over a word that tasted like iron and bedrock, and the windows began to rattle in their frames. It frightened me so much I gripped the edge of the table and began to hum again to stop myself from forming any more words. Bane was right. I had to learn to calm down and stop behaving like such a drama queen before I broke something. Like a mountain. Or gravity. Aunt Lily stared at me with her mouth slightly open.

'May I just point out that minor earthquakes are a natural occurrence,' Mr Beckinsale said as he put a steadying hand on the jug of water. 'Nothing to do with Kolsom's activities, I can assure you.' He gave a short laugh as if he expected us to be amused at the coincidence, but not even the councillor smiled.

I laid my palms flat on the table and recited the list of elements until the ground was still. And then I practised under my breath to make sure my next words would come out in English.

'Take care, Mr Beckinsale. There are more important things in this world than money,' I said, sliding the pile of documents back to him. 'Aboriginal sacred sites are legally protected whether they're registered or not. And it won't be difficult to get this one listed regardless.' I nodded to Aunt Lily to show them the photos. She came to my aid because

I hadn't been confident that I would be able to do it—the cave art was so close to Eden that I had felt the usual guilt just showing her. It must have been necessary though, because I had no trouble talking about it to the suited executive. That gave me some confidence that I was on the right track as to how to deal with this threat. We would have to be careful; the last thing we needed was for a host of people to turn up on our doorstep to check out the paintings. Luckily, there were thousands of sites listed on the register so hopefully one more wouldn't attract too much attention.

The councillor looked uneasy but Mr Beckinsale exhaled like a bull about to charge. Just how hard could I push him? He had invested a lot into this project, and had already risked lives to get what he wanted.

'We can still mine the valley and leave this site alone,' he said.

'But this area is full of cave systems, and the valley has been left relatively undisturbed up until now. I'm certain that my people will want to keep it that way,' I said, to remind him of my heritage. 'Sacred sites don't just extend to rock paintings, you know. I expect that the remaining members of the local Indigenous community will want the whole valley registered given such evidence of cultural significance.' Thank you, Nalong College curriculum.

He leant towards me, eyes full of malice. 'From my understanding, there aren't many members left. The government probably won't act on your word alone, given the conflict of interest you have in this matter. I suppose we could consult with Harry Doolan, if he was available?'

My heart skipped a beat. If he started to ask questions regarding Harry's whereabouts things would get tricky. He had no close family that I was aware of, but that didn't mean that no one would investigate if we couldn't explain where he was.

'Harry is currently on long service leave,' Aunt Lily piped in. 'He's gone Walkabout and we don't know when he'll be back.'

Nice one. If we could establish that the valley was one of the footprints of the ancestors that formed part of a Songline that Harry was following, it would only aid our claim to get the valley registered. The best part was that it wasn't untrue. If the Garden of Eden didn't count as a sacred site, and the path to it didn't count as a Songline, then I didn't know what would.

She continued smoothly, 'I have no doubt that when he returns, he'll be able to provide whatever information the Aboriginal Affairs Department need.'

The lawyer stayed silent. I could sense his fury just barely controlled. I would have liked to have felt smug or relieved that my plan seemed to be working but all I felt was dread.

And when the meeting finally finished, Bane met us just outside the door, and his eyes locked on to Mr Beckinsale's face with a fury I had only seen in him once before. And the dog had not survived it.

Chapter 32

After the meeting we met up with Noah and Tessa by the river, at the same swimming hole where we had spent our fateful graduation afternoon. It was humbling to think I could have been dog meat that day—or at least been seriously injured. Even having a Guardian wasn't a guarantee that nothing could happen to me. My mother's sudden fall down the riverbank that had caused my father's death had highlighted that. As I stared into the reflections on the water's surface I could almost hear her scream as she'd scrambled with me along the river's edge trying to follow him as he was swept away.

Shaking my head, I started humming the first thing that came to mind to clear away the morbid music but it turned out to be a tragic Nick Cave ballad, which didn't help at all. In the past I had never really worried about my own safety but maybe I was finally becoming responsible. Apparently I was needed now, and that made a difference to how I viewed things. I missed the days when I could just fool around. I missed getting into trouble with Noah each time one of us dared the other to do something crazy.

There was a tidy patch of green below the bridge, with a shady picnic shelter that had been graciously paid for by the local council. They did, after all, try to act in the best interest of the community. Apparently. We ate the lunch Aunt Lily had organised and then cleaned up while she went for a walk along the river. I figured she needed time to rant against Kolsom and the council, and freak out about what I'd done in the meeting without having to guard her language. Noah took our rubbish up to the bin on the street—which funnily enough had a bit of a tilt to it—and came back with a soccer ball he found stashed somewhere in his ute. He and Bane soon found a flattish bit of grass to let off some steam, which they both needed to do badly after hearing what Kolsom were doing.

As I shook my head at the waste of water required to keep the grass here alive while so many farmers were struggling to feed and water their stock, I watched my boys kick around the ball, looking relaxed for the first time in weeks. At least there didn't appear to be any more tension between them. Noah had always been pretty easy going, and it was clear that Bane wasn't going to make any moves towards Tessa so I figured the testosterone levels would stay reasonable.

Tessa pulled an ice block from the esky and ran it across the back of her neck while ogling Noah unashamedly, finally able to enjoy watching him play without having to hide her reactions. 'They could both be models. Easily,' she commented as she watched Noah ball up his T-shirt and toss it away.

I nodded appreciatively just as Bane came in for a rough-looking tackle, which made her hiss, but she stayed seated. It was a testament to how hard she'd worked over the years to control her impulses. No wonder she'd always seemed so highly strung.

'Lainie, what do you think my role really is in all this?' she asked, twisting her hair into a casual knot to get it off her neck. Even in the shade we were struggling with the heat. 'It's not like I would actually be able to protect Noah from anything. All I seem to do is get sick and stressed and make him feel bad about getting on with all the things he loves to do. I don't want to be *that* sort of girlfriend.'

'You mean the sort who argues when he suggests jumping from the bridge into the river, or climbing onto the roof of the hay shed to watch the sunset?' Not that any of Bane's arguments had ever stopped me.

She nodded. 'What am I, his mother? He had enough of that with Claudia. I refuse to be the typical nagging ball and chain. No one likes those.'

'Can you tell that to Bane? And use those exact words. Nagging ball and chain.'

That made her smile for a second. 'So what do you suggest I do instead?'

I fanned myself with a leftover paper plate as I considered. 'Let him do whatever he wants, but do it with him. He's going to have to take risks sometimes, just be there to help if things do go wrong, that's all.'

She nodded, and looked down. 'But seriously, Lainie. It really is hard to resist our reflexes when we know you might get hurt. Go easy on Bane, yeah?'

I was trying to. These compulsions were tying us all up in knots and taking away all sorts of freedom. It didn't seem to be fair on any of us, but that's what duty was. Part of the reason I felt such a desperate need to see Eden was so I could appreciate just what it was we were making these sacrifices for.

'Have you healed him of anything yet?' I asked tentatively. It had been a very intimate and personal experience each time Bane had healed me so I didn't know if she would be happy to discuss it, but when she looked at me and nodded, her eyes were ecstatic.

'Just a couple of minor things, but it felt amazing,' she said, then bit her lower lip. 'Well, to be honest, I kind of passed out the first time, but I'm getting better at it. Bane gave me some hints.' She looked as pleased as a cat carrying a mouse. It made me wonder what Bane had told her.

'Still,' she said, 'I wish he'd chosen a safer sport to get addicted to. It should be easier now that I understand why I was so sick every school holidays when he worked at the hang gliding centre but I'm still going to struggle. He loves to fly, and I wouldn't dream of taking that from him. I just don't know how often I can handle it.'

And I had thought Bane had gone through trauma when I was riding cross-country events. I couldn't imagine what it must have been like for Tessa each time Noah had flown. He'd been so proud of the number of flight hours he had logged for his age. Hours that must have been torture for Tessa. I glared in Noah's direction as if it was his fault.

'Has he been talking about going flying again?' I asked innocently, but she wasn't fooled.

'You know he has, Lainie. You both think on the same wavelength, so don't try to tell me you haven't had the same idea.'

I looked away sheepishly, but as guilty as I felt about what it would put the Guardians through, I simply had to find a way into Eden. Maybe if she felt a bit more in control of her abilities she would find it easier to give Noah some space. She didn't really believe she could protect him, so maybe she felt more nervous than she needed to be. A sly smile came over my face as I thought of a way I could prove that she was useful.

'Let's go and play, Tess. I can see you're struggling to just sit here while my Guardian beats the panties off your Cherub.' I smirked as I finished off the apple core I was eating.

She laughed and ran after me as I took off towards the boys. Noah automatically tried to team up with Tessa against Bane and me, but I quickly bullied them into swapping partners. Noah and I had played together for years and it was time I showed Bane what I was capable of. Besides, this way I could take advantage of the fact that Bane would rather let me have the ball than risk me getting injured. We played for a few minutes, laughing at the complexity of a game where Bane was trying to protect me, Tessa and Noah were trying to protect each other, and I didn't really care who I hurt. Perhaps our carefree days weren't entirely over. Each time Tessa managed to steal the ball to stop Bane from needing to tackle Noah, I glowed with satisfaction. She would never have thought she could keep up with a game between those two brutes. My sense of playfulness jumped a level when Tessa and Bane took control of the ball and managed to get past us, racing for their goal. Noah ran to catch them. I was struggling with the heat, and I knew I had no chance of making it in time. Impulsively I took off anyway, running full pelt not towards them, but straight for Noah instead. I visualised myself bowling him over from behind and was gratified to see Tessa almost flip herself over to turn around as she felt the danger he was in. Just a split second before I slammed into him I realised my mistake, as out of the corner of my eye I saw the look on Bane's face as he pelted after her.

$$\backsim$$

'*What on Earth were you thinking?*' Aunt Lily yelled at me when I admitted what I'd done. Tessa had her wrist submerged in the dregs of ice in the bottom of the esky and Noah was pacing. Bane looked both angry and sick at the same time, and was refusing to look at anything other than his feet. He had done well to only injure her wrist when he'd picked her up and thrown her off me. I felt terrible. It wasn't the first time one of my pranks had backfired but usually I had Noah on my side as I faced the consequences. This time I was well and truly alone in my disgrace. So much for being carefree.

'I'm so sorry, Tess. I really am. I acted on impulse and I stuffed up. I didn't mean for you to get hurt, I promise.' I hovered around her, wishing there was something I could do. She glared at me again, but then slowly started to smile. When she began to chuckle I started to breathe again. At least she could see the funny side. I hoped that meant I hadn't done our relationship any permanent harm. After all those years at school together I was finally starting to like her. Now I just had to make it up to Noah and Bane.

Luckily Tessa's injury didn't seem to be too serious. We came with her to get it X-rayed just in case, which took ages. At least it was cool in the hospital. Tessa insisted that she was a quick healer and that we were all making too much of a fuss, and I wondered if fast healing was a side-effect of her role. That could be useful to know but I wasn't about to suggest any experiments. I was in enough trouble already.

Finally the doctor gave her the all clear. He explained that there was some soft tissue damage and gave her strict instructions to keep icing it as much as possible. I apologised to her again as Noah bundled her carefully into his ute to take her home. She was not looking forward to explaining it to her parents.

It wasn't until we were out finishing up the evening feeds that I had a chance to apologise to Bane. I couldn't believe I'd done it to him again. Yet again I'd forced him to become someone he wasn't. There wasn't a violent bone in his body unless I was nearby. What I was doing to him was far worse than just trapping him in Nalong.

'I really am sorry about what I did today,' I said as I bundled up the net wrapping from the hay and tossed it onto the back of the ute.

'Don't apologise. You're not the one who threw aside an innocent girl like she was a paper doll. I should have controlled myself better.' He latched up the back of the tray with far more force than it required.

'It was my fault that I put you in that situation, though. You couldn't help what you did.'

He spun to face me. 'Couldn't I? How is this compulsion any excuse to hurt Tessa? She's been through enough already. She didn't deserve what I did. I should have been able to hold back.' He had the same look on his face that I had been so familiar with back at school.

I glared right back. 'I wish you had! Then she would have given me what *I* deserved. But then you still would have suffered. I'm the one who messed up. I didn't think through the consequences. I just wanted Tessa to see that she really was capable of protecting Noah. I guess even I underestimated how effective she could be.'

His expression softened a fraction. 'She *was* pretty fast. I nearly didn't get to you in time,' he admitted. 'Does she really doubt her ability to protect him?'

'Probably even more so now,' I sulked, 'given that she was the one who ended up injured.' I'd made a complete mess of things. Poor Tessa.

Bane leant against the ute, still frowning, but thoughtfully. 'I wonder if she would be interested in doing a bit of training with me. Just some basic combat techniques. And some self-defence.'

I raised my eyebrows at him. 'Who would you ever need to fight? No one's likely to attack us, you know.' Even Mr Beckinsale wouldn't go that far, surely.

Bane just shrugged and jumped into the ute, slamming the door. He wasn't going to forgive himself that easily, but at least I'd managed to get him to talk to me again.

∽

My valley.

Looking down into the dense foliage the following day, I reflected that the valley owned me far more than I owned it. Deep down I was beginning to understand the relationship my people had with this country. Dry gusts of wind made a symphony of dancing leaves in every direction, as if the eagles were conducting an orchestra of trees right across the valley. My hair apparently wanted to dance to the music too, and refused to stay in its ponytail for longer than a minute at a time.

With his shirt sleeves rolled up and sweaty hair messed from his helmet, Noah was methodically walking along the edge of the ridge, with Tessa hovering behind. Every now and again he would stop as if trying to sense where the boundary was. He noticed my puzzled expression.

'I'm trying to feel where the Event Horizon crosses over the cliff,' he explained. I raised an eyebrow at him. 'Think about it. If it sometimes crosses inside a cave, and Harry was sometimes able to feel it on his side of the cliff face, then the most likely explanation is that the boundary runs in a clean straight line. This ridge is uneven, so sometimes the edge of the cliff will be on one side of it, sometimes the other. If we can find a spot where the cliff juts out a bit, we should be able to cross over.'

Sometimes Noah accidentally revealed just how smart he was. How careless of him. I followed him up the hill. It would be a huge advantage if we could see where we were trying to get to. Even I hadn't been keen on the idea of jumping into the complete unknown, even if Harry did say it was an open landscape. Bane found my hand and gripped it, and I squeezed back reassuringly. It hadn't helped last time, but if it made him feel calmer I was happy to oblige.

It was another half an hour before we found what we had been searching for. I was watching a giant wedge-tailed eagle fly out from the cliff when it suddenly vanished in mid-air, as if to show us how it should be done. I had no idea what the rules were for animals crossing the boundary, but if any were to be allowed in, it would be those amazing birds. And possibly doves. Suddenly I heard Tessa cry out as Noah disappeared from view.

'Calm down, Tess. Don't get too close to the edge trying to find him, it won't help,' I called, hurrying to where he had vanished. I had *felt* him disappear as well and I realised now how disturbing it was.

Bane pulled me up short. 'Lainie. Please be careful. I can't help you once you cross. Please don't get too carried away.'

I gave him a quick kiss on the cheek, which startled him enough that he let me go.

'I'll only be a few minutes, I promise. I just want to have a look.'

He took his watch off and strapped it to my wrist. I got the message. Then he nodded and planted his feet, standing with his arms crossed and looking seriously vigilant as if on sentry duty. I smiled at him, winked, and then stepped across the boundary into Paradise.

Chapter 33

Once again I felt the peculiar feeling of something moving through my skin and wrapping itself around some hidden part of me, as if part of my soul was being held back, unable to cross. The dry wind fell flat, replaced with a sweet humid breeze that I couldn't help but inhale deeply to catch the floral scent. My mind was momentarily blank as I stared out across the valley, until I noticed Noah sitting at my feet with his legs dangling over the edge of the cliff and silent tears streaming down his face. There was so little space between the boundary and the massive drop below us that I had to move very carefully.

I cautiously sat down next to him, trying not to crush the delicate flowers that had somehow managed to grow right up to the stony edge. Intense beauty slapped each of my senses as if scolding me for taking so long to arrive and appreciate it, and in that instant everything I thought I understood about perfection changed. The prettiest diamond, the most breathtaking view, the most delicious chocolate and the softest silk all suddenly stank in my memory in comparison to what I was experiencing of Eden.

Noah and I stared, overwhelmed by the beauty that was inherent in everything we saw. We had to keep blinking away the instinctive tears that came from the profound realisation that we had come home. My mind struggled to absorb the dichotomy between the two worlds. It was as if all the best fantasy writers and movie artists from around the globe had brainstormed together to create the perfect faerie tale land and then handed their ideas over to God, who then surreptitiously chucked the whole lot out while they weren't looking and made Eden instead. It was a thousand times better.

Every one of my pores was busy trying to absorb the heavenly fragrance of the air. Honey-sweet and delicately perfumed with spicy blossoms, I would have paid a fortune for even a tiny bottle of such a scent. It was so very *real*. Where my mind had naively imagined a pink sky and sparkling rainbows, instead I saw natural grass and trees and rippling fields. It was Earth. But it was perfect. It was also huge. Clearly Eden was so much more than a small valley of manicured lawns. We could see majestic snow-capped mountains in the distance where a moment ago there had been dry dusty plains. There were thick forests to the north full of huge trees and birds flying everywhere. I could see magnificent herds of animals below. Some I recognised but some I didn't, and I was itching to get closer and see what they all were. There were so many that it reminded me of the start of the *Lion King*. If there had been a lion cub handy I would have lifted it up to show them all. It was all simply spectacular. And at the heart of it all was a wide river that embraced the land in its soft curves. No. It wasn't a river, it was *the* River. It was so majestic that it defined the word. And apparently I wasn't the only one who felt the need to redefine my language.

'*Ambrosial*,' Noah whispered. 'I get what it means now.' He took my hand in his. We had shared so much of our lives and I was deeply gratified that he was with me for this. His presence was so comforting now that I was faced with the reality of our task. This place was sacrosanct, and needed to remain a secret. There was no doubt in my mind that if the human race knew all this was here, they would stop at nothing until they found a way in. And that *could not* be permitted. I rested my head on his shoulder and stared out over Paradise.

Despite my intention to only spend a few short minutes there, when I checked Bane's watch I realised that more than forty minutes had passed since we had first arrived. Even then it was difficult to feel any sense of urgency. I knew the other two would be frantic but it was so hard to focus on why that was such a big problem. They would want us to cross back.

'So is it possible?' I asked Noah quietly. He knew what I meant. We were both impatient to get down there.

He nodded. 'Very possible. There are plenty of places to land and plenty of birds to show us where the thermals are.'

I stood and pulled Noah up with me. 'We need to go,' I told him.

'Already? Why?' he asked sounding surprised and slightly annoyed.

'Tess will be worried.'

'But I'm fine. Why should she worry?'

'Because she doesn't know that you're fine. She will want you to come back now.' I tugged at him as I tried to concentrate on how the others must be feeling. I didn't want them to feel bad and that seemed to be the only thing that mattered to me. I dragged Noah away from the view. A moment of confusion made me pause as I came to terms with the fact that the view behind me had also completely altered. Lush forest growth begged for exploration, and just a couple of metres from where I stood a giant lace monitor clung to the side of a ridged tree trunk. There was no evidence to suggest that I couldn't walk straight up to it. Suddenly concerned that we had somehow become lost, I stretched out my fingers to feel for the boundary. Did I even want to feel it? A very dominant part of me wanted it to be gone so that I could just step forward and be part of this new world. A tingle met my touch, and I sighed in a mixture of relief and disappointment.

Remembering how Bane's hand always dissolved out of my grasp as I crossed over, I pushed Noah through from behind so I could be sure he wouldn't get distracted again. The second I crossed over I was hit by such a crushing wave of guilt that I started trembling. I had promised Bane I would be quick. I'd wanted to show him I could be trusted, but I hadn't counted on the complete lack of focus that I'd had once I crossed over. It was incredible that Harry had made it to our meetings at all.

It looked like Bane had been pacing along the ridge because he spun around as soon as I appeared. He was visibly struggling not to run over and throw himself at me like last time, so I went to him instead and hugged him an apology. He held me for what would have been considered far too long in polite company but I was in no hurry to move. I could feel his heart thumping in his chest, subsiding as his anxiety lessened. My body yearned to hold him closer and my mind struggled to remember why that was a bad thing to do. All I could think of was kissing him again as I felt him stroke my hair, and I started to turn my face towards his, but then he let me go and I almost cried. Perhaps my feelings were magnified by the fact that I had just walked away from the most spiritual experience of my life, because it was physically painful the way I ached for him. Just as well he had pulled away. I crossed my arms to prevent myself from reaching out to him.

Noah and Tessa showed no such restraint. It was even worse than when Claudia had been all over him. Claudia had kissed him in public to show the world that he was hers, but Tessa kissed him as if the rest of the world didn't exist. A small wave of jealousy washed over me, but I wasn't sure if it was because she was stealing my best friend away or because what they had was so refreshingly uncomplicated. Probably both.

'So what's it like?' Bane asked, distracting me from my thoughts. I looked up at him dreamily. I wanted to tell him it was like looking into his eyes when he smiled at me. It was beautiful and peaceful and easy, and full of exciting promises.

'It's amazing. It's so pretty, and real, and ... huge.' I stumbled over the ridiculously inadequate words. I wanted so much to be able to share this with him. If only he could see it. Guilt welled in the back of my throat at the thought. He couldn't be allowed to know! I couldn't tell him anything. My head was filled with such conflicting thoughts. I desperately wanted him to experience Eden and yet I felt appalled at the thought of allowing him to know any details. It made no sense but that didn't change a thing. It was such a fundamental part of who we all were and I couldn't even begin to explain it to him. Now that I had experienced Eden for myself, I understood why our lives had been turned upside down, and all of it seemed such a paltry price to pay to safeguard something so precious, but he would never know. I just kind of sobbed and exhaled in frustration while he waited for me to say more.

'You can't tell me,' he realised, with only the slightest hint of jealousy. 'It's okay. I understand what that's like. I can see it was a profound experience for you and that's all I need to know. If you want to get into Eden then I'll do what I can to help you. Just don't try to tell me it's for my benefit.'

I nodded soberly. There were so many reasons for me to get into that valley; if he didn't want to hear my main one, that was fine by me. I had plenty more.

Chapter 34

By the time we met Harry again, we had a plan more or less finalised. Noah would 'borrow' the tandem harness he'd been practising with at the training centre and attach it to his own glider. If anyone ever found out, he could kiss his licence goodbye, but Noah never let anything stand in the way of what he wanted for long. He assured me that he could safely take us both on a short flight with minimal risk, but he would have to return the harness as quickly as possible before anyone noticed it was missing. I was curious as to who he would have to charm to get away with such a stunt.

Harry was happy to scout out a suitable area for landing, and he and Noah spent considerable time discussing the safest way to do it. Meanwhile, I was rapidly becoming more worried about getting out than getting in. Tessa suggested that if our abilities were based on the need to protect Eden then perhaps they could engineer a threat that would force us to come out. Her reasoning felt ridiculously flimsy to me, and naturally Noah and I hated the idea, but Bane and Tessa ignored us. They schemed between themselves, explaining that the less we knew about it, the better the threat would work, as we wouldn't know if the danger was real or not. I argued that I already knew the threat wouldn't be real so it wouldn't work anyway. Tessa just smiled secretively.

The biggest flaw I saw in their plan was Sarah. If there was a Cherub available outside Eden to stop the threat, then we wouldn't be needed, so we wouldn't be compelled to force our way out.

'I'll talk to her,' Harry stated. 'She's never wanted anything to do with Eden so it shouldn't be hard to convince her to leave the area.' He looked sombre, as if he was unhappy with her, or perhaps, like me, he was simply uncomfortable that we were planning to deliberately leave the place unprotected just so we could manipulate our powers in order to get home again. Harry's rock fall had not been a bad idea, and he wouldn't have been able to do it if he hadn't believed it was necessary. And if Kolsom did get their licence approved and send people into the area, then the last thing we should be doing was trying to remove it. We'd sent a well-worded email with a few photo attachments to the Office of Aboriginal Affairs, which seemed to have achieved what a host of community rallies could not. Kolsom's licence application was immediately put on hold while our submission to have the valley listed on the Heritage Register was being processed. That whole afternoon was spent doing nothing but eating gelati and listening to Tessa's trip-hop music playlist to celebrate, but Aunt Lily warned us that there was still a lot of work to do before the process was complete.

'It would be easier if Harry could talk to them,' she said to me that evening when we were picking the first of the plums in our little orchard. 'He's got a way of talking to people that makes them see things his way, and he's the recognised Elder for this area. Do you think you can really bring him home?'

I thought about what Sarah had said to me, about how I shouldn't try to talk him into coming back if he didn't want to, but Aunt Lily was right. He was needed here. 'That's why you're letting me go, isn't it?'

She put her bucket down and turned to me. 'Lainie, we both know that I couldn't stop you from going, nor would I. Your authority far exceeds mine when it comes to Eden. I have to trust that you know what you're doing.'

'I'll come back. I will.'

She hugged me. 'If you can.'

❧

Everything happened quite quickly after that. Noah and Tessa took some tandem flights together under the supervision of Noah's instructor at the hang gliding centre. Part of the idea was that Tessa would hopefully feel more relaxed about him flying once she grew accustomed to how safe it really was. I wished I could do the same for Bane. Then Noah 'accidentally' brought the tandem harness home instead of his own. He hoped that would buy us a bit of time. I hoped we would be forgiven for lying.

My own preparations basically consisted of spending a whole after-noon locked away in my room so I could draft a letter to Aunt Lily, thanking her for everything she'd done for me over the years, just in case we couldn't return. Or in case I went loopy. It was a good letter. I made myself cry. I also left her with the Army Recruitment letter for Bane, with strict instructions to make sure he got it if I didn't come home. And if that happened, what would my aunt tell everyone? So I put together a rather vague fake plan to go backpacking around Australia. It was a credible thing to do between school and uni, and it could last for as long as I needed it to.

The most frustrating part was having to wait for the weather. Summer in the Wimmera was pretty predictable but it could get very windy. It felt like a lifetime passed before Noah finally declared that the conditions were adequate. We had both developed an uncanny affinity for the weather since the day we had called the storm, but just because I could sense changes in air pressure didn't mean I could tell when it would be safe to jump off a cliff. Noah's confidence was contagious, though, so when he called after dinner to confirm that the weather was still on track for the following morning, I did a little happy dance.

Aunt Lily tried to look enthusiastic about it. She was holding up well, considering how little detail we'd been able to provide her. On Harry's suggestion, she was taking Sarah with her to the city to try to ratify our submission to the Aboriginal Affairs department, and Caleb and Liam had offered to take care of the farm. They'd teased Noah and me about taking Tessa and Bane away for a few days to an undisclosed location, but it was easier to let them think what they wanted. At least it meant they didn't try to pry for details. Well, not much anyway. Nicole was ecstatic at being asked to take over the care of the joey.

That night I lay awake, stressing about how I really needed a good night's sleep, and tried to imagine what I would say when I met my mother. All these years I had thought she was dead, and she had appar-ently thought the same about me. Is that why she never came back? Had I been deprived of my mother all my life because of a simple lack of communication? But Noah's mum had mentioned my mother had thought I was dead when I was a baby, sleeping in her arms.

Staring at the ceiling, I tried to control my nerves. What if she didn't remember me? What if she didn't *want* to meet me? What if she did want me but we didn't get along? I had a hundred different scenarios whirling through my mind, some of which belonged in musical theatre, most belonged in a dinnertime soap opera. Eventually there came a gentle tap on my window.

'Bane! I'm keeping you up, aren't I? What are you doing outside?' I opened the window and a thousand tiny bugs flew in and dazzled themselves in ecstasy around my bedside lamp.

'I couldn't sleep either, not your fault,' he assured me. 'Come for a walk?'

He'd thrown on a pair of jeans and a loose white shirt, which made him look like he'd misplaced his luxury yacht. I glanced at the clock—it was well after midnight. I had never been on a clandestine night-time adventure before. Not even with Noah. A small shiver went up my spine at the thought of Bane inviting me to sneak out the window. Of course, had she known, Aunt Lily probably would have encouraged it, which made it not quite so thrilling, but still.

My old boots looked terrific with my Tintin pyjamas as I clambered through the window. Bane eased me to the ground far more gracefully than I would have managed on my own and then took my hand and led me to the top of the hill behind the house. The smell of honey drifted in with the warm night breeze. Nearby amongst the trees I could hear possums jumping between branches and a koala roaring. The world came alive at night as the industrious societies of native animals went about their business, completely indifferent to our meaningless day-time activities. In some ways I wished I could join them.

We found a flat bit of dry grass to lie down on and stared quietly at the sky bling for a while. Nothing else existed in the world except the feel of his presence beside me and it was all I could do to stop myself reaching for him. With a sinking feeling I realised how foolish I had been to come out here. The way my blood was singing, it would proba-bly only lead to more confusion.

'Lainie, are you really planning to come back?' he asked softly after a few minutes, snapping my attention away from the feel of his shoulder touching mine.

I sat up. 'Of course I am! This is my home. I'll find a way back some-how.' Did he really think I would abandon this world so easily?

His shoulders relaxed slightly. 'And what are you hoping to achieve

by going? Is it really just about your mother, and bringing Harry home?'
He sat up as well and looked me in the eye. 'Or is it me? I can leave if
you want me to, Lainie. You don't have to risk your life to get away from
me. I can manage if I stay in town.'

I gaped at him stupidly. Me get away from him? These days I struggled
just to leave a room he was in. My brain had been having panic attacks
whenever I tried to imagine letting him go permanently. When had I
become so dependent on his company? I hadn't planned on it, and I had
barely noticed it happening, but now that he said it like that, I couldn't
begin to imagine what my life would be like without him around. How
could I ever make him leave? The problem was, I couldn't afford to let
him know how I felt, but I couldn't make myself lie to him either, so
instead I just stared at him like a startled rabbit with my heart thudding.

His mouth began to curl up into *that* smile.

'I knew it. You don't want me to go.' He looked triumphant.

'What makes you say that?' I squeaked.

'Your heart rate. I'm getting more attuned to you every day.' He
picked up my hand and ran his fingertips lightly from my wrist to my
shoulder. They burned deliciously, and I quivered. His touch thrilled
me—and he could feel it. There was a profound promise there.

'Listen, I understand that you need to do this. You need to experience
Eden and find out who you are. You should find your mother, and maybe
you'll even find a way to resolve the sadness in the river music. But please
don't think you're doing this for me. Just because the link is broken when
you're there doesn't mean I'll stop feeling what I feel.' Leaning towards
me, he waited until I was brave enough to look him in the eye. 'I want
to stay with you. I love it here.' He took my hand again, entwining our
fingers. 'And I love you.' His voice was soft and confident. 'I couldn't let
you go without telling you. I don't care if it's pre-destined or if I'm just
the world's luckiest guy; I'm just grateful to have had this time with you.
I keep waiting for the bubble to burst. For my life to go back to the way it
was, and I'm dreading it. Please just let me stay a little longer?'

Reason had vanished into the depths of his silver eyes, his long eyelashes making them seem large enough to drown in. It would be so easy
to give in to this feeling. It was right, and natural, and exciting. But was
it real?

Gathering my wits together was like trying to hold ten puppies at once. 'Bane. I want you to do something for me. When I'm there, when you're not under the influence of this compulsion to protect me, I want you to step away for a while.'

He froze.

'Just for a few days,' I qualified. 'Go into town and spend some time with other people. Talk to a stranger. Do something you've never done before. Get some perspective back and then examine how you really feel.' I clasped my arms around my knees and studied my old dusty work boots. 'I'm nothing special, Bane. I'm just me. If you find that without the compulsion you stop feeling this way, then I promise I'll stay away from you and let all of this become just an embarrassing memory. A secret that I'll keep. No one will have to know how you almost fell for Lanky Lainie. I'll find a way to let you get on with your life.'

He looked exasperated. 'And if I still feel the same?'

I smiled wistfully. That would be far too good to be true. I just hoped that when the time came, he would be honest enough with himself to admit I was right.

The next morning Sarah's Pajero rumbled up our driveway road just as the early sun was glowing through the dust. I could see Noah and Tessa cuddling in the back seat. The plan was for us all to leave at the same time, so that everyone would assume we'd all gone together to the city before parting company. Tessa got out hauling a huge backpack almost bigger than she was. She was planning to stay in the cave until we found a way to come home. Bane had packed too, but not as heavily; he'd agreed to go to Horsham to see some friends. The Ashbree twins weren't due until late afternoon so he would have time to come back and get his sedan. They would just assume we'd taken that car too.

All too quickly it was time for Sarah and my aunt to leave and I hugged Aunt Lily far too tightly but she didn't seem to mind.

'Come back to me,' she whispered, a tremor in her voice betraying her worry.

'I will. Even if I have to dismantle the rock fall one pebble at a time,' I promised. I glanced at Bane lifting her suitcase into the Pajero. 'Just in case I don't, you'll talk to Bane like we discussed?'

'Of course. But I can't make him do anything. He needs to make his own choices.'

'I know. That's the whole point,' I said with a wry smile.

'Take care of my son, won't you, Lainie?' Sarah asked as she gave me a quick hug. As if he wasn't the one responsible for both our lives as we jumped off a cliff.

'As always. And good luck with the registration process. Hopefully it will get these miners off our backs for good so we can get on with better things.'

She nodded, looking eager and determined. She was probably grateful to be able to finally contribute something useful to protecting Eden without compromising her family.

As they drove away, I reflected that there was a very real possibility that I would never see either of them again. Or my home. Strictly I disciplined my thoughts to focus on the task at hand. If I let myself dwell on things too much I would never be able to follow through with the plan. Even so, I couldn't stop myself looking at each shed and tree and gate we passed, thinking that it might be the last time I saw them.

When the four of us made it to the top of the ridge, the last few tufts of early morning mist were only just managing to grasp at the tree tops below us. There was a light southerly breeze that promised to give a little relief from the heat later on. I began to help Noah unpack the glider, but he stopped and gave me the same look as when I'd tried to help him set up the tent the last time we went camping. I was perfectly capable, but he could be a bit of a control-freak sometimes. Still, he had a point this time. Hanging in the air strapped to a hang glider was probably not a good time to discover I had put the right pole in the wrong place.

Bane pulled me aside. 'I have something for you to take,' he said, handing me an envelope. I peeked inside. He'd printed off a few small photos of himself, Aunt Lily, and even some of the Ashbrees that had been taken at Christmas. 'Just to help you remember,' he said seriously.

As if I could ever forget the people I loved—but I tucked it into my back pocket, hoping that it wouldn't be all I was left with if things went wrong.

'Thank you, Bane. I know this isn't easy for you.' I leant forward and whispered in his ear. 'Just for the record, how are you feeling? Do you honestly feel that I'm in danger?'

A mix of emotions crossed his face. 'I'm so tempted to say yes,' he admitted. 'And to say that I can't help but do whatever it takes to stop you from taking this insane leap of faith. The truth is, I don't feel anything compulsive. I still want to stop you, but only because I don't want you to leave.' My shoulders relaxed slightly. 'Lainie, that doesn't mean much. It could just be that my pre-cognition can't see what happens to you past the boundary.'

Hmm, good point. He had obviously been thinking this through a lot. I had come to rely on his senses to keep me safe, but I was about to jump into the unknown with no such reassurance. He noticed my worried frown and his face became gentle.

'Listen, I trust Noah. He knows what he's doing. It's only a short drop really, as these things go.' He squared his shoulders. 'And you need to do this, if only so I can prove to you that what we feel is real.'

I hoped he wouldn't be too hard on himself when he came to his 'real' senses. I looked over at Noah. He'd finished setting up the rig and was checking the harness and safety gear. It had taken less than ten minutes, and it had gone quickly. It was time to find out what reality was like.

What I hadn't been game to mention to Bane of course, was that the cliff was much higher in Eden than it appeared from this side. Noah didn't seem fazed by that though, so I had no reason to worry. So my head told me.

We cleared the take-off site as well as we could, moving away branches and rocks that could trip us over. We would need a good run up to launch, the idea being that we would be more or less airborne before we even reached the edge. That, of course, meant that we would be crossing the Event Horizon partway through the launch. Bane and Tessa would have no idea whether we managed to even launch safely, let alone land.

As Noah strapped me into the harness I tried to stop myself from shaking. It was more in anticipation than fear, but I still hoped no one would notice. To distract myself, I whimsically tried to imagine what the Eden locals would think when they saw Noah and I descending like a giant winged bird. The glider was not exactly discreet; it was white and yellow with a large picture of the manufacturing company's winged eye logo on each side. In wry amusement I wondered if that meant that technically we had two sets of wings, like the Cherubim in the Bible. Our helmets alone made us look like creatures from outer space.

Finally Noah was satisfied with our preparations. He gave Bane a solid slap on the shoulder, and Bane nodded and looked at him meaningfully. It was clear they'd had words, but I was glad they had done it in private. Tessa was holding up well, back straight and her chin held high, determined not to appear weak. I couldn't believe the change in her since school. A few months ago she would have been swooning in fear. Finding out the truth about her role had given her more freedom to be herself, not less, and I was glad for her. Noah swept her up in a tight embrace, whispering in her ear, and she smiled coyly in response.

I glanced over at Bane only to catch him watching me with his arms crossed. Tension knotted his jaw. 'You're humming again,' he said. 'Are you certain you want to do this? It's not too late to pull out, you know.'

I poked my tongue out at him, trying to appear nonchalant, but he wasn't fooled.

He gave me a quick kiss on the cheek before I could protest. 'Stay safe, Lainie. Come to the cave as soon as you can. I'll be waiting.'

And that was it. Noah had drilled me on what I needed to do and I'd even had a few practice runs from the top of the hill paddock at home. It seemed fairly straightforward. Noah would do most of the work; all I had to do was keep up. Unfortunately I was now regretting the night I'd spent watching YouTube videos of all the things that had gone wrong for people in the past. It had seemed funny at the time.

We positioned ourselves carefully and Noah finished his final preparations before gripping the frame ready for launch.

'Ready, Lainie?' He grinned at me, his eyes ecstatic. This was the Noah I knew, ready to experience something new, and ready to take me with him into the unknown. I smiled back and nodded.

He counted down from five and then we were running, and in just a few short seconds I could feel my feet lifting off the ground. We passed through the boundary so fast that I hardly had a chance to register the feeling, but I certainly noticed the sudden change of scenery and atmosphere. Even the wind was different, which gave me a brief moment of panic, but it was far too late to pull out. Why had we even bothered waiting for the right weather conditions? They meant nothing here. With my heart doing backflips in my chest I hoped desperately that Noah would be able to keep his focus better than the last time. The edge of the cliff came rushing towards us and then it was gone—and we were flying.

Chapter 35

Like the first shocking gasp of a cold shower on a sweaty day, my entire body felt washed clean and crisp as we crossed out of our world. I felt as though I had suddenly woken up, and whatever I had been dreaming of mere seconds beforehand had become completely obsolete. I caught my breath as the valley opened up below us, shining joyfully in the bright sun.

Instead of the expected sound of the wind roaring in my ears as the air rushed past, it was actually very quiet and serene. Gently Noah leant to the right and the glider started to turn. The view was overwhelmingly magnificent. It was a good thing there was not much Noah needed to do to keep us safe, because everything around us was really distracting. Everywhere I looked there was something amazing to see. A wedge-tailed eagle soared ahead of us, as if guiding the way. In fact, there were so many birds in the sky that I was grateful the eagle was there to keep them away. The last thing we needed was to land in Paradise covered in snarge.

As we circled back towards the cliff I could see how different Eden was from the world we knew. The bright snow-topped mountains to the north eased down to a wide grassy plain, but the cliff blocked the rest of the view. I stretched my neck to see where the River cut through the cliff to the south, wide and sparkling and sapphire blue. Easily the most brilliant and captivating treasure amongst a wealth of stunning images, it made the river back home look like a pathetic brown streamlet.

Noah craned his head back to me and laughed. 'You can stop strangling my shoulder now, Lainie, the hard part's done. So what do you think of flying?'

We were strapped in not quite side-by-side, and so I let go of his

T-shirt and rested my chin on his shoulder instead. 'Why haven't I done this before? You should have told me,' I accused. 'This is brilliant! It's nothing like I expected … it feels so natural.' As he laughed I was hit with a sudden insight. 'Do you think maybe Cherubim are supposed to fly? Maybe it's like a primal instinct. Maybe when we die we'll revert back to our natural form and do this all the time. I hope so. I could definitely get used to this.' All my nervous anticipation had dissolved away like a snowflake in the sun and I was feeling utterly euphoric.

Noah let go of the bar and I glared at him in a panic. Had he lost his mind? Become so overwhelmed by the transition across the boundary that he had forgotten he had to steer?

'Have a go. It's easy.'

I grabbed the bar in a death grip.

'Just lean the way you want to turn.'

I leant. We turned. I let out a not so quiet 'woo-hoo'. It really was very simple and Noah's laugh was contagious.

My eyes drank in all the sights, desperately trying to absorb all the details. I felt as if we could just fly over to the mountains and land on a snowy outcrop, or dive down and skim the surface of the lake to the west. I could see herds of grazing animals down below, completely unaware of our presence. Part of me couldn't wait to get down there, but at the same time I wanted to keep flying forever.

After a few minutes Noah took back the controls and let the glider circle gradually down, making minor adjustments as he began to aim for the landing site.

'Lainie, can I ask you something?'

Great. I had thought this might happen. 'I guess so. Now is the time, I can hardly go storming off if you offend me, can I?'

He smiled an evil little smile. 'Why are you so reluctant to admit you have feelings for Bane? Surely you can see he's smitten with you, so it can't be the good old fear of rejection stopping you. What's the problem, exactly?'

Good gracious. Straight to the point. The razor sharp pointy point. He looked at me with his blazing green eyes and turned on his most dazzling dimpled smile. He knew perfectly well he could get away with trampling my most personal barriers when he did that, and I gave in and fell for it, as usual. Maybe it was because we were in Eden, and my inhibitions were as lost as a lamb in a gully, or maybe I had just had enough of trying to protect other people's feelings, but all I knew was that I wanted desperately to tell my best friend everything. The whole truth, for better or worse. So I thought for a few moments.

'I don't trust it,' I admitted. 'I don't trust his feelings. I mean, look at him, Noah. As if someone like him would ever fall for someone like me under normal circumstances. I should probably just count my lucky stars and make the most of it, but that would be horribly unfair to him. Imagine if I'd done that with you? Any girl in town would have given their right arm for an opportunity to get as close to you as I did. Imagine if I'd taken advantage of that?' I had a vague far off feeling that I was saying way too much, but I couldn't seem to remember why.

'I don't understand. Are you saying you would have gone out with me if I'd asked?' His emerald eyes searched mine.

'Hell, yeah! I've loved you ever since I can remember. But I would never do that to you. So no.'

He looked even more confused than I was. My brain was fuzzy. Was it the altitude or just Eden?

'What if I asked now?'

I looked at him. 'Do you mean hypothetically or are you asking me out?'

'Maybe that depends on your answer,' he replied, sounding unsure himself.

I thought for a few long seconds. 'No. I wouldn't. Everything's different now. We had our chance, and neither of us took it. There has to be a reason for that.'

He nodded. And I nodded. At least now we knew.

Harry had chosen a nice clear landing site for us near a loop in the River. It was easy to locate, which was a relief given that he couldn't even draw us a map. Finally I spotted him, waving his arms above his head. Noah eased the glider towards him and released our legs from the harness. I relaxed my legs like he had instructed me, even though I felt as though the ground was about to punish me for leaving it. Noah pushed the bar out slowly and the glider flared into an upright position.

We slowed so gently to a stop that I hardly needed to take a single step. A bit of an anticlimax, really. Just the way I wanted it.

Noah started to unstrap my harness for me, but then Harry reached us and caught us both in a massive hug that was rougher than our landing. It was unlike him, and it felt wonderful, like it was the most natural thing in the world.

'I've missed you, Harry!' I cried, tangling everything to hug him back.

'Sorry I left you,' he apologised, looking almost teary. He helped to extricate us from all the straps. 'You have no idea how long I've waited for this moment. How was your flight?'

'Exhilarating! I want to go again!'

'Beware flight addiction,' Noah said sagely. Like he was one to talk. I punched him on the shoulder. 'Ow! What was that for?'

'For not taking me up sooner,' I grumbled, shaking out my helmet hair and choosing to ignore the fact that I had been too stingy with my money to accept any of his previous invites. He just shook his head at me and continued to dismantle his rig. Now that we had landed it was easy to let go of the melancholy we had experienced earlier. There was far too much here to distract us.

Actually, I was impressed with his ability to focus on the task. I was impatient to have a proper look around, but I also knew it would be best to pack the glider away before too many of the locals saw it. Already I noticed a man coming towards us with a curious expression on his face. He had long dark curly hair and large brown eyes. Everything about him looked innocent, with none of the defensive or cynical body language that most people our age had developed. It made him look very young, despite his short beard.

He greeted Harry with a funny looking wave. 'Like a … bird,' he said, flapping his wrists to demonstrate. 'Can I do it?'

'Not today.'

The man didn't argue, or follow, as the three of us lifted the gear and walked away from the clearing. I whispered in Harry's ear. 'Aren't you afraid he might experiment and get hurt?'

He laughed. 'You have a lot to learn about Eden. You can't get hurt here. Unless you want to.'

'And how does that work exactly?' Noah beat me to the question.

'See those trees? The giant ones with the yellow fruit?'

They were everywhere, and they were easily the most beautiful species of tree I had ever seen. We walked over to the nearest one to examine it more closely. It had a massive silver trunk and long willowy branches that started high over our heads but were weighed down with clusters of golden fruit, each about the size of a peach. The leaves looked grey-green and feathery, and they smelled spicy and minty and intoxicating.

'The Tree of Life grows on each side of the River,' Harry explained.

Wow. I had assumed there was only the one. I'd never expected the Tree of Life to refer to a whole species. What about the other tree? The Tree of Knowledge of Good and Evil? Was the damage already done or would there be dire consequences if I accidentally ate the wrong thing?

'The way I understand it,' he continued, 'is that the Fruit contains something fundamental to life itself. Eating it heals everything that's physically wrong with you. It can even resurrect the dead.' He reached out a trembling hand as if to stroke one of them, but stopped just a few centimetres from it. 'I think it might even do more than that. I believe that eating it makes you forget all sadness, all worries, and all grief.' He exhaled and drew his hand away. 'It's like the perfect drug. It gives instant pain relief, instant healing and makes you feel good. Apparently you can remember that you were hurt but you just can't quite remember what hurting felt like. And there are no real side effects. It even stops you from ageing. It's 100% good for you.'

I looked at him dubiously. 'So why won't you touch it?'

His fingers twitched slightly, but he drew them away. 'Because I'm choosing to remember some things that aren't good for me,' he said drolly.

'Did my mother eat the Fruit? Is that why she went crazy?'

His reply was too sharp for such a serene setting. 'She's not crazy. This place changes you, but she's not crazy. And she only started eating from the Tree recently.' He tucked his hands under his elbows. 'All of Kolsom's recent mucking around nearby awakened compulsions in her that she didn't know how to handle, so she chose to forget instead.' He turned to look at me directly. 'She's here, Lainie, and she knows you're coming. I expect she'll come and find us at some point ...'

I could sense his hesitation. 'But, you don't think she'll remember me?' I guessed.

'She remembers you as a baby. She might not believe it's you. She still insists that you're dead.'

Lost in thought, I stumbled along behind him as he wove his way through a herd of grazing antelope-like creatures. What was I supposed to say to her? I felt as if I should be nervous about meeting her, but it was difficult to feel nervous about anything here. Besides, our first priority was to get to the cave. We had to let Bane and Tessa know we were all right. And hide the glider. And then work out how to get home. At some point. Only problem was, Noah had just put down his end of the glider and had started to climb a tree.

'Wow, Lainie, you should try this. Look how high I'm getting!'

Harry just shook his head. 'Noah!' he called enticingly. 'Tessa would like to see you. Please come down so we can go to the cave.'

'Right. Tessa. She wants to see us. I'll come down.'

I watched him climb down, making the branches shake and drop spinning seedpods. It did look kind of fun. Harry glared at me sternly. Right. I had to keep my mind on the job. It was important that we got to the cave as quickly as possible—just as soon as I had a drink of water from the River.

It must have taken a good hour for Harry to coax us all the way to the cave. Luckily we didn't see any other people. I wouldn't have known what to say.

'Harry, how is it that the people here speak English?'

'They don't. They communicate mostly in sign language but they learn fast. I've only spoken to that man twice before. He was interested in my language so I spent some time teaching him. He remembers everything.'

Mentally I berated myself for making the assumption that the young man must have been a bit slow-witted because he hardly spoke, when really the opposite was true. We shouldn't have taken so long to get the glider out of sight. I hurried the rest of the way to the cave entrance, relaxing only when we entered the chilly tunnel.

This side of the cave system was much the same as the other, except that there was a lot more light, so the sparkling glitter of the stalactites was even more beautiful than on the Nalong side. Even the walls looked like they were made from thousands of miniscule Christmas lights. Everything was enhanced here. It even smelled better. Like chalk mixed with marble and ancient secrets. The walls felt so smooth and cool, and tiny bright-winged insects flitted about like they were dancing …

Harry gripped my hand and dragged me along. Poor Harry. It must have been like trying to herd sheep, keeping Noah and me on track. It was difficult enough to get the long glider through the winding tunnel even when we were paying attention.

Eventually we rounded a corner and I felt the hot blast from the sword. Able now to see it close up in its full glory, I stood and stared at the entrancing way the bronze and golden flames curled delicately around its white glittering edges. It was so beautiful.

Harry put down his end of the glider and eased his way past the giant weapon, shielding his face from the heat. He disappeared mid-step.

Bane would be close. Just on the other side of the boundary. A smile crept over my face and my blood started racing in anticipation of seeing him again. It had only been a couple of hours, but I missed him so much. Part of my brain told me I should stop thinking like that, but I couldn't work out why. Why shouldn't I admit to myself that I missed him? I wanted to see him. Immediately. Rushing past the sword, ignoring the sting of the heat on my cheek and brow, I felt my skin tingle as I crossed the Event Horizon. Suddenly I saw a gap in the wall beyond, which hadn't been there a second ago because it only existed on one side of the boundary. Bane's face was crammed into the hole in the rocks and I laughed openly at the expression on his face. I needed to kiss him and tell him not to look so worried. I took two quick steps but then stopped as if I had been slapped. What was I doing? No kissing! That wasn't the plan. I wanted him to forget me for a while, didn't I? Two hours was nowhere near enough time for him to really think things through.

'I'm here. We made it, no problems. Everything's fine. Sorry we took so long,' I said, trying to disguise my internal confusion.

He threw me a relieved grin. 'Actually, we only just made it here ourselves. Tessa has great reflexes but she's never ridden a dirt bike before, and her wrist is still a bit tender, so we had to take it slow coming down from the ridge.'

He hid his frustration well. I could imagine him trying hard not to rush her.

'And now you know we're okay, will you leave?' I asked, trying not to sound wistful.

He shook his head. 'It's not necessary. I know what I feel. I really would be much more comfortable staying here in case you need me.'

'Trust me, I don't need any help right now. This place is … Anyway, you promised. You have to get away from here. At least for a few days. Please, Bane.'

He took a deep breath. 'Two days. And after that, when you come home, don't make me leave again.'

'Unless you want to.'

'Unless I want to,' he conceded.

I gave him my most reassuring smile and melted back across the boundary.

Noah passed me as he crossed over to talk to Tessa. I was a little nervous about what he would say to her, thinking of the conversation we'd had during our flight, but as soon as I re-entered Eden the thought was lost. It was time to explore.

Chapter 36

Noah ducked behind me, nicked my hair tie and shook out my braid. Then he deliberately wiped his sticky fingers through my hair, and when I tried to evade him he took another piece of melon and squooshed it right onto my head, laughing. Then I got him back by squeezing juice from something like a giant orange down the back of his shirt. We both already had juice all over our faces and running down our forearms.

Harry had assured us that every other fruit we found would be safe to eat without affecting our memories, and each one was more delicious than the last. Noah was in the process of taking up my challenge to try every new type we came across, and had been keeping up fine until now. I was tempted to wrestle him to the ground and sit on him for messing up my hair, but that would mean letting go of the orange, and I wanted to eat some more. Besides, nothing he did could upset me at the moment. This place was too amazing to waste time feeling bad about anything, so I ate down to the unexpected pip at the centre, and threw that at him instead. He dodged it and then pounced on me, tickling me mercilessly. He hadn't done that since he was ten years old. I kicked and squealed and rolled him off me, tearing my top in the process, and then we were chasing each other, laughing and dodging trees and pretending to hide even though that never worked. It didn't matter because it was so much fun to just play. I even remembered how to cartwheel.

A little while later he motioned me to stop, and I heard the sound of laughter ahead. And splashing. There were people playing somewhere, having fun. We looked at each other, and then raced to find the source of the mayhem. Neither of us considered for a moment that there might be consequences to our actions. There was fun to be had. So we went.

Noah got to the River first, dive-bombing into the middle of a group of people who all appeared to be in their twenties. There were seven of them, four guys and three girls, some laughing, some singing, and all stark naked.

Without stopping to think about it I stripped off my clothes and jumped into the water too. It was cool and fresh, and so clean that I could see the bottom clearly where tiny fish darted around in schools, reflecting sunlight off their shiny blue scales, and I ducked my head under to watch them better. The song of the River overwhelmed my senses, but instead of the grief-stricken heartbreak I had become accustomed to, the melody was the most astoundingly joyful noise I had ever heard. It sounded as if each water droplet was adding a harmonious note to a great symphony. The sound was one of pure delight, like a baby's first laugh. Enraptured, I stayed under the water listening, and I understood the meaning of bliss. Even the dancing fish were part of the song. One of the girls ducked under too, to watch me watch them, her long brown hair floating softly around her face. I looked curiously at her, wondering if I had done something wrong but then she smiled, and bubbles poured from her lips as she started to giggle. We both stood up, spluttering as we tried to breathe and laugh at the same time and she reached over and hugged me as if we had known each other for years. Noah looked startled as he watched us and I dimly tried to think about how it must look, both of us naked and hugging. It didn't feel weird at all though; certainly none of the others looked particularly surprised. Just what had we gotten ourselves into?

Then a girl with long black hair tugged at Noah's T-shirt and waved her hands about as if inviting him to dance, but he backed away out of the water and ran off into the bushes. I started to wade after him, but then stopped. Did he want me to follow? I probably should go after him, but why? Why go if he didn't want me to follow? I wanted him to be happy. He'd run off pretty quickly, so he probably didn't expect me to go with him. Good. I would stay then. That would make him happy. The girl splashed me to get my attention. I splashed back.

＠

Tessa dumped her backpack on the floor of the cave and then flopped down onto it, panting inelegantly. She had finally started to put on a bit of weight lately, much to her mother's relief, but she still got tired very quickly, and two hikes to the cave in one day was more exercise than she had ever done in her life. After talking to Noah through the gap in the rock, she and Bane had headed back to the farm for her supplies and he had driven her part of the way back again before he'd left for Horsham. Then she'd hiked with her heavy pack on her own. She'd even managed to wrestle the canoe up the bank, although she couldn't get it up as far as the cape wattle where it usually hid. At least the trail was getting easier to follow; they had worked out the best ways to avoid the worst of the blackberries, and had been coming so often that the path was easy to find.

By the time she finished setting up camp it was early evening. She was exhausted, so as soon as she finished her soup she curled up in her sleeping bag. Even after she moved the worst of the rocks aside, her thin hiking mat was not nearly enough to keep her from feeling the lumps underneath. Still, she couldn't deny that it was a perfect spot to shelter in if you didn't mind the fact that it was freezing—it still surprised her every time she stepped from the searing dry summer heat into the cold cave system. And tomorrow she could have a lovely lazy day reading her book. It would be light enough in the mouth of the cave, and not too hot. If only this really had been a weekend away with Noah like everyone assumed. Never mind. She would wait patiently for him. She was used to that.

We lay on the sweet grass, letting the sun dry us off. The sunshine here had *texture*. And it was kind. The others had all left, leaving just me and the girl who had hugged me. I had dressed again, grateful that my thoughtless strip down had at least saved the photos Bane had given me. The girl was still naked but it didn't feel in the least bit strange. Thinking back, I realised that the man we had met when we first landed in Eden had also been naked. I simply hadn't noticed at the time and I had no idea how that was possible. It just seemed so natural here. There was certainly nothing inappropriate going on. I'd just spent two hours swimming with a bunch of nude young adults and didn't get so much as a leer. Only the completely innocent hug from this girl. It felt like we could be sisters, except I had no idea what that would be like. I peered sideways at her. She had long wild hair and dusky skin a similar colour to mine. Her eyes were much darker than my tawny speckled ones. She was pretty in a comfortable, familiar way, and looked to be just a few years older than me, but her eyes seemed more mature. They had a depth to them that spoke of something profound and hidden, maybe grief? And yet she moved with such energy and innocence that it was hard to think of her as anything other than totally carefree. She noticed me watching her.

'Hello,' she mumbled shyly, fiddling with the ends of her hair.

That was odd. Not just that we had spent the last couple of hours together and she was only just now saying hello, but also that she sounded shy. No one here was shy. It sounded weird. And how did she know English? She sat up straight and looked at me seriously, taking a deep breath as if trying to find extra confidence.

'You really are Lainie,' she announced, as if I might have forgotten. 'I'm Annie. Harry told me you would come, but I didn't believe him. You're a lot older than I expected.'

And she was a heck of a lot younger. I had finally met my mother.

Chapter 37

I stared at her blankly for a few moments. My mouth opened and closed a couple of times but nothing came out. Finally a tear betrayed me as it rolled down my cheek. I didn't know how to respond to her.

She noticed the tear. 'I've made you unhappy!' she said, looking around until her eyes rested on one of the Trees of Life. When she looked back at me her face lit up with excitement. 'If you eat the Fruit, you'll come back to life and then I can keep you!'

Keep me? She was halfway to the Tree before the rest of her sentence had a chance to properly filter into my brain.

'Wait! Please! I can't eat that. Annie … Mum, please!'

She stopped and looked at me, confused.

'I don't want to forget. I need to remember. Please, don't make me eat it.'

'Make you?' She pondered the words as if she had no idea what they meant. 'Oh! I want whatever you want. If you don't want to eat, just don't. But why would you want to stay dead?' She came and sat back down in front of me.

'I don't understand what you mean. How am I dead?'

'You came from across the Skin of the World.' She grasped my hand as if she was breaking terrible news to me. 'Everyone on the other side is dead.'

For a second I panicked, imagining that some worldwide catastrophe had occurred, or that maybe we were in some sort of time-distorted dimension and hundreds of years had passed without me knowing. But then reason returned. Hadn't I just seen Bane a couple of hours ago? We had almost beaten him to the cave so time must run the same on both sides of the boundary. Otherwise how would we have been able to meet with Harry each time?

Her hand around mine felt cool and familiar, and I didn't let her go. For a few moments we just sat there, staring at our clasped hands while images flashed through my mind. Her memories, not mine, but I felt them like they were my own. There was no deceit in her, only … something … guilt?

'You feel hurt,' she stated. 'I can help take that away if you like.'

'No, you can't,' I said, snatching my hand away and feeling somehow violated. 'Because you're the one who hurt me.' Now why would I say a thing like that? 'I'm sorry, I didn't mean that.'

Her smile was wry. 'Yes, you did. There is no place for dishonesty here. In Eden, you say what you mean. That was always a tricky thing when I was here with my own mother.'

'Why, did she leave you too?'

This was not how I had rehearsed it. Not even in the daytime soap opera version.

'Yes.' Her eyes kept flicking towards the nearby Tree but she tucked her feet under her and clasped her arms around her knees as if forcing herself to remain seated. 'We all lose the people we love, and I didn't want to put you through that.'

'So, what, you thought you'd just leave when I was a baby so I wouldn't have a chance to love you?' My words felt hot as they left my chest. Dragon-breath words.

Her words bit back, snappy and sharp. 'Lily tried to hide it, but I knew how she felt whenever I came back for you. I couldn't be what you needed.' A trembling breath, and then she peered up at me from under damp lashes. 'Has she been what you needed?'

Her eyes were so full of desperation that I couldn't deny her the reassurance she was craving. 'Aunt Lily has been a wonderful mother.'

Her face softened.

'But you left me for dead.'

She didn't speak.

'I don't understand,' I pushed. 'How can I be here talking to you if I'm dead?'

She shook her head slowly. 'You haven't stopped yet, but you are dead. Unless you eat some Fruit.'

'Oh. I get it. Death is inevitable outside of Eden, so anyone out there is as good as dead, right?'

Something shut down behind her eyes, and she became so still that for a few awkward seconds I thought maybe I'd broken her or something. She was like a toy that had just run out of batteries. But then she replied with another soft-spoken 'Yes,' and her voice held all the grief that I had slept with for so long. And then I knew. The sadness in the river back home had somehow come from her. Harry had told me that she'd only started to eat from the Tree when Kolsom started poking about, and I would have been willing to bet my entire music collection that the river had become sad at the same time. I needed to talk to Harry, and Noah.

I sat up urgently. 'Do you know where Harry is? I think I'd better tell him I've lost Noah.'

Her smile unfurled again like a morning tulip. 'I can always find Harry. And you can always find Noah.'

She stood up and helped me to my feet, and then confidently turned and walked off through the trees, so I followed.

The old sedan spluttered its way into the service station and Bane groaned in a mix of relief and frustration. That'd be right. He could finally make it out of town without feeling like either throwing up or passing out, and then his car goes and gets sick instead. He popped the bonnet and stared dejectedly at the steam rising from the radiator. It was a good thing Lainie had taught him a bit about engine care or he might have been stupid enough to try to open the cap. He went inside to buy a cold drink instead.

Horsham was hot and sleepy. No surprise there. But it was also a bigger town than Nalong and there were plenty of things to do. He had been many times before, of course. It was about the only town close enough to home that allowed him to be well enough to function, but he had always been uncomfortable staying for too long, and had never felt particularly eager to waste any time there. He usually came, ran the errands he needed to, and then headed back home as soon as possible. This time he would take things much slower. He had a few family friends he wanted to call on, and was considering catching a movie or visiting a music store. There might even be a local band playing somewhere if he was lucky.

Once his car cooled enough to top up the radiator, he took it to a mechanic near the centre of town and then booked himself into a cheap motel. With no clear sense of purpose, he began to walk along the main street, browsing at the shops, and was struck by the sheer number of options there were for him to fill his time with. There were bookstores, music stores, dance lessons and even a martial arts training facility. Which way would his life turn? What did he really want? If the world was truly open to him, what could he achieve? He didn't even know where to start. He had assumed Lainie wanted him to explore the idea of meeting other girls, but maybe it was more than that? Perhaps she wanted him to think seriously about what else he wanted from life. Farming was great, but he probably wasn't really suited to it after all. He enjoyed it because she was there, not because of the work itself.

Looking reflectively at a couple of tourists taking photos of a church, it struck him how little of the world he had seen. He'd always assumed he would travel one day, perhaps in the army, but not necessarily. Would he have gone through with his army plans if he hadn't been linked to Lainie? Could he still? Lainie wouldn't just drop her life here and stay in Eden indefinitely, would she? She had plans too. He certainly couldn't let her sacrifice everything she knew just to let him join the army. That would be ridiculous. But the question remained, what *did* he want out of life? And how was he supposed to work it all out in just a couple of days?

He passed a few more shops, and loitered in the window of a small art gallery. It appeared to specialise in Indigenous artwork, which immediately sparked his interest. So much for exploring other ideas. As soon as anything to do with Eden appeared he lost all ability to focus on anything else.

The dot paintings were beautiful, full of earthy tones and swirling lines that mesmerised him. Some were contemporary, some more traditional. None looked much like the cave drawings. Those told a story, these ones were more for decoration. Suddenly startled, he noticed a familiar figure inside the shop, talking to the owner. Mr Beckinsale was smiling, obviously sweet-talking her into something. Bane moved closer to the open door to listen.

'How can one authenticate a particular piece of work?' he heard him ask the owner. 'I wouldn't want to pay for an original only to find it was done by some student out for a quick bit of cash. Nor would I want to offend anyone by trying to purchase a piece that might be considered sacred by your people. Is that ever a problem?'

The elderly lady squared her shoulders, her dark curly hair shot with grey and held back with a colourful scarf. 'All the paintings here are genuine. I either painted them myself or they were done by members of my family or clan. They wouldn't be offered for sale if they were sacred,' she said, as if that should be plainly obvious.

She was right. There was only one reason that slinking fox would be asking such questions. What was he hoping to prove? That the cave paintings weren't genuine?

'Of course,' he agreed humbly. 'So if you painted these, could you tell me what sort of paints you used? The colours are amazing! Are they made from natural materials?'

She looked a little more mollified. 'Historically most paint was made from various shades of ochre, mixed with blood or saliva. Colours were traded between tribes depending on what was available in each area. These days we mostly use acrylic paints,' she smiled sardonically. 'Hardly any blood.'

Turning from her to inspect the largest painting featured on the wall, the lawyer's eyes deadened in response to her subtle condescension. 'Thank you, you have been most informative,' he said, far too smoothly, and turned to leave.

Bane ducked away from the door before he could be seen. After a moment he turned and watched the man order a take away coffee from a nearby café before getting back into his blue Land Cruiser and driving off. The man was planning something, surely, but what?

All Bane wanted now was to get his car fixed and head back. He had no interest in chatting up strangers. Not now, not ever. He would finish his time here as promised, but not a moment longer.

We found Noah and Harry sitting under a tree whose base was wider than Harry's cottage. It was one of many clumped close together to form a natural shelter from the elements. The dirt underneath had been cleared of leaves and sticks and was more or less level. It reminded me of a fantasy world in a computer game—there were even elven-like people pottering around at various tasks, talking to each other in what I now realised was an intricate sign language. Every now and then I would catch one of them watching us curiously, but they seemed content to give us some space. The people here were definitely human, but different enough to what I was used to that I could happily pretend they were magical creatures who could shoot an orc at fifty paces and never need to brush their hair. And there were enough of them gathered here that I had to assume we were in some sort of village. The tree shelter was on the edge of a native bushland that looked more like a Queensland rainforest than anything else. It gave the impression that these people resided here, although I was yet to see any sort of housing.

Noah looked up at me. 'I'm sorry for running off. I was just a bit startled but I'm okay now, I promise.'

'I'm the one who should apologise. I didn't even realise what I was doing until I saw the look on your face. It was all very innocent, but unfair on you, sorry.'

'Hey. Apparently there is no right or wrong here. What you choose to do is your business. It just surprised me, that's all.'

Wow, he really must have had a shock, seeing me hug a strange naked girl. I started to feel my cheeks turning red as my sense of propriety finally reasserted itself, and I could see Harry trying hard not to laugh at the awkward moment. Thank goodness Noah had found him; they had clearly been having a bit of a man-to-man talk.

'Noah, this is Annie. My mother,' I explained, trying hard to ignore the fact that she was still naked as I was introducing her. And then it was my turn to try not to laugh as his face changed from shock to confusion, and then embarrassment. As if he could possibly have known!

He stood up and glanced at Harry who nodded, and then he stepped forward and kissed her on the cheek. 'Pleased to meet you, Mrs Gracewood,' he said softly, as if he expected her to run away.

'Mrs Gracewood! Blah! You make me sound like I should be making jam for the Nalong Show.' She was right. It seemed a ridiculous title for someone so young looking. Then she beamed at him. 'Noah Ashbree! I remember you. You were such an adorable baby. You had soft white curls and such bright eyes—a real Cherub!' She giggled delightedly. 'How are those two terrible brothers of yours? They used to love eating my chocolate chip cookies when I babysat them.' She sounded so typically middle-aged all of a sudden that Noah and I just stared at her helplessly. The idea that this faerie-like naked girl had ever baked cookies—let alone looked after Caleb and Liam as toddlers—was difficult to assimilate.

'Uh, they're fine,' Noah replied uncertainly. 'I have a sister now, too. Nicole. She's nearly fourteen.'

'Yes, of course. I forgot about the baby ... Wonderful! Sarah always wanted a girl. I am so pleased for her; she was pretty unhappy for a while.'

Interesting. According to Sarah it was my mother who suffered from depression. I wanted to know more but was reluctant to pry into the past in case I said something to upset her again. Obviously Noah felt the same because he changed the subject.

'Annie, could you please tell us where we can find some food? I enjoy the fruit and all, but I was wondering if there was anything ... else?'

Poor Noah. Personally I felt as though the fruit here would be more than fine for breakfast, lunch and dinner for eternity, but he would never cope.

'Of course,' she assured him. 'Growing Cherubim like you need much more than fruit. Let me see what I can find.'

It seemed as though the more she interacted with us the more naturally she was able to converse, although for some reason I got the impression that she might just shatter if we said the wrong thing. I hoped we would only trigger her happier memories because I was enjoying the idea that I might have the chance to get to know her.

She led us deeper into the trees until we reached a sheltered clearing, where tantalising cooking smells made me reassess my earlier opinion of eating fruit forever. It appeared to be a communal dining area. The branches above had such thick foliage that it seemed unlikely that any rain ever got through at all. The trees themselves seemed to help this process by growing their branches all at the same height, crisscrossing over each other to form a stable-looking ceiling. It was as if the trees had grown that way on purpose, just to form a pleasant space for humans to gather in. A garden created for humans to dwell in. I was starting to understand just how significant that was.

Everywhere I looked I could see works of art. Mosaics and embossed clay slabs, paintings and giant sculptures, everything made from natural materials and everything made because it was beautiful, not because it was functional. Apparently the culinary arts were taken seriously as well. There were people preparing meals, shaping vegetables with short knives into tiny animals and flowers. They were laughing with each other, delighting in showing off their creations, and what they produced was being handed out freely. Harry selected a bowl for each of us and found us a large rock so we could all sit together.

'Some of the food can be very rich if you're not accustomed to it,' he warned as he handed us our bowls. My bowl contained a portion of white meat with a deep red sauce and some carrots carved into perfect star shapes on the side. It was garnished with actual tiny yellow flowers too. It was far too pretty to eat.

'They eat meat, then?' Noah asked.

'Yes, they do. Not much, but they do,' he replied.

We looked questioningly at my mother for more details.

'We only kill animals that are ready to die,' she clarified. 'The ones that are sick or old and come to us for help.'

'And this is how you help them?' I asked, confused. Growing up on a farm, I was under no illusion as to where our food came from. I had learnt how to slaughter and dress lamb years ago but somehow I just couldn't quite picture any of these gentle people doing it. It simply didn't fit.

'The Fruit doesn't work on them, so sometimes they want help to stop. It's hard for them to leave this place, even when it hurts to stay. The instinct to live can be too strong, so they come to us.'

'And how does it make you feel to kill them?' Noah asked curiously. It was such a blunt question that I froze, but she just looked at him as if it should be obvious.

'It feels good to help. It doesn't matter if it's a person or an animal. We want whatever they want.'

'So what if a human wanted to die? Would you help?'

'We don't kill humans, but we do help. We sang someone across just last winter. It was a wonderful party,' she told us dreamily, staring into nothing as if remembering.

I was confused. 'But I thought no one could die here?'

'Of course we're free to die!' She giggled at me as if I had been telling a joke, but something deep in her eyes looked … tortured. 'Imagine how awful it would be to be trapped here forever?'

I looked around at the smiling faces and picturesque scenery. Not that awful, I would have thought.

'Besides,' she said, with her mouth full of celery, 'it would get terribly crowded here if no one ever moved across.'

She had a point. A race of true immortals would have some serious logistical issues.

'So you can die if you choose. But does anyone ever die by accident? What if you can't get to the Fruit on time?'

She shook her head. 'Even if your heart stops beating and your brain ceases all activity, there's always enough life left if you want to stay. Even if you stop for a long time before someone finds you and helps you to eat. The man who moved across didn't want to stay, so he went to sleep in the River after his party. He didn't want us to bring him back.'

It was disturbing how happy she sounded as she described this man's death. 'You don't seem sad at all. Don't you miss him?'

'A little. But it's only for a while. When I go across I'll see him again. Even you must know this, Lainie,' she berated gently.

I had a million more questions but she had spotted someone she wanted to talk to, and without another word she stood up and took her empty bowl over to a stream that ran along one edge of the clearing. She scrubbed it out and laid it back on the table for someone else to use, then left to talk to her friend. I ate my delicious meal in silence. There was a lot to ponder.

Chapter 38

Bathed in gentle warmth, I was woken the next morning by the intoxicating feel of sunlight on my face and the sound of gently rustling leaves all around me. Before I even opened my eyes I could smell the delicious fragrance of the tree I was hanging in, like a peppermint gum only sweeter, and I was content to just lay there and relish the moment. My ears were still filled with the memory of the lullaby my mother had sung me to sleep with. I had slept through the night. Deeply. No sad music. I'd almost forgotten what it was like not to wake up crying.

We had stayed up until the early hours of the morning, singing and dancing with the people I was happy to think of as elves. Not because they looked any different—they were more human than I was—it was just that they were everything the flawed human race on the other side of the boundary *wanted* to be. They were kind and carefree, and intrinsically incapable of being selfish or cruel. Nothing they did seemed like work, only fun. I knew they were creative and intelligent, even though I couldn't really understand their language yet. I was now certain that when fantasy writers wrote about elves, it was because they wanted to imagine a race of people that were everything humans should have been. And they were here.

For a while I just lay there, breathing in the sweetness, letting the sounds and scents soak into my bones until my mind began to twitch with curiosity about all the strange things I could hear. I stretched and yawned in my hammock, and marvelled at the way my body ached from all the dancing. These people danced almost as well as Bane. Almost. Throughout the evening I'd kept expecting to turn around and see him there, with his piercing eyes and hidden smile, holding out his hand and inviting me to dance with him again. Rummaging around in my back pocket, I pulled out the little photos he had printed for me and smoothed them out as best I could. Then with tender care I tucked them between some vines so the faces of my friends and family could look out over Eden. I couldn't share this with them, but at least their photos could be guests here. For a long time I stared at Bane's picture, mentally running my fingertips along his perfect jaw the way I craved to do in real life, and wished with all my heart that he could see what I saw.

Today I would head back to the cave to check on Tessa, and to make sure Bane had gone into town as he had promised. I felt so torn as I lay there. I wanted him to be free and happy, and I also wanted to stay in Eden because the thought of ever leaving this perfect world just seemed incomprehensible. But I also wanted to see him again, to feel his arms around me and his breath on my neck and his lips on mine …

A passionate yearning welled up from the exact centre of my diaphragm with such sudden intensity that it flipped me right out of the hammock. My body seemed to be under the impression that I could just run to wherever he was and throw myself into his embrace, and I had to cling to a nearby branch to stop from launching myself straight off the platform.

Everything seemed so simple here. I wanted him. He wanted me. Why did it all have to be so complicated? I wanted whatever he wanted. That seemed to be the only guiding rule here, if it could be called a rule. Everything here was motivated by what made me happy and what would make others happy, and they never seemed to be in conflict. Not in Eden anyway. Home was a different story. Somehow I was going to have to learn how to keep the two sets of principles clear in my head.

Noah was still asleep in the next tree, looking so peaceful that I left him snoring and went to find the others. Harry was talking quietly to my mother by the streamlet, which sang a dainty sonnet as it danced across the rocks. The second she saw me, she jumped up and threw her arms around my neck with such exuberance that we both nearly ended up in the water. It made me wish Aunt Lily could see where I got the same trait. We sat down laughing and she handed me a cup of fruit juice. I peered warily at it.

'It's okay, Lainie. It's not Life Fruit. It won't make you forget,' she assured me.

I bit my lower lip. The whole concept of distrust seemed ridiculous here, but I was worried that she might have had a different idea of what I really wanted than what I did. I glanced at Harry, who gave a short nod, so I took a sip. The juice was lemony and refreshing and by the time I finished it I didn't even feel like I needed to brush my teeth anymore.

My mother stroked my hair as we sat in the sun, soaking up each other's company and I realised that I no longer felt angry with her. Okay, so maybe a part of me was still resentful, if I was honest, and it would probably take a long time for us to properly resolve that, but the more time I spent with her, the harder it was to let my imagination make up nasty stories about her 'selfish' motivations. I could read her at least as well as anyone else, and I knew that she honestly believed she had done the right thing by leaving me with Aunt Lily. And I also knew that leaving me was part of the reason for her grief. I'd known it ever since that dream I'd had of her, on our first night at the cave. Perhaps that was why Harry had wanted me to come. To help resolve her loss. I smiled as I felt her fingers gently begin to untangle the ever-present knots in my hair.

'We should go and check on Tessa again this morning,' I said reluctantly to Harry. My mother tilted her face curiously. 'Tess is Noah's Guardian,' I explained to her.

Harry shook his head quickly, warning me not to say any more, but it was too late. Her back stiffened like someone had just poked her with a sharp stick, and she refused to meet my eyes. Instead, she stared with a haunted look on her face out towards where the silver River glistened through the trees, and then wordlessly got up to leave.

'Annie,' Harry said, holding her back and looking her right in the eye. 'Remember what we talked about?'

For a moment she seemed rebellious, but then she laughed. 'Of course. I just need some time away from all these eyes.'

He nodded and let her go, and she wandered away into the trees.

'What did I say?' I asked.

'It might be best not to talk about the Guardians. It brings back painful memories for her. Things she wants to forget.'

'Has she gone to find some Fruit?'

'No. But she doesn't like crying in front of the people here. She'll be back soon. Don't worry.'

His eyes were such a familiar soothing brown that I didn't. There was simply no room for worry in this Garden. And yet there were things that still nagged at me. Questions that needed answering. Questions that didn't worry me, exactly, but still made me restless. My mother should not be eating the Fruit if that was what was causing the sadness in the water, and yet there was no right or wrong here, so how was I supposed to stop her? And there were other questions I had put off for too long. I looked down at my little cup to try to find some moral support. Its tiny embossed patterns didn't reply to my silent plea. I went ahead anyhow. It was time to ask him once and for all.

'Is it my dad's death that upset her? She seemed so accepting of death last night.'

Harry sighed, and genuine regret was exhaled with it. 'Lainie, a death here is by choice. Your dad didn't choose to die. He drowned saving you and your mother—she'll never get over that.'

I looked him squarely in the eye. 'So Lucas Gracewood really was my father?'

His eyes widened in sudden understanding of why I had found it so difficult to speak openly with him, then softened in apologetic sympathy. 'Yes, he really was. He loved you both very much. It crushed Annie when we lost him.'

Truthful honesty fell around my shoulders like a security blanket as his simple statement untangled the knots that had filled my mind with so much conflict. And as effortlessly as that, a new peace settled. It was such an elegant and beautiful anticlimax that I felt pretty stupid for ever even questioning the truth. Why did I always have to make life so much more complicated than it needed to be?

Harry drank the rest of his own juice, and sat lost in his own deep thoughts while I watched my mother wander away to find healing and comfort. She looked so directionless. Was that my future too? Would letting go of Bane damage me in the same way? Eden was a glorious place, and my mother seemed happy enough, but could I really live like that?

I had a lovely lazy morning watching the people around me converse with each other in subtle signs and gestures, and was just starting to figure out a couple of phrases when I finally saw Noah emerge looking like a child lost in a toy store. He pottered aimlessly around as he became distracted by each new thing he saw, so my mother, who had returned after about half an hour, rounded him up with a familiar sharp whistle. It was the sheep dog command for 'Bring 'em in nice and tight'. Noah laughed and came over before she had to start nipping at his heels.

My best friend looked radiant. I hadn't realised how stressed he must have been lately but his sleep-in must have done him bucket loads of good because he had the sparkle back in his bright green eyes and polished off four bowls of cereal. He even started telling bad jokes again. I hadn't really noticed when that had stopped, and I laughed at them more because he was so happy than because they were at all funny.

The moment he finally relinquished his bowl my mother got up and skipped away through the trees, so I jumped up before she could disappear.

'Wait ... Mum?' She ignored me. 'Annie? Please wait,' I called, stumbling after her.

She turned to me, laughing. 'Of course. You will want to see this. Come *on*, everyone!'

Clearly there was no point trying to call her 'Mum'. It was probably as foreign-sounding to her as it was to me. 'Annie' suited her much better anyway.

We made our way back towards the River, gaping at plants that visibly grew as we passed them. A flock of tiny sparrows landed on us as we walked—literally, right on our heads and shoulders, unafraid, and very noisy. Their feathers brushed my cheeks. Many of the animals we saw I was familiar with, but not all. It was very probable that a lot of them were extinct on our side of the boundary. For a brief moment I whimsically toyed with the idea of taking a photo of a Tasmanian tiger if I could find one—it would certainly stop the miners in their tracks— but would also attract a whole lot of other attention we didn't want. Pity. If not for the gut-clenching guilt that dwelling on the idea was rapidly producing, it might have been kind of fun.

Crashing awkwardly into Noah as he stopped in front of me, I peered around his wide shoulders to see what he was staring at. There was a dead tree next to the River. It looked so out of place that we both just stared at it, confused. Plants and animals still died here, so why was it so disturbing? Annie glanced at it and looked away quickly. The expression on her face was one of remorse. How was that possible? There was no right or wrong here, and certainly no shame. The way I understood it, Adam and Eve were cast out of Eden to make sure of it.

There was, however, no denying the fact that the tree was *wrong*. Everything about it felt deeply disturbing. Other plants that died in the Garden didn't look like this. Each fallen tree I had so far come across had been covered with the fresh green growth of smaller plants and mosses in a healthy cycle of abundant life, but this tree looked ... deader than dead, somehow.

Annie hurried on, so we followed, but as we went past I stared at it more closely and realised that it had once been a Tree of Life. How could such a sacred Tree possibly die? It was supposed to be a source of Life itself. Noah opened his mouth as if to ask her about it but Harry motioned him to stay silent.

Eventually Annie led us to a path that ran up a hill alongside the magnificent River. We raced each other up until it got too steep to run, and then we clambered up on all fours. The waterfall that the River formed at that point was spectacular. Rainbow mist hovered all around us, full of exotic birds that danced in elegant playfulness. At the top of the falls we rested for a few moments, absorbing the view, until Annie again pranced away. The watercourse curved around a bend and kept climbing.

Suddenly a young woman appeared in the water from around the corner, squealing and tumbling past us as the current swept her down the hill. Noah didn't hesitate. He kicked off his shoes and jumped straight in after her. Crazy idiot! What was he thinking? As if he could help her now! Where was Tessa when I needed her? Just a few seconds' warning might have made all the difference, but as it was, I lost sight of Noah's pale hair beneath the swirling current almost immediately.

Sliding recklessly back down the hill, I searched desperately for some evidence of either victim while my imagination was busy being overwhelmed with images of bodies smashed against rocks at the bottom of the rapidly approaching falls. A nauseating flashback of tumbling through the maelstrom at the base of the waterfall near the cave ripped through me and I screamed Noah's name in blind panic. Vivid memories engulfed me, of not being able to breathe or even work out which way was up until Bane had lifted my head above the water. This drop was *much* higher. With stifling distress I realised that even from the base of the falls I might just be too afraid to go in after them.

Gasping, I skidded around the bend and peered into the water at the base of the cliff, scanning the water for evidence of a body.

Long seconds passed.

Flashes of movement kept catching my eyes, but each one was a false trick of the turbulence and froth until finally I spotted the clumsy girl who had caused Noah to risk himself. A pathetic squeaky whimper of relief escaped me as she started to backstroke lazily towards the edge. Noah's head broke the surface a few moments later and he gasped in a deep breath before flicking his blond curls out of his face.

He was perfectly fine.

My knees quivered so much from the fright he had given me that I had to clutch at a tree for support. His bright eyes looked up in amazement to see the size of the drop he had just plummeted down, and then he noticed me and gave me a wide grin. Not unlike the one he had given me after his first ice-blocking run. Right before I had broken my arm. If Adam and Eve had been kicked out for discovering the difference between Good and Evil, I wondered what would happen if I throttled my best friend.

As my heart rate began to slow, I peered hard through the mist into the water. Not one rock. The pool was as clear as glass and flowed gently, with nothing to hide. The riverbed on either side looked pale and sandy, deepening to soothing indigo under the curtain of falling water. Then I examined the River above the drop. The base there was all bedrock, worn smooth by the water. It looked more like a water slide than a river. A garden designed for humans to dwell in? More like a giant playground for cherished children. A slow smile crept across my face, chasing away my recent fright. Eden was *fun*.

By mid-afternoon I was the only person I knew who could say that my mother had taught me how to do triple-saults off the edge of a waterfall. She was an even worse show-off than I was and it was fun trying to keep up with her, but I eventually retired to the warm riverbank with Harry to watch everyone else play.

Throughout the day there had been maybe twenty of us playing at any one time. Some would come for just one turn, some stayed longer to perfect a new trick. Often I noticed people getting out of the water with a slight limp or nursing a bruised elbow. They didn't look upset at all; they just wandered over to one of the plentiful Trees of Life and ate a piece of Fruit, or just rubbed the sore spot with a leaf. I was used to having Bane heal me so it seemed perfectly natural now to see so many healings take place before my eyes and I was very tempted to try some of the Fruit myself just to ease my bruises, but Harry's warning made me wary. If he refused to eat it, then I would follow his lead.

I tried to imagine what it would be like if these Trees existed in the world across the boundary, but my mind just refused to go there. Tainted humans being able to live forever? That held too many ramifications for my intellect to even begin to absorb. It was simply not permitted. Every fibre of my being, and every instinct that I had agreed. No matter how much I wished it could be otherwise.

An iridescent dragonfly danced for my entertainment as I lay in the shade of a giant fern. Who needed holidays when this place was so much better than anything I had even heard of back home? It was good to know there would be some perks to being a Cherub if I was compelled to stay in Nalong my whole life. But what about the Guardians? What did they get in return for all the restrictions they had to put up with?

Thinking of them made me remember the many questions I had been longing to ask Harry. Many of them were answered now that I'd experienced Eden for myself, but not all. I took the chance while I had it.

'Harry, will you come home with us?' I thought I'd start with an easy one, but he sat silently for so long that I reassessed my assumption.

Finally he nodded. 'Yeah. I won't abandon you just yet. Especially not with Kolsom still a potential risk to our secret. Besides, you and Noah haven't had a chance to finish growing up yet. There's plenty for you to experience of the world before you get bound to Nalong too tightly.'

I had a feeling it was already too late for that, but I didn't argue.

'So we're the only ones? No other Cherubim I don't know about yet?' I was pretty confident of the answer, but thought it was worth checking. He smiled ruefully. 'No others, I'm afraid. No duty roster either, sorry.'

'And what about the Guardians? How tightly are they linked to us? You seem to manage all right without one. Do they have the freedom to choose their own path?'

Harry froze, his face lined with grief and a longing that I had never before glimpsed in him. Clearly I had touched a nerve. I so badly wanted to know what had happened to his Guardian but at the same time the impulse to only do what made him happy wouldn't allow me to ask anything else that might upset him, so instead I sat quietly and waited.

He ran a finger along my bracelet, reading the inscription, and his voice was rough when he finally answered. 'We are bound *very* tightly to our Guardians.' He glanced over to where Annie was teaching Noah another way to fly by doing backwards twists off a rock. 'Forever. Even if they die. You don't want to know what it's like to have to live without your soul mate. You really don't.'

Disturbing thoughts swirled through my head, but I didn't try to stop him as he left to grieve in solitude. Harry was obviously still very much in love with his lost Guardian, and Annie had all but lost her mind when my dad had died. The idea that Harry could have been my father now seemed ludicrous. Those were thoughts that belonged in another world. In this world people fell in love, and bonded for life. No matter how long or short those lives were. I was beginning to accept that without Bane I would be as lost as my mother, and I had to assume that it would be the same for him. We were *supposed* to be together. The idea that I wasn't attractive enough, or clever enough, or that I somehow wasn't worthy of him—those ideas also belonged to a fallen world. Enough was enough. If by some remote chance he still wanted me, then I was his. Forever. The decision settled into my heart with a soft bump, like a boat coming home to the pier. This was easy. This was *right*.

As I drifted off to sleep my mind was filled with the image of Bane's light grey eyes, bright with the profound joy I'd seen only twice.

Chapter 39

At two o'clock, when Bane opened the door to the waiting room yet again, the mechanic practically threw him the bill and his keys. He had to force himself to drive away slowly.

Lainie was not stupid, but this time she was just plain wrong. She didn't trust his feelings for her, and he didn't blame her for that one bit—not after so many years of having to deal with his vicious temper. He understood why she kept pushing him away. That girl had proven repeatedly just how well she understood him, and she was far wiser than she let on—their ridiculous fight over the fencing had taught him that—which was why he had agreed to her proposal. Deep down he knew that she wasn't just being a silly teenager suffering from low self-esteem, although he had damaged her enough in the past for that to be a contributing factor. The truth was, she was being uncompromisingly rational in ways that he just didn't have the courage for. What he felt for her was so foundational, so consuming, that he had to be absolutely certain of its validity before it was too late to turn back. They both did.

That was not what she had been wrong about. She had simply been wrong to think there was any chance that it wasn't already too late.

Two days, he'd promised her, but it had only taken a day and a half to find out for certain what he already knew. His place was with her. It always had been. It had never done him any good to try to fight it, and he was heartily tired of trying. He now knew it wasn't just the compulsion, either. He craved her company. Her insane practical jokes. Her unreserved and undeserved friendship. The sight of her mischievous smile and golden eyes and out of control hair. He even missed her constant grazing on whatever fruit happened to be within reach. He had known since the first steps of that fateful dance. He was hers, whether she wanted him or not. He would keep his distance if she asked, but he wanted more. Much more.

Relieved to feel certain of himself finally, he stopped only long enough to buy a few supplies in case the stay at the cave stretched out longer than anticipated, and then he started back for Nalong.

❧

Driving home with the car radio up loud, he thought some more about their plan to bring the rock fall down. It was dangerous, and he didn't like it, but he just couldn't come up with anything better. The safest way to remove the rocks was to get the Cherubim to use their powers to clear it, and apparently that could only happen if the secret of Eden was under threat. With Sarah too far away, one of the Cherubim would have to come out to deal with the hazard. But there were too many variables. What if they didn't believe the threat was genuine? Or found a way to deal with it without coming out? What if they fortified the rock wall instead of clearing it? Tessa had been convinced that was unlikely. There was a reason the path existed at all. God could have sealed the whole thing off permanently in the first place, but he hadn't. He'd gone to a bit of trouble to make sure Eden could still be accessed from both sides, and guarded, so surely He wouldn't let it be sealed off altogether.

So the plan was simply to bring in an outsider—someone who would trigger their protective impulses but who could be convinced to leave before actually finding out anything too important. It wouldn't take much to lure Nicole out there to nose around. The tricky part would be to get her to leave at exactly the right time, and yet make sure that she would be enough of a trigger.

Bane gripped the steering wheel harder. Who were they kidding? Were they actually trying to trick Lainie, Noah and Harry, or were they trying to fool God himself? Neither option seemed at all likely. The only other suggestion they'd toyed with was to set off a bit of ANFO explosive—it wasn't exactly legal to blow up tree stumps these days without a licence, but that didn't mean that farmers had forgotten how to do it. But setting off explosives inside a cave? Good way to collapse the entire system, which would be somewhat counter-productive.

It was almost four-thirty by the time he reached Nalong, but even on a sleepy Thursday afternoon he still felt very conspicuous driving through town. The place was too small to risk having someone mention they had seen him. Besides, he'd never liked the idea of leaving Tessa alone to guard everything, and so he took the road that ran through the state park behind the farm, planning to park as close to the cave as possible but still stay out of sight.

He crossed the bridge and began looking for a place to pull off the road and hide the car. If he hadn't been purposefully searching for such a spot he never would have seen the navy blue Land Cruiser with the Kolsom Mining logo that was nestled in the bushes.

∽

My dreams became increasingly restless as I slept until finally, gasping, I woke to feel my skin crawling with the sense that I was being watched. I had learnt to recognise that feeling, and I knew it meant trouble. Looking around for the others, I could only see my mother.

When she noticed me, she reached up into one of the majestic Trees and picked a piece of Fruit, then stroked it as if trying to decide what to do. 'Should I come?' she asked with childlike worry.

As tempted as I was to bring her with me, I knew she didn't belong in Nalong anymore. 'No, Annie. It's my turn now.' I hugged her tightly. 'But I'll be back,' I promised.

'You'd better go,' she advised me seriously. 'They think they are there to protect you, but they aren't always safe either.'

And then somehow I was running.

I wasn't sure exactly how to reach the cave from where I was but that didn't hinder me in the least; I simply followed the sense of someone approaching an area they weren't supposed to be. Like a fish in a reef, I darted through the trees, ignoring the smiles I received from the people I passed. They probably assumed I was playing a game.

When I reached the cave I caught a glimpse of Noah just as he disappeared into it. I bolted in after him with a growing sense of threat like electricity at the base of my spine. Whatever this scheme of Tessa's was, it was certainly working. I had a brief thought that it was too early, that we were supposed to stay for at least one more day, but the Guardians had been so careful not to let any details slip that I had to assume there was a good reason. I was so keyed up I felt as if I could smash my way straight through the rock to get to where I needed to be. They had better not have created too real a threat to Eden. Nothing was worth risking the sanctity of this place. Nothing.

I spun around the corner, hardly noticing as my bare feet were torn by the rocks underfoot. The sword was just ahead. And it was spinning so fast that it just looked like a giant ball of flame.

Tessa was polishing off her last packet of Twisties when she heard something that made her block up the hole in the rock fall as quietly as possible, plunging everything into complete darkness. Definitely footsteps. Echoing down the tunnel. Then a splash and a muttered curse as whoever it was must have missed seeing the puddle by the second bend.

Bane had messaged her on the sat-phone a few hours earlier to tell her he was coming back early, and to ask if there was anything she wanted from the shops, but something primal inside her knew it wasn't him approaching. Her bones knew it. Her suddenly tense muscles knew it. Even her teeth knew it. She was filled with a familiar but unusually fierce sense of protectiveness, despite the fact that Noah was across the boundary and the link was broken. Whoever was there was a potential threat to him. She would bet her life on it.

A clatter of small rocks echoed down the tunnel.

She thought about reaching for the phone, but even a sat-phone couldn't get reception in a cave. Besides, the only people she could call for help were Bane, Lily and Sarah, and they were all too far away to help. Stumbling in the dark, she felt around and grabbed the only thing she could find that she could possibly use as a weapon. The rock was a bit too large for her to grip well, but it was better than nothing.

As the figure rounded the last corner she crouched, silent and still. Strike now, her instincts told her. Before he knows you're here. The man was not as tall as Bane. He moved slowly, using his torch to inspect the walls. Deep in her soul she was so certain this stranger was dangerous that she didn't even hesitate. She threw the rock as hard as she could at the man's head.

It missed by miles.

If she survived this she was definitely going to follow Bane's advice and learn some skills, she decided, as the man spun around and shone the torch directly into her eyes.

Bane pelted through the bush like a fox with its tail on fire. Blackberry thorns tugged on his clothes and skin and his lungs burned, but he couldn't slow down. He was realising just how careless they had all been to let the path become so obvious. They had travelled to the cave so often lately that anyone could follow their trail. And someone had.

He reached the base of the waterfall, hoping the man might have lost the trail there, but one look at the badly hidden canoe on the other side made that a vain prospect. There was a wet garbage bag on the other riverbank. It was obvious someone had crossed over, probably using the bag to keep something dry. He plunged into the water without even bothering to take off his shoes. There simply wasn't time.

'Just show me where the paintings are and I'll let you go,' the dark-haired man said to Tessa reasonably. At least it would have sounded reasonable if he hadn't been threatening her with a large hideous looking knife at the same time. He had pulled it out of a satchel he was carrying as soon as he'd found her cowering in the dark. Then he'd cut the straps off her pack and used them to bind her wrists. Perhaps if Noah had been close she would have put up more of a fight, but the link was broken and she was terrified and alone in a dark cave with a man holding a knife.

'Who are you? Are you the guy from the mining company that Lainie met with?' she sobbed.

He wore jeans and an expensive-looking cotton shirt with the sleeves rolled up. He looked like he'd just stepped out of an R.M. Williams cata-logue. Except he had obviously just swum the river and was sopping wet.

'Sshhhh! Never mind who I am,' he said in a silky voice. 'I'm just here to see those wonderful Indigenous works of art. But who are *you*?' he asked, lifting her chin with the point of the blade.

'T … Tessa. I'm a friend of Lainie's. We're camping out.' Should she make him think that Bane was nearby too? Would that help? She couldn't think. 'Why do you need to see the paintings? Are you going to destroy them? You're too late. Lainie's aunt has already taken the photos to Melbourne to get the site registered,' she told him, trying to sound confident.

He made an impatient noise. 'I wouldn't dream of destroying something so old and authentic. No. I just want to improve them a bit. There are some very nice modern ochre pastels I've brought with me to bring out the colours. I'm sure when I'm done they'll look just like they did when they were first painted.'

Sneaky bastard. He planned to make everyone think the paintings were fakes, as if the Gracewoods had painted them just to stop the mining acquisition.

Messing with the paintings in any way was a federal offence. He could kiss his mining career goodbye if he was found out, which meant that he wouldn't be letting her tell anyone. Worse still, Lainie had warned them that he was capable of violence. Her whole body trembled as she desperately tried to think of something she could do.

'You can't kill me,' she insisted, trying to sound like the brave people did in the movies and failing badly. 'A murder investigation would really mess up any chance you might have at getting that stupid licence.'

He actually laughed. 'Murder? No. Accident. It's not like I actually need to use this knife. Perhaps a broken neck from a fall down a shaft? Or you could drown in the river. Either option is easy to fake. Lainie could get killed trying to rescue you too, if she's really around here. In fact, the search for you both might just uncover what the two of you were up to in here. Especially when the police find your art supplies in here.'

He had thought it through far too much for her liking. As much as the idea pained her, she actually considered showing him the paintings, because if she did, there was a chance he might just do his dirty work and leave quickly. All their recent planning had been based around manipulating Noah and Lainie to use their powers to break down the rock barrier and come home, but now that there was a real threat, all she wanted was for Noah to stay right where he was. Where he was safe.

Perhaps Bane was right. Perhaps Noah would be compelled to keep the rock fall intact in order to prevent anyone from getting through, even if they knew she was in danger. And the worst part was that she hoped that was true. The last thing she wanted was for Noah to come anywhere near the cave while this man was here. Despite the fact that she was alone. And she was probably going to die.

As Harry crossed the Event Horizon, the anxiety he had been sensing morphed into a feeling of fury so powerful that it hit him like a slap in the face. Mere metres away. Just on the other side of the rocks. Two people were there. One was hostile. Every bone in his body screamed warning of the danger that the invader was bringing to Eden. How had they thought it would be all right to leave the area unprotected, even for a day? Outsiders were not allowed to be so close! He put his hand on the rock where he knew there would be a gap if only he could push it out of the way, but his hand stayed fixed on the wall.

He could not reveal the sword to this stranger.

Extending all his senses, he could hear a young woman crying on the other side. Tessa needed help. His mind reeled at the conflicting impulses he felt. Eden instincts as well as basic decency warred with his compulsion to keep the sword hidden, and he despaired. She was a helpless young girl and he was standing uselessly on the wrong side of a wall.

Noah ran straight past the angry burning sword, hardly noticing the speed at which it was spinning because Tessa was in danger.

There was a stranger. He could feel his presence like acid on his skin and the thought that Tessa might be forced to reveal the truth about Eden woke something powerful, deep inside his chest. Words he had never before uttered tumbled from his lips as he demanded a way through.

Far below him, the deep roots of the mountain groaned as it woke to his urgent call and daintily shook its peak, the unburied fragment, in an obliging shiver. Rocks began to tremble and tumble and bounce like popping candy on a tongue, and he noticed Harry trying to duck as far away from the wall as he could. Even though there wasn't a lot of space between the wall and the angry sword, Harry seemed unable to make himself back further away through the Event Horizon again. In bleak fury, Noah began to shout, vaguely aware that he should control the flying debris but not having a clue as to how he should go about it. Pebbles showered down and plinked in every direction.

Tessa was in danger.

A gaping hole opened up in the rock fall as the stones rolled away, and for a second the remaining rocks framed the scene dramatically before the rest of the wall exploded outwards in deafening surrender to his reckless injunction. He spoke again as he ran. Words of power fell from his mouth like fiery comets as he tried to spin the rocks away from Tessa, making them crash even more unpredictably, but he didn't care much because through the chaos he could see a man on the other side of the cave, standing behind her with a knife held to her throat. Her hands were trussed together in front of her but her wild eyes immediately locked on his. At that moment all words froze on his lips. She was staring at him with such a fierce look that he gasped. It was the same flash of fury that had ended so badly for her in the soccer game and he knew beyond doubt that she would do *anything* to end what she obviously perceived was a threat to him, regardless of the consequence to her own safety. He couldn't let her. Rocks pelted him and he lost his focus, which added to the desperation he saw in her dark eyes.

Between one step and the next, he forced himself to stop moving, realising that approaching them would only make things worse. With obstructed fury, he watched Harry dive through the gap just as Tessa elbowed her captor in the belly. The man doubled over in pain but still didn't let her go. Instead, he tried to slash at her with the knife, but then Harry was there, grabbing at the blade with his bare hands to deflect its course as Tessa stumbled backwards out of his reach.

Rocks flew everywhere, spinning like shells tumbling in the surf. Each one appeared to be randomly inventing its own individual laws of gravity in protest of the fact that he had given them such incomplete directives. Noah scrambled over boulders to get to Tessa, who in turn was madly trying to reach him, hampered by her tied wrists, but then something shoved him from the side and he saw a blade flash towards his face.

Harry's angry roar reverberated from the walls as the farmhand slammed into the man holding the knife, and the three of them went toppling into the chaos. And the sound of Tessa's anguished cry shredded the air from where she was still struggling to reach him.

Chapter 40

'INGVS!'

Hundreds of flying rocks froze in mid-air in a snapped instant. The sudden absence of sound and movement was mind-numbing. All was eerily silent.

Alex Beckinsale stared slack-mouthed at the sight of Lainie Gracewood standing in her denim shorts and torn black tank top, feet apart, hands held out in front of her as if she was a conductor ending a song. Her eyes flashed as she spoke again, in a language unpronounceable and foreign and yet somehow deeply cogent, and the floating rocks began to slam violently against the walls of the cavern and then fall still in a shower of dust and cold rubble. Even the floor was cleared at her command.

Alex knelt, awestruck by the sight of the creature who had ordered the rocks to move. Something large and bright hovered behind her, spinning faster than the eye could see. Her tawny brown eyes blazed with fury as she stared accusingly at the knife he was holding. It was covered in blood. He looked down in confusion. A dark-skinned man lay in front of him, twitching, with dust and crimson stickiness coating his chest and running freely down one arm. The man meant nothing to him.

'What is that?' Alex asked, pointing to the spinning ball of flame suspended in mid-air. As nervous as he was of the powerful young woman with the wild hair, he still knew that there was money to be made here somehow. No. Not just money. Power. The air practically buzzed with it. Raw power and transcending authority. Everything he'd ever wanted.

But her answer was yet another spoken command that made the hairs on the back of his neck try to run away. She had to be obeyed by every strand of his DNA. His vision blurred, so he wiped at the warm liquid that was running down into his eyes, and then the cavern began to sway. His head really hurt. He remembered a lot of heavy rocks whizzing around in the air, so it didn't surprise him that one had hit him. Possibly more than one. But why couldn't he see? Perhaps he was already dead. Perhaps that was why the Angel of Death had turned up. The last thought he had as he lost consciousness was that the fiery angel was not at all pleased with him.

⌒

'Harry!' I screamed as I ran over to him. He couldn't be dead. He was Harry! Shoving bits of rubble impatiently out of my way, I knelt and cradled his head in my lap. He was still breathing, but it was laboured. His hands were cut badly and there was a deep gash across his chest. Blood covered everything. Panic stricken, I noticed a spot under his arm where it was pumping out in time with his heartbeat, and so I tore the loose strip from my shirt and pressed it against the wound. Beside me, Noah grabbed the knife from Alex Beckinsale's slack fingers and cut away the straps holding Tessa's wrists. She immediately placed her hands against Harry's chest and I held my breath but after a moment, she just shook her head. She had no healing for him. A few moments later the sat-phone was in her hand and she was dialling.

'I have to get out of the cave, there's no reception in here,' she cried, running for the tunnel.

'Tell them we'll meet them at the Gracewood's,' Noah called after her. There was no way an ambulance could get anywhere near here, even if we had been able to allow them to.

I shook my head at Noah, tears streaming down my face. I could feel Harry's blood pushing straight through the cloth. So hot. So much of it. 'There's no time. He's cut an artery.'

Noah rummaged in Tessa's pack for the first-aid kit, tossing aside her other belongings before finding what we needed. Wadding up some bandages, we held pressure on the cut as best we could. It felt as though my veins were filled with pure adrenaline as I struggled to focus on what I had been trained to do in such an emergency. He needed medical treatment—fast, but how were we supposed to move him in this state?

Fuzzily, I tried to remember how to speak the words that had come so easily a moment ago, but I might as well have been trying to speak Welsh. How was that possible? How was it fair? We *needed* Harry. Eden needed him. Angry tears streamed down my face as I realised that with Sarah, Noah and I, Harry must now be considered unnecessary.

I looked back towards Eden. The sword had slowed to a silent angry growl the moment the lawyer had passed out.

'We need to get him back across the boundary,' I managed to choke out.

Harry groaned feebly, but Noah nodded. 'You keep holding the bandage. I'll lift him. Try to keep the pressure on,' he urged as he tried to work out the best way to carry him without moving his arm too much.

'No, don't move him,' a gentle voice chimed in. Looking around in surprise I realised that my mother had arrived. And so had Bane. Panting with exertion, he was standing at the end of the tunnel with such an acute look of distress on his face that I almost ran to him to reassure him that I was okay. He looked dreadful; his clothes were drenched and he had bleeding scratches across his face and arms. Watching me like a hawk, he stayed back to allow us to deal with Harry, leaning with both hands against the wall and gasping as his body struggled to recover from its extreme oxygen debt.

Annie smiled and stepped lightly over to us, peeling away some of the skin from the piece of Living Fruit I had seen her pick earlier. She moved my hands away from Harry's wound, revealing the grisly cut muscle underneath. She squeezed the skin so that a few drops of juice fell onto the gash and I sucked in a hopeful breath as the blood flow slowed then stopped. Within moments the wound began to close. Harry groaned again. Annie held the Fruit to his lips but he tilted his head away. She tried again.

'No. Please, Annie,' he whispered, brushing her cheek with his good hand. She looked as confused as I was.

'Harry. You can eat. You can go back to Eden, we'll be all right here. Please!' I begged him.

'No,' Noah said, pulling me back. 'Don't make him eat. It's not what he wants.'

I glared at him. Eden had addled his brains. I didn't care if Harry was too macho to want to accept healing. So what if he forgot a few things? It was worth it to save his life. Life was precious, far too precious to lose for the sake of pride.

'Lainie, I'm serious. He doesn't want the Fruit. He thinks it will do Eden damage if he eats it.'

My mother cringed away and I looked down at Harry, confused.

'The Trees. You saw what happens,' he groaned, his speech slurred. 'There's too much guilt and grief in me. The Fruit was never designed to have to deal with those. If it tries to heal that, it will be washed into the River.'

Guilt and grief? Like my mother's? Was it really true that her newly-woken grief had somehow damaged the Trees and the River as she sought healing? I thought of the remorseful look on her face when we had passed the dead Trees.

'There's always a choice, Lainie,' Harry whispered tiredly. 'It'll be okay. The juice has done enough already. I'll be all right.'

It was true, he did look a little better. His face was still deathly pale but the wound had all but stopped bleeding. Craning his neck, he looked painfully over at the unconscious form next to him. Alex Beckinsale looked like an untidy suit that someone had left on the floor. His limbs were all askew. Annie was looking from the injured stranger to the Fruit in her hand as if she was considering giving it to him instead.

'No, Annie, not him,' I said, pulling her hand away. If Harry was worried about infecting the River, I could only imagine what damage the corporate lawyer's psyche would do to it. No wonder Fallen Man had been exiled from Eden. Who in this world was ever completely free from guilt? The responsibility weighed heavily. If we ever allowed the world to find out about Eden, they would eventually find a way in, and the Trees would not survive that. Nor would the peaceful Edenites.

'What did you do to him, Lainie?' Noah asked, prodding the man with his toe.

'I didn't hit him with the rock. I think that was one of yours,' I defended. 'But I did send him blind. It was the only thing I could think of—but I was a bit too slow.'

'He saw the sword,' Noah confirmed.

'And he saw me moving rocks around with nothing but my freaky brain,' I added miserably. The five of us stared in dread at the intruder slumped before us.

'What happened, Harry?' Noah asked. 'I thought you had him?'

'I did,' he croaked, 'but I couldn't follow through with it. I was going to kill him, but I just couldn't do it.' His voice was weak and slurred.

I'd seen Harry slaughter sheep and even put down our old sheep dog, but this was a whole different situation. He turned to my mother with confusion in his eyes, as if seeking vindication. 'I mean, I really was prepared to kill him, but somehow I just *couldn't*.'

'Of course not,' Annie said to him. 'We are Cherubim. We can't kill humans, otherwise how would we be allowed into Eden?'

Tessa came back down the tunnel, breathless. 'How is he?'

'I'm okay,' Harry replied, trying to smile.

She leant over to catch her breath. 'I've called an ambulance. They're on their way to Lainie's. They wanted to know what happened but I just said there was an accident. I didn't know what else to tell them.'

'That's perfect, Tess, thanks. We haven't worked out what to say either,' Noah reassured her as he gathered her into his arms. My mother stared at her with wide curious eyes and Tessa peered back at her in confusion.

'Tessa, Bane, this is Annie Gracewood ... my ... mother,' I stammered. Still stark naked, she walked over to Bane, hugged him, and kissed him on the cheek. The poor guy looked like he wanted to run for the hills, but he bravely stood his ground, smiling back at her as politely as he could while still panting, with sweat running down the side of his face.

I watched my mum carefully. I had expected her to run away again as soon as she realised they were Guardians, but instead she seemed totally unfazed by everything that was happening. In relieved astonishment, I smiled as she skipped across and gave Tessa the same treatment. Back in Eden she had struggled at just the mention of the Guardians, so how was she coping with this on top of the bloody aftermath of an unexpected battle? It was all such a contrast to the serenity and peace on the other side of the boundary that I couldn't even begin to come to terms with the violence. Maybe she had snuck a taste of the Fruit before she'd arrived, after all. I marvelled at her calm smile. She looked like she expected everything to work out fine, as if the River really had washed away her depression. Or perhaps her confidence was simply logical. We had amazing powers available to us, limited only by need. There were four Cherubim in the cavern, and we needed this man to forget what he had seen.

'Annie, what do you think we should do? About this man who has seen what he shouldn't?' I asked. It was time I stopped treating her like a mentally ill child and started trusting her. She looked down at him with a puzzled expression.

'I wish I could give him some Fruit, then he'd feel better, and maybe forget,' she suggested, but she sounded unhappy with her own proposal. She hid the Fruit behind her back as if suddenly worried he might open his eyes and see it. Clearly her instincts were kicking in again quickly. 'He *is* badly injured. Maybe he won't wake up?'

We all studied his unconscious form for a few moments, trying to come to terms with the seriousness of our predicament. No matter how dangerous he had been mere minutes beforehand, the idea of murdering someone was simply unthinkable, not to mention unhelpful. The last thing we needed here was a police investigation.

'I know!' she exclaimed, 'I'll sing to him. He'll forget *and* he will heal. We *need* him to not die, or others will ask questions.' She knelt down and began to stroke his face with her fingertips, almost lovingly, while I stared at her, astounded by her confidence. As if it could just be that easy.

But then she began to sing the lullaby she had sung to me in the Garden, only the words began to quiver and shift into the same language we had used each time we had needed supernatural help. Listening to it carefully, I still couldn't understand so much as a single word and yet the song's meaning was clear. Her voice coaxed and soothed. Power dripped from the mystical lyrics. We really did have unlimited resources available to us, when it came to protecting the Garden. As I watched his wounds begin to heal, I kept an eye on the sword. It still spun slowly, as if it was holding back and waiting to see what would happen next. Bane bent and picked up the revolting knife and tossed it aside, well away from the man's reach.

Eventually he began to groan and stir. Still the sword stayed calm.

When Alex Beckinsale opened his eyes, they were completely white. 'Are you an angel, too?' he whispered to Annie as her soothing song faded into silence.

'No, silly. I'm a Cherub,' she chided. 'You'll have to start behaving much better if you want to see an angel.'

It took another ten minutes before Harry felt well enough to be able to move, during which time Bane and Tessa had healed all our minor wounds. We half lifted, half carried Harry out of the tunnel. He managed to walk a little once we were in the open, leaning heavily on Bane and Noah, and even managed to speak to a frantic Sarah who had been trying to call—she must have felt the threat, despite her distance.

By then we had established that Alex Beckinsale had forgotten everything, including his own name. He was unlikely to ever be a danger to us again but we were still reluctant to say too much in front of him. We certainly didn't want to remind him of what had happened, so we had to wait for a better time to share our stories. Amazingly, he seemed to be completely relaxed about the fact that he was blind. I felt pretty certain that he would get his sight back in time, but in case I was wrong I didn't want to give him any false hope.

He clung to my mother like a toddler and she stroked his hair and told him to be a good boy. He told her he trusted her and would do anything she asked. So she asked him why he had come. Opening and closing his mouth a few times, clearly struggling to recall what had happened, he started to cry because he couldn't answer her question. Tessa let out a little grunt of satisfaction at the sight.

'It's all right,' Annie soothed, 'my friends will take you home now. Don't worry about trying to remember.' The last words were said with a hint of command. There was still a trace of power, even in English. He nodded happily.

'Come on, Alex, I'll lead you,' I said, wanting to get Harry back as soon as possible.

'No, not you!' he recoiled, clinging to my mother again. So he still remembered my voice at least. Tessa came and took his hand instead. Watching her lead him, I was immensely impressed with the way she was willing to help the man who had held a knife to her throat less than half an hour earlier. I would never think of her as cowardly again.

As soon as they moved off, Annie gave each of us another quick hug, headed back into the tunnel still clutching the Fruit that Harry had refused, and was gone.

When we reached the river, we settled Harry into the canoe with

Noah. Bane pushed the boat off and Noah began to paddle it downstream. Harry had assured us that there were no more waterfalls, but it would still be a rough ride.

'What was he doing here, anyway?' I whispered to Tessa. Mr Beckinsale was sitting down on the riverbank taking off his shoes and socks like he had been asked. 'Surely he couldn't have known about Eden?'

Tessa explained what he had said to her and then Bane added what he had heard in Horsham at the gallery. I glared at the man through narrowed eyes. He looked completely harmless now so I had to trust that everything would work out all right, but I felt deeply offended.

Chapter 41

Liam and Caleb were relieved but confused to find us all rocking up at the house two hours later. It had been a torturously slow hike back with a blind man. They told us that the trip down the river had opened up Harry's wounds pretty badly. Because of the cuts on his hands, he'd struggled to brace himself properly as the canoe had bumped him around, and by the time the ambos got to him he was slipping in and out of consciousness again. Noah had gone to the hospital with him.

The first thing I did when I got in the door was to call Senior Sergeant Loxwood. When he arrived in a dust cloud of lights and sirens, I had no real explanation to give.

'You say you found him trespassing?' the police sergeant asked.

'Yes.'

'And now he's blind?'

'Yes. But seems okay other than that.'

'Anything else you'd like to tell me?'

'Harry's hurt. Badly.'

'I know. I heard the call.' He waited, but I didn't have anything else to offer, so he crossed his arms. 'After you've seen Harry, all four of you will come straight to the station and make a statement. I'll be there as soon as I've had Mr Beckinsale seen by a doctor.' It didn't sound like a request, which worried me because I didn't want to lie but would have no chance of speaking or writing the truth either.

Harry was unconscious when we finally reached Nalong Hospital. There must have been some internal damage that the small amount of Fruit hadn't healed, and he had lost a lot of blood. The surgeon was perplexed by his wound. She said he was lucky to be alive and couldn't understand how he had sustained such a serious injury and yet had somehow managed to miss cutting an artery. I nodded but couldn't look straight at her, because it hadn't missed being cut at all.

Aunt Lily and Sarah met us there shortly after. They had only been booked for speeding once. Aunt Lily had been driving, luckily, because Sarah was shaking like a leaf in the wind. We told them everything that had happened, and Sarah spent a long time at Harry's bedside, not speaking but holding his hand, while my aunt paced around the halls looking for doctors to interrogate. Eventually we had to leave them there to watch over him so we could face up to Sergeant Loxwood's third polite summons.

'You claim Mr Beckinsale attacked you?' he asked as we all crammed into the tiny interview room at the Nalong Police Station. Tessa was the only one who looked vaguely calm. I had no idea what to say.

'We were camping,' she explained. 'We knew Harry was due to come back and we were hoping to meet him on his way home.' Which was sort of true, but I couldn't believe how easily she lied to the policeman. 'Mr Beckinsale found me alone and tried to make me tell him where the cave paintings were. He had a knife.' Her voice was shaking at the memory, but I knew she was more angry than frightened. I could always tell. She swallowed and continued. 'I think he was planning to do something to them because he had a satchel with some ochre paints inside. He must have been trying to discredit the paintings as fakes.'

'What did you do?' the senior sergeant asked, flicking his pen around his finger. It was a gesture that was made to look casual, but I could almost see his brain taking copious notes as he studied each of our faces out of the corner of his eye.

'I didn't have a chance to do anything because Harry turned up and made him let me go, but then they fought, and ...'

Noah helped her out, catching the policeman's eye. 'We heard the commotion but by the time we arrived, Mr Beckinsale was unconscious and Harry was injured. We called the ambulance and told them to meet us at Lainie's farm. There was no way they would have been able to get to us where we were, so we bound Harry's wounds as best we could. He was awake and I thought he would be fine but now ...' His distress was not faked.

'And what about Mr Beckinsale? How do you explain his blindness and amnesia?' the sergeant asked, turning back to Tessa.

'I have no idea. Perhaps he hit his head? He woke up after a few minutes and his eyes were completely white! Does he really not remember anything, or was he faking?' she asked intently. We all leant in a little closer to hear his reply.

Sergeant Loxwood blinked. 'He can't even remember his own name. And yet the doctors have found no evidence of a head wound. Where's the satchel now?'

'At my house,' I replied a bit too eagerly. 'We looked inside but didn't touch anything.'

'And did you find the knife that wounded Harry?'

'I threw it away,' Bane interjected. 'I wasn't sure what Mr Beckinsale would do when he woke up. I could go and find it, I guess.'

The police officer nodded. 'So none of you have any idea what happened to him?'

Tessa's eyes widened as she clutched the sides of her plastic chair. 'Harry Doolan is an Elder in this community. Lainie told me. Do you think he cursed Mr Beckinsale for trying to mess with a sacred site?' She looked like a child being told a ghost story.

The sergeant put down his pen. 'Tessa Bright. This is a serious investigation. Please don't try to confuse things by bringing up conjecture about the supernatural. If Mr Beckinsale has suffered some sort of medical affliction then the doctors will find an explanation. My job is to establish whether or not a crime has been committed. I cannot fathom how Harry Doolan could possibly be responsible for Mr Beckinsale's condition, so unless the medical experts are able to shed some more light on the subject, I will *not* be chasing up ghost stories.' He placed his palms on the desk in front of him and looked at her seriously. 'Do you want to press charges against Mr Beckinsale?'

Her mouth opened, and she glanced over at Noah, who looked very conflicted. It would have been very satisfying to send him to jail, especially after what he'd done to Tessa and Harry, but the idea of having to explain what had happened to a judge without revealing anything about Eden felt very complicated.

'No,' Tessa said firmly, obviously coming to the same conclusion. 'I don't think he'll hurt anyone again, do you?'

The policeman closed his folder. 'Then unless Mr Doolan wishes to lay charges, I will write up a report and not take the matter any further.

For now, I would like you all to go home and get some rest. Mr Millard, could you please go back tomorrow and check to make sure the cave paintings have not been damaged, and call me when you've located the knife—*but don't touch it.*'

We all sat there stunned for a minute. How had Tessa managed it? By bringing up the idea of the supernatural while sounding like a young foolish girl she had effectively managed to steer the sergeant right away from any such ideas. She'd even managed to keep the lies to a bare minimum. We would have to watch out for her. She was really sneaky and I completely adored her at that moment. All of us owed her, big time.

Chapter 42

The heavy night was waiting, and I nearly made it all the way home before I started to seriously fall apart. For some reason the leftover Minties wrappers on the back seat of Aunt Lily's car reminded me of the white butterflies that had danced around me by the River that morning, and then it was suddenly all too much. The vast disparity between my time spent in Eden and what had happened since was just too difficult for me to integrate. My heart was still full of joyful songs and exuberant play but then I had been smashing rocks and pressing my fingers against a severed artery.

My aunt had told us that Harry was still unconscious. I didn't know what that meant. He'd seemed so much better when we'd left the cave. Was the healing power of the Fruit only temporary? If only he'd agreed to eat it. If only he still had a Guardian. Both Bane and Tessa had tried to heal him but felt nothing—apparently they really could only heal the Cherubim they were linked to. Trusting that everything would work out fine seemed a long way from feasible all of a sudden. I only noticed how violently I was trembling when Bane moved across the backseat so he could wrap me in his arms. A tired part of my brain tried to warn me that I should probably push him away, but I couldn't stand the thought. I needed his secure hold, and I needed *him*. And until he had a chance to tell me he was leaving, I would take full selfish advantage.

When we arrived home, Caleb was wonderful. He'd done all the chores, made us cups of tea and even cooked us a late dinner, although I struggled to eat. We told him that his mum had decided to stay with Harry, despite the nurses' orders. She'd announced in no uncertain terms that she considered him as family, and she would never leave a member of her family to lie alone unconscious in a hospital no matter what the rules said. She could be fierce when it came to family. The nurses had backed off.

'Do you want me to come with you tomorrow to bring back the camping gear?' Caleb asked Noah as he took away his plate. We all stared at him blankly. 'You know,' he continued, 'if you're going to have a dirty weekend away, you might want to think about taking Tess somewhere a little more classy than Nalong State Park. Have I taught you nothing?'

Of course. We had all appeared out of the bush so suddenly he would have assumed we were all camping out there together. He took my plate next and polished off the rest of my stir-fry. 'I could bring Nicole along to help. She'll be stoked. She's been asking to see the cave paintings but Mum wouldn't let her,' he suggested.

'No!' Noah exclaimed. His brother paused mid-bite, looking confused.

Bane cleared his throat. 'Actually, Caleb, Sergeant Loxwood has requested that I go and locate the knife. He told me not to touch it. I think he wants to make sure the scene is left undisturbed, just in case.'

We all sat silently as his words sank in. The only reason the policeman would request that was if he thought it could become a murder investigation. 'Just in case' meant 'just in case Harry died from his wounds'. I left the room.

Bane found me in Harry's cottage, staring listlessly at the stupid note on the fridge. I had planned to do some tidying up because I wanted to believe Harry would be moving back in soon, but instead I'd just stood there numbly, staring at his annoying scribble as my mind kept oscillating between hopeful expectation that everything would be fine and razor sharp grief that kept trying to convince me that he was already lost.

'There is always a choice,' I whispered, over and over. Harry had chosen not to eat the Fruit. Had he chosen death? My mother had sounded so confident when she'd explained about people choosing to 'move across', as if they were choosing to take a holiday or a really long nap. Was that what Harry wanted? I shook my head. Again with the wanting. Eden rules. If he wanted to die, I should not only be happy for him, I should help. But what about what *I* wanted?

Behind me I heard Bane enter and lean against the doorframe, waiting for me to say something. I put it off for as long as I could but eventually I turned to face him and took a deep breath.

'I'm ready now. You can say what you need to.' Pressing down a bit of the curled up grey lino with my foot, I tried to sound more composed than I felt but I could hear the tremble in my voice.

He tilted his head. 'What is there to say?'

Oh, I don't know. Maybe how angry you are at me for ruining your life and embarrassing you in front of all my friends and family ...

Looking up at him boldly, I clutched the back of one of the chairs. 'Tell me what you need from me. I said I would help you leave Nalong but I honestly don't know if I can now. It depends on Harry.' There was a good chance that the mining threat was now over, but even if it was, I still couldn't leave Aunt Lily to run the farm on her own. Good farmhands were not easy to come by, let alone finding one we would feel comfortable with living so close to Eden. If Harry was unable to work ...

'But I'm not leaving Nalong,' he said, his slate grey eyes fixed on mine.

My heart was in turmoil. I was thrilled at the idea that I could still see him but I knew it would only be harder on me. The only way I knew of to break the bond was to cross into Eden. Would he stay on as our farmhand if I left? Was that his plan? I was so tired I could hardly think.

'I will always allow you your freedom,' I resolved. 'I need you to believe that.'

He gripped the doorframe in frustration, looking as grumpy as he had all those times when I'd tipped his locker forwards to make his books fall against the door. Was he going to yell at me the way he always had back then?

'Lainie, you can be incredibly infuriating sometimes.' It wasn't quite a yell but I still cringed. 'I'm not going to leave you. Not unless you tell me to. I know you think I need my freedom, but I'm telling you I already have it. And I will *always* allow you yours.' He pointed in exasperation to the writing on the fridge. 'I have a choice. And with or without the bond, I'm choosing to be here, with you.'

I was stunned. He still wanted me? Could it really be as simple as that? As simple as Eden?

'Look,' he said, clearly trying to be patient. 'I don't blame you for doubting me. And you were right to make me leave for a while. For the last ten years I've treated you like dirt. I hurt you in every possible way

I could think of.' His face had taken on that bitter, self-loathing expression again. Humans should never *ever* look like that.

'Bane, I told you I've forgiven you for—'

'I know!' he interrupted, 'but that's not enough. I need a chance to regain your trust, because why would you possibly believe that I won't hurt you again?'

I just stood there looking stupid and feeling scared. How was he able to articulate what I felt when I couldn't even make sense of it myself? I needed to tell him anyway, no matter how muddled I was.

'I used to be able to just let it bounce off me, when you were mean. More or less,' I stammered. Stupid words. I wanted words that would banish that self-contempt from his eyes, not these ones.

'But now you can't,' he said.

I shrugged apologetically.

'Because I matter to you now.' I gave a short nod. He smiled, but his eyes were still very serious. 'I want you to be able to trust me.'

The sign language that I'd seen in Eden could not be manipulated to tell lies and so I knew that everything about Bane's body language was telling me the truth. And I was good at knowing if people were being truthful. He *wanted* a chance to prove I could trust him.

'Bane?' I whispered in a voice that always seemed to go husky when I most wanted to be heard. I was afraid to ask but even more afraid not to. 'What else do you want?'

He closed the distance between us as if released from chains. 'I want us to be together. And I want to help you to do your job. And not just because it's been ordained, but because I've always loved you—even when I was too self-absorbed to see it.'

I could feel his body quivering as he gripped my shoulders. He searched my face. 'But what about you, Lainie? What do *you* want?'

An intrinsic, primal impulse welled up inside me that had nothing to do with Eden, and everything to do with the person I had been born to love.

'I want what you want,' I breathed, and when he kissed me, for just a little while, everything was *just fine.*

Chapter 43

Everything will be fine, I thought to myself as I started to drift off to sleep on the couch. Bane's arms were wrapped around my waist and I could feel the weight of his ankle resting on mine. He had reluctantly cut short my kisses and led me back to the house, saying he didn't want to take advantage of my 'transitioning emotional state'—whatever that was. We each showered away the grime and various remnant bits of bushland that had stuck to us since our afternoon trek back from the cave, and changed into our daggiest old tracksuits, but then I had just sort of gone into hibernation in the lounge room and refused to move again, despite Aunt Lily's best coaxing techniques. Eventually she'd given up and tossed me a spare woollen blanket and a pillow.

Bane hadn't even looked apologetic when he'd pulled the blanket over us both, and Aunt Lily hadn't commented. He couldn't possibly have been very comfortable, but he refused to let me go now that he knew how much I needed him, and the thought of going to sleep in my own bed as if everything was back to the way it had been a few days ago made me feel kind of dizzy. Nothing was the same anymore. Harry was in hospital. Paradise was close enough to taste, and my life had been thrown into utter chaos. My worry for Harry would return the second Bane was not around, I was certain. But with him there, everything would be *fine*.

I let my mind relax, and at some point the line between my muddled thoughts and my jumbled fantasies blurred, and I slept. All night my dreams were cut from sorrow as well as sweetness, both fabrics capricious and yet still somehow harmonious, and both were inescapably woven from threads of love.

The call came at 9.30 the next morning. The surgeon wanted to see Aunt Lily in person, so Bane and I went with her to the small red brick hospital building and she spent a long time in the surgeon's office where she was told the news. Harry's wounds had been healing at a miraculous rate, but when the surgeon had looked at the MRI she'd found something else. A tumour in his shoulder. Further scans had revealed the full extent of the crisis. Harry's body was riddled with late stage bone cancer.

'He must have known,' Aunt Lily sobbed as she told us the news. 'He would have been in significant pain for a while. Do you think that was why he went ... you-know-where?' she asked.

I shook my head. 'Maybe, but then he found out—'

The words stuck in my throat. I couldn't tell her about the Trees. I couldn't explain that he believed eating the Fruit might damage the sacred source of Life itself. After listening to the misery of the River music leaking out from the Garden for so long, I could understand Harry's choice. The blessed Garden was far more important than any of us. It was the ultimate hope of the entire human race. 'He doesn't want to be healed there,' I explained weakly instead.

My world felt like it was caving in as I realised then that not only would I have done the same, but that I would support him in his choice. I wanted what he wanted.

Sarah had spent all night by his bedside. Aunt Lily told me that the nurses had struggled to rouse her in the morning. She was dizzy and exhausted and when she heard the news she became so distraught that the doctors ended up giving her a sedative and made Aunt Lily drive her home.

Bane and I waited at the hospital for Noah to arrive so I could tell him in person. His tears were like a contrasting reflection of the tears of joy and wonder he had shed when we'd first sat overlooking the glory of Eden. Tessa called him on cue, as if she could feel his distress the way she felt his pain. I could hear her stammer when Noah told her about Harry. I knew she wanted to ask the same thing Aunt Lily had—whether we should get him back to Eden—but she couldn't get the words out over the phone and Noah didn't want to argue with her, so he told her he'd see her later.

The hospital facility was small but efficient. The faded walls and dated furniture were typical of a rural town with a small state budget allocation. Harry was still unconscious, and the nurses in the Intensive Care Unit were reluctant to let me in because I wasn't a direct family member. At least I was certain about that now. Bane waited in the hospital café while Noah bullied the nurses into letting us in to see him anyway.

The sight of Harry's slack features and weathered but healed hands outlined against the stark white sheets bothered me a lot. His chest was no longer even bandaged, which made him look like he was ready to just open his eyes and tell me off for hovering over him when there was work to catch up on. Even the few drops of Fruit juice had worked miracles, but it was still not enough.

They had him hooked up to a bulky heart monitor with white lines that waltzed across the screen and made noises that were even more annoying than a phone. If he'd been awake he would have complained about that. He didn't belong here. It brought home to me the fact that despite all our powers and authority we were still human, genetically at least. Spiritually? Not as vulnerable, possibly not even able to be tempted to kill another human, but where did that leave us? I felt human. I certainly felt anger, and grief. I didn't kid myself into thinking he would recover, and I wasn't even sure he wanted to. He had been to Eden. He knew how the people there viewed the passing of a loved one. He would finally be reunited with his Guardian, whoever she was. It would be a joyous time for him, and for his sake I needed to see things the same way.

Noah clutched Harry's hand in both of his, and I thought about all the times Harry had told us off for misbehaving as well as the times he'd made us laugh. He'd grown us up, and we both owed him so much. I would miss his laconic steadiness, and the way he took everything in his stride. He acted like a true Sentinel—confident, determined and capable. How would Noah and I ever fill those shoes?

'Thank you, Harry, for everything,' I whispered, kissing him softly on the cheek. There was not much else to say. His story was finishing. I would have to tell him mine the next time we met.

When we came out to the café Noah's phone rang again. We would have to find a better way for Tessa to contact him or one of them was going to develop epilepsy or something. After only a few seconds, he hung up and looked at me apologetically.

'That was Mum. Nicole's run off again, and I'll give you one guess as to where she's heading. I *knew* she would get nosy when she heard we'd been out there again.' He swore under his breath. 'Why does she always have to be so selfish? She knows Harry's in a bad way and that Mum's not taking it well. Why does she have to pick now to misbehave?'

Probably because she assumed we'd all be too distracted by Harry to care what she did. She would have been right, except that she was doing the one thing we couldn't ignore.

'Do you really think she'll find it on her own?' I asked. 'I don't feel like anything's wrong out there. How long ago do you think she left?'

'She was still at home when I left to come here, so maybe she isn't close enough to trigger our warning senses yet. Mum seemed pretty certain about where she was headed though. She's closer, and she would feel her if any of us can.'

'Lainie, I think we'd better go,' Bane said seriously. 'We're already nearly an hour from the farm. The sooner we get back the better.' He had come to stand closer to me, and his fingers were twitching. I knew those signs. We were headed for trouble again. Even as I thought it, my spine began to prickle. It felt like someone was following me down a dark alley, and the hospital felt very stifling all of a sudden.

Noah drove us home, where Aunt Lily explained that she'd brought Sarah back to our place so she could sleep somewhere quiet while the sedatives wore off, but that she had woken and left to look for Nicole. Even the strong medication wouldn't have been enough to calm her with both her daughter and Eden at risk. Maybe she would manage to head her off in time, but Nicole could be pretty quick when she wanted to be.

I drove much farther up the river than usual, dodging the bushes that were too solid to plough through, until the paddock basher started making a new unhappy grinding noise, and then the three of us piled out and began to scramble our way upstream. I was so tense that I jumped a mile when the sat-phone Bane had thought to bring along started ringing. I looked hopefully at him. Maybe it was Noah's mum calling to say she had found Nicole. Wrong again.

'Hi, Tess,' Bane said. 'No, he's fine. Just some scratches. Nicole's gone snooping around the river so we're going to look for her … Of course, but I suggest taking the normal path. The short cut is pretty wild. Don't rush so much that you get hurt.' He glanced my way as if he was trying to make a point but I ignored him and kept pushing through a stubborn cape wattle. 'No, they won't wait for you, but you'll … Of course I will.' He frowned at Noah at the last part, by which I assumed that Tessa had just instructed him to keep her charge safe until she arrived.

Scrambling along the riverbank was tough. Much of it was so steep and overgrown that we had to wade through the river to get past. I had never needed to get there in such a hurry before and it felt as if it took forever. It was hard to stay patient and test how slippery or wobbly the rocks were before trusting them with our weight. With each passing minute I felt as though the danger was increasing and I pushed my body to its limit trying to move as fast as I could. Bane was so anxious he couldn't even let go of my hand, which made it more awkward to clamber across the chaotic terrain, and I tried not to think about what sort of danger I must be getting myself into. Surely it couldn't really be that bad, though. It was only Nicole, after all.

After what felt like hours, we finally heard the sound of the waterfall up ahead. By then I was stumbling more than walking, certainly no longer jogging. Bane was practically carrying me over all the fallen logs. This would have been a good time for one of those unexpected super powers to manifest. They only occurred 'as required', but I couldn't very well do my job if I went into cardiac arrest just trying to get there, could I? I wondered what Bane would do if Noah and I took to the air and flew the rest of the way, but sadly that wasn't to be and when we finally made it to the bottom of the falls we all collapsed, panting, by the edge of the lagoon.

There was no sign of Nicole, but I could see wet footprints on the rocks on the other side of the river. Noah took off his boots and I started to do the same but Bane grabbed my wrist.

'Lainie, please, not yet. You won't make it as you are and I won't be able to get us both across until I've had a couple of minutes to rest first.'

I watched Noah tackle the current with flailing arms that betrayed how exhausted he was and I knew Bane was right. Sitting there would hardly be restful, but my lungs were already desperately trying to suck in enough air as it was. It was the first time I had ever felt I couldn't keep up physically as well as the guys could, and I wanted to scream.

We watched Noah being swept much further downstream than usual and I decided it was a good thing that Tessa wasn't with us. She wouldn't have tried to stop him, but she would have let herself drown before leaving him to cross without her.

As I sat, gasping, on the rocks, it occurred to me that Noah's dad might be here somewhere too. Or perhaps Sarah wasn't in any danger. We were still a bit hazy regarding the rules of these compulsions. Maybe he was on his way, stumbling along our usual trail. So many people's lives were affected by this place, and no one seemed to have any say in it. Bane had me cradled against his chest as if I would fade out of existence if he let me go. It was torture for him to be so tightly tied to me, no matter what he said. He should have been off doing army training, meeting girls with fake eyelashes who would swoon over a sexy man in uniform, not being compelled to run madly through the bush trying to protect a girl in a flannel shirt with broken wattle twigs in her hair. What had seemed so simple the previous night was beginning to feel complicated again. Was I really doing the right thing?

Pushing back my sweaty hair, I plucked out a couple of hitchhiking leaves and took a few more deep breaths. I had made my decision, and I would stick to it. Right and wrong were not concepts I felt like dealing with right then. I had work to do. No more time for reflection.

My legs had almost stopped shaking and I was only dizzy for a few seconds when I stood up and stuffed my socks into my boots. I let Bane throw them across the river because in my state they would have been lucky to have made it halfway.

The icy water felt wonderful as I slid my way into the current. I could hear the music calling me. It was much less sad now, and yet it still sounded like a funeral march. I rolled onto my back and kicked my way across, trying not to care how far downstream I went, so long as I made it to the other side using as little energy as possible. Bane swam ahead of me so I didn't even have to watch where I was going. I just kept kicking, strong fast kicks. I let Bane worry about steering, and focused only on keeping my head above the water. Finally I felt him lifting my shoulders and I found I could touch the rocks at the bottom again. He practically dragged me out of the river—it was becoming a habit here.

As soon as we managed to force our wet feet back into our boots, I bounded up the tiny streamlet, all tiredness forgotten as I was overwhelmed by a fresh sense of urgency. Bane had to run to keep up.

∽

Noah stumbled his way along the tunnel without any method of illumination. Bane was the one who always thought about practical things like bringing torches. But he didn't need to see, because he could sense someone up ahead, someone who shouldn't be anywhere near here, who had to be taken away from this place as soon as possible, so he followed the sense of wrongness like a kelpie on a rabbit trail until he rounded a corner to see the glow of the cavern ahead. The sword was spinning faster again. Its heat slowed his shivering but the tension in his body didn't ease. His mum was waiting for him.

'Noah,' she gasped, rushing over to embrace him. Her pale hair tangled around her face, making her look more flustered than he had ever seen her. 'Nicole's crossed over. We have to get her back. I've never been past here, honey, but you have. I thought it would be best if I waited so you could help me find her.' She took his hand in both of hers and led him closer to the spinning weapon. The massive sword slowed slightly as it recognised the presence of the Cherubim.

'She got past? How? I thought the sword would have stopped her somehow …'

'She was already halfway across when I got here. The sword would have killed her if I hadn't commanded it to let her through,' she entreated, looking nervous about his reaction. It could be commanded? He would have to find out how she had done that.

The thought of Nicole in Eden sent violent shivers down his spine. What were they expected to do with her? Even if they did manage to find her, what then? Could they just bring her home and pretend it never happened? What if she ate some of the Living Fruit? There was too much he still didn't understand about how this all worked. What would happen to Tessa if he crossed over again? After yesterday he had vowed to himself that he wouldn't leave her alone here again. He couldn't even call her to say goodbye. But he had to find his sister.

Together they headed towards the Event Horizon, the quiescent sword revolving within its halo of flames.

Chapter 44

As I stepped under the rocky overhang Bane yanked me to a halt.

'What's wrong?' My body was quivering with the need to keep moving.

'I can't let you go in there.' He pulled me behind him as if to shield me from whatever was inside the cave. 'It's too dangerous. I have no idea why but this is stronger than anything I've ever felt before. I just can't let you go in.' Turning towards me, he tried to push me back.

'Bane,' I said, standing my ground, 'I understand exactly what you mean because I feel it too. It's so strong. I *need* to go. You said you would help me to do my job. I need you to let me do this.'

He clenched his jaw. 'I have no choice, Lainie!' The sopping wet hair that fell across his face did nothing to quench the fire in his eyes.

'Yes you do. There is always a choice.'

Fear and frustration warred in his expression as he remembered our pact to always allow each other our freedom, and he reluctantly released his hold. As soon as he let go I fled into the darkness of the cave.

As I stumbled out of the twisting tunnel I felt the heat of the sword even before I saw its light. Rounding the last corner, I was blinded by the contrast of the bright flame against the blackness beyond. Noah and Sarah were about to cross over.

'Noah, wait! Something's not right!' I shouted. 'Sarah, please, just wait a minute. Hold on!' Sarah tried to keep moving but Noah held her back with a tortured look in his bright eyes. 'Noah!' I panted, tripping over the uneven floor of the cavern. 'You can't let her cross. She's not one of us!'

With a painful mental slap I had finally worked out what had been bothering me since I'd seen Harry at the hospital. His hands had not shown a trace of the wounds he'd sustained from the knife fight, but my mother had never touched them with the Fruit juice. Also, Noah's dad was nowhere to be seen, nor had he ever said even one word to any of us about a place that was such a significant part of all our lives. Mr Ashbree had nothing to do with Eden.

In the Bible there were two Cherubim appointed to secure the entrance. And now I knew what that meant. Two in each generation. My mother, Harry, Noah and myself.

And each of us had our own Guardian. We had been lied to, and even I had missed it, passing off the hints of deceit I had felt from Sarah as something else because I hadn't wanted to mistrust her.

'She's right, Noah,' Bane gasped as he ducked beneath the last stalactite. 'Your mother is a Guardian like me and Tess. She's not a Cherub.'

He tried to catch my hand but I evaded his grasp.

'It explains why she was so dizzy this morning at the hospital,' he continued. 'She tried to heal Harry but couldn't. She's suffering because there's nothing she can do to heal him from the cancer.'

I thought back to when I had overheard Sarah talking to Harry in his cottage. 'You tried to heal him before he even left for Eden, didn't you? Why didn't it work?'

She seemed to deflate, and once again I saw that self-condemnation that should never exist. That taint that had exiled countless generations from their true home. 'Harry said my gift had weakened because I resisted the bond for too many years. I wanted to be free from it more than anything, but not at the cost of his life!'

Free from it? So I'd been right all along.

'Don't you see?' she cried. '*I* did this to him!' She gripped Noah's wrist and began to drag him towards the sword like he was a reluctant toddler. 'But it's not too late. There's more than one way to heal someone.'

Eden. Sarah had been trying to get into Eden to gain access to the Living Fruit. She intended to use it to heal Harry. I leaped quickly to block her path to the sword.

'Nicole never even came anywhere near here, did she?' I accused. How had she been planning to get past the sword? Of course. If Noah took her across willingly, the sword wouldn't protest. Maybe. But Noah looked as horrified as I felt, and I doubted he could have let her get much further even if we hadn't worked out the truth.

It was time to speak out a new solution.

There were a thousand words I could use to repel Sarah from the Event Horizon. I wanted to do it gently, so I took a deep breath and tried to think, but then she made a sudden lunge towards me at exactly the same time as Bane tried to grab her. From nowhere came the slash of a knife as Sarah sliced ferociously at his arm. It was the same blade that Alex Beckinsale had used against Tessa and Harry. She must have found it while she was waiting for us. He snatched his hand away and lunged for her again. It was too late. She had already grabbed me and had the knife against my throat. I didn't even get a chance to flinch. Guardians were *seriously* quick. Her arm pinned both of mine painfully behind my back, but all I really felt was the cold metal against my skin. How had she learnt to do that? She had moved so nimbly. Like a trained fighter—or a supernatural bodyguard.

'Guardians have no problem killing people to keep their charge safe,' she reminded us. 'You won't come any closer, Bane. If she takes me across, she'll be just fine.'

Noah held him back, looking completely torn. This was not a situation his soft heart could reconcile. Bane's wrist and hand were bleeding profusely, splashing sanguine drips onto the flowstone floor.

Sarah started to back us away towards the sword. It was still revolving slowly.

'Please, Sarah! You know I can't let you cross!' I begged her to understand. This was *Noah's mum*. The woman who had cleaned and dressed my skinned knees and helped me kidnap my Barbies back from the twins when they'd held them for ransom. Her current actions seemed incomprehensible, and yet entirely predictable given what I now knew about her. 'I won't be able to help it,' I pleaded. 'I'll have to stop you no matter the cost.' All too quickly we were level with the sword and I could feel its heat like sunburn on my skin.

'No,' she declared, her voice cracking. 'After everything I've done to Harry, I can't just let him die. I don't understand why he didn't eat from the Tree when he was in Eden, and frankly I don't care what self-sacrificing reason he might have given you. Someone needs to protect him from himself because he deserves so much better than dying in some stupid hospital!'

'It's his choice,' I croaked, but it sounded weak, even to me.

'Well sometimes we don't make the right choices, do we?' she cried, and with her words came a flash of insight. A memory of a night and a day spent locked away from the rest of the world. Two people losing themselves in something that was bigger than both of them. Something that should have been pure and beautiful but was tainted with the weight of a choice to be made. And she had thrown it away and chosen to marry the wrong man for all the right reasons.

I caught Noah's eye, and told him with silent words, in our long-practised language that felt entirely natural. It wasn't a complex language. All I said was, 'I'm sorry.'

'Noah is Harry's son,' I whispered, still staring at him, and the knife at my throat nicked my skin as her hand shook in reply.

Her voice sounded utterly defeated. 'There's nothing you can do to stop me, Lainie. You told me yourself when I arrived at the hospital yesterday. Cherubim can't kill. You don't have a choice. You'll have to let me through.'

I took one last look at Bane's bleeding hand. I would not let him get hurt again. Then my eyes locked onto Noah's shocked face and my tears begged his forgiveness for what I was about to do.

'You're right. In this there is no choice,' I said to the woman who had once taught me how to flip a skateboard.

Even though it was deliberate, when I thrust myself forward I was still astonished by the sheer level of pain I felt as the sharp blade sliced into my throat. And yet I kept pushing against it with all the strength I could find. Hot blood sprayed, filling my vision and my mouth. As I choked, I tried desperately to yank Sarah away from the boundary, my fingers scrabbling to hold on, but I knew it was pointless. She dropped the knife to pull away from me and it skittered away across the floor and then my fingers could no longer grip anything.

The second our skin no longer touched, the sword flared to life, spinning so bright and fast that it looked like an exploding sun. I wanted to do something. I wanted ... but I was locked. My body wouldn't move and my thoughts refused to exist in the same space as that pain ...

A full-throated scream erupted from Sarah as the flames engulfed her, and like an extended flash of lightning, the unnaturally hot fire burned away her tainted flesh within the space of about ten fading heartbeats.

The sword had no trouble killing people either.

As I collapsed into blackness, I could hear Bane shrieking my name.

Chapter 45

Noah flew after Bane and tackled him ruthlessly to the ground, pinning him there as he watched his mother's lifeless body burn out of the corner of his tear-blurred eyes, and Lainie's crumpled form twitch grotesquely. Blood was spurting across the cavern floor.

'Bane! Please, listen to me. *BANE!*'

Bone hit bone painfully, as Bane's elbow connected with his jaw but he managed to keep his hold. Just.

'I can help her, please, listen!'

Bane's struggles slowed a fraction.

'I need to see if she's alive, but *you can't follow,*' Noah begged. 'Please! Do you think you'll be able to help her if you're dead? The sword doesn't distinguish motives. If it did my mother would still be alive. *If you get too close it will kill you too.*'

The distraught Guardian stopped moving, squeezing his eyes shut as if he was trying to sense her. His whole body was shaking and his skin felt like it was on fire.

'Bane, listen. You still feel Lainie pulling on you, don't you? You still feel the urge to heal her. That means she's still with us, but we don't have much time. I need to go to her.'

His friend stayed rigidly still, breathing hard and obviously trying to control his compulsion. At least he was starting to think again, and wasn't trying to bite him or anything. Nervously Noah released him, watching him carefully as Bane opened his eyes again to stare at the crumpled and bloodied mess on the floor. His body was convulsing and he was trying to dig his fingers into the flowstone, but other than that he didn't move. For a broken moment he remained frozen, but then his eyes rolled back into his skull and he slid, unconscious, to the cavern floor.

'No no no no no!' Blood slipped under his boots as Noah scrambled over to where Lainie had fallen. It soaked through her shirt and across her face, chest and shoulder. One look at the gaping hole in her neck was confirmation enough. She was no longer bleeding or breathing. She was dead and he was too late. Bane would kill himself trying to heal her. There was only one option available.

He hauled her up and cradled her against his chest, then took one long look at the smoking corpse that had once been his mother before he turned and stepped across the Event Horizon.

Chapter 46

Tessa had been staring at the burnt body for too long and knew that the sweet meat stench of it would never leave her. The corpse lay level with the sword and was as unreachable as the moon. She'd been warned when she'd tried.

It was not him. It couldn't be. She'd felt the danger to Noah like an erupting volcano in her chest, and had driven her mother's poor little Honda right through Lainie's place, across the paddocks until she reached the other car. Then she'd run like she'd never run before. And then the feel of him had disappeared.

It couldn't be him. That boot. Melted and charred. It looked like a girl's boot, didn't it? God, did she *want* it to be?

A low groan broke her out of her stupor as Bane finally began to stir. She'd tried to make him as comfortable as possible, resting his head on her knees and wrapping his bleeding forearm in a strip from her shirt, which was still wet from crossing the river. It didn't seem to have helped much.

She watched him take a hitched breath, regaining consciousness and blinking, but then he jumped to his feet so abruptly that she yelped in surprise, and only just managed to catch him when he began to keel over.

'Whoa, Bane. I've got you, just sit.'

But he didn't. Instead he shook her off and began to stumble around in a total daze, searching for something. Then his eyes reached the corpse. With a furious yell, he launched towards it, but the sword flared such a violent warning that he skidded to his knees.

'Bane, no! What are you doing? It won't let us get that close!' She grabbed his elbow and dragged him back. It wasn't that hard—he was as weak as a day old chick. And then he threw up and she almost did the same, but she forced her trembling voice to work.

'Is that ... who ... ?' For at least ten minutes she'd sat in a cave, staring at a corpse, with Bane out cold and no one to tell her where everyone was. Noah, Lainie, Sarah, Nicole ... what had happened?

'It's Noah's mum,' Bane whispered eventually.

Choking sobs erupted from the seething volcano inside her. Despair and relief smashed against each other. 'Are Noah and Lainie safe? They crossed over, and they're safe, aren't they, Bane? Aren't they? Where's Nicole?' She pulled him over to the stream and helped him wash his face.

'Nicole was never here. Sarah lied.' He tried to stand up again, but landed in the water instead.

Tessa hauled him up, sat him against a boulder, and made him look her in the eye. '*Where's Noah?*'

'He took Lainie's body across to Eden. She's dead, Tess. I felt her die and I couldn't stop it, I just watched, I just ...'

'No.' Horror caused her voice to crack.

'She's gone, Tess. I failed her and she's ... she's ...'

'She's gone looking for dragons,' a jaunty voice interrupted.

'Noah! Oh my God, Noah! You're okay!' Tessa threw herself at him and he caught her and laughed. *Laughed.*

'She's fine, mate,' Noah assured Bane. 'A bit loopy, but fine. She just needs some time to—'

But Bane had passed out again.

Tessa breathed out heavily. 'He said he felt her die.'

'She did. But I made her eat ... you know ... from the ... the Tree.'

She gasped. 'But Harry—'

'Harry said that the Trees were never designed to have to deal with guilt and grief. Lainie isn't guilty. We have the authority to enter Eden, and she deserves ...' He let her go, and the joy that was behind his eyes began to dim. She wished she could trap and keep it for him but knew she couldn't. Would the transition between worlds always be this difficult for him?

'I just know,' he insisted after a long moment. 'She can eat it. Harry and Annie, they both have reasons why they can't ...' He swallowed. 'She doesn't have their baggage. I can feel that it's okay. I just know.'

Was he convincing her, or himself?

Just then, his head jerked up, and his whole body went rigid. 'Someone's coming,' he said. 'Still far away, but coming.'

'It's Lily. When I saw ... I had to call her, Noah. I'm sorry, but I had to. We can trust her.'

That was when his eyes finally drifted over to the hideous pile of ruined flesh that still smoked where it lay. 'Can we?' he croaked. 'How can we ever know who to trust?'

❧

A while later Tessa broke Lily's gaze away from the life-changing spectacle of the miraculous sword. 'Help me wrap her up,' she requested softly. She'd had to ask Noah to move his mother's corpse away from the threshold so they could deal with it, and somehow he had, and she knew he would never be the same. Then she'd sat him down next to Bane who had woken up again and was staring a spot on the ground that was slick with blood.

They set to work with the woollen blankets Lily had brought, wrapping the body and tying it up with hay band so would be easier to carry, and Tessa wondered when she had become capable of doing such a thing so calmly.

Then they all began the death march back to the farm.

❧

The engine revved loudly while the blackened corpse in the driver's seat flopped to one side and leant against the window. From where they stood on the grassy verge, the face was the most gruesome thing to see, and Tessa gripped Noah's right hand even more tightly as his words began to falter.

'Necessary,' she reminded him, yet again, wishing she could do more to help.

'Come on, Noah. It's nearly done. You're doing great,' Lily added, coming to stand on his left side and placing her hand on his shoulder. They would have been utterly lost without her—she'd known exactly how to fake a death, having already arranged one with Harry's help, decades earlier.

Bane stayed back, leaning against a tree. They had dosed him up on the extra sedatives that the hospital had sent Sarah home with, but they hadn't done much, and he'd insisted on coming along.

Closing her eyes, Tess focused on sending healing warmth through Noah's skin, but there was nothing physical for her to heal. She let out an impatient breath. She didn't want to rush him, but if anyone drove past now, things would get very, very complicated. Not that there was ever much traffic along the road between the Gracewood and Ashbree farms, but their luck lately had not been terrific.

Finally, sorrowful words sprang forth from Noah's lips and the engine revved again and then the car began to roll. There was no shouting, only quiet, heavy command. The four of them stood vigil as the Pajero sped down the road with no living person inside. By the time it reached the next bend it was travelling at well over 100km/h. Noah caused it to hit a large rock, so it flipped over before smashing into a tree, back end first. The fuel tank ruptured immediately and it only took a simple word for a small spark from the battery to ignite the vehicle. He let the resulting fire burn itself out naturally, with just a little help. Finally, as he sank to the ground, Tessa held him in her lap like a child as they watched the car burn.

As soon as they returned home, Lily called Sarah's husband and lied to him. She said that she'd left Sarah asleep and gone to work outside, but had just come in to find her missing, and her car gone. She told him she was worried because Sarah had been given such strong medication that morning. Tessa wished she could shut her ears, but they were her lies too. She would repeat them if she had to, for Noah's sake.

David Ashbree made the dreadful discovery soon after.

Harry never regained consciousness, so he never knew what his Guardian had done to try to save him. Tessa waited uselessly when Noah fled back to Eden straight after the second funeral. The revelation that Harry was his real father was just another thing that seemed to push Noah further from reality—she knew he needed to get away for a while.

Everyone seemed to accept the explanation of Lainie's disappearance. Losing both Harry and Sarah in the same week was reason enough for her to have withdrawn from everyone's company, and when Lily told everyone she'd decided to leave to travel around Australia, everyone accepted that she obviously needed to get out of Nalong for a while. Nicole was the only one who refused to forgive her for missing her mother's farewell.

Epilogue

The young wallaby moved restlessly around her pen. It had been good for Nicole to have something to care for in the month since her mum's death, but she'd started school again and no longer had the time to devote to her. Tessa watched the joey's dainty mouth tug at the short grass, her long black claws digging easily into the dry soil and her muscled tail balancing her like a third leg. She no longer needed to be bottle fed, at least. Perhaps it was time.

She watched Bane fiddle with the envelope he was holding, running his fingers along its edge, but he still didn't open it. Then he jerked his head up as he heard someone approach. Tessa already knew who it was. She'd been waiting impatiently since the moment she'd felt him return from across the Event Horizon.

Despite his time away, the last few weeks had taken their toll on Noah's demeanour. She would miss that air of playful carelessness that charmed everyone he met. Having to keep the truth from his family about how his mum had died had definitely messed him up.

Bane took a deep breath as his friend came to stand beside him. He seemed afraid to ask, and Noah didn't make him.

'She's decided to stay in Eden. I'm sorry, mate.' Noah's breath sounded shaky as he exhaled. Then he turned his deep green eyes on Bane. 'She's living under a much more graceful sky than this one.'

A graceful sky. Tessa's mother had once told her that swear words were precious, beautiful things—like diamonds. They were not for everyday use. They were to be saved up for when you really needed someone to know how strongly you felt. When you heard a sweet old lady swearing, you knew she meant it. In the same way, Noah's elegant phrasing sounded so unlike him that it hit home in a profound way that was not to be refuted.

Bane gripped the edge of the pen tightly, as if fighting his reflexes to prevent himself from tearing it down. 'I nearly had her, Noah. I was so close. When she came back from Eden she saw herself the way I see her. Just for a little while. She understood, and she believed me finally ... I nearly had her.'

He sucked in a calming breath and forced himself to let go of the rail. 'Does she even remember me?' he asked after a moment, staring at the contented joey.

Noah shifted uncomfortably. 'Less and less. She remembers nothing of the events from that day. The Fruit did its job well.' He swallowed hard, and reached into his pocket. 'She asked me to give you this.'

Tessa sighed as the delicate golden bracelet fell into Bane's palm. The word '*Shalom*' reflected too brightly back at them. It had been his wish for her, and now she had it. Peace and healing. Rest and restoration. Under a much more graceful sky than this cruel one. She watched as he slipped the jewellery into his pocket with the letter from the Army Recruitment Agency that Lily had given him.

Then he opened the gate and let the joey run free.

Acknowledgements

So the time has come when I can finally thank people properly for being so good to me (at least in regards to the creation of this book—no one wants to read the long list of people who have ever been nice to me, even if they happen to be on it). So here goes. Firstly, all my wonderful beta readers: Nickie, Kim, Maree, Zoe, Terri, Lyndel, Vron, Bianca, Hollie, Colin, Addie, Sophie, Al, Blaire, Alex, and Bek. Also Jemma, for her priceless advice on sheep farming.

Okay, so I know that is a lot of people, but some of us need a lot of help. The wide range of suggestions and opinions have been invaluable, and helped me to keep things in perspective. Without all your encouragement I never would have had the audacity to see this through.

I also owe a huge thank you to Sarah Endacott for helping me turn my manuscript into something worth submitting—I am learning so much from you.

Michelle Lovi of Odyssey Books deserves blessings untold, for putting her faith in this project and being so patient with me.

Lastly, I need to acknowledge my precious family: Miche, Brian, Dania, Arden and Paul, who couldn't be more supportive if they held me up on stilts (except for that one time I made the girls late for gymnastics because Lainie was having issues getting her words right—sorry 'bout that, hope you didn't have to do too many extra push-ups).

And if any of you readers have been interested enough to read through these boring bits, then thanks to you too. I hope I've added something to your day, because you've added a lot to mine.

About the Author

Carolyn lives on a small hobby farm on the outskirts of Melbourne. She has a science degree, far too many pets and a fear of the ocean that makes her Mauritian mother roll her eyes. Somehow between her mortgage-broking job, driving her kids crazy (mostly by asking their friends' opinions about the Singularity) and feeding 63 baby axolotls, she has managed to write short stories for *Aurealis* and *Andromeda Spaceways* magazines. She is currently working to complete the fourth and final book in *The Sentinels of Eden* and after that she has promised that she will finally vacuum the bedrooms.

Printed in Australia
AUOC02n1053030117
281802AU00006BA/21/P

9 781922 200600